Cyber Kill

Cyber Kill

E Jason Williams

Ordering Information:

For orders and inquiries, please contact:
1-888-404-1388
www.goldtouchpress.com
book.orders@goldtouchpress.com

Printed in the United States of America

CHAPTER

1

I t is amazing how far we have come in the last fifty years when taking the time to think about life, especially as a young child. In many ways the world has made major advances with violent crime virtually non-existent. There are still a few cases each year in the Americas, nothing like what Tim's parents' memories dredge up. We have computers running everything. I cannot remember any moment during my lifetime when computers were not used. Now they control entrances and exits to every building in the world, including every residence. The newer versions include retina scanners. Of course that became common to financial establishments first, then it became necessary to use retina scans for any monetary transaction. It eliminated most fraudulent transactions like stolen credit or debit cards. It is pretty tough to scam retina scanners.

Makes me wonder what happened to the guy who ran that large software company the government broke apart. Probably took his money and retired to a cozy life in some tropical paradise. Although, it would have been nice if those people were a little more security conscious, but it was finally better after 2050. That was the year of the mastermind plot of its time. Leave a little program on every server on the Cloud, and cause every server worldwide to shut down at precisely noon on that day. April 1, 2050 was one April Fool's Day that will be remembered for a long time. Imagine the planning that was involved to connect to every server in the cloud (as it was call then), plant an obscure program in the normal flow of data that hid in memory until the correct time. That person was never caught, because no organization existed to monitor the network and its systems. On the positive side of that, a computer security expert had the idea that had become Global Security Corporation. I have always wondered with security being as relaxed as it was at that past time, whether our founder did not plant the program to get his own company started. Rather unlikely, as it was before his time also. That is still the way computer security functions, hackers try to find ways into systems. If never caught, go back to those involved and show them how to prevent a catastrophe from reoccurring. I suppose it depends on a hacker's area of expertise. Today, most hackers seem to be after diverting monetary funds to acquire a large income to live on, but computer programs are far more sophisticated, which makes it tougher than ever to lose track of large sums of money. As long as AI systems remain under the scrutiny of governments, hackers will have a continued livelihood.

Last person suspected to get away with a major diversion of funds did not target the entire financial industry. Robin Torry has become a much sought after consultant in the payroll banking community. His brilliance insures financial transactions are, if not entirely secure, at least completely traceable. His suspected break into the business occurred approximately 4 years ago while amassing a 22 billion WC nest egg. Instead of going after financial institutions, he tapped into company payrolls of multiple large corporations at the source banks. Estimates affected half a billion employees and he merely rounded off the payment to no cents. Diverting anywhere from one to ninety-nine cents on each employee for a period of over 3 years and six months. Since each individual found nothing major missing, all assumed it was a minor tax change and it went unreported. When the time period was completed, Robin moved the entire fund to a highly secure facility. That amount was over 22 billion World Currency. When he made his actions public, he did not need to return the money. I guess when you go to the company and show them how to prevent a security breach from happening again, it must help. He is very good, and Global Security has him involved every now and then when the company uses his consulting firm.

In this year of 2143, the criminal element has become wiser and more sophisticated, by definition the crimes are "victimless". It is believed the judicial system should get better terminology, since all crimes have victims. The best hackers attempt the crimes of this era. Some people still desire to prove to the world they are the best. Maybe it is ego that takes them over the lines of legality, or maybe it is the mere potential of quick fame and wealth.

Tim was starting his first day as CEO of Global Security Corporation, and time to head into the office, being one of the few who cannot perform his role from home. It was time he concentrated on what today might bring. Most likely the 300 security analysts will have another busy day chasing hackers away from the Information Gateway. IG is what the cloud had become and nothing in the world happens without going through the Information Gateway. It was absolutely marvelous the speed at which countries could get information around the world. Certainly with the transmitters running at light speed, and sending everything to positioning satellites to bounce to the intended destination, eliminates cross feed. He wondered what could go faster yet, since the world would want it. The company's primary duty has been to police the IG, and that by itself could be more than just a little complicated.

Seattle remained one of the best places to live as long as you could tolerate the gray morning sky. They did get a fair share of precipitation; but seldom was the ambient temperature extremely hot or cold. Go to nearby mountains for skiing and other cold weather activities or nearby beaches, which are open year round for warmer action. How many places in the world could be so accommodating and had an office with a view over the Sound? Nice view really from the 35th floor, where Global Security is located. The trip in was pleasant, since most people could perform business duties from the comfort of their home. The compensation was stupendous, but the risks are also extremely high. All analysts feel they could reach that magic plateau of ten years for a comfortable retirement. Kuri and Tim decided that he could have both loves in his life and still help raise the family, and she was due with the first child in less than 4 months. Besides stress was never an issue for Tim. The more advanced the technology, the more advanced the security factors involved. The risk an analyst took allowed a person to retire after ten years of service, but far too few completed the ten-year plan prior to breakdown. Some had even found the stress fatal. No, this is hardly the easy life most hoped it to be, all felt they could survive to that 10 year mark without becoming another casualty of the IG security world. Security has a big appetite for analysts incapable of taking full advantage of technology used at GSC.

As Timothy Frantz stepped out of his transport, he placed memory overload back into a dormant state to become more attuned to the present moment. Upon reaching the office and opening the door, his computer system, (named Nora, because of the feminine voice it was given from the semi-intelligent software package it had,) was screaming like a banshee expecting a response. This certainly was not how he pictured the day starting, which was only a few moments ago. The former CEO Zachery Trask had not arrived yet, and the female robotic computer was acting quite frantic, and Tim said hello to Nora as he entered.

"Here, what do you mean, 'here'? You never told me you left, and that is the only way to realize not to raise my voice for three hours!" was the initial response from the computer.

"Three hours, (that long, he thought) you still have not told me what the problem is." At which Nora proceeded with, "I have detected a major breach in the financial industry that affects International banks, and unable to determine the source. Whoever started this process is using multiple uplinks and divided the code between them. With this method, the person or persons have hampered trace efforts and possibly prevented the full trace altogether. In addition, it is highly probable the actual program does not get assembled until all the individual pieces reach the destination. The receiving network system may inadvertently assemble it, allowing the program to infiltrate."

"Nora, can you determine the exact number of uplinks used?" Tim inquired. Nora states, "Not exactly, but have determined a minimum of six but eight to ten is more logical. The uplinks do not register in the same general population centers, furthermore, one shows in New Jersey, another in Anchorage and yet a third in Bangkok. The remainder are unidentified as locations at this time." At this time, Trask had arrived and was in the office long enough to know something was seriously wrong, and much too soon for Tim to be the sole person involved.

"This would appear to be the mischief of multiple persons, have the other Global regional offices been notified?" Tim's question was answered with, "The other main offices were notified two hours ago, and they appear to have analysts attempting trace efforts to the closest uplinks to each office. As for multiple persons, that can neither be confirmed nor denied, since all that is required to create an uplink is a transmitter and computer. It is possible for each uplink to be established from a single location, using variable times of the day to coordinate with the individual satellites in orbit. Once the uplink is established, the system does not record satellite transfers for communication. A person could wait the specific number of hours to uplink to the correct satellite as long as a separate computer and transmitter is used for each link."

Tim immediately asked, "Are you telling me, one person with eight to ten transmitters and computers at a single location could monitor each uplink. Then wait until all of them are in the correct IG position before starting his program? That requires far more patience than any other hacker has exhibited for more than four years. How long would it take to connect them all?" Nora uses her best you should know this already voice, "First question affirmative, second question twenty four hours. Tim, since that is how long it takes for the earth to complete a single rotation, and the satellites are held stationary. Have you forgotten your early education?" Tim: "Excuse me Nora, besides being too early for me to engage in this type of thought, I have not utilized that portion of my education since I was a child, hence early education. Now give me five minutes to put a plan together and I will let you know what needs to be done and from where."

This allowed Timothy Frantz enough time to determine which analysts needed to be assigned and what needed to be done at the other locations, also to fill Trask in for what he may have missed. It took only a moment to gather his thoughts and decide his top three analysts would be needed to work with the information collected. Also contact each main office to insure the highest priority is given to this case.

Timothy Frantz was regarded as a thorough analyst; this often meant attention to details frequently overlooked by most others in this profession. That was part of the reason his success rate in hacker offenses was exceptionally high during his tenure as an Assistant Director. Although, all the thoroughness in the world did not help him find Robin Torry. It was also the reason why the boards of directors wanted him to stay on to oversee the entire global operation. His primary duty was to be involved with the Seattle Headquarters operations. At the time of his appointment, he made it contingent that certain analysts at each main office were in director positions, because he knew the quality of the work they performed. He also knew a minimum of intervention would be required on his part. This was one of those times when intervention was mandated.

Intellipads are handy little office toys. Just speak to them and they record the information both verbally and in written form. Especially useful if nobody has to decipher handwriting, as the verbal notepad prints in nice legible fonts. He grabbed the notepad from the drawer and spoke," Make a note, contact Ivan, Sooni, Cho and Chaka in conference for getting immediate response and actions taken for the financial security breach." Verbal notepads also can contact other notepads and annoy the individuals until they respond. In this case it merely warns everybody to have their actions already performed up to date, and results from them. He continued telling the intellipad to have Nora direct all available information to each main office. To choose three analysts best for the type of breach from Seattle pool. He finished with a note to self to tell Nora when he was leaving his office. That is the problem with most semi-intelligent computers, they have visual input; but still require a verbal comment. Nora being robotic as well, had visual input but to what degree, Tim was uncertain. Audio is undoubtedly much easier when everything was done from a keyboard and mouse, but maybe it is time to add video, which all AI computers already have without robotic humanoid bodies. For those times, when one is too preoccupied and left without a word. Whoever programmed Nora to learn verbal assault, certainly had all the female charms he learned to expect, maybe just not fully appreciate, but Nora took it upon herself to acquire this talent.

"Timothy, are you there?" asked Nora. "You are two whole seconds past the five minutes you requested and I have already completed the memo task from your intellipad." Tim's first thought was can a computer's ears burn. "Yes, Nora, I am here and this is what I need you to do. Establish the conference call with, Sooni Hakawa in Tokyo, Cho Ling in Hong Kong, Ivan Herbalich in St. Petersburg and Chaka Toukee in Sierra. Have all available data pertaining to this breach up to date in all the main offices by the quickest means possible. Notify the three analysts to come into the conference. Be available for the conference with the data for the meeting. Go."

It took all of thirty seconds for everything to be setup and established minus the three analysts. Trask was watching with intent interest, as he did not think he would have surmised a plan in such quick fashion, but Tim had at least been more in touch with these people than he himself. Seems they are not quite as quick as one computer.

Tim: "Gentlefolks, I hope I'm not interrupting anything more urgent than this breach, which some of you are already working. Who already has people on this?" Cho Ling spoke first, "I have two people trying to trace one of the uplinks that shows to have originated from my domain. It is looking to be false at this time, but we will continue investigating it." Ivan Herbalich chimed in also, indicating two analysts were chasing uplinks to determine origination point, but could only find the link was established when the satellite was somewhere other than over his continent. Sooni broke her silence confirming analysts were working on signal traces. Sooni then added new information to the big picture by saying: 'My team of analysts has some good news and also bad, it seems we are dealing with at least one brilliant hacker. First the signal frequency traced from the satellite is above those made available for normal IG usage. The frequency was within the allowable range to make connection, and allowed our hacker clean signal and highest priority status. An indication the hacker has extensive knowledge of the satellite communications far beyond what is general public awareness, possibly from top secret or covert operations experience. As a result of the range used in transmission, the uplink transmitter has to be custom made, making it a rogue TRU. (TRU, transmitter/responder unit, companies still like using acronyms to identify hardware and software specialty devices). We cannot use normal trace methods beyond the satellite, so the trail has become rather frigid. (Tim gestured the three analysts to take a seat as they overheard the last bit of input.) I have initiated an outside source to research vital components sold here for manufacturing an uplink TRU. That will take a little time. If it was stolen, there is no record on the IG confirming a theft report for TRU's or components for building them."

"Sooni", Tim spoke out for clarification, "Were you aware the search is for between six to twelve transmitting devices when checking the theft reports?" Sooni responded quickly even if a little off guard, "I was looking for multiples, but not really that many. That makes this hacker much more complicated than I thought. More like a genius, if he can custom build transmitters (TRU) very competent with satellite communications, and hack into one truly sophisticated security system. What else do we know?"

Tim: "I believe Nora has forwarded all available data and will continually updating it as it become available. You should have already received that, but may not have had the opportunity to make use of it. Nora is rather quick about those types of little jobs as she calls them. Since it seems all of you have already reacted to this situation, I will just suggest a few alterations to the plan. First trace, second financial and third communications to see if we can narrow down the source of our security breach, and eventually find our hacker or hackers. I will also have Nora post this information on a drop down video and suggest all of you do the same, so we can more easily track what everyone is doing. Nora, have you determined an exact number of uplinks used in this escapade?"

Nora quickly jumps in with an answer, "I have determined a total of ten were used, each on a different satellite. Upon receiving input from Sooni, I found only five signals were above the normal frequency range, and five more were within the acceptable range. None of the ten are registered transmitting devices, which as already stated, makes it very difficult if at all possible to trace to a point of origin. Daisy is making all the follow-up. It may be useful to get the exact time each of the ten transmitters initiated satellite contact, and determine where the satellite was positioned. That will at least decide whether a single or multiple locations were used. Also, it will aid in single or multiple hacker involvement. I do not have immediate access to global satellite positioning information at this time, and must link with a number of secure computers to obtain it all. That may take several hours, as some of the security sites require considerable amounts of authorization code to permit release of the data. You can bounce signals at any time with a registered transmitter; but rogue units are an unknown entity in this scenario. For normal usage, this function is totally transparent to both the transmitter and the computer user. This person or group of hackers may have specific knowledge to satellite positioning information. If it is a single individual, they have this information, if it is a group, they are globally connected. Regardless, we have some very thorough and competent intruders, which bring me to believe we proceed quickly but cautiously. They could very easily have other traps to throw our trace attempts off course."

Tim: "Nora, have the satellite positioning information posted to all the overheads as it becomes available, and team, only work with the closest satellites to your control centers. This will allow each location to perform trace efforts more thoroughly with minimum chance of duplication. Nora will monitor your input and keep everybody updated as things develop from everyone's effort. Nora has brought up one major issue not discussed as of yet. We are in all likelihood dealing with at least one very knowledgeable individual who could have planned for diverting our efforts in locating this person. Please use extreme caution, and verify the accuracy in where the trail leads you. As with any project that requires my contacting you, this is high profile to financial business entities we contract with. Though they expect some losses, this is far too much for any business to consider acceptable. Nora, what is the exact figure of diverted funds as of this time?" Nora responded with, "Approximately eleven billion in world currency; but it seems to be targeting a single source financial firm."

"That concludes this conference, I may be contacting each of you on an individual basis as we progress in locating the funds and the intruder", Tim ended with. The remaining members bid departures and immediately returned their attention to the breach. Each felt positive that they could make progress in locating both the intruder and the funds. The conference concluded, and Timothy Frantz directed his attention to the three analysts parked in his office. They each had a look on their face of intense thought. Seemed they were already devising their counterattack on the situation, as it pertained to each of them. Tim told them, if any more resources were needed, he would get it for them. They seemed relieved the meeting was not a result of reprimand or any similar action, as it rarely occurred in the Seattle Headquarters. Never from Tim at the other locations.

Once in a great while discipline is required in any business environment, but the analysts at Global Security were far more prone to mental meltdown than discipline. The company has become really good at testing people for that possibility and feels a severance package that allows analysts up to two years away from the stressful duties is beneficial. The sad part is most security analysts feel they can make it to the ten years, even when found to be on the edge of breakdown.

Unfortunately, when an individual is released for stress overload syndrome, they cannot return to Global Security Corporation. The stress factors leading to their release would only be duplicated. Tim was well aware of stress factors. As an analyst, when he first entered Global Security some eleven and a half years ago, the company's general theme was stress would be extremely high, due to the nature of this business. The company was only aware of one other high stress job at the time of air traffic controller, and the company stand was that was a walk in the park compared to IG security analyst. In the beginning, Global Security turned a large quantity of excellent analysts into mindless drones. Over two years ago when asked to take over as headquarters director, Tim had made it so all the current systems do 95% of the work load, and stress was reduced 50% across the analysts in all offices.

This had drastically reduced the number of analysts reaching breakdown. The drawback remains that analysts who test positive, are given the two year severance package with the intention the individual will still be able to perform in less stressful environments, and remain productive and healthy. The ones who are released, still fail to believe they could not make the ten-year time for retirement. They typically feel it is a sign of weakness, and few cannot fully understand that a mere five percent actually completed the ten years. Truth is, ego does play the largest part in the denial process. The stress is beyond what a normal person can tolerate, and the brightest people are the most susceptible to stress overload syndrome. As CEO of this global operation, Tim was relieved that under a normal day for himself, stress was not a lingering minute to minute ordeal. Although everybody was under the gun for results, especially when something like this breach occurred.

Timothy took a long look around his newly acquired office, then saw Trask, and asked him what his thoughts were in the whole process he just put into place. The response was he had done far faster what had to be done than he would have, as he was still trying to come to terms with the new breach. The analyst's office environment was so sterile. Everything around them was white, the walls were white, and the internal glass was frosted white, as well as the furniture and accessories. The only color in the entire office complex was that of people's clothing, and sadly most of them had white shirts. He continued this line of thought wondering if some colorful scenery would make the place a little more hospitable. This had always been denied in the past. He assumed too much as he found some documentation indicating this color was optimum for stress relief. The documents were dated from before he was even an analyst, and seldom did he look into files. Simply do not use much paper these days. The computer takes care of all the necessary data transmissions locally and globally. It stores it all and can be asked about anything pertaining to the security once it already took place. "Nora, can you check your records for any information on office ergonomics?"

Nora responded rather quickly with no information found. Tim made a mental note to present the topic at the next board of directors meeting, concerning white as the only color and how about scenic pictures, just to allow people a moment to clear their heads. "Nora, lower the viewing screen please and set up the globe with the satellites displayed so we can starting putting the puzzle pieces together. At each satellite placed, the time connection was established with available places, the orbit locations to coordinate with the times of connection. We may see a pattern before all ten pieces are in place. An eight-meter by 4-meter viewing screen gently positioned from the overhead compartment, with a 3 dimensional view of the earth rotating in real time. At this point the satellites were moved, which let Tim know Nora was still trying to get that information from the secure system the satellites were controlled through. He knew it would take a little more time to complete that link in this puzzle. "Nora, I'm heading to the break room, care to join me?" Nora ranted about how liquid refreshment or caffeine boost was not a requirement for her to keep her attention level high. Occasionally, Tim simply had to have the fun of treating Nora like a person, especially when Nora could rant with the best of them. Normal times in the office, he would have got coffee just after arrival, but today was anything but normal.

As he walked through the office area, he spotted three very busy analysts talking to their computers through headsets and hidden microphones. Each analyst's office was built in solid Plexiglas cubes that were soundproofed to the outside as long as the frosted glass door was closed. The comparison to precious collections was overwhelming. Almost comical, if you considered how it might appear to a new arrival making a first entrance to the 35th Floor. Top floor currently in the building with the additional security of the 34th floor sealed off creating a really peaceful environment. The demand for office space had diminished severely so the owners had no argument about the 34th floor. The lease was less than half of the 35th since minimal lights or other utilities were required, aside from keeping the temperature moderate. Maybe 45 years ago, commercial real estate had a much higher demand, but now it is amazing how many buildings once used for office space, are storage facilities for finished products awaiting shipping containers. Most single floor commercial buildings have been converted to robotic manufacturing facilities.

Most of them are run from home. Just set the production run parameters in the computer and the robotics do the rest. Cuts down on the need for vending machines and lunchrooms, since robots like computers, need no liquids or nourishment. Technology had advanced to the point where seldom repair was required. Surprisingly enough, coffee was still a valid refreshment, even though governments went after them, much like the tobacco industry. The good part is all the medical profiles were inconclusive and most cases never made it to a courtroom. That may never be completely over, since courts have such small workloads with crime no longer a major factor.

Until it was outlawed, Tim would have his coffee. Tim poured himself a large mug from the fresh pot and returned to the 30th floor office. He considered having a brewer placed in his office; but ultimately decided the exercise would be better for him. Upon return to his office, the drop down display already had two of the ten satellites positioned over the southeastern edge of the North American Atlantic Coastline. It was not enough of a pattern to make an educated guess. It was entirely possible for two of the ten to be in close proximity, without assuming there was a pattern. There had to be six in the same general position to decide if this was a group or individual. Nora would let him know when more data became available. Thinking it was best to enjoy some coffee before informing Nora he had returned. Tim bet himself, she had her audio at maximum input to listen for footsteps to make it across the entire office area to the desk. Nora probably could hear a pin drop too, wishing he had one to test that theory. Tim had consumed about half the coffee when a third satellite positioned itself over the East Coast of North America Atlantic. All Tim could think was he hoped it was not another New Yorker from Manhattan Island, because the attitude was not something he needed to add to this problem. "Okay Nora, I have returned." Tim spoke to the atmosphere in the room since the robotic computer did not appear anywhere in plain view. Nora replied, "Yes, Tim I heard you come in the door, how was your coffee?"

(Tim did not state that he knew it, but was still somewhat awed that the audio was that sensitive.) "Coffee is great Nora, you really ought to give it a try some time." The computer went on to inform Tim that liquids were not good for its circuits. Even though it had some protection built into for erroneous liquids spilled, there was no need to take such a risk. Such attitude. (Tim kept to himself, fully aware he instigated the response he received.) "Nora, sometimes I cannot help myself when it comes to treating you as an equal. We humans say things now and then just to see what the reaction will be. You are one hundred percent logical and predictable. Heard any good jokes lately?" This is a first, Nora is not replying. "What's the matter Nora, does that not compute?"

Nora provided an exasperated response, "Tim, you know very well indeed that jokes are not within my programming guidelines. You want jokes, I suggest you get an entertainment programmed computer, just do not expect that from me."

The fourth satellite appeared on the heads up display again within the East Coast region. "It appears a pattern is emerging here," said Nora, "Timothy you had a good idea with narrowing down the satellite times and positions." Tim was rather shocked, he could not recall receiving anything remotely similar to a compliment from his computers in the past. "Thank you Nora, but let's not get too excited until we have at least six satellites in the pattern. As for now, add graphics to show the maximum connect range for each of these satellites and highlight the area that comes into all four satellites." Nora said, "It looks to be all of the North America East Coast, a little bit of northern Central America, Western half of the British Isles and Portugal and Spain." That was still an awful large number of people to have to check into. Nora made all the diagram changes and then told Tim, "You are correct, upon my checking all my past responses to you, I have never given you a single item of praise. That may be because I think of you as a computer, and we are designed to be thorough and accurate."

Tim was at an utter loss for spoken word now, his computer was also a fortuneteller, since he was not verbal about the unexpected compliment. This cannot be a result of asking Nora if she heard any good jokes, he thought. Unless it had to do with the human comment and it reminded her that I was not a computer, but this morning should have accomplished that since computers do not leave. Maybe she thinks I'm a robot. Damn, these computers definitely need better visual input unless that is only available for Artificially Intelligent computers. AI is still not allowed for most businesses as mandated by the various governments. Although, they had received approval for their AI network, as this was the only world security company that governments used. Currently only the medical profession worldwide has justified and been approved.

Of course they use AI for diagnosing and in combination with robotics most surgical procedures are performed. It truly eliminated human error or fatigue related issues. He remembered something about all successfully completed surgery was recorded and documented. The only time a doctor actually performed a treatment of any sort, was when no existing successful procedure was archived in a massive computerized storage facility. Must be somebody seen too many science fictions movies about computers taking over and eliminating the human error factor. He compounded that with too many paranoid people in governments, having seen how many science fiction epics became something of a reality. He believed artificial intelligence in computers could prove truly beneficial in more applications, with the proper safeguards in place, especially in global security matters. Over half the day had already disappeared, and not a single lead to the whereabouts of the financial intruder. Trask had remained intent in the proceedings taking place, and even though he was here to acclimate Tim to his CEO duties, he was finding it amazing how fast Tim got his people working to find an answer.

Nora broke his thoughts by saying, "Timothy, Kuri is on the video communicator for you." Tim: "Good Nora, raise the vidphone at the desk and patch me in."

"Hello dear," Kuri started, "I just thought you would like to know I am requested to fill in as hostess tonight at the restaurant, as it appears the normal hostess is not feeling well and did not want to make the customers ill." Tim told his wife he would see her as soon as they both were home, and to tell her brother he said hello. After that disconnected, the vidphone went active again.

Sooni from Tokyo said, "Time to update you with our findings, or more appropriate lack of results. The traces continue to halt at the satellite. The signal is bounced off two of their satellites to reach its European destination; but cannot quickly be traced back to point of origin. You know this is a difficult trace, and hopefully not impossible, but it will be time intensive to filter out erroneous cross signals to return to its source. Do we have time on our side like a week to ten days?" Tim: "Sooni, since we are the predominant force in global security, we have as much time as it takes. To this point, I have not been contacted by any outside influences, although I suspect Robin Torry would have been contacted by the financial elements to get him involved. If it takes a month, then that is how it will be, but even the financial groups have to realize we are trying to undo what easily could have taken a minimum of two years to plan. We are dealing with an intruder who realizes the risks involved, and wants nothing more than to get lost in the data. Most hackers do not plan enough, and are caught quickly most times before even reaching the objective. We do this quite efficiently, but once in a while, a genuinely bright hacker plans how to get lost in the massive amounts of information exchanged hourly around the planet. I'll even bet money, if we had access to the European Financial businesses affected that our intruder ran several tests on each of the systems. Those tests did not even register more than errant data." Sooni added, "I had not even considered successful testing used prior to the breach, but that does make a valid point. How can we trace those without a time frame to work in?" Tim replied, "We cannot trace them, but the record at the receiving institutions should show increased garbage data hits. To be honest, the only way that information would be available, is when Torry becomes involved. I have not researched any of them to see if Robin has a contract with them. It simply has not been a priority as of yet."

Sooni: "My financial analyst has looked into the data from the satellite and as suspected, it is in bits and pieces, the code was spilt into ten entities and he has imbedded code in every tenth byte using bit position 3. The assembly code is embedded in such a fashion that it would be held in memory until fully assembled. Due to length of time it took to get all the pieces, the receiving computer would then execute the program seeing that it has a valid instruction set and performs the transaction. Who thinks these things up, how could we possible have prevented it?" Tim added, "I had the same thought not all that long ago, but thank you for confirming that our security systems could not have detected this in time to prevent it. From my understanding, AI systems may not have had a valid reference. They probably would not have prevented it, but possibly note that a suspicious transaction was encountered, and get somebody's attention to the problem, while it was still in process. Unfortunately, our systems had to wait for my arrival. I do not believe it is good for all types of business, especially military matters, when the need for bloodshed cannot be avoided, at least minimize it. You know Sooni, when this is all over, maybe Kuri and I can get over to take you to dinner for the help you have given on this intruder breach." Sooni: "That would be nice, but you really should extend that to the three analysts who are providing all this good stuff, I am merely the conduit through which it passes. Additionally, they are all afraid to talk to you, it is that status thing you know. Of course, I do not actually tell them anything to indicate you are a nice guy in order to get them all doing what I need done." Tim replied, "You are absolutely correct to include the hard working folks, as long as you have not told them anything about me that would render them too ill to partake in the festivities. We will continue to stay in touch on this you know." "Without a doubt," was Sooni's parting statement.

*   *   *

"Nora it is time to start assembling pieces on our intruder," Tim said to the wall and continued with, "Add a chart to global graphics displaying:

Expert in financial transactions, line 1
Skilled in Communications, line 2
Knowledgeable in Satellite positioning sequences, line 3
Genius in application programs, line 4
Capable of building rogue TRU's, line 5

Nora what else do we know about our 'friend'?"

Nora merely stated nothing else to confirm at this time, but did point out that security knowledge had to be mentioned. At what level of expertise was yet unknown. To progress to the point of breach detection, which was all ten transmitters online, there had to be more than a casual awareness of security detection systems. As usual Nora was right on the money but what level do we place this person? "Good Nora, thanks for the input and place Security knowledge, line 6 for the time being. We will have to make a more precise judgement later. I see that we have now got six satellites in position, all over the East Atlantic Coastline and the highlight area has now eliminated European countries. That only leaves an estimated fifty to sixty million people to pick from. Start searching the database for people residing in the North American East Coast and Northern Central America for this type of training and experience. We should be looking for a seasoned veteran of 10 years' experience, probable 20 years to acquire all the needed skills in this many areas of endeavor. Ten years allows for an extremely gifted individual, since only a few people in the world could accomplish so much in a single decade."

Nora asked, "Should that be started immediately or postponed until the remaining four satellite positions are confirmed?" Tim: "Try to work both angles; but complete the satellite positions prior to verifying this is an individual. It is possible we have a pair, and the experience level information will still narrow the numbers down for people competent enough to accomplish this breach." Just as he finished a seventh satellite position appeared on the overhead positioned around the Hawaiian Islands, the highlight area included the islands and southern California. "I believe we now have to put a hold on the database search for now Nora." Nora concurred.

Tim reviewed all the information he had and concluded his intruder could well be an individual, possibly a pair, but certainly at an intelligence level superior to the majority of hackers he had encountered over the last twelve years. The silver lining so to speak, hackers could not keep a secret for an indefinite period of time. Nothing so psychological as the desire to be caught, simply in order for them to profit further from their deeds, had to become known to somebody. Global Security Corporation had no intentions of aiding the intruder in that endeavor. Tim would have preferred that nobody knew that security still had some vulnerability; unfortunately, even the best could not comprehend every conceivable prevention. It is not like somebody was never going to try, that would be too ideal, and of course, leads to a lack of employment for a large number of analysts. Tim was not overly concerned about that prospect, but others would be seriously affected. Back on track, where did the day go, he should have taken a lunch break, but certainly too late now? Where could that 11 billion in world currency be? What am I overlooking to get this on a faster track of recourse? Even with rogue transmitters, the signal is independent. That's it!

"Nora, contact all locations tracking the signal, I might have an idea to speed things up a little." Nora replied, "You do, two in the same day, Tim you are going to hurt yourself." Do not remember when Nora learned sarcasm, as she said her programming did not include humor, but she had evolved somewhere along the line since her offline time from the network. "Yes Nora, have the trace group filter out all the registered signal returns from the satellites to the point of origin. With any luck and a little time, we should be able to pinpoint the location of the rogue TRU's we seek." "Excellent input," Nora spoke, "are you sure you're not a computer hiding under human coverings? I have been so occupied with these security codes to get the satellite positions, I have not taken the time to analyze what we can do with the information we already have." Tim said to the ceiling, "Yes Nora, but you are doing in hours what would take humans weeks or months to accomplish, so you truly are speeding things up immensely. I would not be able to perform my analytical duties without you. Even though I am not supposed to be analytical anymore. Forward the information directly to the trace analysts currently working this trace at all locations." "Yes sir!" was all Nora replied with another task completed. All that can be done is to wait for the analysts to find the rogue unit locations. That will still take time, with the computer eliminating millions of registered units over a 24-hour period. "Nora, have each analyst select the best shift replacement to continue with each shift, so we have the analysts working around the clock." Nora did not even respond but she never forgot anything. Tim though about another trip to the snack bar, since Global Security provided all of it without cost to the employees. The corporation's directors felt with the demands of the analysts, they should provide all the possible perks they could to attract the brightest talent around the world. It appeared to work well, since analysts lined up at all the Global Security locations for interviewing with the company. The downside was there always seemed to be a need for more, and the risks up to and including fatality, did not seem to deter any of them from believing they could complete 10 years of service. How foolish we all can be in our youth.

"Nora, I am leaving for the day, hopefully by morning the picture will be less cloudy." Trask said that he could never have handled this any better and certainly nowhere near as quick. Although, he had been out of touch with analysis a far longer period of time. He also asked if his presence was needed, since Tim had such control over the situation. Tim simply said there were many things he did not know anything about yet, and unfortunately this situation was taking away from his learning them.

CHAPTER

2

Tim awoke with his legs stiff and arms lifeless from being propped on the desk, additionally a very sore neck. More evident was the overwhelming need to eliminate the large amounts of coffee consumed during the last evening, awaiting the positions of the rogue transmitters. He came in yesterday morning expecting to have that accomplished, but even he did not know how many registered transmitters existed. Nor the number of times they were used throughout the course of twenty-four hours. He did not remember falling asleep in the chair, and being five floors below the analysts, noise would not have been an issue. Nora did not emit a sound. He almost fell face down in his attempt to hustle to the break area, where the facilities were he needed to indulge in using. He was not accustomed to all the aches and pains he was experiencing and his appendages were revolting in response to the commands his brain was issuing, or at least not performing with normal expected rate of compliance. He did stop to obtain another large mug of coffee on his return to start the process of determining what progress had been made. He checked his viewer remembering that the remaining satellite positions still required three more and they still did. This was so unlike Nora to leave a task unfinished. "Nora, are you there?" he asked the windows.

"Yes Timothy, and my memory banks estimate you would like the remaining satellite positions. Unfortunately, the last three satellite computer systems have been offline for diagnostics, and remain inaccessible for the type of inquiry we need to make. They can have transmitters direct signals from them. Either there is a serious problem, or our hacker planted a diversion in anticipation of Global tracking procedures. Since, I have no additional means to communicate with them, I have kept my line in a continuous loop between the three computers, expecting them to reply at any time. As a diversion, I have been eliminating registered TRU signals from the six completed and have 50 percent removed. Do you have any other means to contact the satellite groups to verify maintenance is being performed?"

Of course he did not, because Nora always took care of all those details. "I will have to look into that Nora, I have always been dependent on your ability to contact everyone when needed. Place a call to Sooni, and patch it to the vidphone, she might know somebody to contact. Which satellites are you trying to contact?" Tim ended with. Nora's response, "The European pair and one Asian, it is possible they share a single security system, since all those satellites were placed in orbit by the same organization."

"Tim you look positively awful, have you been out on a drinking binge?" was how Sooni started from the vidphone. "Only coffee" Tim stated, "But I did spend the night and I really think I need to get better furniture for overnighters. I hope I do not look as bad as I feel." Sooni quickly took the opening, "You in all likelihood look even worse; but maybe some of it is the pixel quality of the vidphone. It is a little early for progress checks, so what's up?"

"Nora has been unable to contact three security systems, it appears they are down for maintenance and have been for well over 24 hours. I was wondering if you knew anyone to contact directly, and Nora tells me one is Asian and the European pair are in question." "Way ahead of you Tim," Sooni started, "before leaving last night for a comfortable bed, I noticed the progress had stalled on the remaining satellite positioning overhead viewer and checked into it personally. It seems that the first thing our hacker or hackers did, was to slip that satellite security system a small virus, and the system has been down trying to reject the virus from within the system itself. After twelve hours, the company's own people could not gain access from their normal home locations, and went to the security system location. They have been working on it since, and the friend I talked with, indicated the problem needed to be cleared by this evening. If that cannot be done, the system would need to be cleaned and rebuilt from the primary backup storage data, which would take an estimated 72 hours. I hope it does not go to that extreme, but our intruder seems to have planned all sorts of nasty traps to prevent us from completing the point of origin details. That means the satellites are usable to all authorized transmitters; but getting information about who used them is out of the question. The worst part my friend told me, if they have to use backup data, they might not even have the information on record for the time frame we need. That depends on when the virus was planted. The intruder has been so concise so far, it would not come as a surprise that virus was planted sooner than the transmissions were initiated. Time will tell, but I would not expect any more information than we already have."

Tim said, "You are just full of information I did not need to hear this morning. We already have the times of contact logged, we simply want to know where the satellite was positioned at the time it was initiated. I assume, which may not be a good thing; it takes 24 hours for a satellite to be in the identical position over the earth. At least Nora has already reprimanded me about the satellites being held stationary it is the earth that rotates in 24-hour cycles. We should be able to obtain that information for the purpose of the graphic viewer; it simply would have been easier to trace to the point of origin. What else you got before I go find a shave kit somewhere close by?" Sooni said again, it was too soon for a progress report.

Timothy Frantz did not really expect this much information; but by shift change he did want major inroads pointing to some location. The virus was undoubtedly a major hurdle, and he had no desire to be waiting three days to resume efforts. I have no more angles to chase. More input is necessary to further the progress, but once we get past this, I do not foresee any more surprises. I wonder why the intruder only infected one system with the virus. I need to think on that for a while longer. "Nora, please call my home and Kuri in particular, I owe her an apology and explanation." Nora had the vidphone already active and made no response to the request. The next voice he heard was a sleepy Kuri saying hello with eyes barely open. Tim said, "I first owe you an apology, obviously for waking you and for my not coming home last night." Kuri said in a very groggy voice, "Not really, at 3 AM when I got home, I was too tired to do anything but remove my clothes, which I think are still next to the bed and go to sleep.

I just assumed you were there and did not even have the energy to check. But if you do not mind, I am going back to bed, I still need more sleep than this." The vidphone disconnected and Kuri did not even let him say goodbye. Tim had never seen her like that before, at least without his help, and that was much more pleasurable than work.

"Nora, I need to step out for a little while, time to find some toiletries to make myself a little more human." Respectable was out of the question with clothing that had been slept in. Nora simply acknowledge that Tim was heading out.

Tim decided while he was out to have a small meal for the first time in more than 24 hours. There was nothing going to happen fast enough in this breach case that could not wait long enough to get some nourishment. If he was gaining ground on this culprit, he might view matters differently. As it were, every step forward so far had major obstacles to overcome. It was as though this unknown person was able to read his mind, or at least probe for the course of action. Every footfall had some adverse reaction planned in its place. Since it was still morning, a good hardy breakfast might encourage him to be patient and let it come to him. He just had the gut feeling; the problems were just beginning, that did nothing complimentary to his digestive system, even with the tasty breakfast from his favorite nearby establishment. He did use the facilities there to spruce up while his order was being prepared. He had arrived simultaneously with the food. Of course it included coffee, real eggs not those genetically manufactured likeness of egg products. They still used real dairy products here, which was the biggest reason for liking this restaurant. A little pricey for most of the young kids weaned from real meats and vegetables; but many of early middle aged and up still enjoyed them. Too many things were fabricated these days, and being old enough to have consumed only the real thing as a youth, synthetic foods simply did not tickle his taste buds. No matter how much healthier they might be for prolonged well-being, and mental states as the medical associations informed us. Certainly had not damaged his parents or grandparents who were doing quite well yet. The family lake property was all paid for with a wonderful little pond that Tim paid to have stocked, since some of them enjoy fishing.

It had taken about 90 minutes of time to take care of all his errands including a deep thoughtful breakfast, but since he had been at the office for more than 24 hours, that was not terribly unreasonable. Granted he fell asleep and probably less than the recommended eight hours. Analyzing traces and digging into financial security systems was not his duty as detailed, 'coordinate security efforts, Tim' was how it was explained. 'Who knows better than you Tim, what is required to perform under the rigors of analysis with Global Security Corporation. You are one of a precious few that completed the time requirements to relax and bask in retirement, but we really need someone exactly like yourself to oversee this operation. Tim, we know you can leave and live a nice lifestyle without any additional stress in your life, but consider staying on as director of global operations and we will make it more than worth it for you.'

Who could refuse? Everybody I was associated with from the beginning until now knew exactly what he or she was going to do when they completed the 10-year milestone. One even knew what part of the tropical island beach the shanty was going to be erected. I still can't figure out what I'm going to do tomorrow. Anyway with the amount of other investments, plus the perks the company provides for extended service, I am insuring that the company, hence my investment will perform above the standards. The vidphone appeared out of the compartment and Nora said, "Tim, a Mr. Robin Torry, has requested an audience with the 'one and only' Timothy Frantz as he stated it." "Thanks Nora," Tim replied.

Robin appeared as if by Nora's command and Tim jumped into the fray, "You're late." To which Robin responded, "I didn't know I was expected. My clients in the European financial district are probing me for input into the disappearance of some 11 billion in world currency, know anything about it?"

Tim said with a Cheshire smile, "Not a thing, missing funds is more in your line of work, isn't it?" Which broke out into mild laughter from both parties, but it was short lived and did not take long to return to the real purpose of the call. Tim: "Robin, we got us one smart intruder, even beyond what you dreamed up. Certainly we have been working on trying to trace the intruder. Every move we have made so far has been anticipated and the doors that we keep opening seem to slam shut almost as fast. This person or persons definitely want to get lost in the information movement with the money. How much do you know concerning this?"

Robin told Tim he had just gotten involved this morning at the financial end and regardless of how much money was missing all the transactions appeared to be perfectly normal. "Sure there are some large transactions, but this is not unusual considering the amount of funds processed here." Robin concluded with.

Tim let him know that the transactions were split between 10 rogue transmitter uplinks and each handled 1 of 10 information bytes transmitted to be assembled as a whole at the financial system, thus appearing to be a legitimate transaction. "My analysts have been unable to complete a single trace back to the point of origin, and needless to say, I am not authorized to divulge techniques. Suffice to say a great deal of information considered confidential to Global, the intruder has placed way too many safeguards in our path. One that is not confidential to us, the weasel planted a virus into one of the controlling satellite security systems, forcing it into maintenance mode sometime prior to getting your financial groups funds." Robin did not make a single sound that would have better explained than the look of total shock on his face. It took a good deal for Robin to be surprised; yet had the appearance of an expert who just faced his better. Tim continued with, "I had truly expected to hear from you a couple of days ago when I was assembling my best teams to get a quick countermeasure against this intruder. Needless to say, there is no quick solution. I must say, I have not felt this overwhelmed since you did your thing six years ago to make your mark into the financial circles, although we never could prove it was you. It is assumed that you showed everyone how to prevent it and since no single individual had any major loss they all let you keep the money as a fee. I honestly do not expect a confession at this stage Robin, I simply wanted to emphasize how difficult this particular intruder has been to this point. I do not believe he can pull off your feat, because he infiltrated financial institutions that would not allow him to keep such large quantities if he went public. Tim explained as much additional information as allowable, knowing Robin was here to assist not hinder, but also had to relate that things were in a holding pattern until the remaining satellite positions could be pinpointed. Robin offered all the assistance he could to help find the intruder and stated from a security standpoint everything and more was already being done.

One hour had passed since the vidphone had return to its overhead compartment. At the very end of the conversation he informed Robin he had no means of prevention for this type of attack, even with an artificially intelligent systems network. The specific application of financials on the IG might be an ideal testing place for its use, and he would appreciate it if Robin could get the word out to the right people. Robin did have far more contacts when it came to this type of need. The last thing said was without being able to obtain all the pertinent data from the problem, he could not tell them how else to correct matters. He also indicated that data would be in their transaction records; but doubted they would want outsiders perusing with the exception of Robin himself. He suggested for Robin to alter things to try to prevent another similar occurrence. Robin had parted with the usual be in touch for updates and would get to work on the infiltration as soon as he got off.

Tim had asked Nora for a progress report and his suspicions were confirmed. Nothing could be completed until the satellite security system was returned to normal operations. Concluding that the most critical issue was stalled, he informed Nora he was leaving to get rested for tomorrow. Nora had ways to reach him; but seldom found anything so important to use them. He reiterated he could be reached should anything pertinent develop prior to his expected return time. Tim left and headed towards a place sure to relieve him of all his pains from the night before. He found his way across town to a professional masseuse he had seen occasionally for the last thirteen years. He went there because the results were always better than anticipated. Explain where it hurts and not only did they make it go away, he felt if he had wings he could fly to the moon. Should a person come expecting more than a massage, they were either turned away or disappointed. Upon one occasion, a rather boisterous customer was escorted from the premises. Needless to say under those circumstances, nothing is done for those types of aches and pains. After an hour wait, since he did not have an appointment, he got to enter a booth for the much-needed rubdown.

Tim completely enjoyed the experience of a true artist each and every time he came to this establishment. Today had been his first trip in quite a while. He attributed that to a less stressful work environment, which was good for all at Global Security Corporation. It has also been a few years since he had worked at his position until he succumbed to fatigue. Today's experience was no disappointment, he felt marvelous and decided he would spend the evening at his family home with the wife.

First thing he checked the pond, found a large number of fish were present and some were getting fairly large. The stock was not depleted and that was good, unless nobody was fishing it. He checked the families and everyone was in good spirits with his unexpected visit. All offered dinner later and he learned nobody so much as suffered a cold since his last visit. He hoped he had spent enough time from the house for Kuri to be a little better rested.

She was up and about, had already performed her morning meditation routine. She was a bit surprised to see him this time of day. They managed to get in the customary hug and kiss before she started with her evening at the restaurant. Kuri said, "I would think that everyone from within a 100 miles of the restaurant decided to have dinner there last night. I cannot believe they are that busy every night of the week. I consider myself relatively fit; but with all the walking I did seating customers, serving drinks and taking care of the charges, my legs ached all the way to my neck, if that is possible. I think even the baby was worn out, she did not even kick until I was in my routine. On top of everything else last night, after closing we had to do full inventory to see what had to be ordered to have everything for today. My brother ran out of sushi just before closing, and he said it had never happened before. As a result, I did not get home until 3 AM this morning and all I could think was sleep. So how is it I did not know you were not home you wonder?" Tim said, "Big problem hit as soon as I walked in yesterday morning, and I kept waiting for some results to go home, they never came and I fell asleep. Sleeping in a chair is not a good thing to do, because nothing works right when you awaken. Since I already woke you this morning, when I left, I went to the masseuse I know of and got all the aches and kinks worked out. It does sound like we both had forgettable nights."

The remainder of the day with Kuri was largely spent relaxing with each of them rather tired out from the night before. Tim did make a nice dinner and got his meditation routine done before they made it an early night, and went to bed holding each other.

He slept like a baby after the masseuse did the magic to not only make the pain disappear, but rejuvenated his whole body like when he was years younger. He indulged himself with special roast coffee when he arose. He only kept that coffee here at the lake property. It just did not have the same taste when using it with the sterile city water, so he was forced to use something else for the other homes. With the fresh mountain stream waters that fed the well here, it was better than anything those gourmet coffee shops ever produced. It took him about an hour to get ready, and most of that time was consuming the coffee to make sure the pot was empty, before he left for the Seattle office. He let Kuri sleep, as it would seem she had an even rougher time the night before than he.

The trip was uneventful. It took close to an hour since there was hardly any traffic at this hour of the morning. It was amazing how people working from their homes became prisoners of their own environment. They purchased everything over the IG and had it delivered. Fuel economy was not an issue, the transports today had an inductor that removed airborne particles and exhaust all the oxygen and nitrogen that went through the system and cleaned it essentially, at least that was how it was explained. There was very little crime to speak of, so what had made the people so reclusive. Most restaurants and shops were attached to homes, so there was no travel for those people. Some of the additional employees may have to travel, but most probably lived within walking distance.

The transport is some marvelous piece of technology in its own right. They are under complete computer monitoring control, and hover approximately 3 feet over the surface of the roadways. Roads remain a necessity for those who still own automobiles, but those roads that have not been updated with permanent surface material can make traveling them less than admirable. Hover transports however are not susceptible to bumps and holes. You do not really need to drive a transport, just inform the computer system to take the best route to a destination, and with instant mapping access it take you there. Surprisingly you still need a driver's license to own one. It does have a manual override for those that need to feel in control, the monitoring system will take over if you put yourself or transport into a dangerous situation. Tim did like to take control most times to remember the feel of driving', but it is not quite the same as an automobile. Today was not one of those days. He simply did not make this trip frequently in sunlight and desired the opportunity to enjoy the scenery before arriving in the city.

Timothy Frantz arrived fully refreshed, and ready to take on the world. He hoped he would make a difference today, he thought as he entered his office. He made his trip to the snack area where the coffee was, and informed Nora he was wide-eyed alert requesting any activity Nora could provide him.

Nora responded with, "The satellite security systems is still offline, but I did complete the signal elimination on six of the seven satellites. I have a total of eleven unidentified transmitters on the six completed satellites. I have not found any government agency admitting to using any of the transmitters, but we know that they have them and should assume some were at least operating. Tim said, "Good Nora, can we determine the exact frequency used on each transmitter and possibly match them to the frequency used on the rogue transmitters we want found. Nora was stunned, if a computer can have such a reaction and replied, "My circuits seemed to have overlooked that, and I cannot understand why that was not the next logical sequence. Timothy, do you think I am due for a maintenance check?" Tim stated, "No Nora, you have performed all your functions perfectly as usual, I believe the real problem is you have never had to go to the extreme measures we currently face. You normally have a hacker apprehended by this time and have no reference to steps beyond that point. You may never have to go this far again in finding a hacker, I have once and I lost. You are far more advanced than what I had to work with then. As an analyst, it took me four weeks to have advanced as far as we did in 48 hours." Nora: "I should be able to get that information within an hour, quicker if I do not keep trying to get the satellite security system that remains off line." Tim: "An hour will be fine, my guess is you will match up at least 10 frequencies on each of the satellites, and some of those frequencies will correspond with the satellites we cannot get information from. That means we should be able to reverse trace to specific points of origin, but we will have to transmit on the specific frequency with a simultaneous trace." "Nora recommends you be the computer from now on when it comes to course of action", Nora said as it was obviously the end of conversation for her.

Tim finished his mug of coffee and headed for a refill. He considered contacting the other offices, but thought better to wait until Nora confirmed signal frequency matches on the satellites. He poured over the overhead video chart for any additional direction to concentrate on while he waited. Once again he was stalled until information was confirmed. It was 57 minutes from the time Nora ended the previous conversation when she broke the silence. "Timothy Frantz, I do not understand why you ask me to do something when you already know the answer", Nora said coldly. Tim had no clue how to explain 'hunch' to a computer so he said, "Nora, suspecting something is not a conclusive answer and hardly proof. I assume you have proven information we can use to start the next operational phase." Nora: "Yes, I do. The seven satellites have a confirmed 12 identical frequency matches on each. I can place the frequencies on the overhead if you like. The previous checks did not locate the eleventh and twelfth until all registered signals were removed completely from the map. Those two signals are below normal but within acceptable range. It is possible one or both of these signals will not show on the three satellites that are affected by the security system that is offline. The frequencies, which can be displayed at the appropriate satellites are at exact intervals of three hours and twenty-two minutes. This is something I could not check prior to eliminating the registered signals. It could mean our intruder is not as knowledgeable as we gave credit, or he may know much more to be so precise with the intervals and mislead us once more." Tim: "It is excellent information to post, Nora please indicate on each satellite the frequencies and the exact time in 24 hour format on the overheads. Once you have that posted contact all the major offices for a conference to get everyone back in the same direction." Nora must be slowing down Tim thought, it took just over a minute for the videophone to appear and all the numbers were updated on the overhead screen.

"Welcome to my parlor," said Tim with slight humor to his voice. "We have received a little more information to go on. Nora should have updated all your overheads to show frequencies and connection time with each satellite we can access. There are still three more which we should get soon, but we do have a total of twelve frequencies to reverse trace. For those analysts who have not performed this function before, the process is a little different. Normally we trace an active signal back to the source. These little culprits need to have a signal generated, I suggest using an inquiry trace or 'are you there' signal to send out for response. Reverse trace that signal to pinpoint the source locations. Our intruder has given considerable thought and planning into our line of reaction, so once again caution is highly recommended. The nicest thing about the TRU is very little power is required to get a response from our wake up call. With any luck, our intruder may have overlooked this feature should the power have been turned off to the devices we seek. I want each office to take the satellite belonging to you regardless of position when time of connection was established. This prevents us from doing the same satellite by more than one office. Start with the signals in the normal frequency range and then we try simultaneously on the higher frequency ranges. This might help cover our tracks in the event our intruder is monitoring his devices for activity. The normal range devices will be harder to separate from all the other activity while the higher ranges will be much more discernible. "Sooni entered the conversation with a question, "Tim, do we need to coordinate the trace simultaneously on the normal range signals?"

Tim answered quickly, "The traces would work more to our advantage if they appear random. I would hope our culprit does not possess too sophisticated of security equipment due to cost. Single traces from various satellites will appear as mistaken identity or erroneous data, unless somebody has equipment similar to our own. I would think the expense would far exceed 11 billion in world currency. If anything at all is used, the most that would occur is a hello that got no response. There should be others occurring randomly throughout the day from mistaken identity or bad data streams, sometime hit all frequencies trying to locate a destination."

Next came Chaka Toukee to speak, "Tim, I'm not sure we are equipped to generate a signal tone from our trace facility here, can you confirm that?" Nora jumped in with the answer, "Your office is equipped with the identical trace equipment we possess, as are all the other offices. If you would like assistance in performing this function, I can uplink with your computer and load the correct parameters required for the necessary signal and procedures. Would you like that done for you?" Chaka made a positive acknowledgement and then Ivan and Cho requested the same assistance. Tim suspected at least half his office directors had never been this deep into trace procedures previously. This was his primary reason for conferencing everyone along with getting everybody back onto the same program. This was especially true, since all may have deviated from it with the time lag and major hiccup in obtaining the information from the satellites. Nora said it would take a minimum of thirty minutes to get everyone the procedures allowing some to proceed sooner than others, which would make it appear all that much more random.

Tim concluded with having everyone contact him when the traces were complete so that the source locations could be posted to the overheads. When everyone had completed, it was vital to have the high frequency signals traced simultaneously. Everyone acknowledged the importance of the timing and made their parting statements. Tim would have Nora trace the low range frequency signals when she had completed her procedural assistance to the other offices. She would most likely be done before any of the offices check in with their task completed. Tim watched the overhead updates with the anticipation of a child on Christmas morning. A low-level transmitter appeared nineteen minutes later showing a trace point in North Carolina's East Coast, north of Albemarle Sound. The position was only accurate to a fifteen-mile radius. Tim then requested Nora contact local authorities in Elizabeth City to initiate a search for the transmitters, which could require resident to resident searching. Also for authorities not to come into physical contact with any devices in case the intruder had rigged the devices for adverse reactions. The search parameters would normally start with vacant and public access buildings first, before going residential. With any luck they would be located without interrupting the normal life of the local citizens. Tim estimated no more than two people involved and becoming more likely a single individual was the intruder. It took ninety minutes for the remaining frequencies to have positions, and Nora was not needed to instruct additional authorities. The vidphone appeared and everyone was there waiting the next stage to be conducted.

Timothy Frantz said, "Thirty minutes from now we want to reverse trace the three high frequency transmitters. It needs to be relatively synchronized in order to achieve the effect of getting closer to our target. Sooni, your group has one of the frequencies, I have my team on the second, and Ivan's group has the third. The remaining offices should monitor the events, just in case you need to use this technique again. It is not a mandatory request, you are invited to monitor the sequence as a matter of interest to those who would like the learning experience opportunity. Nora will transmit video trace information only. This is precautionary, in the event any other perils lie in wait for trace teams. Monitoring personnel will not be fully exposed. Signal Nora if you desire to have the video feed directed to your locations. We will begin in precisely twenty-six minutes. Thank you for all you have done to this point." Tim concluded and left no opportunity for second thoughts, questions or other nonsense to prevent them from keeping the schedule.

The trace parameters were set, the group of analysts from each office were ready, and all the remaining offices were requesting inclusion in the monitoring of the event about to take place. Five minutes before trace time, the videophone dropped from the compartment and Nora said the urgent call was from the site of the North Carolina Beach Resort and Casino. The local analyst who Tim did not recognize appeared on the vidphone. Tim said, "Hello, might I inquire as to your name?" The analyst stated, "Roger Morris, sir. I was told to contact you when we found the transmitter site." Tim:" Yes Roger, what do you have?" Roger: "At this point we have found the location on the roof of a casino and resort on the North Carolina Beach, and are still investigating the area for traps and anything out of the ordinary. The local authorities seem to have more experience with finding devices intended to do harm to persons and property than I do myself. I can say there is more than one item here, but have not been able to get too close for an exact count until the authorities complete their investigations. I thought you might like to know we have at least found something believed to be what you are looking for. I did see at least one remote transmitter and the possibility of other items hidden in venting areas on the roof." Tim: "Good Roger, that means we have at least got a point of access we are soon to trace three more transmitters and just in case nobody gave numbers we are seeking a total of twelve. Since you said one was remote that would probably be a low frequency range TRU, which most likely means our intruder is not going to be there. When you can have full access let me know. Thanks for the good news." Just in time for the reverse trace to start and Tim wanted to monitor it as well. He was not monitoring for an educational experience, Tim needed to insure everything went according to plan.

Nora was going to be involved in synchronizing the inquiry outbound traces and monitoring for responses, all of which would be recorded by the computers each analysts was using to reverse trace. The inquiries went out and it took about a minute for all the transmitters to wake up and then the second inquiry would hopefully generate responses. At the start of the second inquiry all three analysts started the reverse trace. 15 seconds later all three responded and then it did not take long for the results to suddenly turn catastrophic. The Seattle analyst collapsed at his desk. Nora immediately recognized a problem and notified Tim. If anything good came of this, it was Nora said all three reverse traces were successful, but when Tim arrived at the analyst's office and opened the door, he was not overjoyed with what he saw. The analyst did not merely collapse, he was dead. "Nora, halt all operations immediately." Tim removed the headset from his now deceased analyst and saw trace amounts of blood from his ears. "Nora, contact the local authorities, inform them of a fatality, which is likely murder. Then conference everybody into my office pronto."

Tim returned to his office, the vidphone was already down and he inquired to each of the other offices whether the analysts who were involved with the reverse trace were well. No other analysts were affected. Tim: "Okay people, we are no longer dealing with an intrusion. I have a dead analyst, which seriously alters our attack plan. We now know this person or group has no intention of going public, since murder is not a public option. We also need to rearrange our chart and place priority on the individual knowledge. Obviously they have intimate knowledge of security procedures, and seemly specific information on our operations. I am going to have Nora very busy in obtaining records on past employees. It may not be the only option, but someone knows an awful lot about how we step through trace procedures to be able to interfere with our individual stages. Nora these changes need to go into the overhead chart at the top goes Expert security and appears he or they are expert levels in all other categories."

* * *

The overhead video chart included with the satellite position information display showed as follows:

34

Expert security procedures Line 1 (emphasis on GSC methods)
Expert in financial transactions Line 2
Expert in Communications Line 3
Expert in Satellite positioning Line 4
Expert in application programs Line 5
Expert in Technology (rogue TRU's) Line 6

Tim continued, "I would like all the other offices doing a search for a possibly stolen artificial intelligence device. There is no guarantee one will be located, but it would make sense to be expert level at so many aspects of the Information Gateway and the technology used. Nora will be searching for how many people had access to the history files, in particular the one unsolved case that went through many of these identical stages." Nora broke in, "Tim, every employee from every office has had access to that file, because it is used in the initial training, since the case was encountered, and that amounts to over five hundred thousand people. Also the authorities have just arrived and will want to interview you." Tim: "Okay Nora, people this meeting will need to resume at a later time, be expecting it and any input toward finding our intruder will be more than welcomed. Thanks, see you all soon." The vidphone was disconnected leaving no options but to think and wait for the other offices. Tim opened the door for the authorities, but they had not made it to his office yet.

Tim figured the most likely location of the authorities would be the office of the dead analyst, and headed off in that direction. When he arrived to close proximity of the office he was held back to keep from contaminating the scene, as he was told. A more senior person came from the office and toward him. He said, "I am Detective Marshall from the Seattle Police Department, could I have your name for the record." Tim: "I am Timothy Frantz, CEO of operations here."

Marshall: "Can you explain what had happened here and who removed the headset?" Tim: "We were running a synchronized security process and about ninety second from the initiation, this analyst who was the primary person involved with the process, collapsed at his desk as indicated by Nora, my computer. I moved the headset in order to check for a pulse; but saw the blood trickle from his ears and had Nora contact you. He has not been touched by any other person besides myself, which was only to find out if anything could be done for him." Marshall: "You realize that you have contaminated the scene, it could make you a primary suspect in this matter. Can you provide me with any details concerning what your company was doing during the time this person died?"

Tim: "I can to some degree; but most people, do not fully grasp what we do on a daily basis. The procedure was a reverse trace, which sends a signal out on the Information Gateway to a transmitter, in this case used in a financial theft. The signal is intended to wake up the transmitters and with a second trace attempt to pinpoint the location of that transmitter providing it responded to the wakeup call. Do you follow me so far?" The detective gave an affirmative nod and waved his hand in a fashion for Tim to continue. "Upon Nora informing me of the analyst in distress, I halted all operations. I then came to see if there was anything I could do for this analyst. I was not overjoyed about the condition I found him. I would need to know exact cause of death, although whatever killed him came through the head set. I suspected either an audio or frequency that caused ruptures in the blood vessels that were fatal. Since all of the offices are fully soundproofed, whatever it was remained contained to this office. I have not had the opportunity to get with Nora about the results of the process we were running or analyze the recording of what came over the headset. That will be the next thing I have her do, should you decide I can continue with my work." Marshall: "I am afraid we will need to detain you for a little while so as to clear you of any wrong doing. It will be an inconvenience, but my computer records show that this facility has a history of problems, although few have resulted in death, there have been enough cases to cause suspicion." Tim: "What we do here in protecting the Information Gateway has many drawbacks, stress can lead to a number of problems, but there are also inherent dangers from those who seek not to be found. I wish you would reconsider detaining me, as some of the information I can access may aid you in your goals as well." Marshall: "Sorry, can't do that for you. You will come with me while my people examine the scene. That will take several hours and I have noted your cooperation to this point, and may or may not have any further questions for you. You can come unrestrained; but only if you do so willingly." Tim: "Does not sound like I have a choice, can I at least inform Nora I will be out of the office?" Marshall: "You speak of your computer as if it is a living being. What kind of computers do you use here?" Tim: "We are allowed semi-intelligent systems that like most computers these days have audio and speech functions included in the personality application. We have not yet been authorize AI outside of the main network, which could help tremendously in preserving analysts and possibly see a pattern before it become a criminal act." Marshall: "I see, would you mind if my people look around to confirm nothing more that semi-intelligent computers are in this office?" Tim: "Do you have people who can tell the difference, and will they know not to interfere with any of the computers, since most have confidential company information. We are somewhat in the same business; we just stick with policing the Information Gateway. An area, unfortunately, city and state authorities are ill equipped to deal with." Marshall: "I have two computer experts here, and they will only verify that the computers are semi-intelligent, as they have explained to me there is one significant design component that separates the two. It only requires a visual inspection to ascertain." Tim: "That will be fine, just make sure they do not try to interface with any of them, that could make them unresponsive to the assigned user and that cannot happen. I still need to inform Nora I will be leaving." Marshall: "How do you inform your computer you are going?" Tim: "I need to return to my office and tell her, since that is the only audio input I have for her." Marshall: "Okay, we can do that on the way out."

Tim told Nora he was being detained by the authorities and would let her know when he got back. The next five hours were spent going to the police facility, sitting around and waiting. Detective Marshall had no further questions during his waiting and had said nothing until it was time to leave.

Marshall: "You are free to go, I will assign an escort to take you back to your building. The autopsy results are as you suspected, the inner ears were severely damaged and hemorrhaging of the brain vessels were cause of death. The doctors said it took all of fifteen seconds for the victim to succumb to it."

Tim was escorted to the police transport, the day was gone and outside of a couple things to do as soon as he got back, just to initiate some action would take no more than fifteen minutes. When he returned, everything appeared relatively normal, aside from a different shift person in the office where the analyst had been killed. He had Nora contact all the offices to inform them he had been detained, and the conference call would take place tomorrow. His next action was to Nora, he wanted to know the outcome of the reverse trace and positions placed in the overhead diagram. Then he wanted Nora to analyze the last thirty seconds of the recording of the reverse trace through audio and frequency meters with the audio fully muted. He did not know if the sound or frequency used could fry her circuits, but simply did not need to have it happen. Finally he gave her the second part of what would likely be a task that would consume lots of days even for Nora. He wanted every person who had access to the Robin Torry history file, current whereabouts, and by process of elimination narrow down the suspects list, he now thought pointed to a former employee. Just another hunch, but with 500,000 records he did not expect answers in the morning. He also told Nora to access all the medical records to help with eliminating those who could not possibly be responsible for this outrageous act.

With that done he informed Nora he would be back at his usual time in the morning and just to keep her happy told her to have his coffee ready and waiting when he got in. That got the anticipated tirade from Nora he had learned to love.

CHAPTER

3

fter dinner, Tim asked Kuri if she would help him develop a
more substantial meditation routine, and he knew his Tai Chi
was nowhere the quality of her routine. He did say he was not
likely to ever get his leg straight up in the air like she was as certain body
components did not agree with those movements. Kuri said it would take
some time, but she was more than willing to see if she could help with his
various skills from multiple types of martial arts. She did say that her leg
lift was one that took years to perfect and he did not need to get it that
high; but the overall balance and height would help keep very much of his
body firmed, and it was most beneficial to body and mind harmony. She
said she would help as she had seen his routine, and thought it was not too
bad for a mix. Kuri had him do his routine for the evening and tomorrow
she would give him ways to induce other moves within, to keep the flow
continuous. He did his 50 minute exercise and she and he went to take in
a little entertainment, snuggled closely together before going to bed.

He did not see a psychiatrist, psychologist, but had occasionally seen
the acupuncture specialist, especially in the time before he and Kuri were
married, but largely before she accepted his proposal. Global Security had
finally started doing mandatory stress testing with all the analysts, even
he had to see them at the time they wished. They always asked him how
he managed to be somewhat exempt from the stress that had overcome so
many of the other analysts that were involved with security. All he ever said
was he was not ever too stressed by anything on a day to day basis. They

asked what he did differently. He would tell them, since he did not know what everyone else did, he was not qualified to say what was different.

Every day since first joining Global as an analyst he would find moments where he could let his mind wander. Most often he thought about the various advancements made since he were a young child. The food-processing center, transports, medical advancements, technology such as AI computer systems. When he thought about how much easier his life was now, as compared to his youth. He seldom looked back to what it was like for his father or grandfather, and he was sure they could very easily tell him things he would find difficult to believe. He remembered Detective Marshall informing him of the autopsy results that was something he knew little about outside of stories. The medical scanner used by all medical practitioners was a machine that scanned the entire body from head to toe. It produced a 3 dimensional image of every detail of the human body that it had scanned. It could be used to find any anomaly and find them very soon in the stages critical to having a patient diagnosed and cured. The same scanner was used for autopsy work. It was much quicker than having to disfigure a body to find what caused their death. Autopsies were mandatory throughout the Americas, as both a method for determination, but also prevention. Not having been present for any of these procedures and too young to have had a reason to before the medical scanners, the stories were somewhat gruesome to Tim. Cutting into a person to remove organs just to get the weight and also determine if any them failed abnormally seemed so cruel. He remembered that the detective told him that it took only fifteen seconds and he wondered how they could determine that from the images of the medical scanner. Maybe, they could tell how much damage was done to blood vessels, but to determine how long it took, was not something he could grasp from looking at images. Enough morbid thoughts.

Tim awoke an hour before he was supposed to be up. There was no point in trying to go back to sleep. He was fully awake for whatever reason interrupted his slumber. Kuri was still quite a bit asleep, and he did not want to disturb her and got out of bed as slowly as he could, not to disturb her. She slept a little more these days with the pregnancy having some effect, but nothing overly severe. He made his coffee, and sat at the counter with a nice cup of coffee hoping the aroma did not disturb Kuri, although she was more partial to tea.

He picked up with the thoughts he had the evening before, and then something occurred to him. Although he had never spent any time analyzing himself via psychology, maybe, his mental wanderings have been his stress release mechanism that had kept him fully functioning in an environment that few people had completed ten years. He had completed it once. Now into his twelfth year at Global Security he gave a passing thought to retirement when this was over. He remembered when he was a young child and going through the intelligence qualifying tests, they had informed him he had scored the highest I.Q. results ever recorded. He was young, and never really put much stock into the tests, and wondered if the results could be achieved by guessing with random choices. He did remember that in order to achieve his high grades, he never really had to work that hard, everything just came easily and although he did not have a photographic memory. He did have a really high retention of anything he saw or learned. Mostly as it pertained to his work environment, he caught on to patterns in minutes, which others took hours to find. He knew what course of action he could take and when he had made a mistake, it was not repeated the next time he encountered a similar situation. He always switched his mental wanderings on and off throughout the workday, maybe it was his coping mechanism, and what he did differently from everyone else. He thought he might mention it at the next psychological testing. Maybe he would mention retiring too.

Now it was time for his second cup of coffee, and the normal morning ritual of getting ready for another day at the office. Kuri had awakened and he made her some tea as she sat at the counter seat next to him. He placed her tea in front, walked behind and reach around her to hold her as well as place his hand on the now visible baby bump, and told her she was without a doubt the most beautiful woman he had the pleasure to lay eyes on. This got Kuri to give him a nice long kiss that he held for a bit longer, before telling her it was time for him to get ready for another day at the office.

Kuri and Tim had a home in Tokyo, and tried to get there at least once a month. Her father, although now looking around Seattle for his and his wife's home, were staying at his other home and the one he was born in. It would never leave the family as long as he was around. Kuri's father Hiro, had a small chain of restaurants 5 in Tokyo and his flagship restaurant in Seattle. It was run by his son, who Hiro taught to be as much of a master chef as himself, and they had finally found a home of their own, and all of them loved the freedom of being in Seattle. During the five months waiting for the board to finally reach a decision on Tim becoming CEO. He and Kuri had the opportunity to go the home in Tokyo twice for about two weeks each time. During the last trip, while entering the sauna house, Kuri already pregnant but not showing, went through getting Tim and the baby access privileges to the sauna house. It was not a long procedure, Tim being her husband was issued his own entrance identification, but until the baby was 13 years of age, could not enter, even with identification privileges. That made it so Kuri did not complete that portion, since at this point the baby had not even been given a name. It did bring to light to them both, they should give this some consideration in the very near future.

Under normal circumstances, interoffice communications probably lasted five minutes on a monthly basis. Current circumstances were not the normal. It required considerably more interoffice interaction to keep control of all the additional activities for finding an intruder.

Japan had been an economic power for over 130 years. How they had done that had always been to improve someone's technology, usual from the Americas, and design a highly efficient process to produce the technology that others found difficult to compete with. As an island nation, with no real resources of its own, ingenuity had been a key element in the nation's economic success. In the 1950's it started with manufacturing economy class automobiles. Expanding decade by decade with electronics, playing a major part of the nation's success. The computer industry in western America designed most of it; Japan just made it better. The cooling systems used in all computer cases for the main systems or memory and storage devices was designed in the American State of Texas. The dual cooling gas cylinders that keeps the internal temperature of a computer case at 35 to 42 degrees. Small tubing is used around the perimeter of the internal dimensions of a computer case, connecting the two gas cylinders. The gas cylinders require only a minute bi-hourly electrical charge for the gas to remain cold and circulate through the tubing. The design was great, where Japan improved this was if the box were devoid of air, the cooling would effective last fifty years without need of replacement. Japan found a way to create a vacuum after all the pieces were assembled, they also designed the device to remove all the air. Japan then sold it to anybody requiring using these cases. It also made it possible to remove the air should an internal component need to be replaced which was infrequently. Most companies that were in the business of repairing computer systems, found it necessary to obtain this tool whether they used it was not important. Computer business precaution: 'better to have something you might not need, than not have something when you needed it. Computer designers never could find a faster way to get data to the core processor than memory. Japan improved the technology here as well, condensing component size and increasing the amount of memory.

Today's computers have a central processor core and 1 billion terabytes of memory for the semi-intelligent computer. It also has a personality core that can vary in size depending on what the computer's primary function would be. Security computers like those used at Global Security, are some of the most complex personality modules created. Requiring an additional 10 billion terabytes of memory to store the personality and primary functions. Any computer can connect to any other computer as long as both computers can comply with the access verifications. This is a very complicated process with 40480-bit encryption used, and cannot be hacked by an unauthorized computer. This is also a part of computer's personality modules. Security computers have the ability to interface with any computer period, all methods are included in the personality module. Financial computers can only access finance computers, and there is a secondary identifier the computers receive when business is established with each institution it deals with. With most businesses a larger memory container is used, and usually some hard storage for history files. The same computer case is used for these devices and memory storage comes with 100 billion terabytes of memory. Additional memory cases can be added, and hard storage comes with 100 billion terabytes to a disk, and ten disks to a computer case. Most computers are kept within the same room, all have infrared feeds to send data back and forth when needed. Computers outside the room can still use the IG and computer access verifications to transfer data. With the computers cooling system the processor core can transfer data between it and its memory at the rate of 1 terabyte per millisecond. With the central processor design being more like a brain, light pulse replaced hard wire circuits and travel through optical tubing. This allowed computer systems to get over the hurdle of binary decisions.

Sooni was ready to leave and set out for her office, she expected the conference that was interrupted yesterday would resume sometime early in the shift. She wanted to be able to help with this situation, although, she realized she was never going to achieve all that Tim had accomplished. Tim was undoubtedly the best there ever would be in the security business of policing the Information Gateway. She took consolation in the fact there was still a large need for what she could do with her own group.

Tim arrived a few minutes early and as he expected his coffee was not waiting for him. Nora could multi-task better than five people, but hands to perform certain task was just not part of the package. He let Nora know he was in and going to get his coffee before getting down to business. He no sooner got back in, (which meant Nora had her audio input amped up for the door to open and close), as she spoke. "Tim, yesterday while you were being detained, Roger Morris, the analyst investigating the North Carolina Casino resort, called for you and wanted to report his findings. I can contact him if you wish." Tim: "Yes Nora, that would be excellent, I need to know what exactly he found though I have my suspicions based on what he had reported. " Nora: "Are these more suspicions that mean you do not really need his answers?" Tim: "I always need confirmation Nora, no matter how accurate my suspicions may become, until proven, they mean little or nothing at all. You are almost always my best source of confirmation, but if it were not for your wonderful ability to multi-task for me, I would not have time to concentrate on suspicions." Nora made no reply and the videophone appeared with a Roger Morris looking a little bit tired. Tim: "You did not stay on this all night, did you?" Roger: "Yes sir, I did not know when you would call back and it helped me condense my findings." Tim: "When you complete your report to me, tell your team leader the CEO said to go home and get some rest, you're no good to anybody, especially yourself getting overly fatigued. Give me the condense version." Roger: "The roof top of the Casino had a total of eleven transmitters, one for each computer and a single remote TRU. All the computers were wonderfully concealed with infrared access ports with unrestricted views to its own transmitter and all the computers could reach the remote. The computers were hidden in rooftop access ducts and venting areas and the person who placed those, assembled custom holding brackets to keep each computer completely stable. All of the devices including the computer were custom made, none were rigged with any traps. Although the computer cases are a little older, they appeared to have been updated to current configurations. Finding all the computers proved to be more time consuming than I anticipated. I am unable to determine where the remote transmits. Very nice work, your person or persons are very professional." Tim: "That confirms my primary suspicion that the intruder is not at your location, he contacted all the computers via the remote TRU to start the process. Unfortunately, that means the intruder could be just about anywhere on the planet, which get us no closer to apprehending or identifying this culprit. Thanks for your help, now, go home and get some rest." The call was completed and he told Nora to contact the team leader of the office Roger came out of. "Inform the team leader I insisted on Roger leaving and getting some rest." Nora complied.

Trask arrived and asked how everything went yesterday while he was being detained. Tim told him they did not ask a single question while he was there for 5 hours, and did not truly understand why they had to detain him. The autopsy gave them the answers they were seeking. Trask informed him that the procedure he was running through currently is nothing he would have ever had to do during his time as the premier analyst in security. It just proves how out of touch he had become with what he was the best in the world at doing. He felt like he was back in high school, looking into the direction he was going to take when he found he could not be the musician he was hoping to be.

Next Tim needed to get updates from Nora concerning yesterday's departure requests. Tim looked up at his video overhead and notices all the satellite positions and the connections times and finally noticed all the trace points were set. The two additional remote transmitters were added, and the ten computers all showed to be in the 15-mile radius of the North Carolina Casino and Resort that had already been identified. The second remote trace went to Southern California area near San Diego. There was no computer signal from this location, but there had to be a computer to connect to the others in North Carolina. The fact the single remote transmitter trace was pointing to Southern California was a fair indication this was the source of initiation to the financial fund diversion. It also meant the intruder was an individual not a group. Although, the intruder could have had other unknowing people perform some of the preparation tasks.

45

Global Security Corporation employed over fifty thousand people. Most of these were analysts, but support staff still had to include the psychologists and financial personnel for tracking payroll and income. Tim, as the CEO, also was responsible for International operations. It was because of his active involvement that his input was highly sought after by the rest of the board. It also entitled him to know how the company got its income. Every TRU ever sold included a security fee in the sales price, this was the money that helped start the company. In addition every month the Information Gateway funded the satellites and the security monitor company from sales revenue, all users had a monthly fee like any other utility. Global Security Corporation was the only IG security company worldwide, although many smaller consultants worked for businesses that wanted additional measures in place. The amount of money set aside for security from IG revenue was staggering, but then so was the monthly payroll. Global Security headquarters offices in Seattle were populated by 40 analysts on three shifts every day of the week. With a total of 300 analysts to cover a 24 hour seven day a week operation. Each main office had additional analysts to allow for 15 people a week off, five to a shift, and also to rotate into the time frame that limited everyone to a forty-hour workweek. It came to a little over 200 analysts per main office, plus support personnel. Global also had secondary offices in every major city in the world, with 5 to 10 people on duty at all times. Each office has a team leader who got directions from main offices closest to their location. The next stage was decided and Tim called out for Nora.

"What did you find from running the reverse traces recording through spectrum analyzers?" Nora: "What you suspected, it was an ultra-high frequency audio signal. I have the exact range in my memory banks assuming you want further research into this. What I do not find logical, Tim, is this audio signal is so high on the scale, it produces no sound the human ear can detect. So how can something a human cannot hear kill a human being? "Tim: "Exactly how, I do not fully comprehend myself. In general terms, even though a human cannot detect sound, the audio signal still penetrates the inner ear. In this case, causing significant damage to the ear and then allowed the high frequency sound to start rupturing blood vessels in the human brain, causing death in fifteen seconds. You are quite right that this will lead to more research, specifically medical research records on ultra-high frequency sounds that can cause nearly instantaneous death. My guess is the only people who would have done this kind of research for this purpose, likely this is military or some government secret. You may even find it necessary to check military research, since they are likely to find easy ways to kill the opposition without retaliation. I would assume you will be able to find every computer that checked these records in the last three years to be on the safe side. Hopefully, these are all registered computers and most will be people who had legitimate reasons to access the records. You are looking for someone who was not, and with any luck the computer, if registered will belong to somebody who once worked at Global Security Corporation." Nora: "What if the only thing I find out of the ordinary is an unregistered computer?" Tim: "It will mean our intruder is still ahead of us in this search. Also, I am sure you still have plenty of records to work with before completing the former employee list, which we will need to verify the whereabouts of all of them. I will have you delegate the verification to the closest main office. We still need this list complete, so do that first." Nora: "I have been working on that between the other tasks and have completed the number of people who were employed which came to exactly 525071 persons. I have not completed the medical cross-reference on all of those people because so many different computers are involved in the medical record status of former employees." Tim: "I would like you to separate the voluntary leaves from the remaining number of people, if you can. The people who volunteered for Stress examination and left willingly, are not highly likely to be involved. There is never a guarantee, so keep the names separate until all other possibilities have been eliminated. I will be having the other teams trying to chase the money trail to see if that leads anywhere, but I will need to clear that with Robin, and Ivan would be most adept in aiding, since financial is his area of expertise. Let start things rolling by getting Robin Torry and finding out if he wants our assistance and will make records accessible."

Nora performed her usual magic and within 45 second the vidphone dropped out its compartment. Robin was looking a little bit weary, the video was too good of quality for Robin's appearance to be a result of the picture. Tim started with, "Hello, Robin have you had any better luck than we have in finding answers?" Robin frowned and said, "I have been at this almost nonstop since we last spoke, and whoever did this is quite the illusive magician. Obviously he did not place all the funds into a single account, which would be way too easy." Tim interrupted with, "Yes I had given that a little bit thought and eliminated a single account, eleven accounts and figure more likely a minimum of 1100 accounts since 10 million per account would more likely to go undetected. He has planned quite well for most measures we would take, and even killed one of my analysts to keep us off the scent." Robin: "I did not know, sorry you have lost a team member, can't say that much deterrence has been place in my path. I had not considered breaking down the transactions as far as you think it may go, why would you think that aside ease of hiding a smaller amount?" Tim: "Our little culprit has planned for every possible action security would employ in locating an intruder. First he used custom built unregistered transmitters and computers, I now find out. He may well have had help from people who had no idea what the plan was, but I believe this entire operation to be the plan of a single individual. He also used two remote transmitters in his elaborate scheme. All the computers and TRUs were found on the coast of North Carolina with a second remote somewhere in San Diego, there is no footprint to follow on the San Diego computer. Leads me to believe, he has an AI computer at that end. He killed my analyst using ultra-high frequency sound transmitted from the TRU that was being reversed traced, and by sending out the wakeup call and initiating the reverse trace, it triggered the high frequency sound. My analysts never heard what killed him in the total time of fifteen seconds. This intruder has no intentions of going public with a murder in the picture. He has been a step ahead of us the whole way. Do you need any other reasons why I think 1100 minimum is the focal point?" Robin: "No, I quite see your point." Tim: "Anyway, I wanted to know if Ivan could be of assistance in tracing the money flow, but that would require you opening up the records for him to access. He could probably get at least half of his twenty analysts involved on all three shifts, to give it round the clock coverage until all the transactions can all be traced to an account. He is in the St. Petersburg office and financial is his field of expertise. He could still take direction from you to safeguard your customers. What do you think?" Robin: "I like it, this is far too much data for me and my three members to go through to find the anomalies, and so I guess the more the merrier. I know your company and reputation for keeping confidential data completely confidential. That would be a concern for most offers of assistance, but I do not see that as a concern with you. When did you want to start this up, if you couldn't tell I could use a break?"

Tim: "I sort of noticed you were looking a bit weary, and I intended to go next into the game plan conference, that will take at least an hour. Allowing for questions and answers, I could have Nora get Ivan with you in roughly one and a half hours and no more than two hours. You could get some rest in that time or go whole hog and delay it up to 22 hours, when he would back in for a new day. I apologize, this is Friday and Sven gets weekends off to match my schedule that would make 70 hours." Robin: "No, I do not believe it can wait that long, so as soon as you get him to contact me through Nora, we can get the plan in action. I assume that he has analysts that pick up the program from shift to shift." Tim: "Absolutely, we as a group here have individual offices assigned to a group of analysts that fill each other in at shift change, it works quite well since analysts of various areas of expertise only work in an office with analysts of the same field. I will have Nora get things going at the conclusion of the conference." Robin: "Good, and thanks for the help." Tim: "No need for thanks Robin, at this stage my single highest priority is apprehending that 'sonabitch' that killed my most senior analyst. You will be hearing from Ivan with Nora's assistance, talk to you later."

"Nora, it is time to get the conference going" Tim said to the robotic female within the rather large room. Thirty seconds later the videophone drop out of it compartment and everybody was present.

Tim started the conference once again, "For the delay yesterday, I was detained by the local authorities which Nora informed you late yesterday evening, but some of you might not have got that until this morning. The game plan is set, everybody will get to help Nora once she has compiled a list of former employees who had access to the Robin Torry's files, as I like to call it. Nora said every employee who has been accepted as an analyst since that case was filed has seen it as a part of training. Did not know that, since I had not been in training for quite some time, and it did not exist then. I am quite familiar with it, since it was my one and only unsolved case. I am informed that every stage of my attempts to find solutions were documented, and used as a sort of guideline for future events. Guess we have one NOW! Nora is going to remove all the people from the past employees listing that voluntarily submitted to Stress Overload testing and were dismissed. The names will not be eliminated entirely, just held out until all other possibilities have been exhausted. Each office will be responsible for determining the whereabouts of those on the list they receive. For those institutionalized, it should be a simple matter of verifying the person is still in the facility. You will be relying heavily on your computers to track down last known address and so forth, to insure each individual can be cleared of the current case. It will probably take even Nora a much longer time than normal to provide you the list of people to track. This is still based on a hunch, but anybody that can block each and every stage of our process, would certainly appear to have inside knowledge of our security procedures. Nora is also supposed to be checking the medical records files, to identify those people who have been institutionalized, that should help some; but we still have to verify that person still is a resident. It is highly unlikely that someone could have recovered from a broken mind, but medical advancements continue at an amazing pace. I do not hear of all of them. Next on the agenda will pertain more to Ivan, and his group than the rest. I talked with Robin just before starting this meeting and Nora will get Ivan in touch with Robin. I have requested from Robin, access to his financial records concerning this theft and volunteered Ivan and his group to give all the assistance they can in following the money trail. Sorry Ivan, you can blame me for the additional workload. You and your group of analysts have always had a higher degree of interest in financial matters. I assume that it kind of goes with the European system of heavy banking interests by many of the member of that group. I did give Robin my input of having a minimum of 1100 different accounts the money was moved to, and it could be even higher. It seemed with all the other precautions our intruder has taken, making it harder to track the money would have been in his plans. Any additional input at this time will be welcome." Ivan:" Since you believe a large number of accounts are involved, do you think any of them would be easily traced?" Tim: "I firmly expect all of them to be numbered accounts, where personal information is held secret by the individual banks the account is set up in. Some banks have numbered accounts that required no personal information whatsoever, as long as funds are established in the account. I do not believe our culprit will make anything easy for us. Ivan, just so you understand, once you get involved with Robin, he will determine what he wants you to do, and for all intents and purposes for this particular part of the case, he's the boss. I provided him my hunches concerning it, and it will still be his decision on what, if anything will be done with it. He does welcome the help, use as many of your analysts in this as you see fit. Twenty-four hours a day in finding where the money went. Any other questions or input that might be useful?"

Cho Ling spoke up, "I see that from all of the satellite information on the overheads that there remains one transmitter not located, anything I can do to assist you with that?" Tim: "I believe that the location is San Diego area and the authorities and a local analyst have been assigned to locate it, I have not had any feedback from them as of yet. San Diego will have lots of places to hide a transmitter and computer." Cho: "That reminds me, we have found no missing AI computers reported anywhere on this side of the planet, which includes all of the Asian nations and Russian Republic as well as the Middle Eastern groups." Tim: "That was kind of expected, although I wonder if our intruder was able to custom build one. I still have a suspicion that an AI computer is as much involved as anything else, it just makes sense that with all this planning a computer would be better to carry it out. Anybody have other thoughts on this?" The response was 100 percent negative. It seemed everyone was in full agreement an AI computer was at the source of this.

The rest of the next half hour to forty-five minutes were spent with everyone laying out the follow through; so nobody was repeating what another group might have done. Much of it was establishing territory for areas that were gray for group responsibility, should it be necessary to investigate into those areas. With the conference concluded, Nora initiated the contact between Ivan and Robin. Tim expected to at least get some feedback on the plans.

Ivan Herbalich worked in the St. Petersburg office of Global Security Corporation as the director. He has a master's degree in financial security administration. He could have easily gone into any financial house in the world and made somebody else lots of money. He was more intrigued by what he could do to keep everybody's money safer. Only Global Security Corporation offered something he never found lacking of intrigue. Investment banking offered some challenges, but nothing compared to a single day in the security of the Information Gateway. Like many of his country people, he enjoyed winter sports. He kept himself relatively fit with cross-country skiing. Flying down steep mountains at break neck speeds was a sport for younger skiers, and it was difficult to use as an exercise technique. In the non-snow months, he resorted to inline roller blades and that was his method of getting to and from the office. On weekends, he could still get out and roll a good 26 or more kilometers to build up stamina and mostly to forget about the past workweek, and look forward to a fresh one.

He did not feel anywhere close to Tim, Kuri or Cho's overall security insight, but did feel he had an advantage in the financial area. He was somewhat happy that Tim thought of him for helping Robin Torry. Robin was considered by many financial institutions in Europe to be a respected genius in financial circles. Ivan hoped he was up to the task. He had not practiced making daily financial transactions, but monitored large numbers hourly. The intruder's transactions did not raise any alarms because they all appeared perfectly normal, except the funds were not the intruder's to use. Ivan had just completed the conference and was about to get a beverage from the snack area when the vidphone dropped out and his computer announced Nora had Robin Torry ready to forward to him. It was not like it was unexpected, although this would be his first time working with Robin.

The snack area was just outside his door so he decided to quickly get some bottled water before announcing he was ready. Robin appeared, and Ivan introduced himself and they exchanged the normal pleasantries between people meeting for the first time. Common before getting to the business aspect of the call, which was started by Robin.

Robin: "Tim tells me you're quite good with the financial side of security and told me I had no worries over the confidentiality of the information I am going to forward to you. I will be the first to admit it is overwhelming for two assistants and myself. To give you an overview, in the twenty-four hour period that these fund diversions took place, my clients had over 400 million transactions recorded over the IG. To be honest, it has taken us this long just to get a firm number on all the transactions. Pattern search and recognition have not even been attempted, but comparison figures to other twenty-hour periods put the number of transactions for all my clients at about the same number. Tim had the insight to fill me in on the individual who planned this and as a result I have to concur that this individual will have used a large number of accounts to divert the transactions. Bottom line is, I need help. There is simply too much to work with for three people to find quick answers, and my clients are being rather persuasive about the return of their funds. The constant interruptions are simply causing this to slow down more than ever, but I do have to reassure my clients we are trying to get it resolved. Any suggestions from you and your staff will be highly considered." Ivan: "I can have my staff, 5 people to a shift a total of fifteen plus myself looking through the transactions for patterns and where the funds may have been diverted. Simple things like duplication of account numbers or money was moved in a multiple transaction. I have one question that may help speed this task up considerably. Do you know how many transactions occur daily to numbered accounts?" Robin: "I have had a rough figure of between twenty and twenty five such transactions in a 24 hour day for the last two years, with little fluctuation and all the numbered accounts are reputable companies who want to keep liquid capital numbers from public information." Ivan: "As you know numbered accounts have special routing numbers to separate those funding transactions from account numbers. This information can be used to find how many of the 400 million transactions went to numbered accounts. I keep a listing of all the special routing numbers for those banks that offer this service. Most of the banks are in Hong Kong, with some in the Cayman Islands and Bahamas. I am not aware of any in Russian financial groups, and the government has not yet implemented it into their banking system, but I suspect that will change in the near future. I am also betting that the 400 million transactions of the period under review will have between four and five thousand numbered account transactions." Robin: "You have obviously done this before, what makes you think you will find that many transactions?" Sven: This individual as Tim has told you is doing everything possible to get lost, you cannot get lost with standard bank account numbers because identification is required by all bank. All banks have a tendency to make that identification public knowledge, if you know where to look. Numbered accounts are secured by offering this service at a price without standard identification. Identification could be a number, a pass code, a password, or some special symbol allowing the bank to draw funds from the account when presented with the proper identification code. Accounts can be opened without even being physically present at the bank, and as you know, identification for any account is not required to deposit money into it."

Robin: "It seem you have a good idea what to do about the pattern recognition, since I have records of approximately two hundred numbered accounts, all verified, once you have your pattern and separate the numbered account transactions we could use this list to find out which accounts are new. I will unfortunately have to do that myself, because of my contractual agreements with the clients involved. I will have the records transferred to you to start immediate course of action, that will be through Nora, as Tim has arrange all this to be done. Ivan keep me more up to date with your progress. I image with the number of people you have working this and if your pattern holds true, this will take you less than a week." Ivan: "I will keep you up to date, and I am pretty sure about the pattern, without any problems should have the answers in five days. I will have Nora reach you in say 48 hours for the first update, you can relax a little now."

Robin: "You are the second person today to say something to that effect, do I look that tired?" Ivan: "Do not take this the wrong way, but I have seen corpses with livelier eyes. If you were working for me, I would send you home for 36 hours mandatory rest." Robin: "Thanks, I'll take it, talk to you in 48 hours."

Ivan wasted no time picking his analysts for the extra duty, and filled them in on the patterns he anticipated finding with the recorded transactions, which would be here shortly. He let his group get their energy foods and drinks and distributed the records to teams thirty minutes later. The game was afoot. Searching 400 million transactions was a tedious affair. The first thing that came to light was the significant number of transactions that went to numbered accounts. Ivan was looking through the sixth hour of transactions, and he had given hours one through five to the other analysts. It had taken them about six hours to complete the pattern recognition on each of their parts of the records. Next thing to do was record the numbered accounts, and have that ready to go to Robin to compare against his verified list and find the discrepancies.

Tim was dealing with Nora over the personnel records, she had questions concerning those who were deceased and institutionalized, but had not compiled a complete list to work with, which he really did not expect for another week. Nora always proved to be far more efficient than he anticipated. Tim called out, "Nora, do you have a moment?" Nora: "Always a moment." Tim: "Can the high frequency audio signal that killed my analyst cause damage to your circuits? Nora: My design is immune to that and utilizes a number of less damaging high frequency tone for moving data. The audio signal that killed the analyst is a sound I can interpret, but I would not recommend playing it for you for any length of time. I have had a chance to get to some of those records and so far only authorized doctors and military personnel, also mostly doctors, have accessed it from the sources I have been able to check. There are many more medical facilities to check around the world and I am still trying to connect to different systems."

Tim: "With all that said I guess it is time to leave for the weekend, I cannot accomplish anything more until more information comes available. I can only guess you will be working all weekend." Nora: "Yes, I will and you know that I do not take time off."

Trask had left an hour earlier saying Tim had things moving faster and farther along than he would have ever been able to get accomplished. It was obvious his reason for being present was in a holding pattern so he would get an early start on the weekend with the wife. Tim departed for the lake property residence, he planned to do nothing more than spend quality time with his lovely wife of less than 6 months. He was hoping he could do the one thing he wanted to do for her pleasure, but she had to tell him if it were possible. He did not want it so intense the child growing inside would be in jeopardy. He would still start with making one of his special dinners, largely of the Chinese variety but not excessively hot.

Ivan decided to put in some extra time going over another hours' worth of transactions that took him and the next shift eight hours to complete. That included recording the numbered accounts, with twelve hours completed there was over two thousand numbered accounts, and only two on his two hours' worth were used more than once. With half the task already completed, the pattern was pretty clear that numbered accounts were the key, which made this a shorter process than he expected. He decided to head home for the rest for the weekend, and thought it was quite possible the remaining transactions would be complete by the time he went to work Monday morning, even though he would have to stop in for a short time Sunday to make contact with Robin. Ivan planned to get something to eat, relax a little and get some sleep. Tomorrow he would take a 30-kilometer run on his in line roller blades, just to clear his mind and that always did the trick. Then he would spend time in the kitchen preparing his meals for the entire week, something he enjoyed doing; but never had the time to do every day.

Tim arrived at the lake property residence, he had a drink and ask Kuri if she cared for something and she accepted a little bit of Cognac. Tim started preparing for a Chinese dinner, which was one of his and Kuri's favorites. He went a little milder with the chili pepper sauce in case she had a change in her tastes with the small package of joy she carried. It turned out to be just right for her and he could have done it hotter for himself, but it was still quite tasty and just what he was looking for. After taking care of the cleanup and all the dinnerware and utensils in the sanitizing unit for a good cleaning. He asked Kuri if it was possible to provide her some pleasure, starting above the waist instead of the toes. She said it would not be as intense, and may take a little longer to reach a fully aroused state, but it would work. He said he did not know if her being with child, it would be good to start in the normal places. Before they were to have pleasure time, Tim needed to go through his mediation routine. It was now common for them both to use the computer room, as it had plenty of room for the exercise and it was a little more secluded on the lower level. Kuri came along to help him modify his routine. She started with letting Tim start his routine in his normal fashion, and when it got to a point where Kuri thought his routine did not flow properly, she had him drop a maneuver, and showed him one to take its place. This shorten his routine a little bit, the finish would increase his routine to over an hour overall once he was able to hold the positions for the full 5 minutes. She had Tim for the final moves raise his leg as high as he could in a full standing position, without using his hands or arms, it needed to be fully extended regardless of the height. Then she had him lean back with his leg forward into a position that would resemble a T. Tim felt every muscle twinge in response, and it was a strain for him to hold it longer than 2 minutes. Kuri said once he could hold each leg forward 5 minutes, the reversal of leg behind and bending forward into another T position would complete his routine. also held for 5 minutes each leg.

Kuri explained in these positions his mind and body would more likely find harmony and then he could be anywhere his mind took him. He simply had to have been there once with a picture in his mind. After a short rest from his meditation routine, besides having muscles used he had not fully used before, his legs were a little weary.

They did make it to the bedroom, where Tim decide he wanted to pleasure Kuri to a point that would not cause problems for the new life soon to enter this world. It was not intended to bring himself or Kuri to the edge of erotic madness; but to a least have some such pleasures to allow her to feel loved.

He did find with her being pregnant she was a little more sensitive to arousal, and she did experience orgasmic responses rather quicker; but no violent shudders although the last one did last longer. He also noticed that with her pregnancy, her already perfectly proportioned body was growing slightly larger in the breasts to what he thought, if he took measurement was now 35D. He told her he thought she was getting larger upstairs, and she said she thought she was too and does not think it from her meditation exercise. She was not exhausted nor he; but were both pleasingly satisfied, and that was what he had intended to accomplish. She held him close and thanked him for being such a wonderful husband. After an hour they got up and Tim asked Kuri to join him in the computer room. They descended into the lower level where Tim had Kuri take the chair, while he activated the desktop video with a touch of his finger.

Tim said, "In light of recent events, I think you should have access to this information, in the event something unforeseen should happen to me." He first brought up his investment account, which now totaled a little over 23 Million World Currency. He gave her the access code to it. Kuri said, "I hope I can put it someplace and never have reason to use it, as she would much prefer to have him than all his money." He did not have any such morbid thought until this week, but he said it could have just as easily have been him instead of the analyst. He never would have considered his headset to be a lethal weapon before the death at Global." He then entered his information to his interest account, showing he had regained much of his payment for the restaurant to be constructed, it was at 8 Million WC, where his regular account was up to 450,000 WC above his normal 200,000. He said tomorrow he was going to contact his investment person and move half his interest account and start having half of his monthly pay placed there also. It would still leave them plenty of funds every month to do what needs to be done and still have all kinds of extras. Kuri said, "Is that really necessary, you already have me saving my entire retirement money in the samurai investment. Although it does not rival your interest account, it is earning quite well?" Tim replied, "It just seems logical to let it earn as much as it can while we have no real need for it, do we?" "No, we have plenty more than we need even with a baby on the way. It just seems getting more makes less sense than leaving it where it is."

Next morning when Tim arose the coffee was made and he started with making an old fashioned breakfast that would have the medical profession declaring him dead in a week. The eggs were fresh and the bacon went on the grill cook mode in the device used in most modern kitchens. He made enough for the both of them and he decided on sunny side up for the eggs, having the bacon cooked to his liking not too crisp preferably chewy, but fully cooked which meant a low heat. Using the drippings from the bacon the eggs were made and the excess drippings ladled over the top to cook both sides while three pieces of rye toast were getting bronzed in the toaster oven, Kuri arrived with the finishing touches of breakfast being dished out. She said it smelled too good to consider going anywhere else than here and they savored every morsel. They cleaned up the utensils required for breakfast. Poured a cup coffee and made Kuri tea.

Ivan had taken only two hours to complete his 30 kilometer in line roller blade trip, and when he got back and cleaned up, it was time to check the condition of his equipment. Since roller blades were not the most easily acquired item these days, he had learned where to get parts and repair his own blades. Mostly it was worn rollers and bearings that needed to be addressed. He had traveled quite a long distance since he last repaired his blades, and toward the end, felt the wobble of one or more rollers reaching the limit of use. First he replaced both the rubber stops used for breaking and found three of the rollers were worn unevenly on each of the blades. It took about an hour and half to remove and replace the worn components. It used most of his stock and he went to the computer to order replacement quantities of rollers and stops. Then he used a family old traditional lanolin and silicone based cream, to keep the leather uppers supple and soft. This cream gave it a slight shine; but more importantly prevented them from becoming brittle and cracking. Then he put them away until the next use, if it was tomorrow, it would be the shorter 5 kilometer run that was more his daily routine. Ivan decided he wanted to go visit the local sports bar to be among his neighbors, which he got to see less frequently than he would like. It was not just his schedule, everybody has commitments including himself. He got to get there with a soccer competition playing on the sports entertainment overhead screens. Had a couple drinks and conversation between the game's actions.

Got with the only other single member of the group, and somewhere along the line they decided after the game, they would head off for a bite to eat at a local restaurant that serve only the best foods from around the world. The general idea behind the establishment was not so much a regular menu as to sample different foods from far and near. Ivan was always willing to try something he never had before, and this place catered to a culinary adventurer. The menu was usually written on a board as you entered, and the servers told you more about the daily offerings. It could be interesting, and the policy of the restaurant was anything you did not enjoy would be free. They did not have to give much away. People who do not want to try different tastes, seldom frequent this place; but all with an adventurous flare for food rave about it.

One week may be Chinese cuisine and something from the Cajun selections, the next week German and English specialties. It all depended on what the restaurant could acquire from one week to the next, but the lists seemed endless. Some spicy, others exotically seasoned but sweet and pungent. Some were more practical in everyday tastes, but if you wanted your taste buds to sample variety, he was not aware of any place like this one. He and his friend were not on the prowl for companionship for the evening, but wanted a good meal. They both had wanted to go here because of its unique qualities.

This evening's choices were several Cajun recipes all with warning over the hot quality of the pepper spices, and all included a large helping of shrimp jambalaya, a rice side dish. There was also some Indian cuisine that was a little milder and served with white rice. Nothing on the menu tonight included potatoes, but Ivan had no complaints with Cajun rice dishes and wanted something flavorful, even if he had to down a gallon of water with it. Cajun food had that effect for him and even though his temperature went up with intake he marveled over that wonderful taste that accompanied the heat. Ivan did not know what kind of wine, if any, went with Cajun entrees, so he inquired from the server what would be best with his food. He was surprised that the server did not recommend a wine, but rather a good beer from all places the Americas. He knew many of the world best beers were from European countries, like Bavarian beer makers and good English Stout Ale but he agreed to try it. He waited until his meal was served before sampling the beer, he started with the rice dish and found it spicy, but the sensation of a burning tongue quickly subsided and the dish itself was not as spicy as he expected. The main course on the other hand made him go for his beer rather quickly, and although it did little to tone down the burning sensation, he had not expected such smooth and flavorful beer to come from that side of the ocean. After consuming his main dish and two beers, he found the remainder of his rice dish actual soothed his burning. Learning this too late he asked for another side of shrimp jambalaya and learned that the rice like many starches lessened the effects of peppery food. The desert choices were not in line with main dinner choices. As always there were strudels and some tarts but also coconut cream pie. He did not know if it would go with the meal, but it sure sounded like something to give a try at. He ordered the pie and when they were done they decided to have their nightcap here as opposed to going back to the sports bar.

Like most restaurants a small bar was setup, typically for those waiting to be seated. Although it was getting later, the restaurant was still doing unusually brisk business. They told the server they would go to the bar for a last drink to allow the table to be freed up for someone else. Ivan ordered another beer, he found it quite good actually, one of the best he had in a long time. He tried to get the server first and then the bartender to tell him who made it. The answer from both was that this was the only place in all of Russia that sold it, and they wanted to keep it that way. It was very good for business. They had as many people come in just for this beer, as they had come in for the unusual food entrees. They could also serve the beer much later than the food. Also because it was an import that could get premium WC for it. When Ivan got his bill for the evening he could see they got more than a fair price for the beer, but it was actually worth it to him, he might consider coming by a little more frequently just to have a beer. Ivan and neighborhood friend parted ways, and went home late enough for Ivan to go to bed.

Ivan did not rise exceptionally early but hardly an unreasonable hour in the morning. He got up and used the food-processing center for orange juice and buttered muffins. Ivan thought synthesized food was pretty good, and was happy that no matter what he requested it was healthy. It had essential vitamins and minerals for a respectable diet. He had to go into in the office long enough to see where things stood with the financial records, and needed to call Robin. He decided he did not need to wear normal work attire for the short interruption to his free time. He made the trip with the normal roller blade excursion, which usually accounted for his daily exercise. Once there, he first check on the progress of the records that his analyst were going through and found two hours, had not yet been completed, this was on account that daily security business was not overridden by any protocol in this case. The problem with weekend security detail was that hackers, who had free time from the normal week of activities seemed intent on getting caught. The hackers were caught, since the weekend type seldom had any real plan other than to see what they could get away with. Penalties for hackers varied from fines with restrictions on computer usage, to five-year bans from using a computer or transmitter. The later was for multiple time offenders, and with retina scanning as the means of identity, they could not obtain a computer or transmitter from any reputable business. They also were unable to obtain components to build something on their own. Business penalties for selling or manufacturing rogue equipment were so severe, that no business risked taking the chance for even the best of profit margins. That left hackers to their own devices for obtaining things to make a computer or transmitter. Very few had a good enough understanding of the technology to endeavor into it. Theft was a possibility, but components had tracking and registration numbers that made this difficult. The business merely had to report the theft and number ranges that were missing. If the identity number showed up on the IG, it was found. Very few hackers had the knowledge or special equipment required to manufacture the components from beginning to end. A limited number had access to facilities and the knowledge, but still had to perform the process without anyone noticing them doing so. Not impossible, but by no means a simple task.

Ivan placed his call via Nora to Robin Torry. It had taken less than a minute for the videophone to drop and show a much more refreshed Robin than the last time. Sven: "I have good news for you concerning the records we have been going through. Sometime tomorrow morning, I will have a complete list of numbered accounts for you to compare to your list of verified accounts. By my estimate at this point we are in excess of 4000 account numbers showing up in the 24-hour transaction period. Will that be good for you?" Robin: "That is sooner than I expected and I will be happy to get the list. I do apologize for bringing you in on a Sunday, I did not realize when we first discussed this that the time frame of the return call would be a weekend. Hope I did not inconvenience you too much. Once I have your list, provided the individual responsible has not moved the funds from the accounts in question, I can at least get the financial groups holding the fund to freeze them, so they cannot be accessed. I do not know how long before I can get the funds returned with the various numbered accounts, since like most banking institutes giving funds up is not as easy as depositing them. I do thank you for your expedience in this crisis and expect to hear back from you tomorrow morning sometime."

Ivan and Robin exchanged parting pleasantries and disconnected. Ivan went back to his home to complete his weekend.

Kuri's parents were in Seattle, so Tim arranged to go over to see them at his spare guest home where they were at the moment. He told Kuri to get ready for her little surprise and did not tell her exactly where they were going. Since being in Seattle, Kuri had learned to wear some undergarments although she wore no brassiere, she found ladies lingerie quite sensual. The chosen items in her clothing was largely for keeping the draft from her jade gate as she said it. Tim had of course seen them, and they surely could not be called panties as it barely had enough material to cover what she said it covered. They were very sexy and Tim did not think any article of clothing would possibly improve her loveliness; but he was proven wrong. Once they got into the transport and on the road, Kuri figured out where they were going and asked if this was to check on the property. Tim said sort of and left it at that. She did not like him being evasive; but was always happy with the results, as it was always so far from what her imagination had led her to believe.

Once they arrived and Kuri saw a transport in the driveway she knew somebody was there just not who. Her brother and his family had already found their home. They should have everything already moved as the furnishings were all a part of the house. Tim knew if the security system was set it would have announced the transport arriving. When they got out of the transport and near the door it opened, with Lian standing there to greet them. Tim gave her a little kiss and hug, which she no longer was embarrassed about, and Kuri got a much bigger one. Hiro was just getting to the door and they all entered, it was largely a catching up on all that was going on in the restaurant business and his thanks to Kuri for helping out when it was needed. He had way too many students working in Seattle, but had no way to get around the issue; but had to have Kuri in much too frequently. They all made some comment about the baby bump; but was amazed at how Kuri was still in such good shape for a woman in her condition. Hiro was learning to enjoy his new function in his restaurants, and not having to work a kitchen, except at home. They spent two and a half hours chatting and Hiro made it definite that he was going to buy a home in Seattle, and spend a week each month with Lian in Tokyo. Checking the other restaurants to insure all the menus and foods are absolutely correct. So far, he had had no discrepancies and wanted to insure it stayed that way. He and Lian had decided that their home would be in the Japanese section of Seattle, as even those from Japan have become more American than Japanese.

Lian was much more relaxed in Seattle than in Japan. She said she could truly get spoiled by the way people treated her here as opposed to Japan. She said it had improved somewhat after Tim and Kuri made such pageantry of his proposal. Hiro said he may have to revise his original restaurant to private booths, so couples could display affections with a little privacy. He said there was more kisses and hugs exchanged there than all of the rest of Japan combined.

The remainder of the weekend went by for all Global Security Corporation personnel without any problems.

CHAPTER

4

Monday morning started out with nothing but normal routine for everyone at Global Security Corporation. Nora was still compiling the former employee list and separating the voluntary and medically released personnel into separate lists. Nora stated if everything continued at this current pace, Wednesday would be when lists would be ready.

Around 10:30 AM the vidphone dropped out of its ceiling compartment and Nora announced analyst Tom Woodridge from San Diego was awaiting. Tim acknowledged Nora and the video went active. Another analyst Tim did not recognize; but there was no way of knowing all 50,000 or so. Tim: "Yes Tom, what can I do for you?" Tom Woodridge was a little hesitant and started with, "I thought you were the person who asked for the investigative team in San Diego to locate equipment, am I mistaken?" Tim: "I am the person who requested that a number of days ago, yes. Have you found something to report?" Tom: "Sorry it took so long, San Diego has quite a few public locations to hide this kind of technology, and the team from the local authorities is not platoon size. The transmitter and what I believe to be a computer have been located on the roof of a large public office and apartment complex. The authorities have found no external wires or triggers and have cleared us to take a closer look." Tim: "You said what you believe to be a computer, can you explain that please?" Tom: "It is a computer type case; but it is not of any design I have ever seen before, I can't even begin to say what level computer it is unless I open it; and examine the components. I certainly should not be doing that in this location."

Tim interrupted, "Tom, I would not advise opening the case under any circumstance. You may not have been informed prior to now, but the individual that assembled that case, has already killed one of my analysts, and I do not want to risk another with a case that could be rigged internally to do something lethal. What might be more advantageous is to setup a video surveillance system, well-hidden but able to detect any movement or computer and transmitter activity. Can you accomplish that, Tom?" Woodridge stated, "I believe I can; but it will take about a day to set up and get the proper equipment from the San Diego office, who would you like monitoring the system and from where?" Tim: "I think your office would be the most suitable location to monitor the site. That is assuming your office has somebody that can be assigned to the job. If not I can get somebody from one of the major offices to transport in and monitor it, but the feed would need to go to a close by hotel. What do you prefer?" Tom: "My preference has never been asked before, but I agree that it would be best handled from our office, and we have a team that can do the shift work for 24-hour coverage." Tim: "Good, that's settled, just let us know if you need anything or get something to lead us further. You can relay all of it to Nora unless you need to speak to me personally. Thanks for all the hard work." The conversation was concluded and Tim went back to needling Nora for progress knowing he had a couple of days to wait.

Ivan had Nora contact Robin as soon as he had the completed list, it was around 11 AM, and this list showed 4212 numbered accounts. Ivan had already transmitted the list to Nora so she could forward it to Robin. The videophone conversation between Ivan and Robin did not last more than five minutes. At the end, Ivan told Robin if he needed any other assistance to just ask, and he would receive. Ivan then contacted Tim to let him know the list was complete and the offer was made for additional assistance should Robin need it. Tim was always happy to get important matters finalized before going to the next stage.

Wednesday morning and the lists from Nora were finally complete. There were 124361 names on the medical list, which required confirmation on the mental condition of those listed. Functional enough to take care of themselves was not anywhere close to pulling off two plus years of planning. There were another 202300 names on the voluntary list. These people were not likely to hold a grudge for not being able to complete the ten-year requirement, but interviews would need to be conducted. There was also 1250 deceased and that would not require any further investigations. That left 297160 candidates for the person who pulled off this diversion and murder. The good news was Nora was further breaking down this list for each of the main offices to handle what was closest to them, and they were still to be investigated by the closest city offices. Tim called out to Nora, she did respond quickly. Tim: "When you have finished dividing these lists into appropriate offices, I need to see the HQ lists."

Thursday morning brought the final breakdown on the lists that needed to be completed through the Americas with Seattle being the main office. Once again Tim required Nora to send the information for the subsidiary offices in all the major cities, still leaving a rather large number to be completed from Seattle. The initial investigations could be accomplished with computer assistance in tracking the last known whereabouts of the individuals. Once that was all assigned, Tim finally got a chance to look over the lists with a little more detail. On the medical list one name stood out, Charles Burroughs. He remembered Charles as a sort of mentor, but really just someone that Tim learned from during his initial couple years as an analyst. Charles Burroughs had previously been doing computer security for an individual company. He had done so for about three years before Global Security Corporation had formed to monitor the entire Information Gateway. He said the rules were different for individual companies, but the monitoring was the same concept, just a whole lot more of it. He did not like being called Chuck and Charlie was only passable, Charles was his preferred moniker. Tim learned quickly to comply, because a single Chuck put Charles in a foul mood for the entire day. Tim remembered him as being fairly high strung and feeling responsible for everything that took place on the Information Gateway. He also remembered the day that Charles broke completely, sitting at his desk with a completely blank expression and drooling rather badly. He did not acknowledge any audio input and made no sounds of his own.

It was a sad day to see one of his closest peers in that state. He was taken to a mental rehabilitation facility and had remained there since. Tim had no desire ever to visit those who had fallen to Stress Overload

Syndrome. In the first ten years of the company, that ended up being 25 percent on all the analysts hired. Charles was probably the worst of all the cases he had witnessed during the time period. The problem in the first decade of Global Security Corporation, was severe enough that the mental assistance facility was being considered as a company acquisition. Tim had worked with Charles for about five years before his breakdown. He learned a lot about security and nothing much about Charles. Tim was certain he had parents but no clue about siblings. Was he the oldest child, only child, youngest child was not a topic that Charles ever cared to discuss with business associates? Tim did not know if Charles was married, single or engaged. It was amazing that during five years, nothing other than security was discussed, even though they had worked in the same department of security for the whole five years.

With Charles gone, Tim remembered changing departments to get experience with other aspects of the business, and before his ten years was up had been involved in every department prior to becoming operations director. That made him an excellent generalist that knew enough about the various operational departments, that he could relate to the much bigger picture easier than most specialists. There were specialists in the departments that knew far more than he about procedures for that department. Most of them were entirely lost when it came to interdepartmental operations. As with any generalist, it was the whole picture that truly told the story, and was often how you finally got your intruder cornered.

Tim went about with having Nora contact the mental assistance facilities to verify how many of the analysts who were taken to the local facility were still in residence. It took two weeks to get the confirmations of the 55000 analysts that came from Seattle to the rehabilitation facility. There were a total of 225 still in residence, Charles Burroughs was one of them and the other 55000 were released with improved conditions, but none could perform more than day to day activities beyond exercise and taking care of themselves. Global Security Corporation continued to pay for these people to live a quiet and sheltered life. It was advantageous to the company, setting up apartments and providing the income to maintain a normal lifestyle was far less costly than providing 24-hour care. In talking with the staff members to confirm the status of the 55000 patients, all of them were required to report to the facility on a regular basis. Some weekly, others monthly and some only had to report in every three months. It did require the patient to show up in person for both physical exam and mental testing to make sure no relapse had occurred. All the patients had made the scheduled visits and all had been progressing, but incapable of doing anything as stressful as work. In the opinion of the staff, none were capable of planning a single phase of the intricate plan that Tim was trying to find the originator of. Tim did not give them any information pertaining to the case, but had ask questions similar enough to form his own conclusions. The results from the other offices were all the same and as Tim had suspected these former analysts had never really been suspects, just that every person had to be confirmed.

It was going take even longer to confirm those who left because they failed to pass the stress testing process. They were still capable of performing tasks and planning in what they decided to do after working at Global Security Corporation. Tim was not so much as losing interest in finding the culprit who had broken the financial scheme, but relegated to the facts that it was now going to take a great deal of time. To find the individual that killed his analyst, he would find him some way or another and hold him or her accountable for the needless loss of life. This was definitely becoming personal. He was not going to accept anything other than a successful conclusion to the events that started over a month ago.

Robin did call to say at least the funds were frozen, but did not relate to how long it would take to recover those funds. He did indicate that some 3 billion in world currency had been moved several more times and may be unrecoverable, since he had trouble tracking it beyond the fifth move. Tim surmised at least 8 billion was acceptable, frozen and any attempt to move them now would lead directly to the intruder. He also came to the conclusion the intruder knew this and was unlikely to make the attempt.

It had taken a month before the first of the interviews started appearing as completed with only 100 hundred of over two hundred thousand eliminated. Tim also realized it was stress he was placing upon himself, nothing else was to be held accountable for the tensions of his own doing. He was at least self-aware enough to know he was currently his own worst enemy, and sought to relieve himself of the problem. He announced to Nora he was leaving for a period of time and went to the medical staff to see the acupuncture specialist for possible relief.

It had taken an hour and half to get treatment. The session took over two hours and the acupuncture specialist commented upon how tense he was. That was something that Tim never recalled hearing before. At any rate, the specialist performed his magic and Tim felt reborn. He returned to the office to find only a couple more names were eliminated, and since it was the start of the weekend he was going to get started on something other than work. Tim decided he needed to go to the lake property to get completely out the work frame of mind, and seeing his beautiful Kuri should certainly do that.

The trip home took very little time and he was at the house without even noticing he got in the transport, and told it where he wanted to go. First check of supplies told him he would need to go to the local store to restock for his weekend. He found Kuri resting which he had never seen before, she always seem to have limitless energy, and asked if everything was okay. She told him the baby was a little more active today, and it just seemed to wear her out. She had done her routine this morning, which was modified as suggested by her doctor. She had to adjust her leg raise to what she had him doing as the doctor thought it might cause her to break water too early. It could start a premature labor and birth. That would cause a much longer stay in the hospital for the baby, and possibly other health issues for any baby born too premature. She was starting her seventh month, and the baby bump was no longer a bump. Kuri said it was now a full grown melon and would be overgrown soon.

He was about to leave the lovely lady he married to start his own routine, and she gave him a smile that was far more than a simple hello. He asked if she had something else in mind before doing his routine, and then getting kitchen supplies restocked for the coming couple of weeks. She did; but said it was not something they really could not do and told him to go about his routine while she rested a bit longer. She hopefully could regain enough energy to go with him to the grocers.

His modified routine now took 1 hour and 10 minutes, since he was able to completely fulfill all the final moves. He could see he had gain considerably more muscle tone when in the positions he found so difficult when he started. Kuri was right he had much better harmony between mind and body, but even that was insufficient over the stress he had subjected himself too in the last month and a half.

Tim completed his routine, and checked on Kuri who was now sound asleep. He quietly left to the grocers and got everything they needed. He returned back to the lake property home and put the supplies away. Kuri finally stirred from her sleep, and asked if he just finished his routine. He said he had done that, found her sleeping and went to the grocers, returned and had it put away.

He said he got enough steaks and extras for dinner for the whole family if she felt up to some entertaining tonight. Kuri said she felt much more herself now and that it would be fine with her. She asked if he wanted her to make the calls to everyone in the property around the lake. It would be his sister Jackie and her husband Tom with the two kids Mike and Michelle. His parents, but his grandparents were off in San Francisco visiting his brother and his wife and child as well as other friends who still lived there. Kuri made the invites via vidphone and Tim started his preparations for dinner.

Once everyone arrived which was in relatively short order, Kuri was the center of all the conversation. Largely how lovely she look even though she was 7 months pregnant. It appeared the only weight gain she had was largely the other life growing inside. If it were a wager contest they would have selected a date and time after the expected date of birth when she would look exactly the same as before she was pregnant. Since Tim did not have the full 24 hour marinate time, he learned he could speed the process by placing the steaks in marinate and using the warm setting on the computerized cooking device for one hour, and achieve virtually the same results. This was accomplished at the very beginning of his preparations. Kuri was keeping the conversation going with at least the rest of the ladies, while the men decided to check out the entertainment center for the current sport. Something was always in season when it came to professional sports. Tim was in a world of his own for the time being making sure all the food for dinner would be ready at the same time, his hour was up for the steaks. He removed them, found it had absorbed all the marinade and he placed the steaks in the computerized cooking device and set it for grill. The other items set for the correct settings including the time to be completed by 6 PM. He cleaned up what he used for preparation, and placed them in the sanitizing unit until the remainder of the dinnerware and utensils were ready once everyone had eaten. Tim even remembered to get the banana cream pies that Kuri always liked for desert after this meal.

He finally got to give his little kiss and hug to his mother and sister, with a better one for Kuri. Went over to the men and got time to shake all hands and see who was playing what sport, and it was baseball season and not one of Tim's favorite sports. He found it a rather dull experience as a spectator sport whereas, basketball and football were far more entertaining to him. He decided to place himself in the lounge chair that was near both groups in order to be able to contribute to either or both conversations. The women unfortunately were talking about baby clothes and such stuff, which reminded him, and he had to interrupt the conversation long enough to inquire if his sister Jackie would like the bedroom set that was purchased for when they stayed here for the holidays. She said she did like it quite a bit and did not know if Tom was that thrilled, but they could talk about it. Tim asked they let him know if they could use a new set, and that had not been used but maybe half a dozen times. He said to let him know tomorrow because it was time to arrange the other rooms for children and not guests, and his brother and his family would be here permanently fairly soon.

Kuri had said she almost forgot they would need a nursery soon, and Tim said it might as well have a child's bedroom set in the other room for when the baby was old enough to move from nursery to bedroom. Kuri even went so far to say by that time, the nursery may have a new owner in waiting. Everyone asked if she had it all planned out already, and Tim only knew she was capable of doing it. He just knew she did not want two so close together as requiring continuous attention at the same time, but having a three year old with second child in waiting was quite possibly something she could do and plan. Kuri went on to say it was not so much planned as she knew she would not want to have them so close together, and both requiring continuous attention. When one is ready to go to a bedroom, though the attention time is not so high and she did want at least three. That was largely because in Japan, more than two was severely penalized, as it was frowned upon by the Japanese government, but not banned as it once was.

The ladies asked why that was, and Kuri said it is simply there are already too many people in a small space, and there is nowhere to expand to accommodate more. For those who have a third, there is no government assistance of any sort for that child. All costs from medical, education, feeding, clothing and care has to be absorbed entirely by the parents. So only the really wealthy members of Japan can truly consider a third child, and most of them do not, as it would infringe upon their life style too much.

The computerized cooking device announced dinner was ready as it was 6 PM. Tim and Kuri were already able to expand the table to accompany eight. Jackie and Tom got the kids to put their games away for dinner, and Tim seeing them had forgotten they were even here, they were so quiet. He told them it was nice of them to come up for air long enough to eat, and they were in for a real special treat.

The steaks and deep fried mushrooms were perfectly done, the wild rice mix got Kuri's immediate attention, and she asked what was different, whatever it was it made it even better. Tim told her it was the first clutee from the garden, and apparently the richer soil in Seattle gave it a hint of mushroom to its nut flavors. She asked if her father knew this and Tim said he did not, because he did not think if they turn every available inch around the property not in use to growing them, it would not be enough for all the food that is served out of that restaurant. She laughed and said she did not consider that. She said she did not think she would use them for her fruit covered waffles though. Tim said, if it were the imported ones she might like a banana split waffle some morning. Kuri asked what that was. Tim said it would be strawberry and banana topping not figuring she would want chocolate or fudge on a waffle, and topped with whipped cream. Kuri said it sounded delightful, maybe she would try it. The kids both said if she did let them know too, they would be more than happy to help Kuri eat them. Which got a nasty look from his sister, but mostly directed at her two children. Tim got a fist wave from his for bringing it up at the table.

The dinner went quite well, and the finishing desert made the kids and Kuri quite happy to have something sweet to finish the meal. Drinks were served and the kids went back to the games, the rest to the entertainment room, and Tim cleaned up. Started the sanitizing unit to take care of the dinnerware and all the other items from the meal. About an hour later, everyone was ready to return to their own homes. Jackie said her husband said the bedroom set would be fine, and they certainly could use a better one. Tim arranged during the week for movers to place both bedroom sets in his brother's and sister's respective homes, all within close proximity to his own. Kuri and Tim had enough free time after Tim got home to locate and arrange delivery for the nursery and child's bedroom sets. It would be there the following week. Kuri was quite happy with the items selected, leaving Tim one last thing to do prior to Kuri and the baby returning home. It would be to set the home monitoring system to listen in for any disturbance in the nursery, to insure the child could be attended to when it became necessary.

There were other things to obtain, but that could not be done without some idea of the baby's dimensions once home. But it would be needed almost immediately when the time arrived. Tim and Kuri did check for the items Kuri felt would be best for a baby girl. Tim made a note of where to get them in the proper size once the baby arrived.

The extensive search for possible answers to the intruder that was responsible for the death of his analyst was slow and progress was just as slow at Global Security Corporation. Under all normal conditions, Global was not responsible for locating and apprehending the criminals who committed financial theft. This was more than that, and the authorities did not have the resources to perform such a large task. Tim took responsibility for the death, and put all the needed search squarely on the shoulders of himself. The company was adamant once found, they were still not to apprehend the suspect. It was solely for the authorities but a suspect had to be located.

Tim had made sure that Trask would fill in for him when his five days of paid time off arrived for the birth of his and Kuri's first child. That time had come long before the long list of names to verify the whereabouts and actions of those whose names were possible suspects.

When Kuri went into labor Tim got her to the hospital and made sure she was attended to before he called Trask to tell him his wife had gone into labor. Trask would need to keep track of what was going on in the search. The rest of Global was running like a clock, no other issues went unresolved. Tim was in the delivery room with Kuri for 8 hours, before the newest arrival to the Frantz family entered the world. Tim was amazed at how even as a newborn infant he could tell she was going to have Kuri's beauty. He also realized he was going to need to have a big stick to keep the boys away until she was truly ready.

It was decided by Kuri and Tim the girl would be named Liani, largely for Kuri's mother with I from Kuri, at 6 pounds 5 ounces on August 9th 2144, the first child was born at 2:01 AM. The first thing after the birth, the child was cleaned up by the nurses and attending personnel, and returned to Kuri for her first feeding. Kuri was thrilled she could do what was necessary and even though quite tired and sore from the events, she remained rather happy to have the first child of theirs. The nurses told Kuri the baby would be taken to the nursery afterwards and brought every 6 hours for the same process to allow her to get some rest, and return home in a couple of days. Tim was only allowed to stay with Kuri until she fell asleep so she could get some well-earned rest. It was not very long after the baby was fed that Kuri entered her slumber. Tim left the hospital and went to obtain the necessary items for Liani to come home and have enough to make it through a week for cleansing and start over. The disposable diapers were listed by weight for infants. Tim obtained enough for he hoped for two weeks, with the chemical to use in a toilet to dissolve and make it something the in ground treatment equipment could take care of.

He also was advised to get a room air purifier as no matter how far we had advanced as a technical and computerized society, nothing else would eliminate the smell, a newborn infant could make when it was time for diapers to be changed.

Although Tim was not concerned over the costs, he wondered how people making far less than he managed to cover how much upkeep was involved in a new born child. Some families making ten or less percent of what he made every month. He and Kuri could not spend the amount he did not invest and still regularly moved the over 200,000 WC from his primary account to his earnings account. He figured although he did not ever inquire into Kuri's investment account, which it should be at least between four and five million WC. Considering how long she had her bonus money working and her entire retirement being added each month.

It took Kuri all of a week after Liani was home to look as if she had never been pregnant, except for her more ample breasts. She was told it would not ever be exactly the same after having given birth, but for subsequent children in her future, they would return to the shape they take after the first child. She had grown to a little over 35 D and the doctor said the best she would get, is back to 34 but D, no longer a C. She should still have her figure she was familiar with, just a bit more width. Which the doctor said herself included, would be a body that most women would envy. It took Kuri a month from child birth to have all the tenderness dissipate for her to resume her normal leg lifts in her routine. Even after the child was home, she made certain she did daily. This accounted for her appearing nearly exactly like she was prior to her pregnancy. It gave her the 19 inch waist line and same size hips as before but a few stretch marks would take a little longer after she resumed her normal meditation routine. The baby did keep them occupied for the first 3 months, with waking in the night to either be fed or changed or both. Kuri was not overly run down by it and Tim helped when it was possible, knowing he could not feed the baby if that was the reason. They could not tell any difference in the noise that Liani made to either event.

They had obtained all the necessary accessories for Liani to go shopping with her mother which at 3 months, required larger infant wear and diapers as she was growing rather quickly, but nothing beyond what was normal. In the meantime, Tim had returned to Global Security Corporation to resume his CEO duties. After getting up to date with Trask, it allowed him to return to his semi-retirement state, knowing he would need to return when this problem reached its end. Tim, still had not really had the opportunity to know his systems people like he should. Although they were kept busy with keeping the AI network running optimally as well as the semi – intelligent systems in all the offices, they had nothing new to work on. Tim had not the time to go looking for new technology that would further enhance their system. During Trask's 5 days he had taken the time to get robotic systems ordered for every analyst employed at Global Security Corporation. He saw major benefits for the wellbeing of his analysts. Nothing had been completed other than a number of potential candidates were eliminated, and there were still plenty more to locate and question, which was as Tim had anticipated. It took nine months to locate and question all the candidates on the first list from the time Kuri went into labor. After a year from the start of the list, they were back to square one on the candidate who might be the culprit in the death of his analyst. The baby Liani had reached the age where her mother, Kuri, was going to bottle feeding. At six months was eating that stuff they called baby food. Tim even acquired a couple of small infant size utensils for that purpose. He and Kuri took turns every night when he was home for who got to feed Liani.

As far as Global was concerned it was time to initiate phase two of the search. It would indeed require far more research from his analysts, before ever initiating a single person being questioned.

CHAPTER

5

T im called for the meeting with all the main offices of directors and supervisors, and stated what had been discovered over the last year of investigating. He also let them know they would not likely need to participate in Phase two at this time, as all the TRU's discovered were in the United States, and likely only the offices in North America would be needed in the further investigations. Should someone on the list currently reside within any of their territories, they would be made aware of it, however unlikely it would appear at this time. It was not a long meeting as there were lists to have Nora, Daisy and Anabelle to start breaking into regions first, and then find other family members beyond the person who was in the employment of Global Security Corporation.

Tim laid out the groundwork for the AI and network to follow through with. This consisted of lots of research into immediate family of the 124,361 former employees, who were entered in to medical support facilities for what would be lifelong care. The list needed to be divided into sections first, the list needed to be narrowed down to those employees that were in the US, and the remaining could be separated into a single group of other countries. The list was not to be ignored entirely, as the younger or older brother or sister of one such member, could now live in the US. It would not be used until all the US members were eliminated. After the two lists were separated, then immediate family members needed to be determined as either suspect or not, based on this criteria. Unless there was an overachiever like himself, they needed to be at least 28 years of age. They had to have military time involved in medical research. This was the only documented medical function for the method used for killing the analyst in Seattle. Tim felt this was largely his doing, having introduced audio analysis to the standard procedures. The second requirement would be for the same person to have a computer related background, which would need to include hardware design or engineering. The ideal candidate would be a specialist in electronics, as the military was never one to have the latest terminology in the world of business. This same person would have also been involved in medical research as a part of their electronics training and skills. This would be the two skills involved in the high frequency audio signal that instantly killed one analyst, simply doing his function as he knew it. If this did not produce a suspect, the other two lists would be researched in much the same way, and the last one would be for family members who wanted revenge for the death of their brother, sister, son or daughter. These identical skills and having revenge as an additional reason for such a cowardly murder. Tim was truly hoping he would not need to go to this list, and do the research for these people. They could not be interviewed by GSC people, and they would have no option, other than waiting for the authorities to conduct interviews.

It took Tim nearly an hour to have the AI systems with all the parameter, and have them keep Nora up to date on the progress while Nora would keep Tim updated. After that was done, Tim contacted his person in the local authorities who detained him in the very beginning. His call went directly to Detective Marshall. Tim thought he should give him an update into their findings having eliminated over 400,000 people from past employment, that were not involved in the crime committed. His computer systems were once again researching for potential candidates that were initially considered unlikely, but now the research was into immediate family members who may have had the skills, to exact their version of justice on the company responsible for the condition of one other family member. It would take time to narrow the list down based on the parameters he set for the AI Systems to research. He honestly did not expect anything concrete to work with for at least 2 to 3 months, but AI systems could access records that even the authorities could not without legal process.

Marshall appreciated the update and would look forward to the next update, and asked at what point in time he may be needed. Tim told him first the suspects would be interviewed once determined they had the skill set needed, and an itinerary could place them in the cities to prepare for what turned into a crime. Since the exact whereabouts of the suspect were unknown, but if in Seattle, he did not have an accurate time frame to give him. It would not be prudent of him to guess if he even would be needed, until the suspect was apprehended outside of Seattle, and then forwarded to his facility by the other authorities. Tim understood enough about cybercrime that the location of the crime had the highest priority in the actual conviction. It meant that Marshall at some point in this process would meet the suspect face to face.

Tim from there found JP was in the offices nearby performing once again at his talent search functions, and had to get out of the office for some air and lunch. He asked JP if he was up to it, JP said he never turned down the chance for good food at that little restaurant. He said he thought it was even his turn to cover the charges, but Tim said it was not necessary, he had no problem asking, he should take care of them.

Tim told Nora he would be back after lunch and may even have a drink with it. JP and Tim went to lunch and JP asked if he was serious about maybe having a drink too. Tim told him, he was stating he needed to dull his over worked thoughts on this problem that has almost made it a year. He had hardly even used any of his paid time off as a result, only taking the 5 days when Kuri went into labor. Although he was not sure how strong cognac was over wine; but told JP he was welcome to indulge also, if he cared to.

Lunch was wonderful as always, with this little gem of a restaurant in the heart of Seattle. He also commented on the fact that he could see Trask had made a few more visits to have his brand of cognac kept in stock. Which got a definite confirmation from the waitress, but asked where he was, as he had not been in for quite a while. Tim told her he was in semi-retirement and in all likelihood, if he and his wife had been in, it would be after she had finished for the day. He would be here only at dinner these days. During lunch, Tim and JP came to the decision that he could take a couple of weeks away from the office, as he did have plenty of paid time off. JP could cover his desk for that long without being too worn down, and since everything was going to be awhile to get research completed Tim should take a break from the insanity of finding the person responsible for the death of an analyst. He finished the last couple days of this week before taking the next two weeks off.

During the last couple of days Tim found nothing new to report from either location of the computers, and TRU's that were being monitored for any activity. Since it had been nearly a year, and the 8 Billion WC that was in the numbered account and being monitored, had no attempt to be acquired by the intruder, the authorities convinced the bank to return it to its rightful owner. It did involve Tim telling the banking firm that as a Global Security Customer he could, if necessary, drop all coverage if they refused to cooperate. He could go as far as to make it a public announcement, leaving the bank vulnerable to all sorts of intruders that they could not possibly deal with.

The bank although reluctant, did return the funds as the consequences were too high for them to do otherwise. Tim informed Nora he would be away for two weeks, and if anything were to happen let JP know. He would be able to contact Tim immediately. Also the lists for the research were being formed by the AI as to the number of families research would need to be done with. As Tim suspected, the Seattle Headquarters that employed far more analysts than any other office, had the largest number to research. Of the 124,361 names 83,152 were from the Seattle headquarters. Tim knew the biggest reason was that everything in the world went through the AI system in Seattle. It would be several months for research to be completed, even with the AI systems doing it. There was too much information to obtain to just start interviewing potential candidates for the crime committed. He departed to his home for two weeks away.

When he arrived, he told Kuri he was home for the next two weeks and hoped she did not get tired of him being home. She gave him a big hug and kiss saying she doubted that it would ever happen, and two weeks was nowhere near enough time for it.

Liani was sleeping, but for how much longer Tim did not know and went about preparing a quick but good meal for dinner. Liani woke in her usual fashion, just as Tim and Kuri were finishing the meal. Kuri checked to see if it was time for a new diaper or she was hungry. It was the latter, so the high chair was brought to the table by Tim and Liani received one small bowl of mystery food, as Tim was now calling it. A little bottle of warm milk, although she was not able to feed herself at this stage. Tim and Kuri took turns feeding Liani and she appeared to be making a game of it by swiveling her head to where the next spoonful was coming from. Tim by no means thought it looked or even smelled appetizing, but Liani was eating without any difficulty. After half the bowl, it was time for a little milk still warm. Kuri held it for her and let Liani take what she wanted before continuing with the food. Once Liani was fed, Kuri took her into the entertainment center room and put on the entertainment center and simply held Liani in her arms and let Liani decide if what was on interested her. Tim went ahead and cleaned up the kitchen from all the dinnerware utensils and cooking implements, got the sanitizer running, and joined his girls in the entertainment room. He was surprised that what kept Liani's interest was the evening news, not the animated children's programming. After food and 30 minutes of news, Liani was back to slumber land. Tim took Liani from Kuri gently, and took her to the nursery, and laid her in the infant's bedding.

During Tim's two weeks off, Hiro called not expecting Tim to be the one to answer, but it was just as well, he wanted Kuri and Tim. Since he was available, to tell them if the house they were looking at was fairly priced, and it was in the Japanese section not terribly far from the restaurant. They had to be there in one hour, and he gave them the address to meet Hiro and Lian there. Tim and Kuri agreed, and got Liani ready to go for a ride, and since Kuri had the larger transport to accommodate the hover stroller, it was placed in the transport. They got to the house address with all of two minutes to spare. Hiro and Lian had just arrived, as the salesperson was a few minutes behind. It gave Tim and Kuri enough time to get the hover stroller out, and Liani in place.

Before going in, Tim asked Hiro what his intentions were about buying the home if that were the case. Hiro told Tim he was planning to buy it outright, he had the funds from all the restaurants doing so well. Tim said to let him know where it stood before he said yes today, to see if there was any negotiating room. The outside resembled Japanese architecture, but the materials were not from Japan. It used a number of woods with a mix of redwood but it was not teak. Although other woods were just as durable, the color created was not natural. It still look quite nice for its appearance and Tim knew it was going to be different than Hiro might have expected.

The inside was definitely more of this country than Japan, as it has solid walls like most homes in Seattle. It did however have sliding rice papered doors, but it has some insulating and soundproofing internally. Unlike any home in Japan, it had a lower level that was purely Seattle architecture. With the laundry area and environmental control partitioned off with a large recreation room and a rather large other room, with a small sanitizing and bathroom partition next to it.

It meant the room could be used as a bedroom or office or computer room depending on the needs. From what Tim could determine, the house was not more than 5 years of age, based on the condition of the computerized kitchen, laundry devices and environmental controls. The rear of the house had one of the most beautiful rock gardens Tim had ever seen. The bridge over the manmade stream from ponds on both side had carved samurai for posts, at the four points of the bridge entry. It had a three tier arch with the first and last the same height and the middle a good foot taller. Tim still did not know how to read Japanese, but he assumed the poem had to do with honor and samurai. The pond and stream were not more than 6 inches deep, but the material used as the solid base gave the illusion it was much deeper. The in ground system made it appear like the water was moving from one pond to the other at a gentle pace. A large number of perfectly kept bonsai trees were all around the rock garden in particular the ends of the ponds.

Hiro said he and Lian liked the house and knew they would not find true Japanese architecture, but in many ways it was more solid and quieter than a true Japanese home. Tim said he would like to ask a few questions of the salesperson first if it was okay with him. Hiro said by all means if you think it will help. Tim said it could not hurt to try.

Tim inquired with the salesperson with Hiro involved in the questions as a listener. Tim first asked if the house had very many prospective interests. The salesperson said the house had been on the market for two months, and its uniqueness had limited people interested, largely as a means of respecting the population of the area. Tim asked why it was for sale, and the salesperson said the owner was transferred to San Francisco by the company he is employed with. This told Tim that in all likelihood the company would insure the sale would not be at a loss to the current owner, and in all probability would cover the difference to market value. Tim asked what the asking price was and it was 510,000 WC. Tim next question was if there had been offers on it. The salesperson said not as of yet. Tim said, considering its uniqueness and the neighbors also being unique, the home might be difficult to sell quickly and would offer 465,000 WC cash. The salesperson did not have authorization to accept that; but could call the owners. She stepped into another room and used her mobile vidphone, came back three minutes later and the said the owners could go no lower than 470,000. Tim asked Hiro if that was acceptable and Hiro was happy. He was fully prepared to pay 510,000 WC. Hiro said it was quite acceptable, and he and the salesperson completed the paperwork, transferred the funds, and had to wait one week. For the sale to be recorded, but the owners have already moved to San Francisco. They could move in next week once the salesperson confirmed the sale had been recorded. She would call them when it was finalized.

Hiro said to Tim they had no furnishings in Seattle, and he did not intended to completely abandon their home in Tokyo, and said he had gotten a little spoiled by the furnishings Tim had in his house. Especially the bed that did not require him getting onto the floor, since the accident it was not so easy anymore. Tim fully understood and said they could either take him to the stores he got his from, or give him the address after he and Kuri got back home. Liani was ready for something to eat, and nothing was brought so Kuri fed her in the transport on the way home. It was something only a mother could do.

At their arrival more mystery food was given to Liani by Kuri, while Tim got information for Hiro, and the place to check for furnishings. Making sure he gave them the store for the bedroom sets and the bedding used in his homes. The other locations was for the other furnishings as well as an entertainment center. If Hiro decided, it would be used by them, knowing he would still be in Tokyo at least one week each month to check his other restaurants.

Also during the two weeks away from GSC, Kuri and Tim reacquainted each other with pleasures that were more in line with the way it was prior to her pregnancy. Liani only made a few interruptions to the pleasure times. It was wonderful to both of them and the love they shared was only getting stronger with each passing day.

At the end of his two weeks, it was time for Liani to only be bottle fed, and starting to get her first teeth in, she was rather cranky; but it was all part of the growing process. Tim hoped he was not so busy with this problem at Global to miss her first words, which he figured should be soon, if she was like her mother.

He returned to Global Security Corporation, said hello to JP who had very little to report concerning the research. He had no other activity with the sites being monitored. Tim informed his robotic computer Nora that he was back, and she said the only thing to inform him of concerning the research from the AI was that of the 83,152 names on the list, was 511 have been eliminated. The employees were the only child, and none of the parents had any of the skills to be responsible for the acts that have created such concern to him and the company. Tim was nearing his end of the first year; but he was not going to let this rest, until an apprehension was performed over the needless death of his analyst.

His first year came to an end with John Thompson bringing him his next year's contract to view. Tim and Kuri both knew he was not leaving until he had closure in the death of an analyst. He signed it without a second thought, and the change was an additional 50,000 WC a month, because he was the only person who could have accomplished what has been done in the death of an analyst. This was per Zachary Trask, and fully acknowledge by all the board members who were also the 10 owners. His last payment of the first year had additional money that was for his unused paid time off, and he decided he was not doing that again this year. He really needed to have more time with his wife and daughter, who was now seven months old and said her first word the week before; but it was not what he was expecting.

It took four months for the research to be compiled into a list of 5700 names that required further interviews and investigating to determine if they indeed were the suspects responsible for the a senseless death. 1500 names were from the east coast to be divided among the offices closest. Although none of them had flights scheduled to both cities, all had been to the west coast. They could have easily used other transportation to the Resort Casino that housed the largest number of computers and TRU's with a remote transmitter.

There were another 1000 names from the list for satellite offices around the west coast. With the remainder being in Seattle's area of investigation, his analysts were going to be busy for quite some time. He had Nora determine which names went to which office, and start contacting the various people who had responsibility for the respective offices. His own supervisor would have the remainder and determine which analyst should go where. His supervisor knew if it was a satellite office under Seattle's control whom to involve to expedite the interviews. It would take 4 months for the west coast satellites to complete the interviews of the 1000 names. They had determined none of them were the person Global Security Corporation sought. At six months the same results were concluded with the east coast.

During this time, Tim had taken 50% of his 45 days paid time off and the last being a mere week before. Liani had taken her first steps, and was learning to talk with more than single words. She knew who her mother and father were, and also both her grandparents. His brother and his family had finally arrived to the family properties, and Tim had insured them that there was no need for them to repay him a single cent towards the homes they had built. It was the last installment of his Christmas gifts to them and the rest of the family got something they could use, but he had run out of big expensive gifts. Tim also decided the next week he took off that the 3 of them should go to Tokyo for the week. See the people they knew, and check on their house to make sure nothing had occurred to be a problem, although he had not heard anything to indicate such was the case. Neither had Kuri, not everything that happen in Tokyo made the nightly news broadcast.

Tim was beginning to think he was going to have to go to his last resort to find the culprit behind the loss of his analyst. He had hoped it would not come to it, as this was the one group of people he could not expedite in the process of interviews. Nor any other type of direct contact from Global Security. He was well aware of the fact that the authorities did not have the resources to accomplish it in a timely manner. As a result of his thinking, he asked Nora if the 1250 names on the deceased list had the research done for potential family members to have been involved in this crime. She confirmed his suspicion that they indeed were not, and Tim had the AI system start the research in additional family members of each one that may have a grudge with Global Security Corporation. For reasons beyond the person who was employed was made well aware of the risks, and what steps to take if it was beyond them to deal with. They had a medical staff that was there to help them, and if all else failed, they could voluntarily leave with a GSC assistance to gain employment at a level they could handle, or even additional training to change into some other area of the Information Systems environment.

Granted none of them would compensate them at the same level GSC did; but it would mean doing something that did not lead to total breakdown or mentally broken. One week before the final group of interviews would have been completed, Tim took his week off, and had the company jet ready to go. Tim had everything ready and in the larger transport that Kuri had, she met him at work at the exact moment he was leaving the building. The transport was pretty well packed, the big advantage that Kuri had was with Liani growing, and now over 1 year three months, all the clothes packed for Liani were all purchased over the last week. She had outgrown most of her other clothes, and it was not practical to buy them so large to get long times of usage from them. Beside babies could soil clothing quite well with food that did not stay in her mouth once placed there. Of course having too much in a diaper to contain without seepage and staining. Usually with the latter, after cleaning and still not get it all out Tim was not so light in funds that discard and replace was a problem.

The crew was prepped and knew they were expecting three, and a few items for a young child still considered an infant; but close to toddler age. Once they all got to meet the newest member of the Chankwan – Frantz family, Tim wondered if they would ever start the engines much less taxi and get airborne. After 30 minutes of fussing over the lovely little girl, and even they could tell she was going to be as beautiful as her mother if not more so. The pilot and co–pilot finally headed to the cockpit, and shortly after, the attendant was ready for them to board. Once seated, the attendant made sure that Liani had everything she could possibly need or want, while they were in the air for the next 5 and half hours. She did occasionally see if Tim or Kuri needed anything, but it certainly seemed to Tim that the attendant was definitely due for her own family, so she could spoil her own child. The attendant did leave long enough to heat and serve the meal, which included something that Liani could eat, and it was warm; but not hot along with a bottle of milk. Liani was like a little angel when she got to have her own little piece of banana cream pie. Although the graham cracker base had to be broken into small pieces for her, she completely enjoyed it and showed with the amount that covered her face when she was finished. She was cleaned up by Kuri and the attendant.

The first thing done after landing in Tokyo was Tim renting the largest transport available, which happen to be a newer one that had three seats and a raised top, which retracted into panels to act as a seal behind the seating. If it needed to remain open for taller cargo to be moved. The hover stroller would fit with it closed, as well as the luggage and the child safety seat in the third seat, and locked into place. Liani was curious about where they were so she watched as much as she could, once they got under way. Kuri, as they drove past the Tokyo Global Security Office told Liani that was where she worked when she met her daddy. Liani did not really understand; but acted like she did. Kuri asked if they could drive past the restaurant, and show Liani where her granddad restarted his restaurant business. Tim complied with the request, and Tim was surprised to see that even with the expanded seating, there was still a small line out front. Kur noticed it too, but told Liani that this place where people were lining up to get in, is the restaurant that her grandfather launched his business. Neither Kuri nor Tim had been to any of the other restaurants, and did not even know where they were located. They knew there were four others, but did not know if they were all in Tokyo or whether some were outside the major Tokyo area. They got to the house, found everything was not only repaired; but in excellent condition. The rock garden was fully restored and looked even better than before, as the replacement bonsai trees were larger and nicely shaped.

With all the luggage brought in, the first thing being the hover stroller with Liani aboard. She got to see the rock garden and bridge for the first time. She was rather happy to see it; but did not understand it just yet. Tim figured at some point Kuri was going to teach her about her ancestry, and the importance the Tokyo home rock garden represented.

With all the clothes hung, and Kuri still had some here as Tim had a suit, Liani's clothes were placed in the dresser as none of it required being hung. Tim told Kuri to call Sooni when she was ready, and see if she would like to have dinner here as taking Liani to a restaurant near the office may not be easy during lunch. If she needed transportation to get this far from Tokyo, one of them could pick her up and bring her here. He also said if there was anyone else she would like, they could come also; but he did need to know how many to cook for. Kuri said it would only be the two that came to the wedding, provided they were both still there. Sooni had completed her first year as director as well as Tim as CEO and she may have left for retirement. Tim did not think about that when he signed his next year, and since most all the work was within the North American continent, it never occurred to him to check. With that in mind Kuri had already contacted Sooni and she had resigned for another year as director, and her other friend had left to take advantage of her retirement. She moved to a more secluded part of Japan where she was living up to her father's expectations. To marry a man from a family that would help her father grow his business in the cloning and stocking of fish to help feed Japan. It was not being done out of love, but she had found the man her father wanted her to marry was at least a gentle person. He was not prone to abusing women, which was something she could become accustomed to. She did not know if she could ever truly love him, but she could find she could respect and honor him as her father wished. It was also helpful that she could have a fair retirement income to take care of herself if need be. Sooni did not know exactly where their friend went, and she had no means to contact her since being told what was happening just before she left.

It was arranged for Sooni to come for dinner the next evening, and it allowed Tim the time to see what would be needed for restocking and dinner. He was happy to find the computerized cooling system had kept everything quite well, and he found the fish was in good shape for the quick dinner he had in mind and it was something that Liani could eat until the mystery food was obtained. It was not going to be too much as the next time they got to Tokyo, Liani would likely be able to eat regular food stuff. He was disappointed with baby food, since on top of it all being mixed into a single container, it was synthetic food, largely because of the big push over the health benefits all governments claimed it had. Tim had never seen anything released by any government to actually provide proof to this claim. He figured it was more to insure there was enough food for all the people around the globe, to insure they had something of nutritional value.

Before heading to the grocers, which Tim only knew of one in close proximity to the Tokyo home. He called Cho Ling to verify he was still with Global Security Corporation as the director in Hong Kong. Cho was relatively quick to respond to his vidphone and started by saying, "Tim, has been a while since I heard from you, how are you doing?" Tim said, he was currently in Tokyo at his and Kuri's home, and he had been pretty preoccupied in trying to find resolution to the meaningless murder of his analyst. Signed on for another year as he wanted closure, and would settle for nothing less. "How have you been and are you still director in Hong Kong?" Cho replied, "Yo-li has sort of gotten accustom to the nice pay, and insisted he stay on at least another year, so in fact he was. Yo-li is considering to revise the trace program to account for AI systems, and to streamline that portion of the code, to take advantage of the decision making of the AI itself. She also wants to incorporate a number of enhancements to take advantage of the most current technology. She is looking for seed money so to speak, and since Global already has exclusive rights. She wanted me to ask if it would be something they would like to continue to have, by providing her with a purchase of the completed code. If Global accepts, she is considering leaving the university and concentrate on the code exclusively, and when completed and fully tested, she would like to start raising a family, before as she said, 'she gets too much older'." Tim said, "The best I could do was propose it to Trask and the board to give him an answer, I am not permitted to make such a decision without going entirely through their process, as a requirement for my position." Cho asked when that would be. Tim said he thought the next board meeting would be the week he was back in Seattle. He could not give him a time frame concerning the decision, as they could take a good deal of time discussing the benefits and the costs involved. In some cases they could make quick decisions. They may even want to make it a requirement for Yo-li to work directly with the company code specialist for that particular code. Cho understood, and simply asked to let him know how it turns out, but hopefully not too long, as Yo-li would look into alternatives.

The call concluded with quick parting statements from both. Tim went to spend time with Kuri and Liani who were in the entertainment room. This time at least Tim found them watching animated children's programming that was a little bit educational, and Liani was paying close attention at least for the time being. Children under the age of three had very short attention spans, largely a result of seeing something else that got their attention diverted from the original.

Tim only asked what time to expect Sooni, and whether she needed to be picked up. Kuri said she had her own transportation now that she was making the big money, and said around 7 PM. He already had his list of items to get, which included hopefully already corn starched chicken in stir fry portions, along with some soy sauce that was nearly gone and fruits to go with waffles for Liani as well. It was not extensive; but necessary to have food for the week. The largest part of his list other than fruits, was a few different meats for relatively quick meals, except for chicken breast and Swiss cheese and some hams. He had everything else he needed for the meals, and hopefully enough things that Liani could eat. He obtained a few fresh vegetables, specifically for the nights stir fry. Since he did not have clutee or the citrus flavored vegetable from Helsinki, it meant he would not make his Teriyaki steak and sides that went with it.

Upon his return, he got all the fruits ready to process, and put the remaining items into the appropriate compartment in the environmental cooling system for foods. Tim checked to see if Liani and Kuri were still in the entertainment center room and they were, but only one was up and gave Kuri a kiss and asked if she would like lunch shortly. Something simple like mixed salad and some fruit. Kuri agreed it would be best if he was cooking up dinner tonight. He sat with Kuri for a little while with Liani curled up next to her on the other side. He could not figure out why youngsters required so much sleep, but could not remember himself at this young age either, to make any comparison to contradict it as normal. He asked Kuri if she thought if Sooni and she got to go the sauna house, if that would be enough payment to watch Liani long enough for the two of them to go while in Tokyo. She did not know, as Sooni had never been to her sauna house, and all she could do was ask, but Sooni might have other plans for the rest of the week. She is after all a single female, who make excellent money for anyone in Tokyo, much less a woman. Tim agreed it was quite possible, but it would not hurt to ask, he did know Liani would not be allowed into the sauna house. Kuri said not until the age of thirteen, as by that time most Japanese children could be controlled by parents. It was supposed to be a place to completely relax, and running, playing or screaming children were not a part of that equation, nor tolerated.

Tim also decided once he was back to headquarters, it would be a good idea to visit all the major offices, have a lunch or dinner with the current directors. He would space it out a little better by going to one city each week, and return to Seattle instead of making it into a single long trip away from his family. He would need to check with his parents to see if they could watch Liani, while he and Kuri went to the various cities for a couple of days each week. Allowing enough time to travel both ways, and have lunch or dinner with each director, to make sure he knew all the people he would need to count on for the time he remained CEO. His first stop would need to be Chaka in Sierra, and see how he and his wife were doing as long as he was still director. Find out if his government got the schools built for him to be a part-time educator, as he was planning to do. Chaka did say he might leave altogether to become a volunteer professor, to help advance his people into the modern world. Tim did not know which way he decided, and if the schools were even in place as governments are rather slow in completing endeavors of the magnitude Chaka had indicated.

Tim started the dinner preparations around 6 PM, expecting Sooni at or before 7PM. Kuri was keeping Liani occupied, and starting to teach her some basic language skills which were only English to start. No need to create more difficulty in Liani's learning by added a second language at this young age. Liani was learning at a fair pace, and understanding what different animals were, and other things she could relate to. It was still a one word at a time approach, and the intellipad was a good tool to use for visual reference for Liani to see. Although, it did include the name in print, Liani was not at the point of learning the writing skills. It was a start as far as Kuri was concerned. Kuri fully intended for Liani to be able to start her early schooling by age 3, which is where she would learn to write and understand the written language. Japanese would not come into play until age 6, and it was not a quick process as Kuri remembered it. It really took her until she was at high school levels to completely comprehend the written language, whereas verbal was relatively simple. She could speak in both languages by age 9.

Tim had dinner completely ready just about the time Sooni arrived, and of course the first thing she had to do was meet Liani who was not too shy about meeting new people when she got the chance. Tim had made Liani some fish from the fish used in the rice dish, which he used white rice a little teriyaki and soy with pea pods also used in his stir fry meal with several other vegetables suitable for such meals. There was sake that Kuri said was good for stir fry, and it was a good sake at any rate. Liani got a bottle of milk slightly warmed to go with her bits of tuna and salmon, and a very small portion of the rice mixture. She was now at an age where she could use the utensils with a little assistance, but she still preferred fingers over utensils. Sooni once seated at the table, asked Kuri if she could borrow the pleasure master for a few hours, which was apparently Tim's new moniker in the Tokyo office. Tokyo, still had a large portion of women employed, like 80% of the office. Kuri was at least kind enough to say although there were many things she would share with her friends, Tim was not one of them. Sooni did continue to ask until Tim told her he could pull rank and use his influence as CEO to put it to rest. Sooni decided it was best not to continue with anymore requests. Although his moniker told him not to enter the Tokyo office without personal security people.

Everyone enjoyed their meal including Liani, and Sooni asked Kuri if Tim did all the cooking, and where did he learn to do it so well. Kuri said, that he had taught her to make some things without assistance, but he was much better than she. Since Liani was born, she has not had much opportunity to expand her cooking skills, but still made an occasional breakfast that Tim showed her to do. It was quick and very tasty, and not Japanese. Kuri asked Sooni if she took her to the sauna house for the most honorable samurai, whether it would be sufficient payment to have her watch Liani for a couple hours a couple nights later. So she and Tim could visit it, since they usually did when in Tokyo. Sooni had always wanted to go to the best sauna house in Japan, and said she would as Liani was too young to go, and understood why she was being asked. It was arranged that it would be a lunchtime day on Tuesday where if she was a little late getting back it would not be a problem. That way, she could watch Liani on Thursday evening after work, as long as Tim had something cooked up for her, while they went to the sauna house. It would take them at least an hour to cover the distance there and back and a little more than an hour in the sauna house, so she figured no more than 2 and half hours would well be worth it.

Tim did not know what was on the menu for Thursday, but figured there was enough fish in the house to accommodate one additional plate.

He would need to see what the chances were of finding banana cream pie. This would be something to ask Kuri, if she had any idea if he could get it in Tokyo. After dinner, Tim got to do the cleanup while all three ladies took up seats in the entertainment room. Liani of course needed a change in diapers, which she had been starting to go through the process of learning not to use them. There were still times it did not give her advanced warning for the avoidance of using the diaper. Tim got the kitchen all cleaned up and the sanitizing unit started before joining them, to find they were watching something on the entertainment system that was a Disney movie. It seemed no matter how long there were movies since they first came into being made, there would always be Disney movies which seemed timeless. Some were as much as 200 years old, and still children from around the world wanted to watch them for their wonderful story telling. As well as the imagination in presenting something virtually from a child's perspective. It remained one of the oldest film companies in the world, and to this day still came up with something new for children of all ages, that could let their own imaginations become a part of the story. How it was that Disney was able to find such dedicated help with the skills to present a story from a child's eye, was way beyond Tim's comprehension. Tim did not interrupt the interest in the movie, and took up a seat nearby on the pillows that served as chairs in the room. He still had a difficult time adjusting to getting on the ground in order to sit or sleep, but he was not so old as to have it pose painful as a result of physical failings or ailments.

After the movie, which was about a 90 minute animated fairy tale story that could only come to life from the world of Disney. Aided by the amazing people that continued to find their way into carrying on his legacy. Sooni decided it was time to leave, and Liani said goodbye to her new friend, and Sooni gave her a little kiss on the forehead. Said her goodbyes, and Tim made sure she got to her transportation, which to his surprise was a transport unlike one he had seen. It was a two seat with some additional space in the rear, but it was narrow to resemble a motorbike, as they were called in Tokyo and Hong Kong. It appeared much safer than a motorbike and nowhere near as drafty. Tim went back inside once Sooni pulled away from the house. He really expected no trouble of any kind in Tokyo, he was trained as a youngster to make sure to accompany a female until safely in her vehicle before going inside. He learned it so well, he did it without thinking. There were a few days to the week that had no immediate plans. Tim and Kuri decided with Liani sleeping through the night most times for the last few months, to take advantage of it for their own pleasures. Tim was continually amazed at how many ways Kuri could surprise him pleasantly, with the different ways she could devise for the means of pleasure. Regardless of the means, her vision of loveliness was a sight that always took his breath away, and it was always delightful for them both. The next night was far more time consuming and extensively pleasurable. They exchanged pleasure points not completing the entire sequence for either, but more than sufficient to achieve far more than either had expected. They had become more familiar with each other's bodies and points of pleasure through nerve endings, much like acupuncture specialist used.

Tuesday Kuri left at 11 AM to go to the Global Security office, and meet Sooni for her hour in the sauna house. Kuri had stirred up enough interest in her husband and made no mention of the night before. Not because she was shy, she just did not need to get more attention to Tim and fantasies from the women at GSC Tokyo. Sooni was overjoyed with the sauna house, having never experienced anything like it before. She had been to her sauna house regularly, but the difference was like night and day. She told Kuri she envied her for being able to come here whenever she wanted. If possible next time she was here, she would watch Liani for a whole week if this were the payment. She went so far as to say she would even learn to change diapers if necessary.

During the time Kuri was in Tokyo, Tim and Liani found entertainment to please Liani. It was the enhanced version of a classic Disney movie which was animated and fully restored, called Sleeping Beauty. It was a long standing Disney classic that never seemed to get old to anyone who ever watched it. Liani was quite taken by it, and stayed attentive for the entire movie. Tim found it amazing in itself, as children her age seldom had anything keep their attention that long. Tim did not hold her on his lap, but she sat right next to him. He had his arm around her to keep her close; but also so she did not fall over or lose her attention. When the movie was over, Liani got up and gave her dad a kiss on the cheek. It was quite a shock to him and his response was to pick her up and give her a little hug. When that was over, Tim asked Liani if she needed to use the bathroom. Liani nodded her head to say yes, so Tim took her to the room, put the child seat up and helped her with her diapers and pants so she could use it. It took about 10 minutes, but when all was said and done, Tim got her back to normal. He took her in his arms to the computer room, to show her the computer, and see if there was anything of interest for her there.

Liani quickly learned if she touched the screen, it would jump to something else and in her touching it came up with an article concerning GSC. Tim drew Liani back from the screen long enough to read the article. It was from a banking firm that had taken every possible means they had to avoid using GSC for the protection they desired. After countless consultants claiming to have something just as good and being a purchased product that required configuring, and a small fee to keep it going. They quickly learned from each, that it was nothing in the league of what they originally stated they needed. So, with recurring configuration fees, and multiple attempts with each consultant to get it working it the way they initially said it would, they all failed to provide them the solution they needed. In the end, after nearly three years of trying to avoid GSC, which as it turned out were ultimately cheaper than each of the other consultants, had the most superior system in the world. They wished they had just done it first, instead of trying to avoid the inevitable. The rest of the article went on with accolades and how marvelous the people at Global Security Corporation were in making them aware. And tracing any problem that occurred within their financial transactions, which in all cases were resolved completely within 3 months. Tim forwarded the article to Nora to post to all the analysts, and board members including the system people. He then let Liani play touch screen bingo some more. Kuri had snuck into the house and he did not even hear her when she said from behind, "It figures I would find you two in here, and what is she doing to my computer?" Tim said, "Liani has learned the screen will change with the touch of her finger, and seems to find a joy in it, even if she does not understand what is says."

Kuri just stood there and Tim got Liani to stop, and picked her up and he and Kuri with Liani went back to the entertainment room, and Kuri asked if Liani had her nap. Tim said she had not after watching the entire sleeping beauty movie, and going to the bathroom. After, we went to the computer only for about 15 minutes I think. Kuri ask Liani if she was ready for her nap and Liani did not seem ready just yet. Tim asked her if she enjoyed the sauna, and Kuri said it was much nicer with him; but yes she enjoyed it. Sooni said she would watch Liani for a week and even learn to change diapers, if the payment was another hour in the sauna house. Tim laughed and said it does have some marvelous results.

Liani was ready for her nap 30 minutes later, and Tim made a quick lunch for them. Leaving some fruit for Liani when she awoke, which was getting shorter, since she slept through the night. The next couple days was spent relaxing with night time pleasures. The best would come on the weekend, which would leave Kuri in a rather lengthy state of arousal for the next two weeks after returning to Seattle. Thursday Sooni arrived to watch Liani, and Tim made sure there was a nice meal with pork, although it was more of a Chinese style meal than Japanese. A little bit of Chinese Chili pepper mixed into a teriyaki sauce, which was spicier than most Japanese food, but nowhere near as much as true Chinese. Tim was quite in need of some sauna house time, and the results as always left him feeling both relaxed and invigorated. When they returned Sooni and Liani were watching a movie, although it seemed more to Sooni's liking than Liani's, as Liani was asleep. Tim gently picked up Liani, put her in her bed, and thanked Sooni for watching her. Sooni said it was no problem, if she ever had a baby, she hoped she was just like Liani, she was quite the little doll. Once again Tim made sure Sooni got to her transport safely and inside, once she pulled away he returned to the inside of the house.

After an absolutely wonderful week in Tokyo. Sunday morning had arrived and after breakfast which pretty much deleted the food stocks in the house, Tim made a note on his intellipad. That the restocking would be necessary the next time that they got to Tokyo. The clothes were all packed, and most had been cleaned the day before. The transport loaded up including the hover stroller for Liani, and the house secured. They left for the airfield where the private jet was for the whole week awaiting their arrival to return to Seattle. Tim unloaded the transport at the airfield made sure his lovely wife and child were inside the waiting area. He returned the rental transport and took care of the charges. He then walked to the waiting area, and the crew had already put the luggage on board as well as Liani and Kuri. They were simply waiting for him to board the jet. His absence allowed the crew to be with Kuri and Liani, although it was obvious when he returned, it was not Kuri that was receiving the largest portion of their attention. He being merely the CEO, was of no concern for the time being. Tim did make sure that Global Security had taken care of all their meals and accommodations before the engines were started, and he had taken his seat with his wife and daughter. Liani got to be by the window to look out and see all the tall buildings of Tokyo, just before reaching the clouds. She found she could not actually touch them, although she tried to. She was stopped by the window, which Tim though was made of a translucent aluminum, as opposed to glass or clear plastic type material. He did not know if they were completely shatterproof, but considered if a truly catastrophic engine failure occurred, it would still likely tear through the body of the plane. It was something that rarely occurred; but was always considered a possibility. The trip back to Seattle was uneventful, and the only thing during the flight was the meal. This included something just for Liani, which she seemed to enjoy, although Tim could not truly identify it, although he was sure it did not come out of a container.

Once on the ground in Seattle, Tim got the transport, loaded it up, and got Kuri and Liani inside to return to the lake property. Which he found to be spotless, since the robotic sweeper had no toddler making a mess for an entire week.

CHAPTER

6

im's first day back after a week and telling Nora he had returned, brought several things to light. First, the board of directors were meeting the following day at 1 PM and he was expected to be present. The AI systems had produced the first 1000 of what would be slightly over 6000 names from the list of former deceased GSC employees, the cities were around the globe, and no flight information was performed as it was not requested. Tim asked if the last known address was discovered for these people, and it was included in the name lists. Tim had Nora forward a full copy to Detective Marshall for him to coordinate with the other authorities, to perform whatever needed to be done to find or eliminate them as suspects. Tim did not expect this would happen in quick order although a few might. The AI system had determined a total of 6024 names were to be researched, but the remaining names still needed more research to provide a more substantial means to locate, interview or interrogate as the authorities deemed fit.

Tim's next call was to Detective Marshall to inform him of the first part of the list of names would be forwarded to him by his computer Nora. He could determine what to do from the last known whereabouts of those names given. Tim said unfortunately he could not have his people do the interviews, as they had no formal training in self-protection, in the event any one of these people were willing to murder again. The people from GSC were not expected to put themselves in harm's way, as it was far beyond the normal duties to have conducted all the previous interviews. Since the person or persons they sought had already killed once, if it would be possible to escape from further action from authorities, they were inclined to do so again. Detective Marshall fully understood, and was appreciative of all that GSC had done to this point in narrowing down the list substantially. He would be in contact with Tim as the investigations were in progress. Tim had Nora forward the first list of names and let the detective assign them to the authorities deemed most appropriate for the last known location, but with 3 billion WC at their disposal, they could be hiding anywhere.

The mere fact that they find a person who still resides in the last known address, greatly reduced the chances they would become the suspect. The investigation would not rule it out entirely. Detective Marshall had also been able to identify the accounts that were targeted by the culprit. They were former covert government accounts that were from a government fund that was off the record. It meant that the government did not know the funds existed. Some of their former covert operation used nefarious means to obtain them, and the covert operation being disbanded long ago. The funds were apparently forgotten about, and never mentioned to the government that originally had people that kept it from becoming a part of the record. With that bit of information Tim wondered if he could research who actually had it, for what purposes, but some covert groups of various government were so secretive, that only one person in the entire government would have known it existed.

From his conversation with Detective Marshall, Tim inquired with Nora whether she could research and access information from the US government for covert operations. Those that have been disbanded over the last 75 to 100 years as this would have been the time frame for the start of a world government. Nora said as long as the information did not require an AI system, she could have something in the next 24 hours. She went to work on it after Tim told her to keep him up to date on the groups she had found.

It was not long before she came back with three groups that were unlikely what he was looking for, as they were within well-known government branches. But the FBI, CIA and Homeland Security all had covert departments, largely dealing with infiltration and deep cover agents, used for the ultimate purpose of derailing terrorist activities within and outside of US borders. Tim told Nora unless they got funding through less than legal means, she would be correct in them not likely what he was looking for. Three hours later, Nora came up with another covert operation, which did receive funding from sources outside of the then US government. Largely from obtaining funds from the drug cartels they infiltrated, and brought to justice and used their money to fund the take down of other such cartels. Tim told her to keep it in storage, but did not believe that the government would have been unaware of the funds from the beginning to the end.

Tim went to the break area to get something to eat and drink, and he thought it was long overdue for a good cup of coffee. He also got a hot sandwich, which was toasted and actually not too bad. He did eat in the break area looking out over the ocean view that he really missed, being 5 floor below, and on the opposite end of the building. After lunch and the remainder of the day, Nora had nothing new to report; but she only said she should have something within 24 hours, not everything in that time frame. She already found 4, although none were truly likely. His trip home was uneventful as always.

He did get home to give the two ladies in his life a hello kiss and a hug from his daughter which he did not mind one bit, but wondered what he did to earn it. It was a short hello as his next chore was to make dinner. Since there was baby food for Liani as well as some fruits, he made a rather spicy Chinese meal that he simply had a taste for and had not had in some time. General Tso's Chicken was a versatile dish as far as what type of vegetables he could include, and he did it full tilt tonight with broccoli, pea pods, carrots, some of his citrus blend from Helsinki and clutee for what turn out to be a very good meal, with the spicy chili peppers and sauce. Kuri had her days where spicy was just the thing to have, and he knew she could tolerate it, if it was not one of her days. She was middle of the road today, although Tim did notice her breasts were still jutting much farther than a completely normal day. He and she both knew after the weekend in Tokyo, it would take at least another week for her sensations to subside some. All and all it was a very pleasant night with his lovely girls, and he got to perform his mediation routine an hour after dinner, when Liani took a short nap on the sectional with her mother right there. He had made it a point to do his routine daily, and with Kuri not always arising when he was ready to leave, his was evening while Kuri still did hers each morning, although he was never sure if it was without interruptions.

Tim's next day started at home much the same as they usually do, except this morning Liani was up, although not making any fuss, so he picked her up gave her a little kiss on the cheek. He took her to the kitchen and put her in the high chair to give her some fruits she liked for breakfast, while he got his breakfast made. He made a little game of feeding her by acting like the small spoon was a plane, and fly around her and landing in her mouth. His meal was already cooking, and would not take long, as it was some hash brown and bacon with an English muffin to make more like a breakfast sandwich. Therefore the hash browns were in deep-fry mode to get them fairly crisp on top to hold better on the muffin. Liani was done with her fruit dish before Tim's was ready to eat, and after a bit of warm milk, Liani was ready to go back to bed. When Tim returned his meal was ready, and he ate and cleaned up the kitchen. He left Kuri a message on the intellipad built into the environmental cooling unit, saying that Liani had some fruit for breakfast. He then went through his sanitizing ritual completely. Once dressed he gave Kuri a little kiss to let her know he was leaving, which did not wake her; but it was enough she knew it was him. He left for work which had nothing really happen until the board meeting.

It was headed by Trask, if that is what you want to call 11 people who all knew it was more of a family meeting, than a board of directors. He started with asking if there was anything new to be presented. Tim waited a few moments to see if anyone else had something to say before he began. Tim: "While in Tokyo last week I had the opportunity to talk with Cho Ling in Hong Kong, which was for the intention of just checking to see if he was still director there. He said his wife Yo-Li, was considering leaving the university to start a family, but had one more proposal to make it a better life for having children. For those of you not familiar with Yo-Li Quan, she was Cho's professor when he attended university, and Yo-Li was the person who had her entire class for four years put together the ideas into code that became the IG trace program. This is the trace code GSC had eventually obtained exclusive rights to. She openly admits when she compiled the code, AI was not considered for the code, since the use was so restricted.

She intends to revise the code to work specifically with AI separately from the semi-intelligent systems it was originally designed for. Considering how many changes have come in other technologies, there will be numerous enhancements to account for those changes as well. Since the

AI side utilizing the decision making capabilities it will be based more on parameters, than code. Cutting down on the storage overhead for fully coded programs required for the semi-intelligent systems. I did tell Cho that you may, if you decided to keep exclusivity over this code, that since our code specialist has already modified some of our code, largely at the insistence of the AI systems themselves, you might require Yo-Li to work directly with our specialist. I did not get enough time to get more details or how much Yo-Li was looking to get for this revision. I was told that if GSC did not take up the exclusive rights that the revision code would be sold to other possible companies. I propose you seriously consider Yo-Li's offer to maintain exclusivity. My assumption is someone would want to converse directly with Yo-Li before a final decision is made."

Trask: "I will make the contact and I believe we all know in this room the exclusivity of this code has been a large part of both our growth, and continued success. I believe I can offer Yo-Li a price she will gladly accept, but you are correct it would be prudent to have her work with our code specialist. He has learned some by trial and error, and there is no need for the work he has achieved not be incorporated into the revision. This is especially true, since his revisions have proven to be successfully incorporated into a network of AI's, although between the both of them I am sure many refinement can be achieved."

JP asked, "Who is going to get the bonus if this entitles someone to have it?"

Tim: "Maybe give it to Nora, so she get that makeup and perfume she wanted." Trask burst out laughing, and none of the other directors understood what was so humorous to Trask. Trask regaled them with the story behind Tim's comment, pointing out that only the two of them were actually present when Nora, before having her robotic body, evolved on her own into a rather humorous computer. Trask did a far better job of telling it, as everyone including JP found it was truly funny.

Trask: "I know Tim has been pretty wrapped up into this investigation, so I have put the systems people on the lookout for the first batch of robotics being delivered soon. One for each and every analyst over the next 18 months in all the offices. It will keep some of them pretty busy for that time frame, although the code specialist will not need to be involved, since it can simply be integrated into the robotic humanoid. How are things progressing in the investigation, Tim?"

Tim:" Over the last year and nearly a half, we have eliminated the largest portion of former employees with maybe 200 investigations still in process. Yesterday I got the first 1000 names of immediate relatives to our deceased former employees, and handed it over to Detective Marshall to investigate. Since we are looking for someone on the list of 6024 names, I have not gotten more than 1000 from the AI systems. It is likely where our suspect will be found. Not knowing whom it might be in that list of names, I did not want to risk losing another GSC analyst to do interviews, and we are now at the mercy of the authorities in how long this process will take for resolution. It really means that I have no idea how long it will take for the authorities to complete their investigation, or what all it will entail. I do believe that somewhere within those 6024 names the AI systems found, that the suspect will be determined, but as Detective Marshall has expressed, with 3 billion in WC, they could be anywhere in order to avoid apprehension."

Trask: "That almost sounds like I can get back in to get you acquainted with the systems people so you can have full control over the resources you have available to you. Do I read that correctly?"

Tim: "I see nothing that should cause any major interference; but I will likely still need to monitor the situation, and be available to those who might call to update on progress. Or lack of progress, since it seems I have far more of that than real progress."

Redfurd Waters and Thomas Thorn were now both in the UK, as Redfurd had been able to return from his director duties in Sierra, and concentrate on his communication and negotiation skills, in conjunction with JP to find a more suitable approach to finding good talent. In particular the recruiting group to locate over achievers not yet decided on a career path. Redfurd spoke for all three: "Is there any assistance we can provide in this investigation to help speed things up a bit?"

Tim: "I do not believe the authorities will want any influence from us on how to go about their investigation. I am sure their methods are far different from our interview process. We do not have legal guidelines to adhere to and I do not know that any of us fully understand the do's and do not's from a legal prospective. Since I only have 200 interviews in progress, but not completed, it does not seem likely our suspect will be in those remaining. You can offer assistance to Detective Marshall as far as key elements to look into from a Global Security standpoint, as a means of aiding them to have the correct information. To use to determine if they are taking the right approach for the people they question. I see no harm in that, and they can use the information within their own guidelines, to deduce if they indeed have a suspect to further investigate."

Redfurd:" I'll get the number from you after the meeting."

Lou Osaki: "Since I am now back in Seattle, I do not think Finance can be of assistance to you, but in case there is something you need to discuss, you can find me in the offices off from your office."

Tim had completed his portion of the meeting, and with it seeming he was the only one to have anything new to be placed on the table. Trask called an end to the meeting and then came over to Tim. Trask: "Since I am here, you want to go and meet with the systems people today? Or should I plan to start at the beginning of next week to get you up to speed with your additional staff? They work more behind the scenes than up front in the line of fire, so to speak." Tim: "I thought the first thing you wanted to do was contact Yo-Li on the code to determine whether it was worth the investment to keep it exclusively on our inventory of tools." Trask: "I do, but after that I can meet you in your office and get the systems group together." Tim: "That will work, it will give me enough time to see if Nora has any more information for me that she is working on obtaining."

Tim returned to the CEO office asked Nora if she had anything new to report and she said she had found three additional government operations, but has had difficulties in getting to the more pertinent information. What they did while they were active, and even though disbanded 85 to 90 years ago, the documents were not easy to get into, and none of them would have been released publicly. All three were very secretive and still listed as classified by a government that has been revised so much, it does not resemble what it was when these offices were operational. She was still working on getting more details.

It was fifteen minutes later when Trask arrived, and Tim asked him if he would like his seat back or just pretend he was here. Trask said it made no difference, it was not really his seat anymore, and he asked if Nora still could call a meeting. Tim said, as far as he knew she could, unless her other research project was taking too much of her time. Trask: "What research is she performing?" Tim said: "Detective Marshall told me they found the source of the funds, that were taken and why no complaint was lodged to the bank holding them in a numbered account. The funds were from a disbanded covert government agency, which never had the money recognized by any part of the government. Apparently, used rather dishonorable ways to fund whatever function they performed. It appears to be very secret, and even Nora was having a difficult time in finding information concerning the group, and who they may have reported too. Tim said they could not get any more clandestine than this group that was certain. The funds apparently were forgotten about after it was disbanded. Since no other part of the government knew about them, the money was never reported. It makes sense that our culprit found out about it to fund his means of avoiding the authorities. It means the person at some point in time uncovered the information while working for or with the government. Likely in the research for the audio frequency with deadly consequences."

Trask: "We are way out of our depths in this one, as we were never supposed to be involved beyond tracing the money. I could never have considered the approach you took, largely because I would have never thought in those terms. Has it been of any help with all the people doing so much beyond the normal?" Tim: "In the terms of eliminating a vast number of people from the list, and taking more than 5 years off the time for authorities to have done it, I think it has helped. It has not got us any closer to finding who may have done it. Now those left are entirely up to the authorities to locate and interrogate or question. In respect to dealing with 6024 names as opposed to nearly 150,000, it is simple mathematics it was largely a time saving function."

Trask: "I see your point when you speak in the numbers category, and the authorities would not have the people needed for such a large task. To change the subject, I did speak with Yo-Li, and since I still have some pull within the board, I have told her we would like to maintain exclusivity in this source code. The number she gave me was too low for her work, but I did not tell her I would double it. I like to give people surprises if you did not know that. She was told that our code expert and herself should work together in order to induce the short cuts he has already been able to incorporate. He has worked with the AI systems and she has not, I do not believe. She will get started immediately, but will not resign from the university until end of term, at which point she can fully concentrate on the code changes and enhancements she is aware of. She will accept the condition of working with our specialist, as she knows he has as much experience and probably more in real use situations. As of now, I do not have a precise time frame, but anyone who has been involved in this business or technology knows 7 years with the same thing is a lifetime, without having something change. As Yo-li said, she is aware that a 2nd generation TRU has been available and although the first generation are not obsolete, there has to be ways to take advantage of 2nd generation to make the system even more powerful."

Tim: "I kind of thought you would want to keep exclusivity of this code, as it keeps us in the forefront of security. With other people having it, it just opens the doors for competition in our own backyard. I likely would not have known, if I did not try to find out if Cho was still director in Hong Kong. I had planned on going around to the different major offices to reacquaint myself with those who remain, and meet the ones I had not met as of yet. I may not be able to meet every analyst who works at GSC, but I should know who I might need to ask help from. I had planned to only do one office for a couple days in a week, which included travel to and from. Not more than a single office in any given week, except for UK and Helsinki, which are not that far apart from one another. I guess that can wait until we go through with meeting systems people."

Trask: "With what you have had on your plate from your first day in this position, we can do things in what time frame you wish. Meeting the system people are also those you should be acquainted with when you may need help, and these people can help in ways your directors and analysts cannot. They might have some tricks to use in chasing down the hardware used on the Casino resort in North Carolina or San Diego. They may be able to identify the remote manufacturer, and track down who sold them, or even individual components used for the custom build systems. Others can do back door coding to help sniff out where a transaction originated, when no other evidence is obvious. In a sense this is no different than going to Hong to talk with Cho and Yo-Li for an evening, or Tokyo to get to know Sooni, since you stole my other director. Just kidding there, but last I heard you would need to enter the Tokyo office in a remarkable disguise to get out of their again."

Tim: "How is it I seem to always be the last to know these things anyway, I am married to the source. She never said a word about the trouble she cooked up in that office for me."

Trask: "That my friend, is the result of women who talk about everything, and certain nations are more likely than others. Unfortunately, when it come to a woman having been pleased in some ways, they will talk to their closest friends, usually other women even in this country. Let's see if Nora is busy. Nora this is Trask where are you?" Nora: "Trask honey, where have you been, I much prefer calling meetings and having conversation with you over all this work Tim is making me do. I might have fried a circuit in that last one, I just finished getting information about although, I do not think it is the one Tim wants." Trask: "I have been away since Tim is taking such good care of business, I am no longer needed here as much." Nora: "Tim I can see you, so here goes, the second to last government account that has been giving me fits was disbanded 90 years ago as a joint military special operations group. Since all military is funded and known by governments, that would not have had the numbered account. This group was involved in a number of different types of operations. They first and foremost were the first involved in recovering captured persons by what is called terrorist groups. The term with extreme prejudice mean anything to you, because I do not understand exactly what that is." Tim: "It meant if hostile forces were encountered to take similar action, in other words the government sanctioned them to kill any resistance without harming the persons they were to recover. Which could be other military personnel or civilians from our own country." You are correct in assuming this will not likely be the group we are looking for, but what other functions did they perform?" Nora: "They used snipers from long distant to remove threats to the world peace process, as it stated in this report. This was done as either the leader of a group, or country that was standing in the way of peace throughout the world. It sometimes included numerous people, as in the whole upper leadership of certain groups, also considered to be terrorists. They did a few intelligence gathering missions as well, usually preemptive to one of the first two tasks."

Tim: "Thank you Nora, I believe Trask has a request for you as well."
Nora: "Another job, give a girl a break." Trask laughed and said, "I think
you might not mind this one too much Nora, would you call a meeting
please?" Nora: "Trask darling, I would do that for you. At which point,
Nora did her thing and the next thing to happen was heads started popping
up from the doorway on the far side of the office. Trask waved them in,
and stopped them about twenty feet from the desk. Trask: "I believe this
will need to be done one on one, so whether you wander about the room or
take seats in that area or just stand in line is up to you." The first one in line
was motioned forward to take a seat next to Trask. "Tim, this is a man who
has skills in many areas of the systems group, sort of a jack of all trades,
does reverse engineering on technology, has code capabilities, as well as
versed in communication hardware like satellites and TRU's. I would like
to introduce my son, Jonathan Trask, Jonathan, this is Tim Frantz, the
current CEO of Global Security Corporation." Tim shook his hand said
it was nice to meet him and then asked Trask, "If this is your son Trask,
why am I here in this position?" Trask let his son answer. "Jonathan: "My
father is not the easiest person to live up to as far as his accomplishments
are concerned. I did not have an easy go of my education as some do, I
had to work twice as hard to learn what I was good at, and it was not what
my father was good at. I do not have the skills in security or business to
do this company justice, and by no means the diplomacy necessary for
the large number of people that must be conversed with on a daily basis.
My father made a wise choice, although he asked me if would want to do
it, and thought I could learn what I needed to run the company. I found
I am better with computers and other inanimate hardware devices than I
am with people. So I really left him no choice about finding someone more
suitable to the tasks required of the CEO. If it makes you feel any better, if
you were not doing an outstanding job, he would have been here every day
looking over your shoulder, and pushing you into a better decision, that
was more his direction to take. He came home and told my mother that
you were going down avenues he would have never ever thought possible,
and felt out of place in the same room as you. Since I do not live in the
same house, I do still get to talk to them regularly. I think I have about one
and half years of work coming up soon if my father did not mention it to
you. A whole lot of robotic humanoids need to be integrated to computer
systems, and I will be one of the people involved in that."

Tim: "Just out of curiosity Jonathan, if I were to get one of the rogue TRU's shipped from North Carolina, and it is determined not to be rigged in any way, could you reverse engineer it to determine how it was even possible to make?" Jonathan: "I see no reason why not, it will have components that should identify themselves as far as manufacturer, and what companies it was made for. It would also be a means to find out if any components were stolen, and chase an approximate location from where in the country or world it occurred at." It would need to happen rather quickly though, I do not see having much time outside of robotic and computer integration for quite a while, but it is good to have people like me to help out where a specialist can only do one thing good. I can do many." Tim: "I'll see if one can be shipped in quickly, just to see if we can determine anything from it. I believe there were 10 used in North Carolina and 2 in San Diego, but that is in being watched with video surveillance. I do not want to disturb it in the unlikely event the equipment is attempted to be recovered." That concluded the conversation for the time being with Jonathan Trask.

Trask told him he could return to his office if he had anything to do. Jonathan just said he had preparations for robotic humanoids in the works at the moment, and left for his office.

Trask then called a pair of people up who looked quite alike. Trask did the introduction saying, "Tim, this is the Celini brothers. Sal and Roberto, this is Timothy Frantz." Again Tim shook hands with each, and asked how they were doing, which was literally answered in unison with the same word. Trask: "Sal and Roberto if you have managed not to notice, are identical twins, which makes telling one from the other a little more difficult, but after time you spot the slight difference. These gentleman are technically called Security Code Testers, and by many others, our resident hackers. Since they quite literally know what the other is thinking, it makes for a lethal combination when it comes to cracking security." Trask turned it over to them. Sal: "We work in tandem for some things, as it presents a bigger opportunity to crack a customer's security, and we do this quite frequently. We thought we knew a large number of codes for what we do." Roberto: "When you entered all the secondary codes into the system, we found there were a number we did not know, and must say you would have made a good Security Code tester yourself. Between those codes and the occasional new ones that we find out about, we have as of yet, been able to crack security in our own system, which we try about 4 hours each day we are here. On the other 4 hours, we test our customer systems. If we crack one, the customer is notified of their vulnerability and told how to correct it by other code people in this department. If we can crack a customer's security, that means there are others who will find a way to do it as well, so we actually consider ourselves more of public servants, than hackers." Sal: "You may think this is a strange way to look at what we know how to, but considering most financial businesses manipulate other people's money in far greater quantities than their own, it is saving the bank from making people's money public to the wrong people."

Tim: "My experience as limited as it may be, hackers are rather efficient with code, so why when you crack a system do you have another code person inform the customer?" Sal: "Being known for this particular type of work is something we have tried for years to avoid, additionally, we did not learn code for the latest systems, and feel a bit antiquated in that particular area of code. Although, some of the old break codes occasionally return to having success again with the IG. They cannot account for every possible means of cracking security; as a result they often think they are not vulnerable from a code that had not worked for 20 to 30 years." Roberto: "Yes, what goes around comes around and it seems it will always be that way." Tim: "It seems you two get to work largely at whatever pace you decide, and I do not want to interfere with you much, since I cannot fathom any other projects that may come into play for you two." Trask: "They have plenty to do all the time, and I have always operated that same way; but the service they provide is invaluable to this company and its customers." Trask let them return to their offices to go about their business.

Trask next had four people come up in a group and there were not enough chairs around the desk for more than 4 total. Trask: "This is our code team, and they also have some other skills with satellite and TRU communication, as it is vital to know how information is moved in order to protect it. I will let them introduce themselves." First one to speak up was Philippe Gomez. Philippe: I am Philippe Gomez; I work largely on code for the semi-intelligent systems to interface with both the AI and outside communications, which are used for systems contacting the other systems, largely within our own network." Tim had shaken hands and let him go ahead with his introduction. Tim only asked one question.

Tim: "Are you also involved with any of the integration of the robotics and computer systems?" Philippe said only with any of the code changes that involve functions unique to robotic humanoids. Largely video input and motor skills needed for the robotic computers, to know what they can do from sight and movement they never had before." Tim: "Does that mean you will be busy for the next year and a half as well?" Philippe: "No, the code has already been placed in the existing one here, and since it has tested without problems, I will be available for other projects when needed." Next was Drak Johnson. Drak: "Full name is Drake Johnson but Drak has been my call sign since early on in school, and it has stuck. I am a code generalist, I deal with it all. Help in semi-intelligent and have learned to help with the AI systems as well. I also deal with the various means of communication; but more with outside the organization than the internal network, as we as a company must deal with both. Which is how the different systems can make calls to customer for warning or resolution results." Tim: "Do you also work with the voice packages, since you deal with their communications?" Drak: "No, the voice packages are provided by an outside source, and although we helped him in getting an AI system, he did all the code himself, and is the sole owner of that particular code, which I believe he also designed." Tim had concluded his bit and was really looking for a break from meeting all the systems people to digest what he did know already. He suggested to Trask it would be nice if they all got a cup of coffee or snack before continuing. Trask agreed, it was time for such, and said everyone that has not met Tim be back here in twenty minutes, for a drink and or snack from the 35th floor. Tim was ready to go too, when Trask said, "where are you going?" Tim told him he was getting a cup of coffee and Trask said but there is a coffee right here and he thought he told Tim before about it. Tim told him it was news to him and did not even know where it was. In a small room off the office was a coffee machine that made single cups, but had a wide variety of type of mixtures to choose from.

Tim looked through the selection for a simple coffee, which he found with a name like black cow coffee. Who names this stuff anyway, he thought. But it was a very rich coffee that was quite good. He enjoyed it more than even the coffee he made in the morning at home. Tim enjoyed his coffee so much, he got a second one to return to the desk with. It was only two minutes later before the remaining 10 systems people were back in the room.

CHAPTER

7

rask had the remaining two people, Jacki Tomlin and Bill Brown from the code group take seats at the desk just before Tim got back into his. Trask: "Both of the remaining code people are generalist in the code. They can work with most any code with a little direction from others they work with. It can be semi-intelligent, AI, Communications, even Robotics; but they never initiate a code issue." Tim said hello to both and shook hands with each, although he never really knew just how to shake hands with a woman, but was not offering kisses on the cheek in lieu of it. Jacki was several years older; but had the look of a cougar. Figuring she was either still playing her field or between marriages, but the type of woman who easily bored with the same man repeatedly. Jacki: "I do have one other skill that as generalist makes me a little different, and I am the only person in the group that does code for the vidphones. Since they are still computerized, they occasionally need code updates, and minor code adjustments. They just are not as advanced as computers, and the rest of what is in use in this company." Bill: "I simply do anything I can to help with keeping all these computers working optimally. I have learned far more here than any other point in my career, and am just happy to be with such a wonderfully advanced organization." Tim had no questions as it was pretty clear from Trask this pair largely did what needed to be done as the group required, more specific instructions from the person in charge of a project that needed multiple people.

Trask let them return to their offices as long as they had something to do or they could just remain in the room until everyone had gone through the introductions. Next was a single person that Trask said was Jon Franks. Jon: "It is short for Jonathan; but to cut down on confusion I have been called Jon far longer. I believe you are the person who told Trask about my company failing, and see if I would be interested in becoming a part of a team that would make use of my skills. Although I do not believe we have officially met, I do owe you my gratitude for bringing my situation to Trask's attention."

Tim shook hands with Jon and said, "In a previous life, I did have time to keep up with things outside of Global much better than it has been since the first day of taking this position. Have had my hands full in trying to get resolution to the problem that happened almost as soon as I started. One of the reasons this is happening today, as opposed to almost a years and half ago." Jon: "Yes, it has made the rounds in the offices; you making any progress in that?" Tim: "Only slower than I would like, and now it is to the point where only the authorities can go farther and even slower, if that is possible." Jon: "Not sure there is anything I can do from my place in this company, but if you think there is, just let me know. I have learned, and I think largely by your help, the AI's have considerable decision making abilities and attitudes when provoked." Tim thanked him and said he likely has another project coming up which will take a good amount of his time.

Trask let Jon Franks go about his business, as he knew more about what he wanted to do than anyone else. Then Trask had a pair of code people come up next. The next two were Suzanne Collette and Adam Burke, Trask said they were primarily assistants to Jon, they were the IG team prior to Jon, and having the documentation with code for the IG. If he did not remember wrongly, they were part of the team that helped in the week the code was written with the supervisors from the major offices. Tim shook hands with each, saying he was Tim Frantz. Suzanne Collette: I must say I hear some strange things from Tokyo with your name involved. I believe if you go there any time in the future, a coat of armor might be advised. Although, from a woman's point, it does make one wonder after the nickname they have given you." Tim: "Let keep this business related, if you do not mind please." Suzanne: "Okay, my function primarily before Jon Franks arrived, was to find ways to make the code work without having documentation. I am afraid with the complicated code functions and lack of documentation, we did not make much progress. With the documentation, it has not been so difficult, and we have successfully adapted to the AI capabilities in several areas. I am sure there are more ways to improve it. I do primarily this code at all system levels, since we have done away with the prior codes that are in essence obsolete." Adam Burke: "I cannot add too much else to that as far my functions have been the same." Tim: "Will both of you be involved with Jon and the pending code update, coming up?" Adam: "I believe we will be asked for our input with some of the things, we have found we could do in working with specifically the AI's, but as far as working with Jon throughout I do not believe so." Suzanne: "Seems somebody has to keep up the enhancements and adjustments, while Jon works with somebody in Hong Kong I believe." Tim: "That someone is the person that developed the code originally, she had a whole lot of help from college students during the five year process." Suzanne: "Do you know who this person is?" Tim: Yes, and her husband is employed by GSC as well." Suzanne: "Am I to understand you are not going to disclose who this person is." Tim: "That is correct, do not need everyone knowing too much to pass going through the proper channels."

With that small disappointment to Suzanne, Trask let them return to their offices, knowing they were working with giving Jon their input over code enhancements already incorporated, to cut down on the amount of work ahead for the revision.

The last four people were brought up in a group and again there were not enough seats around the desk for everyone. Trask just said from right to left this was the technology/ hardware group. Lonny Ivanich, Laurie Holland, Tim Topeki, and Ralph Mazurski. Tim is supervisor over the whole group, and determines who needs to do what with the skill set they have. It does not take a lot of his time, but occasionally when groups are needed to work a project, he determines who is best suited for it. For instance, we try to have a minimum of 4 people for larger project involving upgrades and changes. Adding storage anyone of these people can handle it, as well as Jonathan. All five will be involved in the robotic integrations of computer to humanoid." This made things easier; Tim shook hands with each of them and asked only one question of the group. Tim: "How many of you are also capable of reverse engineering should there be a need?" All four said it was a part of their area of expertise and education."

With that concluded, Tim and Trask let them go back to prepare for robotic humanoids to be delivered within the next week.

Once the office was clear, Tim and Trask went to the coffee machine, and got the selected brews of their choice. They both returned to the desk and Tim said to Trask," I need to make a quick call to Roger Morris in North Carolina." Tim: "Nora can you reach Roger Morris in North Carolina and put him on vidphone please." Nora: "Sure can honey, I love it when you say please." Within a minute the vidphone dropped down, and Roger was there. Tim: "Hello Roger, I know it has been awhile to get to this stage, but I am wondering if any of the rogue TRU's you found on the casino rooftop, could be packaged and sent to Seattle." Roger: "I believe the authorities have given an all clear. I think they are still monitoring it for anyone that may come back for it. I would need to clear it with them, and just tell me how to send it." Tim: "You should be able to take it to any expedite facility you have close to get it here, and they can have it packaged in a shockproof container that will withstand any type of impact or harsh movement. Just send it to Seattle Headquarters to my attention, and I will get it to the people who might be able to help find out a little more in how it came to be." Roger: "How is that?" Tim: "They tell me by reverse engineering, they can find out where the components were manufactured, and whom they were made for, which will give us a little more information on finding our culprit." Roger: "Good, I should have the clearance and TRU by tomorrow, and sent as soon as I can, once I have it." Tim: "Thank you Roger, it is probably getting close to end of day for you so have a good evening." Roger: "Thank you, and you do the same." The vidphone was disconnected and retracted into its hiding place.

Tim told Trask he should make one more call before getting back to the systems group agenda. Tim took a good drink of his coffee and said, "Nora, one more call to Robin Torry if you please." Nora: "Consider it done." The vidphone dropped down and Robin was there. Robin: "Is this a social call?" Tim: "A long overdue update is more likely. Your banking group with the missing 11 billion World Currency, has had 8 billion returned, even though they had no formal complaint from those who opened the account. I would think the bank was responsible for doing investments with it as well. I am sure there is much more in it than the 11 billion, since the group who had it, has been gone for 85 years." Robin: "And how did you find this out?" The detective involved here for the murder of my analyst, let me know last week the funds were returned. He had to dig into a number of confidential documents from the government to even find out it was a former government agency, but long disbanded. I still do not know the exact agency, and have my computer looking further. It was very deep covert and the government did not even know the funds existed. It told me that it was so covert that they likely used unorthodox means of acquiring funding, which kept the government out of being seen as a proactive. My computer has found five covert agencies, but four have been ruled out as being funded by the government." Robin: "I see, that makes it pre-World Government. Likely up to things to change the shape of the world to get to the point of having a world Government. It could mean some very nasty business dealings for such vast amounts of money to operate with. Any chance of recovering the other 3 Billion, not that the bank will be hurt by it?" Tim said, "That is unlikely, it was removed with the death of my analyst, and my detainment." Robin: "They detained you for what?" Tim: "I was the one to discover my analyst was dead, and I had to remove his headset to find it. They kept me for 5 hours without asking a single question, until they could verify beyond a shadow of a doubt, I was not responsible directly for his death. They have a job to do too, I guess, but it delayed me from getting more answers when I really needed them." Robin: "That would certainly put me in a foul mood, and knowing me, it would take more than a couple of days to get over it. My people try very hard to not be seen when that happens. Although, there are only so many places to hide from me." Tim: "Good thing I did not call on one of those days." Robin: "I do not answer on those days, so you need not be concerned there, but thanks for the information. I am not sure there is much more I can do over that problem anymore." Tim: "Not likely, but if anything else comes up, I will let you know and thanks for your help." Robin: "Likewise, see you later." The vidphone disconnected and retracted to it unseen position.

Tim: "Okay Trask all the overhead is done now with the systems group, how do you handle just talking with a small group, say the technology group for reverse engineering of a rogue TRU?" Trask: "That is simple just have Nora reach Tim Topeki, and everything goes through him as to the specific people to get for you in a meeting in your office. It does not occur as quickly, as with Nora calling for a group meeting, but I do know what you mean as only needing a select few instead of everyone."

Trask: ""By the way I do like the way you handle Suzanne there pleasure master." Tim: "Wonderful, will GSC cover the cost of my armor with a good chastity lock." Trask: "Sorry, you got to cover that one yourself, or maybe have Kuri get it for you unless she wants to share, after all, she did start it from what I heard." Tim: "So it would seem. I remain to be the last to know about these things, and it really is a bit annoying. To think that Tokyo is not going to see me for a long time from at least an office visit standpoint. I may meet with Sooni outside of the office, and preferably with Kuri there also." Trask: "Yes, that would likely be a good way to go about it. At any rate, you think you have a handle on how to deal with your system people, I can tell they have already got a good deal of respect for you, since you have unknowingly influenced a good deal of their needs to remain in this company."

Tim: "Sorry, I do not know how you tell that, as I just met them, and do not know how to read them just yet." Trask: "If they did not have respect for you, they would have given you a much rougher go of it, as that is simply how systems people think. If you ever had a group that knew you had only a minimal idea what it was they did, as occurs in many organizations, they would have ridden you pretty hard. They know who you are by things that have been arranged with your input, and they know you have an understanding of the overall purpose of everything in this company. As a result of your input, this company has advanced way beyond what I envisioned when I first got the group together to form it. The knowledge you have rubs off on everyone, and they make every effort to prove they are worthy of being in the only company in the world to do what we do for the world of finance. That exceeds my expectation of where this company would be at this time in the world of finance. I had expected to have a large percentage of governments; but not everyone and nowhere near as high a percentage of the finance world. If things went according to my original plan, we still would not be doing a trace service, in addition to monitoring the movement of money. With your invaluable input to make the IG code exclusively ours, we advanced further than I considered possible. People do take note of these assets, and how they came to be." Tim: "Is there more I need to know about concerning trying to fill your shoes around here?" Trask: "Funny, I thought I was trying to live up to your expectations for the last several years. As far as I know, the only thing left is really to introduce you to your secretary in the outer office, but that can wait until tomorrow. You already have to handle the incoming customer calls, which have not been many as of late, we have kept everyone pretty happy with the level of service we provide. If it increases, it is a means to measure where improvements need to be made or adjustments. Usually it has to do with stress levels gaining again and I have no more ideas how to lessen them. They now get 2 weeks paid time off, and have mandatory evaluations along with the ability to seek help from the medical staff whenever they feel things getting out of control. With the robotic computer systems coming, short of cutting the time to five years from ten there is no way to change it. Unfortunately five years is not enough time to warrant a retirement plan and stay profitable."

It was time to call it a day, Tim and Trask left the office at the same time. Even had the transportation in close proximity to one another in the parking facility, owned by Global Security Corporation. Over the last ten years, Tim learned that Global Security Corporation had purchased as much of the office space they leased as possible. Only three cities had a major office still under lease. Hong Kong and Tokyo, had far too great of a demand on property on their little islands for it to be purchased, for a price not overly inflated. In all other cities where offices were located, the buildings were now owned by Global Security, as a part of their considerable assets across the globe. The other exception was St. Petersburg, and it was the government that kept that from occurring. Tim arrived home with time to give the ladies in his life a hello kiss and hug. Liani was in learning mode today longer than usual, she was ready to stop for the day. Kuri and Liani went from learning to entertainment, which for some reason the nightly news still was something Liani preferred as opposed to animated shows.

Tim started his evening dinner routine, and Kuri told him she went to the grocers today with Liani. They picked out a bunch of fruit and some vegetables that needed to be done yet, as well as getting the meats and fish they were running low on. She said it was a much nicer grocer facility than any she remembered in Tokyo. Except maybe the open air farmers market, where everything was if you felt like wandering through all the vendors' aisles. Also, since so many things were being cooked, that at times the place did not smell so good when items conflicted between neighboring vendors. Tim found everything he needed as Kuri learned it was easier to put things in specific places to always be able to locate when you needed them. She learned it so well, that the house in Japan was setup the exact same way as both of those in Seattle were. Tim had not been to the other house as a resident in quite a long time. It also had two other residents in that time, and he had not checked it since. He made a mental note to himself that it should be done this coming weekend, just to see if there were items needed to be restocked, check for anything missing, broken or damaged. Get an idea about what may be due for replacement, as far as the house was concerned. It really had not had much done since it was built, and over 30 years that he lived in it, he thought it was built by his parents, but he was the last of the children. He knew for certain that the robotic sweepers were likely due for modernization. They had become even more efficient and enhanced with longer run times before charging. And even more powerful in taking care of the material it collected. He would need to contact the consultant to see if it was something he could do, and determine what was in need of being upgraded and replaced.

Dinner went along as planned, and Tim inquired as to how it was so much fish was needed. Kuri said she was making it for Liani every day for lunch, as she liked it much better than mystery food from a container. Tim could understand that, since he could not identify most of it without reading the labeling. It was getting close to the time when Liani would not be eating it, since it was largely synthesized food stuff. After Tim cleaned up the kitchen, he went ahead and did his meditation routine which took 1 hour 10 minutes, but it kept him focused, and in pretty good physical condition. The evening was spent with Kuri and Liani until fairly late in the entertainment area. After putting Liani to bed for the night, it was snuggle time with Kuri.

Trask had called the next morning saying his wife had arranged for furniture to be delivered, and he would not be in until the next day, as she conveniently had other things scheduled for her day. That would keep her from being home for the delivery and setup. Nothing really happened until the following day when Nora announced she had finally obtained the last covert operation information, and it was really quite nasty. "The group operated only with the knowledge of the Vice President at that time in the past. No other government official or agency knew of it and its purpose. The Vice President at that time had spent nearly 30 years prior to political office in black operations. He felt in office he could do more, by setting up the organization called Clean Sweep, in getting the world more into the World Government mind set. Clean sweep amassed it funds by supplying drugs to various cartels that were still in business, with declining drug needs, as they were being hunted by far too many other governments. They also had an agenda of targeting the government officials, and terrorists that were holding up the formation of world government and peace among nations. Clean Sweep, also obtained funds from other governments and groups by finding those willing to pay for the removal of the problem leaders. They had a select group for assassination, and were paid well by those others who were most affected by the existence of resistance to World Government, and largely dealt with terrorist groups worldwide. They did not just kill anyone who had a price, those assassinated were also on their own list, which was produced largely by the Vice President 95 years ago. The funds from assassination and drugs were used for the operations that were performed. During the 8 year run of the Vice President, they accounted for near 85 assassinations around the world. If a leader was surrounded by other high ranking members to the organization, to insure it would not continue forward in the event of the leader's death, Clean Sweep took out the entire group and sometime even entire families. These did not get officially put on record as only the 85 leaders were accounted for in the 8 years. The funds collected in excess of the cost of operation were invested in numbered accounts. Only two people knew about it, the Vice President and his group leader in Clean Sweep. This would likely be the source of the funds that were obtained by the intruder." Tim then contacted Robin Torry and let him know about the owner of the said funds. In order for them to be discovered, it would have needed to be someone within the military or government, since it was unused for nearly 85 years. It also means that the only people who knew of the account, officially have long been deceased.

Trask arrived just after his conversation with Nora and Robin Torry, and Tim filled Trask in on the details. From there Trask and Tim went to the outer office area and up to the secretary's, although her official title was office manager, and she handle routing all calls within the offices on this floor. This consisted of the 10 board members, the fourteen systems people and Tim as current CEO. Trask waited for her to finish up the call she was on to be routed to one of the members of the board. Trask: "Loretta, I know this is long overdue, but this is Timothy Frantz, the current CEO of Global Security. Tim said, "It is nice to finally have a name to go with the face I have seen for the last 10 years." Loretta said she had known his name for quite some time, but had no idea that hers was not known to him until today. Tim said he would make sure to use it now, when he walked past her to the office area.

Trask was done with his duties in turning over the seat behind the CEO desk, but stayed around until lunch time. Tim had him go to the restaurant with him so he could prove they still had a reason to stock his favorite Cognac. Lunch did include each having a glass of Cognac, and Tim took care of the charges. He let Trask leave from the restaurant to return home early, and only show up for board meetings now and then, unless he got bored. Tim got a little more good news from Daisy, telling him that she had the next 1000 names to forward to authorities. He got the list sent to his intellipad, and then had Nora call Detective Marshall from the Seattle Police.

The department forward him to Detective Marshall's mobile vidphone and Tim saw him just getting out of his vehicle. It was not enough to determine if it was a transport or other type of vehicle. Tim:" Hope I am not catching you at a bad time." Marshall: "Just arriving at an interview in your list, but I have a moment, what can I do for you?" Tim: "I will be quick, I have the next 1000 names for you, and can send them to the same location as the last time. Also, I believe us to be seeking more than one person in this investigation, and since I am down to family members of deceased analysts, I would believe them to be related. There are too many skills involved overall for a single person to be responsible entirely, it required help. Also the final thing to know is the military or government had to be available to these people, as the account that was siphoned for 3 billion world currency, belong to a covert black operations group. It was only known by the Vice President some 95 years ago, and it was known as Clean Sweep." Marshall: "Good information to know for the investigation, I will get the word out and work it from there. I look forward to the additional names when I return to the precinct."

The vidphone ended and Tim's retracted into it hiding place. The rest of the day had no more enlightenments, and not much in interruptions until nearly end of day, when his North Carolina TRU made it in. He had to contact Tim Topeki, even though he knew he needed Jonathan Trask for the reverse engineering. Tim had Nora make the call and Tim specified Jonathan Trask, who Tim Topeki said he would send right to him. A few minutes later, Jonathan Trask appeared and Tim motioned him to the desk and take a seat. He reached down and retrieved the TRU, and said it just arrived from North Carolina and was for him to reverse engineer. Jonathan took one look at it and told him, it looked like it was military. Since every type of information sharing originated from the military in the past, it would not surprise him that the IG was any different. Tim: "What do you mean?" Jonathan: "Part of engineering of this type, is also learning the history, the previous methods being last the cloud and then preceded by the World Wide Web. Both, long before being public, were used by the military as a secure means of communication among all of its facilities, including temporary ones in other countries." Tim: "Just see what you can come up with and let me know." Jonathan: "No problem, should know in a day or two, but I might need to do a little research to be certain." Jonathan took the TRU with him, but only had enough time to set in his space securely and head home for the day. Tim was ready to go as well.

Outside of Jonathan saying everything inside was military issue, and from the information he discovered on their light speed network, it had no TRU address as the military used its own satellites. With only three, it had to wait to be in range for a transmission to take place and or receive. The satellites held the transmission until it was in range for the recipient TRU, although the military did not call them TRU, they called them Laser Light speed transmission unit.

Jonathan went on to say he believed the one he got from Tim was built by the military for their own use. It might be possible that they have a list of 12 or 13 missing from their inventory. It might very well be documented, he did not have access to that type of information. Tim had Nora check into missing Laser light transmission units in a group of 10 to 12 from a single warehouse location.

***

For the next 6 month's Tim felt he was sitting on his hands, and getting nowhere aside from some days off for his paid time off he made no real progress. Only 500 of the names handed over to Detective Marshall had been fully investigated, to end being eliminated, as the source of the problem that was now closing in on two years. Daisy had given him all the names on the list, all 6024 which were all forwarded to Detective Marshall as they were received, but in 6 months, 5524 names still remained. Tim did not know what else he could do to get to the point of resolution to the murder of his analyst. His patience was being worn extremely thin in the slow progress that was taking place, but it would not rest until it was resolved. He spent countless hours trying to figure out what more he could do to eliminate some of the endless hours of waiting. Time and time again without putting more GSC people at risk he came up with nothing that would make the problem come to its appropriate conclusion. He thought he would take a good long break near Christmas, having more than two weeks of paid time off left. It had to be used before that, as he would be due for another contract. He already explained to Kuri until this problem was seen through to resolution, he would not leave for another run at retirement.

As a result he took a week off with less than 3 month before his contract renewed, and 4 month until the Christmas season was in full bloom. Before leaving he had Nora bring up the information that had been initially recorded. He had Nora remove the satellite positions as it was no longer going to produce any additional help.

***

The information remaining needed to be revised.

Expert security procedures Line 1 (emphasis on GSC methods)
Expert in financial transactions Line 2
Expert in Communications Line 3
Expert in Satellite positioning Line 4
Expert in application programs Line 5
Expert in Technology (rouge TRU's) Line 6

Line 1 would remain the same
Line 2 would be revised to internal knowledge of GSC methods
Line 3 would be revised to efficient in communications
Line 4 would be revised to understanding Satellite positioning
Line 5 remained the same

Line 6 would be replaced with Military or inside Government access and knowledge of classified documents

Line 7 would read at least two persons required for all the skills needed to plan this murder and theft (suspected same family)

Line 8 access to military inventory in order to obtain military issue TRU's known as Laser light speed transmission units

Tim asked Nora to update all the major offices, and ask for any input to expedite a resolution. Nora complied and Tim got no response for the remaining day and left for the entire week including two weekends. He arrived home to announce to Kuri he was home for the next nine days, and hope nobody got tired of him in that time. Kuri said she would never get tired of him and wished he were home more. Liani said she liked it when her father was home too. She was now totally off container food and had enough of her teeth in to eat most anything as long as it was cut into small enough pieces for her as opposed to adult sized. She was closing in on her second birthday, and Tim had to ask Kuri what was appropriate to get her for the occasion. He knew instead of a birthday cake she had acquired Kuri's taste for banana cream pie, so that would be served for the occasion.

Kuri said she was already learning her ABC's and it would be a good idea to get her own intellipad, so she could start using it for basic reading skills. With a little assistance from her mother or father, she could start learning to read the simple children's books available through the Information Gateway. Kuri then said, she must have got his brains because she has an excellent memory and learns quickly, and does not seem to need to do it repeatedly. Tim said to Kuri that she was going be a dangerous teen, to have Kuri's looks and his brains he was not looking forward to how many hearts she was going to break, before she finished high school. Kuri said," Bet you can't wait until she starts getting her family heritage training from me". Tim said, " Oh yeah, I can see her knowing how to pleasure a boy by age 10 and wanting to find out how good she is by 12. I just can't wait, and since you train her, how I am supposed to curb her curiosity, which is normal but usually not acted upon."

Kuri said, "Liani will not be that young for that type of training, only meditation routine before age 10." Tim replied, "So you are going to make me replace the big stick with the samurai sword to keep the boys away." Kuri, said, "I hope not."

CHAPTER

8

Tim and Kuri had a good loving session after Liani went to sleep that night into the morning hours. The next morning when Tim awoke, he contacted the consultant to see if he did upgrades as well as construction. The consultant told him he did everything that was necessary to keep a home in top condition, as well as the building of new homes and businesses. Tim arranged for him to meet the consultant later that afternoon at the original home, to see how much was past its prime, as far as environmental and robotic sweepers and the kitchen.

Kuri and Liani awoke shortly after. Tim said it would be nice if they could go with him to look over the original home, now that it was no longer occupied by some of her family. She agreed, and Tim made them all a hardy breakfast and cleaned up afterwards, before Kuri got to do her morning routine, while Tim kept Liani occupied. It was learning on the entertainment system finding a selection that was good for Liani, showing how well she knew her alphabet and numbers. Tim was surprised that she was so far along, and she was having an easy go of it. Kuri finished her meditation routine and cleaned up, got dressed and took over with Liani, while Tim could get cleaned up and dressed. Then it was time to get Liani dressed and ready to go, she was now walking more than using her hover stroller, so they left it home, and went to the old residence to meet the consultant. Once Tim was inside, he noticed the house was a bit less clean than usual and found the reason. One of the robotic sweepers had failed to keep a charge long enough to return to its recharging location. It was an indication that the long life batteries had reached the point of all needing to be replaced, as once one failed, the rest were sure to follow. They were there nearly an hour early, and Tim looked over everything in the house. The kitchen needed restocking, but most everything was where it belonged, and he put those items that were not, into their proper place. Since he had three homes all arranged identically, it was easy for him to remember where the proper place was. He checked the environmental systems, and really did not see where anything appeared to be in need, but the consultant would know best. The kitchen computerized cooling device was rather old, but did not appear to be working improperly. It had to be nearly 40 years old, as with the computerized cooking center, which Tim figured should be replaced with something newer, more efficient and preset for far more food types.

The consultant arrived, and Tim first asked him about the environmental system as to the age, and whether it should be replaced for that reason. The consultant informed him that it was 42 years in service, but just as efficient as recent system. The typical need for replacement is a result of failure and or continual repairs, which can become costly. He suggested leaving it be, as it seemed to be operating just fine. It was decided that the kitchen would get everything upgraded, and the robotic sweepers were indeed reaching an age where they would all stop holding sufficient charge to complete the assignment. The total cost would be 15,000 WC and it could be started almost immediately, taking about a week, as the majority of the work would be with replacing the charging systems in the robotic sweeper locations. They went into hiding when not in use, and the space to work in was rather small. Tim transferred the funds and told him to go ahead, it was time to upgrade it. He said he would check back next weekend to see if it was complete or nearly complete. After the consultant left, Tim and Kuri got Liani away from the entertainment system. Tim decided to get some of his audio disks that were here, and took them to the lake property residence. When they returned, it was a little later than normal for lunch, so it was quick and light, except for the queen of fruit, Liani, who got just what she wanted.

After lunch, Liani was back into the entertainment room devouring anything she could learn, and it certainly had proven instrumental in her speaking. It was getting to the point where reading was going to come before her birthday arrived. Kuri was asked to come to the restaurant and fill in as hostess. Kuri had to leave before dinner could be ready, even if Tim started the moment the vidphone came active and it was too early for dinner. Kuri said she would be able to eat at the restaurant, and to just cook for himself and Liani. It took three hours before Liani was finally tired of the entertainment system, and educational material when she asked, "Why W was called double U when it looks more like double V?" Tim had no answer to the question as he said, "It was possible it once resembled U more than V a long time ago, but I do not know for sure." Tim put Liani in her high chair, while he got dinner ready. He figured it would be wisest to share his meal with her than to cook two portions. He did make a larger portion than he would normally, but he made a fully mixed salad to go with a large tuna steak grilled to perfection, with lemon butter and some deep fried breaded mushrooms as well, and a single English muffin in case Liani was not happy with mushrooms.

Tim ended up eating the muffin, as Liani ate as many mushrooms as she could, leaving him all of about three, while she also had tuna and a small bit of mixed salad. She also ate all the clutee and citrus flavored vegetables from the salad. After dinner, Liani went to the little ladies room without assistance, and Tim waited for her to come back to see what he would need to do. Apparently Kuri had given her little girl panties instead of a diaper, and she was back without any need for Tim. He set her up in the entertainment room; but this time with animated programs more for entertainment than learning. He went to clean up the kitchen while he could still watch Liani. It did not take more than 15 minutes to get everything into the sanitizing unit, and then he was back next to Liani. She lasted only about 1 hour and after having a long day and no nap, she was ready for some sleep. Tim got her ready, changing her over to sleepwear, and put her into the padded infant bed and she fell right to sleep.

Tim thought he would go to the audio room and listen to an album, before checking on Liani, and then getting himself into his routine. He managed to do both in two hours, including cleanup and got into his own sleeping attire, just before Kuri arrived home. Kuri immediately got out her hostess attire, put her sheer robe over herself, checked on Liani, who was still quite asleep and returned. Beckoned Tim to join her in bed. She turned to give him a kiss, and turn back and was asleep before her head finishing making it to the pillow. Tim, in all the time he had known her, thought she had limitless energy. He decided to bend over place his lips on her forehead for both a kiss, and to see if she was too warm to explain anything might be wrong. She seemed perfectly normal from that standpoint, and pulled the covers up and lay next to her until he fell asleep.

Next morning after sleeping with his arm around her, they both awoke about the same time. Tim had to ask, "I do not recall you ever being worn out by anything, even checked to see if you might be a little under the weather. So what got to you last night?" Kuri replied with, "It was a nightmare last night at the restaurant, we had a party room group that took it most of the night, and we served 1000 meals in addition to those in the dining area, which was full from the time I got there until it closed. I even had to clear tables to get space available for those waiting, in addition to seating everyone and taking the payments. I never got to stop for a bite to eat, and did not stop working from the time I got there until it closed for the night. I finished up with clearing tables and final count out for the night's totals. Never seen it like that before, and I hope not again." Tim said, "That sounds rather busy, what was it compared to your early days working with your parents in Tokyo?" Kuri said, "When it was just a sushi bar and café, it would have taken two weeks to serve that many meals from opening until closing."

Tim got up, did his morning hygiene and went to go check on Liani, who was still asleep, must have worn out her thinking cap yesterday, he thought to himself. Went back to the room, where Kuri was already into her meditation routine and she still did it with no clothes. Which always made Tim look in awe at the gorgeous woman he felt lucky to have as his wife. Even though he really wanted to stay and watch, he managed to pull himself away to go start up some breakfast. Liani was awake before breakfast was completely ready, so Tim managed to get her out of her bed, and let her go off to the little ladies room before returning to the kitchen. To make sure it was not over cooking, which it being computerized was never really an issue. He then went to go see if Liani was in need of any assistance. She was fine, and ready to join him in the kitchen.

Kuri was finished with her morning routine about the same time as breakfast was being served. The three of them had a nice meal before Tim got the clean-up detail, and Kuri the learning duties. Kuri had brought her intellipad to change Liani over to basic reading, and the process was now started. The simplest things to start with were pictures of domestic animals and farm animals, with other items like a house and trees and the likes. The program that Kuri used had each picture spelled out, and also had the phonetic spelling to get the correct pronunciation. Even though Liani knew how to say correctly a fairly large number of words. She did not know how to read them, and had no phonetic understanding. So Tim found her another audio and visual aid on his Intellipad that explained the phonetic pronunciation of each letter of the alphabet, in order to help Liani learn her pictures. Kuri had no idea the program Tim found even existed. She thought it was ideal for her to learn her reading skills quicker and easier. Tim then had Kuri let Liani be alone a bit with her phonetic alphabet. He told Kuri in the kitchen where they could watch Liani, but talk for a moment to let Kuri know what he was thinking about doing.

Tim: "I have been thinking what I can do to try to speed up the process of getting to the bottom of the murder of the analyst at work. This is what I have come up with, since I will not risk any other analysts in the interviewing process. I was thinking that the person or persons behind it, did not cause the death by a means of direct contact in any way shape or form. With my martial arts training, I should be a better candidate to conduct interviews myself. I will start with the parents of employees that have lost their child to the stress of being an analyst for GSC. I will try to see if there are any reasons for them to have a grudge against Global Security Corporation, and find out if they might have had a hand in the death of the analyst." Kuri: "I do not want anything to happen to you, but I know you have a routine that should allow you to defend yourself quite well. What if the person you encounter is armed with some sort of weapon, very few martial arts experts are truly capable of dodging speeding projectiles, myself included. Are you sure this is what you need to do?" Tim: "I cannot see any other way and the authorities are simply undermanned to do this in a timely fashion. I want the problem resolved, so I can possibly get back to being a retired GSC employee after nearly 12 years now, and likely 13 before this is finished. I need resolution, and my patience with the authorities is stretched to the point I need to do something, to further this to a point of resolution." Kuri: "It seems you have made up your mind about this already, but just be careful. You have no concrete evidence to support your theory that this could not be dangerous for you." Tim: "I fully understand this is a risk, but I cannot ask other analysts to do it. They have no self-defense background that I am aware of. Who else can I have do it?" Kuri: "I do not know enough of the people in that office to give you a justifiable answer, just if you do this, please be careful. I do not want to be raising a child without you, and it does make it a little difficult to give Liani a little sister or brother also."

Tim and Kuri continued their chat for another five minutes. Nothing new was really discussed; but Tim pointed out it was unlikely the parents of any of the former GSC employees were a major threat to his wellbeing. Kuri finally concurred that he was the most logical person to conduct the interviews, and more his responsibility as CEO.

They went back to the entertainment area to insure Liani was doing well, she was engaged in her phonetic alphabet, and learning it quickly. It was decided the next day Tim would need to acquire an additional intellipad for Liani. Liani was advancing too fast to be able to wait until her birthday, even though it was nearing. Tim also said for her to see if her parents were in Seattle, and have them over for dinner this week, while he was off. He would plan on having the restaurant's biggest seller; but he intended to go all out on the rice side dish. It would have all the additives that make it even better than Hiro's own recipe. Kuri agreed, and went directly to raising her parents on the vidphone. It was not the longest conversation, but Liani waved hello to them before going back to her learning program. It was decided to have them over in two nights and they would not be leaving for Tokyo until the following week, when Tim returned to Global Security Corporation.

Tim decided it would be best to make sure he got enough of everything he needed from the grocer today, before they were here. It would allow proper marinate time of 24 hours. While he was out he would also get Liani her intellipad. Kuri agreed, and said she would keep vigil over the learned Liani, as she would be reading very soon if not today.

Tim departed the lake property home, and his first stop would be for the new intellipad. It was easily concealed in the transport, and posed no theft issues unlike unattended groceries. It was not very common; but still a precaution everyone should take. No reason to tempt fate. His trip to the shop that had intellipads and such items, was not terrible far from the grocer, and since Liani was not in need of vidphone connections at this time, it took a mere 5 minutes to setup for what was needed. It was not too costly, and Tim paid for it from his normal account. He then went to the grocers.

He knew he should get enough steak for everyone that would be present, although Liani would only need something small. She would eat more of the rice dish than anything else. It had all of her favorite ingredients, not to mention the deep fried mushrooms. Tim got six packages of the breaded mushrooms, knowing he would only need two for the meal. Since Liani had acquired a taste for them. He made certain there were plenty to go around. He got enough steaks for two meals, one for Kuri's parents and the other for just the three of them. He knew he had sufficient teriyaki sauce for at least the two meals, but would have to order some from Tokyo. He was not going to find the sauce he knew best for that meal at his grocer. He did not need any more fish; but got some anyway, along with a good size package of shrimp. He also picked up a nice tuna steak knowing the rice dish called for some. The remainder could be used for another meal or several rice dishes.

Once he obtained more than he really needed, he took care of the charges at the checkout and returned home. It took him all of an hour to get it all accomplished. After greeting his ladies and presenting Kuri with Liani's intellipad, Tim put all the food away and got the steaks in marinade. It was time for a lunch also. He decided with all the fish available to cut up some for a different rice dish, using teriyaki of another style, and some soy sauce with clutee and the Helsinki citrus flavored vegetable, along with a few pea pods and carrot slices. Everyone enjoyed lunch, and Kuri even inquired on what he used so she might make it again while he was at work. He let her know and showed her the teriyaki sauce to use, which was different from the one for steaks, it was more for stews and soups, but added just the right flavor for this rice mixture.

He also noticed he was running low on both, although not out, he should order a few of each from Tokyo to be safe. After he cleaned the kitchen, he let Kuri know he would be in the lower level long enough to reorder sauce from Tokyo, and the Helsinki vegetables. Those he could order in large quantities, since they were dehydrated, they would keep for a long time until placed in water. That was something he did only when he used them, and had the correct amount per person to each dish engraved in his memory.

It took about 30 minutes, long for Tim, but he checked the Tokyo IG store to see what other items he might like for future use. He did not really find anything that made him decide to add to his collection, although he considered authentic Japanese soy sauce, but Kuri never noted any difference from what he used locally, and she would certainly let him know if it was different from her father's. Tim also noted he could buy 8 containers of local; for the cost of one authentic, so he told himself it was merely a marketing ploy to make more profit than the item would normally get.

He went back up from the lower level to spend time with the ladies, right up until he had to start dinner. Since steaks were on the menu in two day, he needed to make something different. The steaks were already being prepared as far as the time in marinade was concerned. So he decided on trying to make some sweet and sour pork. He had a good Cantonese style recipe, and all the ingredients; but did not want to make another rice mix side dish. He decided on some fried rice, which was already prepackaged with the extras that went with the rice. Deep fried mushrooms were always good and he had plenty, he knew none of them would get tired of them with two meals consisting of them in the same week. He got to work on the preparations and had everything set in the computerized cooking device within 45 minutes, and set to be cooked in one hour. It would be the normal dinner hour, and then he returned to the entertainment room to check on progress. Liani had finished with phonetic alphabet, and Kuri pulled up the simple children's books she was having a difficult time with before. Tim asked if she should take a break from that for a short time, since dinner would be ready in an hour. Liani paid no attention, and went to sound out words and was getting most of them right on the first attempt. Once she sounded a word out, she said it two or three times absolutely correctly. No one taught her this, but it let her say the word correct and associate with the letters together that made up the word. The amazing part about it would turn up later on in her reading. Once she knew what a word was from this little process, she did not seem to forget it later on. She went through about 10 different animals, and then a couple more generalized items like house and tree. Then the cooking device announced dinner was ready to be served. Kuri had a bit of difficulty getting Liani to put down the intellipad to eat, so from the kitchen Tim announced to Liani, he was going to eat all the fried mushrooms if she did not come and get hers. That got rather decisive movement from his little girl, and Liani and Kuri were at the table, before Tim even had it all served out to take to the table. He decided to use the fried rice as a bed for the sweet and sour pork, with the fried mushrooms on the side of the entrée.

Dinner was superb as far as Kuri was concerned, she knew this was a Chinese meal; but still had a hard time believing they could create such wonderful ways to cook a meal. It was ingrained in the Japanese heritage for some reason, and Tim not being that historic, could not understand how two countries could hold such dislike for one another for nearly 1500 years. It was quite mutual, as he often heard degrading remarks from the Chinese toward the Japanese, while in Hong Kong. Those in Hong Kong were a bit more derogatory than anything that Kuri ever said, but he was sure other Japanese people, were not as kind in their words. Hiro was likely as a master chef open to good cuisine, no matter where it originated from.

Tim cleaned the kitchen, while Liani went immediately back to her intellipad, after making sure she got more than her share of fried mushrooms. She liked the sweet and sour pork also; but hers was cut into much smaller pieces, to make it easier for her to eat. She still preferred fingers to utensils; but that would change as she grew a little older. She was not allowed to touch her intellipad until Kuri made absolutely sure her hands had been cleaned. She still had milk in a bottle; but Tim was reminded he should be getting her some other type of drinking utensil, preferable unbreakable. He asked Kuri if it should have a straw as well, or just open mouth container. Kuri decided both would be nice for days when she started getting juices instead of milk at all her meals.

Tim had another little chore to take care of the next day, and had to think about where the shop would be to obtain such items. It had been a rather long time since shopping for little people, since last one in his life was himself, and his mother knew where all of them were. Problem was that was quite some time ago, and things do change over time. Small home based shops do not always have younger family members interested in keeping the family business going, usually because there are bigger and better things out there for them. He would need to check the IG in the morning before deciding where to go for those items. He was sure it was not in the shops they got Liani's clothes, as she outgrew them. Liani stayed with the intellipad until 10 PM that night, never once taking a break. Kuri almost had to prey it out of her hands, to get her ready to go to bed, and it took Liani fifteen minutes in the bathroom as she had forgot she did not stop in it for quite some time. Kuri asked her if she felt any lighter now after losing so much liquid in one time. Liani only said yes, but it was with a smile, so Kuri understood she knew it was to be humorous also. The little girl was smart as a whip, as the old saying once went.

As much as Liani resisted giving up her intellipad for the night, it took her all of 45 seconds to fall asleep, once placed into her bed. Kuri arrived in the bedroom; but Tim was in the lower level doing his meditation routine, his was not as precise as Kuri's. Her first 10 minutes consisted of rapid movement exercises, which she told him was to make sure her flexibility was optimal for the other portions of her exercise. All the movement from both of their exercise were based entirely upon legitimate martial arts maneuvers, Tim's were all just in a slower motion, as his training for meditation was based that way. He was without a doubt keeping his routine daily without fail, except for the night he fell asleep at the office. His strength had improved tremendously from the changes Kuri had him make. He no longer struggled to keep his final position for the full five minutes, for each of the four positions. He even noticed it was no longer a strain of any type, but did not know if he should lengthen the time. His endurance would increase, but did it offer any advantages beyond what he already did.

Once completed he returned to the bedroom for his other ritual, and once done asked Kuri if he should lengthen the time of the final positions. She told him it would not provide much additional benefit, outside of making his routine longer. In reality he would never need to hold a kick for anywhere near that time. It did however strengthen every muscle in his body, and if required to actually defend himself, he would be amazed at his own abilities, when he needed them. Tim hoped he really would never find out, but took Kuri for being more knowledgeable than himself in such matters. The next two evenings were very pleasurable for them. Not to the point where she would be perky with her parents present; but totally fulfilling.

The next day, with the exception of Tim finding where to go to obtain drinking items for Liani, and going and getting them, was much the same as this day. The other differences were different menu choices for meals. Liani spent most of the day mesmerized by the intellipad and her reading.

The following day was dinner with Kuri's parents, Tim had everything prepared and in place in the computerized cooking device, well in advance of the expected 6 PM dinner time. For lunch they had something relatively light, although something he had seldom used, since having more than one person to cook for. It was a soup, one of the 150 some varieties available in prepackaged containers. This was more like a stew than a soup, the difference being the gravy was not nearly as thick as a stew; but not as liquid as most soups. Kuri had no idea it was even in the house, but since she and Liani both enjoyed it, she asked where to get it. Tim said it was available at the grocer they frequently went to. Granted it had been in the house some time, but unless the container was damaged the shelf life was considerable.

Liani was required to put her intellipad away for the evening, while Kuri's parents also being her grandparents, which were the ones she waved hello to a couple days ago. Liani was cooperative because she did not get to see them as frequently as those in the lake property homes nearby. Hiro and Lian arrived around 5:30 PM, which gave them and Liani the chance to reacquaint themselves. Kuri parents marveled at how big she had got since the last time they saw her. Liani made sure she demonstrated how smart she was becoming also. Kuri even said she was advancing more rapidly than most Japanese children her age, and would have little difficulty in the first couple years of school coming up in a little over a year.

Five minutes before dinner was to be ready, Tim excused himself long enough to get the dinnerware and utensils out for dinner. All the utensils were placed on the table; but he did need to keep the dinnerware until the food was dished out. Just about the time he finished, the cooking device announced itself as being ready. With that, he started with the getting the servings dished out, while the rest were heading for the table. Tim already had the high chair in place for Liani, with her utensils and some milk still in a bottle for the dinner.

It took Tim a couple extra minutes to get Liani's teriyaki steak cut in small pieces; but he did serve Hiro, Liani, and Kuri before bringing the other two plates. His and Liani's were the last to bring to the table. Liani had no problem starting right into her meal. She was much better with a spoon than a fork, but still used her fingers for the steak bites. She also did to help put her rice mix on to the spoon. Still she managed to use the spoon to get the rice mixture into her mouth. The others did not touch their meal until Tim arrived with his. First thing Hiro tried was a bit of his rice side dish, and immediate vocalized, "Why is this even better than my own recipe, I thought I was considered the master chef?" he said humorously. Tim said he was sure he mentioned the Helsinki citrus blend vegetable to him in the beginning in Tokyo; but did not know if it was too costly. Hiro remembered that and said, "There is still something else here that has a mushroom flavor, and I see no mushrooms." Tim said, "The clutee I grow here in the garden, seems to have acquired that extra flavor. I do not know if it is this soil being near the trees, or just richer soil in general from that of Sierra, where it is largely parched desert." It does make a wonderful combination though." Hiro agreed, and wondered if he could achieve the same affect with mushrooms in his rice dish, they were plentiful everywhere, and hardly costly. Tim said all he could do is try, but he could show him how much the citrus vegetable cost him. Tim said, "I only use 3 or four pieces for each person to be served. Since they are dehydrated, they keep for a very long time and the weight is at least three time more after hydration, which only takes 5 to 10 minutes. Hiro said he would like to see after dinner.

The other thing Tim noticed was Lian was finding it much easier to speak up during conversation. She admitted that it was a result of being in Seattle, but had to be very careful when she went to Tokyo with Hiro. Tim apologized for no sushi being served; but admitted he did not know where to get it or properly cut it and it was safer for them all, if he did not. Hiro said, "Sushi is a fish that needs to be fresh for the best flavor, and only mediocre chefs make the mixes with other fish types, and color to account for their poor cutting skills. It is not an easy craft to learn, unless you have a master teaching you, but once again, without continual practice, it could have bad results." The dinner went over quite well, and for desert Tim had got two banana cream pies, knowing he would only use one, but if Kuri found the other, it would not go to waste. Tim served tea, and he had coffee during dinner, but after the desert was consumed, he got out Cognac for each. He also used the straw cup with half full of grape juice for Liani. He did not know if Liani would like grape juice. He explained the straw was like her bottle; but a larger amount of liquid would come through it, so be careful with it. Liani seemed to very much like grape juice. Kuri tried first to taste her Cognac without the pre ritual. Made a funny face and then did the swirl and sniff. She announced, "I do not understand. why it tastes so much better doing this swirl and sniff, but it does considerably." Tim displayed to Hiro and Lian the proper way to drink it, and they both found it quite good. Lian said, "With all the different things you have me try, I may find it difficult to drink another drop of sake." Hiro laughed, and then said he had to agree with Lian after tasting his properly.

After Tim did the dinner cleanup and got the sanitizing unit started, he had Hiro join him to go to the computer room. The ladies went to the entertainment room where they watched some of the nightly news before changing to a movie to everyone's liking. Tim brought up the display and showed Hiro the cost of the Helsinki vegetable. He told Hiro the dehydrated packages were about 8 ounces each, he just order 8 for 30 WC including shipping. Each package contained about 150 pieces of the vegetable, and with hydration grew three times larger, and also tripled in weight. They were a little more expensive than most vegetables, but quite unique considering they came from a country that had no citrus crop. Hiro agreed the cost was a little more than he would consider for all his restaurants, but might include it for the Seattle restaurant, since they profited 3 times more than any other. It was still a matter of whether mushrooms would bring out as much flavor as his clutee. Tim told him all he could do was try first to decide for himself. Tim could not grow enough clutee to provide for one of his restaurants, much less all of them. This Hiro could agree upon, and thought the simplest solution would be to try mushrooms, chopped up in small pieces; but fresh mushrooms were always tastier. After the food discussion, Hiro said he never saw such a desk before and wondered how he might obtain one for the house. He did use the extra room in the lower level as a small office, and a new computer would help immensely. Tim warned him the desk was a little more expensive than just a computer system, but the advantages were obvious to him. He told Hiro where he got his, and did not know if he had travelled enough around Seattle to know where that was. Hiro said his transportation could find anything as he still used auto pilot, mostly to take in the marvelous sites of Seattle when out.

Tim asked Hiro if he used an intellipad and Hiro did, so Tim pulled up the shop information from the computer desk, and let Hiro enter it into his intellipad. He said now Hiro just needed to tell his auto pilot where to go when he could get there to see for himself. Cost usually included setup and delivery for large items such as the desk. After that the two of them rejoined the ladies one level up.

The movie selected on the entertainment system was approximately 15 minutes beyond the start. It was a movie which Tim watched with the rest of them, but not one he would have chosen. Conversation during the movie was largely catching up with what everyone was up to since last getting together. With the exception of Hiro, deciding he was going to introduce the Helsinki citrus vegetable to the rice side dish only in Seattle. He was still in need of trying mushrooms in the mix, to see if it provided the same flavor as the clutee from Tim's garden. He told Lian it would be tested at home before going to Tokyo next week. Lian was willing to be his additional taste tester; but said Hiro had to make the final decision.

Half way through the movie, Tim served another round of Cognac, which finished off his supply, and Liani got another half a cup of grape juice for the rest of the movie. Liani was a little restless with the movie, obviously it was not one of her liking either, but she remained behaved with the grandparents present. She was happy enough to be sitting in her grandfather's lap, since she did not get to see them quite as often. The only thing additional brought up by Hiro was how the Seattle restaurant went through so much food compared to the other restaurants. Even though he had more cooling units in that restaurant than all the others, it seemed they could not make it through a whole week without having to reorder most of the stock to be able to serve all the meals. Tim said he thought there was enough room in the rear of the building to have more added and asked Hiro, if he wanted Tim to see if the consultant could work something out for him. Hiro thought it would be good idea, and told Tim to go ahead and let Hiro know when to expect him. Hiro wanted to be at the restaurant for when it could be planned. Tim told Hiro he would call the consultant the next day.

Kuri's parents stayed until 10 PM, when they decided it was time to let their granddaughter get some rest for the next day. Liani rewarded them both with a kiss and hug upon the decision to head to their own home.

Kuri's parents were surprised that she was such an affectionate child, and responded in kind to her little gift before leaving for their home. After Hiro and Lian had left, it was time for Kuri to get Liani ready for bed. It was not nearly as long as the night before in the little ladies room, but it still took a little bit of time for that, and the nightly hygiene ritual, before getting her into sleepwear. Once again Liani was fast asleep in short order, and Kuri and Tim got to have their night of pleasure.

Tim awoke first in the morning and before breakfast was started, he called the design consultant to see if he could help Hiro add more environmental cooling devices to the rear of the building. The consultant still had the original building plans, and told Tim there was sufficient room for 10 additional cooling units behind the building and it would leave sufficient space for delivery vehicles. Once that was done though there would be no more expansion space available for the restaurant. Tim asked when he could look it over and work with Hiro on how Hiro wanted to go about the expansion. The consultant said he could either be there this afternoon around 3 PM or the following morning. Tim told him he first needed to see when Hiro could meet him there and he would get back to him shortly. This was acceptable to the consultant and the vidphone was disconnected. Tim placed the call to Hiro to see which time would be best for him and Hiro wanted answers as soon as possible, and said the 3 PM time would work best. Tim let Hiro know, if the time was okay he would not call to confirm again with Hiro.

Tim made the follow up call to the consultant, and everything was set for around 3 PM. Tim did not feel he needed to confirm it with Hiro again as the time was one that was offered by the consultant. From there Tim went to the kitchen to prepare breakfast. He made a quick check on Liani to find her still asleep, as was Kuri. With eggs benedict, hash browns and bacon being the breakfast entrée, Tim figured the aroma would get the ladies up in short order. He went about his preparations and once finished started up the cooking device for all to ready in 30 minutes. 20 minutes into the cooking both Liani and Kuri were present for the breakfast to be served. The smell of breakfast was a wakeup call to both ladies.

Breakfast was served, and everyone enjoyed the meal. Liani needed a little help, but that was okay with both Kuri and Tim. It kept the mess to a minimum and Liani made sure she ate every morsel available to her.

After that, Kuri and Liani were taking care of their morning rituals, while Tim got the kitchen back in proper order for the next meal. Once done, he found Kuri and Liani in the computer room and Kuri was going through the finish of her meditation routine with Liani watching, but not ready to start her own just yet. Liani was learning a little about the routine, which Kuri would teach her when the time was right.

Aside from a few honey do's during the day, it was a relatively relaxing day for him and Kuri. Liani was back to her reading with the aid of the intellipad. The only time she stirred from the entertainment area was to have a quick luncheon. At 5 PM, Hiro called to say the consultant and he had come to an agreement on how to expand the cooling area for the 10 additional cooling units. One would be easier as it would be for a constant 68 degrees to hopeful have enough sake to make it through the week, for a change. He also discussed turning the bar into a full service bar; but it would require too much of the party room for it to be changed. Hiro would rather have the seating space, than all the trouble of serving a larger variety of drinks. He did not know he would have to make so much space available to account for all the types of glasses, add an ice machine and coolers to keep beer as well as kegs for those who preferred beer in that form. He had no idea there was so many different types of alcohol available. Additionally the consultant informed him he would need to hire people specifically trained in that area, and they were not as inexpensive as servers and kitchen help. They did require some type of special schooling to be qualified as bartenders, and the demand for those type of services brought higher wages. That really was not too much of a concern to Hiro, but the space required was the biggest drawback. He did not want long lines waiting to get seated in this restaurant like those in Tokyo. So he would stick to simply serving sake at an authentic Japanese restaurant. Tim agreed his space was more important than serving all types of alcoholic beverages.

With only 4 days left of his little vacation, he decided to make the weekend meals some of his best, non-oriental food selections, requiring a trip to the grocer for items he did not normally keep in stock. Saturday's meal had far more cooking time then consuming time; but he had not made corned beef in quite some time. He decided to make them Reuben's, which meant some sauerkraut and just to be safe he obtained additional Swiss cheese. Also he got a nice roast for Sunday that he would make the family recipe garlic mashed potatoes. He decided also rather than a mixed salad for the corned beef he got a large container of Cole slaw. Tim also got two bottles of the Cognac that Trask informed him was the best. It would be a simple type meal from the serving on Saturday; but preparation time was extensive. Made certain he had all the right seasoning for the corned beef, which was vital to the overall taste.

He also took the time to harvest some of the clutee in the garden and reseed for the next batch. He checked the trap that collected all the residue from the garbage units, as he could not remember when he did it last. He found it was just about too long, he had Kuri join him just to make sure she knew to check it, since she spent more time in the house than he. She was unaware of it, and asked how often it should be done. Tim said he was once in the habit of doing it once a month, and the residue simply got dumped into the garden to return it to the ground naturally. Any nutrients left would filter into the soil to fertilize the garden with each rain, until it was completely absorbed. It made for a richer soil over time. He did not know how long of time as it really depended on nature. She understood, and said she would make a point to check it now that she knew about it. She also inquired if the Tokyo home had the same thing, and Tim thought it did; but was uncertain, he did not look for it, although it is usually in close proximity to the rear exit. He said they would check when they were next in the house in Tokyo.

A few more honey dos done before the weekend and wonderful nights of pleasure led up to the weekend. Liani had completed reading 12 children's basic books by the time the weekend arrived, and Kuri was already considering increasing the level of books for her. Tim made lunch Saturday, and when completed with that started up the long cooking process for corned beef. There was enough for the meal and several additional luncheons, should Kuri decide to have them. He showed her the different ways to make sandwiches, aside from the Reuben's that were for the evening meal. He did acquire some really good rye bread for the corned beef, as he was under the impression that was the best way to have that type of food. For the evening meal, he did want the rye bread toasted, which would be little more of a problem for Liani; but he figured he could help her with it. The meals for the weekend were big hits with the ladies and the Sunday evening after Liani was put to bed. Kuri decided to prove to Tim that she had not used all her pleasure tricks just yet, and found an entirely new means to provide pleasure as far as he could tell. It was most erotic and of course with Kuri totally enjoyable.

The vacation did not last long enough for Tim, but Monday morning had arrived with him going through his typical work ritual. He had enjoyed the pleasure of his family and truly did not want it to end, but duty called.

Tim had accomplished about 20 interviews in person, before making it a vidphone interview. He found many parents were seeing the same problem with the son or daughter prior to having a breakdown. He discussed all these symptoms with the medical staff to find it was indeed the symptoms that lead to the mental breakdown. The first indication being a person who was easily agitated by a minor stress issue. Usually by this time, the person had already convinced himself that he could ignore the problem until reaching the time necessary to retire. After enough times of denying the problem, the brain quits asking, and at that point the worsening symptoms rapidly come about. Ultimately, the former employee became their own worst enemy with continual denial, and over riding the mental function that warned of problems.

Tim completed many additional interviews over the phone, and stumbled upon parents who had two additional children who both were in the military. The girl was in military medical research, while the boy was considered an electronics technician, who specialized in communications. The military continued to use antiquated terminology for the various positions. Largely because so many of them were so specialized to specific military needs, the person's training did not truly equate to a meaningful position in the civilian employment domain. This news came nearly 200 names into the list. It was so significant to Tim, he contacted Detective Marshall to have him conduct further investigation. The names of the two in question were Artimus and Rebecca Robbins, or Art and Becky as they were better known. The detective acknowledge the need to talk with the parents personally, and set it into motion as soon as the vidphone was disconnected.

Detective Marshall was back to Tim within 2 hours, saying the two had been released from active duty, and claimed to being travelling around the two coast of the country; but had not been heard from in over a year. The detective said it was likely they could be anywhere in the world; but would start the search with all the authorities around the globe. So the search was on for the time being, and the detective said it could be a difficult process; but got some photos to distribute, and was working his area; but suspected they likely were nowhere in the country.

CHAPTER

9

Tim's next week started with the monthly board meeting where his input was deemed important, even though he had little time to research new technology. Not anything beyond finding the persons responsible for the death of his analyst nearly two years ago. The meeting was opened with anything new to be brought to the table. Once again all remained quiet, leaving Tim to be the person to inform the board of his decision on the analysts.

Tim: "In my interviews with the parents of former analysts who were admitted into extensive care facilities prior to their death, usually by suicide, I found many parents repeat the same problems they noticed prior to the analyst's breakdown. I have since verified with the medical staff that when stress overload syndrome first begins, that the first issue is the analyst becomes easily agitated, as well as becomes despondent. The analyst frequently exhibits being a solitary person, wanting no personal interaction with others, including their own family. This is also a point in the symptoms where after having told themselves to ignore the problem, reasoning is no longer possible within that person's mind. I have also asked the acupuncture specialist if a person in this advanced state can have his treatment to at the very least bring the analyst back to a point of reasoning. The acupuncture specialist said it could be accomplished; but took approximately 6 hours under treatment. I have mandated with the medical staff for those analyst deemed at the point of stress overload syndrome, that the acupuncture specialist perform his treatment. This is to get the analyst to return to the point of reasonable communication for the medical staff to explain to the analyst why dismissal is the analyst's only option. Outside of this environment, the analyst can perform less stressful duties, whether as an analyst in a less demanding position, or additional training to another area of Information systems, as we provide to those who are dismissed. I realize I may have stepped beyond my allotted powers as CEO; but the medical staff agreed 100 percent that this course of action would be better than the one currently in use."

Trask: "Tim, I do not believe you have overstepped your authority in this matter, as you have not put into place anything of financial significance. The medical staff is already in place, and by mandating a process to make the dismissal process more effective, simply means you have found out more about the ways to save the company the expense of extensive care. Again, you have proven to be a valuable asset to this organization and thank you for bringing it to our attention."

Tim: "Next on the order of what I have been working on for the last two years, Detective Marshall had informed me that they are trying to locate the potential persons that caused the death of our analyst. I expect to hear from him today as to whether or not the brother and sister of a former analyst, have retina scans in the local home security system they once resided in. It appears to be the best means to track their whereabouts to apprehend, for further questioning by the authorities. Unfortunately, they have been out of touch with their family for the last year, and current whereabouts are unknown. The brother and sister have the necessary skills based upon their military records, which the authorities are trying to obtain. Both were in classified job positions so the authorities inform me the military is a bit reluctant to release their records, although under the circumstances they will have to. It may take time to get those records. With the whereabouts currently unknown, the authorities can provide no time frame for this to be concluded. I still have nearly 2500 names to give the authorities, but have held back those names to investigate these people completely. They are the first of over 3700 names to have the proper skill set to have achieved the deed that has kept me occupied for two years."

Trask: "Does this mean we have a breakthrough in this matter?" Tim: "As it stands, it is the only people we have encountered with the necessary skill sets to have performed this tragic waste of life. I cannot call it a breakthrough until they can be located. In the meantime, I have continued conducting interviews with parents verifying the skill sets of their children, and have found for the most part, I can now do this with a simple vidphone contact. I have talk to nearly 3 dozen parents and eliminated them as potential suspects as well as their other children, which amounts to nearly as many. Those with a single other child would require a large amount of military time to have acquired all the skills, and I have yet to have found a single person with those skills."

Tim: "I nearly forgot this, which I believe must come to your attention to approve or disapprove. I have the acupuncture specialist checking with his colleagues to see if any successful treatments have been performed on those people institutionalized for, as they call it, a broken mind. If the treatment is possible, it might be some means to cut down on the number of suicides we have among former analysts, who could not cope with the stress levels they were subjected to as analysts. Granted many of them brought it onto themselves by trying to do the work of the computer, or simply ignoring the signs of stress overload syndrome, but if they can be helped we may want to do this for them. If successful, it might mean they can leave extensive care units and go into assisted living, which should be a reduction in cost for each one. Although, suicide is a definite reduction in cost, is seems a bit heartless that we do not take treatment to the level that will be beneficial. I do not have a time frame for this either, and it quite possibly could be treatment is not possible. They say they can treat depression for people under the condition of a healthy mind, but the broken mind, they cannot fix. Since nerve ending are signals to the brain, treatment may not be effective when the mind is no longer capable of understanding the signals. It is for now, something to keep in mind, once I have a more definite response."

Trask: "We will discuss this to determine the best course of action should it be found a treatment can be successfully applied. It is a better alternative to a life entirely under extensive care. Anything else that needs to be mentioned at this point?" Tim: "I have nothing more to offer the board for consideration."

Trask: "Meeting is now closed for any additional input, and the board will now discuss the options on those items presented. Tim you may return to your duties and thank you for your input today."

Tim took his leave, and returned to the office where for the next three weeks he continued with interviews of parents on his list of names. During the interview process nothing new developed. His list of 125 names in the Seattle area presented no additional person or persons to have authorities investigate further, and no other persons with the skill sets acquired to be responsible for the murder of his analyst. Tim did find out the day of the meeting that Detective Marshall had indeed got retina scans from the home security system from the Robbins home, as the children were always welcome there, when they were around. They can use this information to help locate this pair of siblings; but still want military records to see what additional skills they may have, especially in the use of firearms, as for now they are considered armed and dangerous.

Tim decided to leave the remaining names untouched, until the Robbins pair were found and see what proved out, he hoped it was not going to mean he was delaying something that could have been done. He simply felt, the skill sets were not so common as to have another pair of persons, similar to this pair.

At the start of his fourth week without any more names to interview, his vidphone dropped down and Nora said it was the medical staff and the screen activated with the acupuncture specialist and another staff member. Tim greeted them and the second medical staff member said, "Tim, if you do not mind, when the conversation is over please disconnect from you side, so that they work properly afterwards." She then left for her normal duties. The acupuncture specialist went right into his findings saying, "Out of my 50 colleagues in Seattle, 49 have never had the experience of working with a broken mind. That leaves a single specialist, who has successfully treated this condition on 2 separate occasions. My biggest concern, is this specialist is rather ancient, and the treatments may be too much for this individual, although he still has an active practice in Seattle's Japanese area." Tim: "I was under the impression that acupuncture was a Chinese skill, more so than Japanese." Acupuncture Specialist: "You are correct in that understanding, but in Seattle, the Japanese population have learned to appreciate the treatments, since they do not have the sauna houses as in Japan." Tim: "That makes sense, since I have enjoyed that experience immensely myself." Acupuncture Specialist: "I have always wished to try it myself, but having never had the opportunity to go to Tokyo, I have not had the luxury. I hear they are quite marvelous. At any rate, the specialist that has successfully performed this treatment said it takes 6 months of weekly treatments, and precautions have to be taken. Since people suffering from stress overload syndrome that leads to mental breakdown, are prone to fits of rage, restraints are necessary. Since the mind of such a person is easily agitated by pain, and needles to nerve endings are treated by such a mind as a method of administering pain. Each treatment requires 6 hours of treatment. This is after the specialist is able to locate the happy place the individual has. Since this type of person is not likely to provide the input, the specialist must find it through touch, before applying the treatment. The nerve endings for each patient can be different, depending on where the happy place is. To clarify, the happy place is defined as some point of joy within the person's memory, but those memories can be triggered with nerve endings, and it is much easier with a person of cognitive capabilities. They can provide you verbal input to assist in locating such a place in your memories. The other specialist also stated that only specialist's with the most exquisite fingertip sensitivity, can perform this treatment. This means that the specialist can feel a pulse between all the toes on both feet, something I cannot do, and I did not inquire from the others, since I did not know that at the time."

Tim: "Is this specialist willing to teach another specialist his technique, if it is not too much of a strain on him?" Acupuncture Specialist: "I am sorry, I did not inquire, as I did not inquire to the other specialists about exquisite sensitivity. I can get back to the first specialist as to the first question, and if he says yes, then I would check with the others. The specialist who has done this treatment said it would cost 10,000 WC for each treatment, since he would lose an entire day for each treatment. If he is training someone that cost may double, for the other specialist's time." Tim: "Check on if he will train, and if so, who would be most capable, if this goes forward with the board, the amount of people in need will likely be high." Acupuncture Specialist: "I will check on it and let you know." Tim disconnected the connection to the medical staff vidphone and his retracted into its normal position.

That afternoon his vidphone dropped down with Detective Marshall at the other end. They exchanged the normal pleasantries prior to the detective getting to the point of his call. Detective Marshall: "The retina scan input was of great help into getting an idea of where the Robbins pair has been recently. They have apparently gone through the trouble of getting a number of false identification made up, and have checked into and out of quite a few hotels in the southern regions of Asia. First they were in Vietnam, then Malaysia, the Philippines, a few other stops in various locations before ending up in Hong Kong. A very good location to get lost in, if that is their plan. Over a six month period, they were in about 50 different hotels and other types of temporary living locations. Last known whereabouts remain to be Hong Kong, but they have not checked into another hotel for the last 4 months, even though, they did check out of the last one. It means they could have gotten more permanent residency, likely an apartment that does not use retina scan security to access it. I have alerted the authorities there to be trying to locate them. Video surveillance that was obtained from the different lodgings, shows they have not had major alteration done to their appearance other than hair color has been changed. It is just enough change to make them a little more difficult to locate for most untrained people. I am still waiting for military records, although we have submitted a high priority request with justifiable reasons attached. Getting government to act quickly in anything, usually requires some devastating factor and this unfortunately does not reach that high on their list of reasons for quick resolution." Tim: "It is progress none the less, and that is all I can hope for at this stage of the investigation." Detective Marshall agreed, and then disconnected the vidphone connection, as Tim's vidphone retracted into the ceiling and disappeared from sight.

Nothing advanced in the investigation or work for the remainder of the week, and Tim was home at his normal time each evening. Conversation and dinner were typical of the Frantz household, since Liani was the largest portion of the topics discussed.

The Monday of the following week was the next board meeting, which was scheduled late morning, allowing Tim time to greet his office manager Loretta, as he had done each morning since learning her name. This morning, he took a few extra minutes just having a conversation with her and at the end, ask if her schedule was so rigid that she was not even allowed a lunch. She inquired into the reason for asking, and he said he thought it might be nice if he took her to a nearby restaurant, that served very good food, just as sign of appreciation for all she did. She accepted the invite and it was set for lunch the following day, since Tim had a board meeting today that would likely go past the normal lunchtime. Tim checked with all the computer systems, once getting into the office and found they had everything pretty well covered. Daisy said that there was another hacker in the financial investment portion of the business; but not smart enough to get past the TRU trace. The person was found quickly and being brought into the judiciary system as she was telling him. His attempt to acquire 10 million in WC was enough to get immediate attention, and the records were forwarded to the authorities for proof to the people who needed it. All in all just another day in the world of information security, at least when in it comes to people's funds. Tim could not imagine any other area in information security with as much activity, or severity in the information world. If there was one, he was totally unaware of it. It was his job to be aware, even if he had been void of it for the last two years.

He used the rest of the time before the board meeting to research new technological advancement and found one to keep an eye on, but nothing else had any promise. It seemed the world of robotics was getting the most attention these days, but Tim knew the cycle would come back to them sometime, as it always did.

The board meeting opened with Trask asking for anything new to be presented and there was once again nothing. Tim had nothing new to present, but did have more information concerning last month's meeting in which the acupuncture for depressed analysts in life long care facilities was made to the board.

Tim waited a little longer than normal before making his information available to rest of the board members. Trask knew this to mean he had nothing new to bring to the table either, but the other members did not know him quite as well.

Tim rose and stated: "This is not new, it is simply follow up information from last month's meeting. The acupuncture specialist has gotten back to me with more information concerning using acupuncture for depressed long term care analysts currently under our program. Of all his colleagues, only one had attempted and twice successfully treated such a type of person. I was told this particular specialist is rather ancient, these are the exact words of our own acupuncture specialist, and I have him follow up farther on training another specialist or specialists to help with the number of people we have with this specific condition. There are some unique requirements for a specialist to be able to perform the treatments under these circumstances. Largely most specialist know where to search for nerve endings for different ailments based on verbal input from the patient. Since our patients are untrustworthy in this area, finding the appropriate nerve endings must be done entirely by the sense of fingertip touch. It requires especially sensitive fingertips, and many acupuncture specialists are not sensitive enough, although there is a way to identify if they have the touch. I do not think the details in this area are of any great value to your decision, so I will leave that out. The reason for the sensitivity is to identify what the specialists referred to as a person's happy place. This is memory that holds great value in time of joy and wellbeing. Once this place is located, the treatment begins with a 6 hour treatment once a week for six month. This is to convince the less than fully functional mind, which it would prefer to be in a happy place, over a place full of pain and regret. It more or less deceives the broken mind to find this place, and stay there to end the depression. Because they are dealing with less than a fully functional mind, the treatments take longer and come with a cost of 10,000 WC per weekly treatment. This is largely a matter of the specialist losing a full day on a single treatment, including the time to get there and return. This is based upon how much a specialist makes in a single day. It still seems to me, it will save money in the long run, as opposed to long term care facilities for a lifetime, provided suicide does not become the issue. Treated minds have shown no sign of this end result, although hypothetically, an additional traumatic experience could require additional treatments. Not enough is known in this area, as most assisted living facilities, are rather free of traumatic events. Also I need to add that the authorities have a general location for those possibly responsible for the murder of our analyst. The authorities in the general region have been alerted and are supposed to be looking for them."

Trask: "You certainly are full of good news today, do we have any time frame for when the persons responsible might be in custody?" Tim: "No, Hong Kong is a marvelous little island to get lost in, with the large number of people and transients in and out of Hong Kong."

Trask: "Keep us up to date with both, we cannot go forward until we have complete answers."

Tim: "As a personal note, I will be out of the office two weeks around Christmas, likely the week of and after as paid time off, although I do not expect that will be a major crisis time, since nearly every year prior, the hackers seem to take time off as well. Mostly college students, take a break and seem reluctant or unable to spend time hacking systems. I suspect it has to do with having some other family members in nearby rooms."

Trask: "Are you sure about that, I never noticed while I was in that chair?"

Tim: "You have computer access you can ask Nora or Daisy to verify, but it is something I have noticed from being involved directly with analysis."

Trask: "I guess that concludes this meeting, unless anyone else has something to present."

One of the financial members, Lou Osaki, said, "I believe from the number of financial requests lately, that the robotic units are coming in on a regular basis for the migration to be distributed within this office. Am I to expect the same for the other major offices as well?"

Trask: "Eventually every analyst in every office will have a robotic computer system, but since the migration must be performed here I believe the project will take quite a long time to actually complete. I can ask my son how far along we are in the project. Last I heard we had only 200 in place, all just in the Seattle office, with none having been sent to any other office."

Trask called an end to the meeting, and Tim decided to go to the break area to grab a bite to eat, and look out on the wonderful view offered from this one room. He took a full 30 minutes in the break area, enjoying the serene view of the ocean from his perch 35 floors above the ground, or roughly 350 feet.

Tim returned to his office, and once again the remainder of the week had nothing more to offer in anything that required his immediate attention. The following week was much same as before taking his two weeks for Christmas, except for John Thompson bringing another batch of recruits, only 18 this time.

Tim: "Welcome one and all to Global Security Corporation, if John did not tell you I am Tim Frantz currently acting CEO of this wonderful organization. If any of you play your cards right while here in approximately

10 years from today, one of you could be in this very seat. I will say you do have some previous competition for this spot by a little more than a month; but it does not mean none of you might be the one to show you're the right stuff for this chair. While in you first days here, it is absolutely imperative you spend as much time possible, getting to know the technology you have to help you perform your job. Currently, all the computers have voice programs that give you the sense of talking to a realistic person, so it is easy to get to know your computer. The upgrades are coming in quickly, and being distributed to give each analyst a robotic computer system, that will give you a more substantial sense of having someone else to converse with in your own office area. These systems are semi-intelligent, and work in conjunction with an AI network of systems that do 95 percent or more of your work for you. Since they all have real person voice programs, they can make client calls for you at your request. They already take care of the minor infraction that require a customer made aware of it, and a warning to the hacker that is rather severe. Any questions to this point?"

One of the recruits asked, "You are not serious about one of us holding your position in 10 years are you?" Tim replied, "I certainly am 12 years ago, I was exactly where you are right now, except I only got to meet the director, 20 years old fresh from MIT home schooling, and never worked a day anywhere else but here." This got the whole recruit class thinking they could do it too. "Tim continued, "One of the ways to get yourself noticed is to present well-conceived plans to improve things in this company, we are always trying to make your job easier, which in the long run becomes a cost saving means by keeping analysts on the job for their full 10 years. At that point, you can retire or maybe have the opportunity to advance in position, which does not require an additional 10 year commitment, merely one additional year with the option annually to renew your commitment, or retire at a better rate than the year before. Because stress is a very real enemy here, the more ways we find to eliminate it, the better everyone becomes, including Global Security Corporation. Other means of increased profit from concrete plans are other ways to get yourself noticed. Speaking from experience, Global does compensate quite nicely for ideas that prove to be profitable or cost saving. John is there an AD in place here?" John Thompson: "Only a director at this point." Tim: "The 18 of you will be the first to hear this, the first one of you who presents an idea that improves the profits or saves in cost, which is really another means of improving the profits, will get the AD position offered to them. As I said before, your idea has to be well conceived, it needs to be looked at from both the advantages and disadvantage, and then turned into a plan that can be implemented, even if it required modifications by those who will make a real improvement. It is not so simple as to think up any idea, and say this will work, I presented a large number of improvements that this company implemented, such as the AI systems from two different aspects. I also presented the concept of real person voice programs for our computer system, as opposed to the tin can voices they originally had. I even had to come up with the way for the outside consultant to make the voice program advance to reality. None of my ideas were for the intention of being compensated, it was for improving the way we as analysts had to deal with vast amounts of information. This being the only company of its kind in the entire world, presents some unique opportunities, but also many very real obstacles to overcome in the process. So when you get the opportunity to see something that you think could be better for you, and all the other analysts, work it into an implementable plan, and let your director know so he can get it to me for you. Any other questions you might have, feel free to speak up now." No other questions; but the look of mind turning to see who could come up with the first idea, which was a unique experience for both Tim and John. Tim: "Nora, would you come out and say hello to our newest recruits please?" Nora came from wherever she was hiding, which was not entirely abnormal for her and stood beside Tim's desk. Nora: "Hello it is a pleasure to meet you all." They all pretty much just looked and stared with awe and fear simultaneously. Tim: "She does not bite, I do not think anyway, do you bite Nora?" Nora: "I have never tried outside of using a sharp tongue, when you get me worked up, do you think I should try?" Tim: "No, that is not a really good idea, but I just thought I would ask."

Tim: "Nora is my robotic computer system, my biggest aid in keeping track of the day to day happenings within Global Security Corporation, and has a direct link to the AI systems as well. With Nora taking care of most of the activity without my input, it allows me time to talk with you, and others that need to be contacted within the day. She also can activate the vidphone and place the necessary call to make the connection by simply asking. If you get to your office and find you have a robotic computer system or even a simple voice computer, the best way to get to know your own technology is to ask it questions, typical if she or he can do this or that and see if you can find its limitations. With the help of the AI systems, I have yet to have found something that cannot be done, and Nora does things that should probably not be done, but it gets people's attention, which is the purpose of what it so unique about her. Nora I believe has spent too much time with the AI systems, as she has proven to be the only computer system to have evolved somewhat. How well you get to know your computer system will be your biggest advancement in the company from our standpoint. You use your technology to its full potential, and your time as an analyst will go by quickly without any major concerns to yourself. You try to outdo your technology, you will drive yourself into unrecoverable levels of stress that will be your end. Still, the choice is yours to make, so choose the wisest one you can, as it could mean the difference between 10 years of a wonderful position or a lesser time of pure agony."

Tim had completed his little speech, and this time John took his recruits to the outer office and then returned. John: "You were not serious about the AD position were you?" Tim: "I most certainly was serious, since it appears I have been the only person to ever hold the position, there is absolutely no reason why one of your 18 recruits could not change that." John: "Well, you certainly have them all thinking about what they can do to get it that is for certain." Tim: "I rather enjoyed seeing all the gears kick in and start churning, have never seen that from any other group of new analyst I have met or individual ones for that matter." I do hope you're here for the advancement, when it becomes obvious these kids have something to offer." Tim: "I should be, if it does not take too terribly long." John then returned to his recruits, and escorted them to their offices, which John had to answer the numerous questions about the AD position being realistically available to them if they presented a good implementable plan. John told them he made 100 percent sure the CEO was not blowing smoke, and he is serious. He wants to see people last and advance, instead of the alternatives.

Tim had nothing new to raise its head in the last week before his Christmas break, although he knew the first thing to do was get Christmas presents and such. He did have an idea what he would do with his limited time for performing such things, but some would likely require more time away from the house than he would really want, and Kuri, which meant Liani, also would need to go.

CHAPTER
10

Tim started the first day of his time off from GSC with a rather large breakfast, making omelets with bacon and of course hash browns with some waffles and fruit toppings. He knew he made too much food, but he was really hungry this morning for some unexplained reason, and was making too much food as a result. The aroma of breakfast seemed to get the attention of both the ladies in the house, with Liani making it to the kitchen about two minutes before her mother got there. Kuri said, "There is no way I can do my routine with the wonderful aroma coming from this part of the house. Why so much food though?" Tim replied, "I was hungry, and it seems my stomach won out over common sense, but it will not go to waste, even if we have two breakfasts today." Kuri said, "I guess that will work, it is not like lunch has a prescribe food type, although it would be a little different than most days." Tim said, "There will likely be enough left for one of us to have breakfast twice, but the lunch as normal for others. At any rate, we have places to go today, and although I can do one stop without you and Liani, the other stop requires both of you in order to get Liani clothes that fit better, since she is growing like a weed. The other place I have in mind you must choose what you feel is best for you. With Christmas just around the corner, something should be under Mom's tree for you two that would be nice." Kuri asked, "What do you have in mind?" Tim said, "For you or the rest of the family members?" Everyone would be nice to know." For the family members, I was thinking of giving them a 10,000 WC gift card, so they can get whatever pleases them over the next year. You should have a matching bracelet to your necklace, or maybe even one for each wrist.

It really is more for you to decide than me. I would not want to get you something you would not find a use for."

Breakfast was served, Liani got her waffles with fruit, a little bit of hash browns and a single piece of bacon. Kuri and Tim had omelets with hash browns and bacon and Tim also had a fruit covered waffle, with enough left over for a small lunch for one of them It was just a bit too much, but Tim ate more than he normally would, and he expected it was too much for all of it to be gone. After breakfast, Kuri went to do her meditation routine, while Tim did the kitchen cleanup and Liani went about her reading as much as she could comprehend. She was getting pretty good with reading simple books, and it would not be long before she would be moving up the scale. Kuri was not ready to start with teaching her Japanese, it was simply too complicated, although she was working a bit with the verbal skills, so Liani could converse with her grandparents in their native language.

Fortunately there has been no need for Kuri to fill in at the restaurant since her last long and hard night. That had more meals served in a single night than two weeks in her parent's original restaurant in Tokyo.

After the kitchen was cleaned up, and Kuri had completed her routine, Tim got to do his morning hygiene ritual and get dressed, while Kuri got Liani away from her intellipad and into her room. Liani was able to dress herself for the most part, but Kuri still picked out what she would wear. Largely it had to do with what still fit better than other clothes fit. Liani had just about outgrown all her sleepwear, and it was time she got something that was not a single piece suit; but more young girl style. Kuri knew that Tim would need her help in picking what would be best for Liani, and it was going to be a close call on the sleepwear, to wait another week or so before Liani had new sleepwear. Liani was now diaper free, and would need more undergarments as well, although they wore longer than most other things that were affected by length.

Tim had finished getting ready, and would keep an eye on Liani, while Kuri got ready; but he did stop to ask Kuri if her family celebrated Christmas in the same fashion as his. Her answer was that everybody celebrated Christmas to some degree or another. For the Japanese it was merely a time for the family to rekindle their family relationships, and usually a specially prepared meal. In her home, since her father was a master chef, it consisted of fresh sushi for all, with a number of other seafood served with a white rice mix. It included some of each type of seafood mixed into it, with some sauce and often vegetables that were easily obtained at that time of year. Gift exchanges were not a common practice, except maybe among the wealthiest members of the Japanese population. It was largely a family time, with a marvelous meal to celebrate family, more so than an event in Christian religion, as we are largely Buddhist.

Kuri inquired to his asking, and Tim replied, "I was wondering since this is the first year all of your family is here, whether gifts were in order, or even trying to figure out how to include 5 more people for dinner." Kuri said, "I would need to ask my parents if they were intending to have my brother and his family over for the typical Japanese Christmas. If that is the case, it might be good if we at least made an appearance, not necessarily for the meal, but to be present as family members." Tim said, "I did not think of that, something would need to be changed, as we cannot be in both places on the same day, especially with dinner being prepared here for everyone, who would be most open to have one the day before and the other the day of Christmas." Kuri said, "It is most likely that my brother will have the restaurant open on the day before Christmas, so it is unlikely they can change days." Tim said, "I will ask the folks when we get back; but before that you need to ask your parents if they have plans for a get together." Kuri agreed, and went to call her parents before they left, since this answer would determine if the other calls would be necessary. Liani was just about ready, and needed help with shoes; but other than that, she did a wonderful job in getting herself ready.

It was not long before Kuri returned to answer the question, Her parents had hoped to see them, but had no plans for the day, as their son and his family planned to have to just spend some time together as a family, as the restaurant did take up so much of his time. As a result, they would vidphone her parents in Tokyo to wish them a greetings for the holiday. It may be a long call, since they have not seen each other in quite a while.

That made things easier and then he asked, "Would your parents like to join us for the day, and enjoy a different type of meal than they are accustomed to for the holiday. I do not believe there is anything they would find terribly awful, although it is not Japanese." Kuri said she had already asked, and they will be here around 2 PM to meet everyone, as they have not really had the opportunity other than quick introductions at the wedding, which was a bit hectic for most." That was settled now. Tim had one more little chore to complete before leaving. He quickly went to the dinner cabinet to do a quick count of the number of plates for each and as he thought he was short so he would need at least another 4 piece set to match this one, and possibly a 6 piece set if it was available. That was assuming in the future all the family members could gather for the holiday.

Tim got Liani into the transport first, she still had to be placed in the child seat, as required by the law. Kuri was next, and finally he got behind the controls and the first stop, would be to get the gift vouchers for everyone, including ones for his in laws. He was still uncertain how to handle Kuri's brother and his family, so he asked Kuri. She said it would be best not to do anything, as they may feel obligated to do the same and she did not feel it was within their means just yet. Tim understood, since he knew his income was far beyond that of many. He did not know how the Japanese honor system would fall into this idea of a gift. Tim never gave gifts expecting anything in return, and although Kuri's parents had learned to understand this, her brother was relatively new to this concept. His first stop was quick; but costly, getting 13 gift vouchers for 10,000 WC each and paying out 130,000 WC from his normal account. It was not like it was going to cause him or Kuri any hardships, but it was a rather large purchase. This covered his grandparents, parents, Kuri's parents, His sister and her husband and two children, as well as his brother, his wife and the single child as of now. Next stop was going to be to get Liani some new clothes that were more grown up than she had been receiving. Tim knew Kuri would be the one to do most of the selection, including undergarments and sleepwear. It took three hours to find a dozen and a half outfits, another dozen undergarments, which included some with upper under shirts as well as little ladies panties, and another dozen sleepwear sets. Kuri though the items with the under shirts would be good for the colder months, which Tokyo did not have that cold of winter months, although the mountain regions were more likely to have them. The next stop after paying out another 3,000 WC for Liani's cloths was to see if the household store still carried the same dinnerware set, so he could up the quantity. The set was still sold, and they did have a six piece set. It included another couple of serving dishes as well as a large platter, which would come in handy for the turkey to be placed on the table for those to help themselves after the initial serving. He also obtained another 6 piece utensil set that went with the others, so there would be utensils for all to use also. This was the least expensive at 500 WC for all of it, and it only took Tim 15 minutes to get it all taken care of and in the transport.

The final stop before returning home was the jewelry shop that Kuri got her ring and necklace from. It was intended to get her a matching bracelet; but it had to be of the same type to match her necklace. They did have a single bracelet that matched; but not a pair. Kuri decided since the bracelet was a bit small for her instead she would get another meaningful bracelet, and possibly a matching necklace for Liani to show how much she is loved. The necklace was identical to the one Kuri already owned, and it would be a few years before Liani could wear it. She would know its meaning, and why Kuri would hold it for her until she reached an age where she could safely wear it. Kuri decided for herself a charm bracelet that represented meaningful things to her in her life, and it was one that could have additional charms added in the future. It did not have anything to represent a Samurai; but it did have a replica of something Japanese, it had a variety of choices for children to represent number, gender and the likes, and she got something to represent Liani as well as something to represent computers and restaurants. There was also a rather large gem in red to represent Tim to her as the flame in her life. She knew there would be additions later, but for now she was content with the choice on her wrist and in her life. The final tally for both was 5,000 WC kind of cheaper than Tim anticipated; but he did ask if they could be gift wrapped for presentation next week, while they got to rest under a tree until then. That was done at no charge, as Tim had spent more than they required for the additional service free of charge.

Tim felt like Kuri should have something more, so he decided he would go out the next day to just find something he thought Kuri might like, and he could think of things that might work well. He was fairly certain about the size; but he knew certain things needed additional tailoring for perfect fit to her liking. Especially, when it came to an evening dress, which she had always managed to take the breath away from most who lay eyes upon her. She had a marvelous form, and even after childbirth, it did not alter her lovely appearance in the slightest. His idea was to see if she would indeed like some of the more sensual undergarments available to woman, with little to hide from view. A new evening gown, which would still need to be fitted afterwards to her explicit instruction, but something that could only be done with her, and the alterations expert in the store. It would be a requirement for the purchase, knowing that few had waists as tiny as Kuri with all the other portions that accentuate her physic.

Once arriving home, since Christmas dinner was going to be as scheduled, just a couple more added to the gathering. Seating may be a slight issue; but there was enough space with the kitchen stools, which might be best for the youngsters, and the adults at the dinner table. He thought it best to go over to his parents to put Kuri's gift and Liani necklace under the tree, and inform his parents of the two others expected for dinner. It was highly unlikely that any of the family would make them anything but welcome. Just in case, he asked his mother to make everyone else aware of their presence, as she was far more likely to talk to them than the rest. Tim also told his mother that there were going to be a few more gifts for Liani after they got them wrapped, and more presentable for Christmas presents, but most of it would remain home for her to see afterwards. His mother had no problem with that, as she always felt this was a holiday for the very young, as the older folks had more appreciation to the other aspects of the holiday, that being the presence of family and friends and good food and drink.

That reminded him he should get a coupe bottles of a good wine for the dinner on Christmas, plus the other beverages for afterwards. He knew coffee was always good, but upon occasion other drinks were more appropriate for celebration. So he decided to also get three bottles of Asti for after dinner to have an adult celebration that all could enjoy. He was fairly certain he had enough proper glasses for the number to be present, but he would double check when he returned home. His additional conversation was short, and he made sure everything was good at his folks and grandparents homes, before returning to his ladies. He was much too late for a lunch, so he decided to make an early dinner to make up for the missed meal; but he did not think it would take three hours to get Liani new clothes.

Tim check for everything he intended to make, Liani was going to get a nice piece a grill salmon, basted in lemon butter, while Kuri and Tim would have Chicken cordon bleu, all would have a mixed salad, which Liani had learned to appreciate especially with the extra ingredients from other countries. Tim was still able to get some Clutee from the garden, the citrus flavored vegetable from Helsinki was not something he could grow himself, as it was done in specific conditions that only the growers knew, and it would remain so for as long as it was family owned. Tim really had no problem with that, it was important to keep others economically independent besides himself. It did occurred to Tim, he did not check his investment account anytime since he first started his CEO position, and with weekly additions and interest he should find out where he stood in retirement wealth, if he ever got done with this problem at GSC. He knew he would be getting a renewal contract, shortly after his return from the holidays to start his third year as CEO. He knew he would have to accept, it as it was highly unlikely that the murder case would be completed in time. His best hope was it did not go into an additional year.

With all the dinner preparations done, and the computerized cooking device set for a 5 PM finish, he had enough time to check his investments. His last item to prepare was not difficult, it was simply a baked potato for each of them, although Liani would have a smaller potato. He was unsure how she would be about sour cream and fresh chives; but he would find out.

With the dinner all in its appropriate cooking compartment, food type selected and finish time set, he went to the computer room. He activated the console to his computer desk with a simple touch, and quickly got into his investment account, to find his numbers were far beyond his expectations. Adding 325,000 WC for one year, and the 350,000 for another did equate to having nearly 65 Million WC in his retirement nest egg. His investment had more than doubled in two years. That was an awful lot of gain from his view point; but maybe he needed to double check. 34 million with 30 % gain it was actually pretty close when he figured it out he may have had 35% gains, but the numbers were far more than he expected to find. He closed it out and let the video go back to sleep mode, when he went back up to the entertainment room to see what the ladies were up to.

It came as no surprise that Liani was busy with her intellipad going through simple reading books, some she had done enough time to have it memorized, but still practiced it with words to make sure she knew them. Kuri was actually using her own to find the next closest level for Liani to advance to, but it seemed most of what she was finding was a little too complicated for a 2 year old child. Although, by many standards what Liani was already reading was supposed to be too advanced for a child her age, who should simply be working on letters and numbers. Tim went to the kitchen to see where dinner was in the cooking process, and everything would be done in 30 minutes. So in order to be of assistance to Liani and Kuri he went to get his own intellipad to find additional reading material for Liani. He had a little better idea of where to look than Kuri, although when it came to Japanese, he would not have near the clue that Kuri did. Tim found a place that had about a dozen books at the level that he believed Kuri was looking for. Instead of pointing them out to her, he forwarded the IG name to her intellipad, which showed up as a message to her. She looked up at him and simply mouthed the words, Thank You, and went over to Liani, and got it up on Liani's intellipad for her to start with some new material. It was now back to Liani reading out loud, so that if she stumbled, Kuri or Tim could help her with pronouncing the word. For the most part it was common for young readers to misunderstand when letters were pronounced in the hard or soft sound for different words, especially ones they were not familiar with. Kuri had reminded him that in nine months, Liani was school age from a Japanese perspective.

The computerized cooking system had announced dinner was ready, at which point Kuri got Liani to stop her reading. Kuri got her to the eating area, where Tim had the meal served up for all. Tim helped Liani by getting her salmon broke into small pieces, and cut a small piece of his chicken cordon bleu for her to try. She seemed to like the cheese, was only okay with the chicken, and not thrilled with the bit of ham. And went back to her salmon steak with lemon butter. She did seem to like her little baked potato with sour cream, but all the chives got pushed aside as the first one she ate, was not to her liking one little bit. Food was still an experiment for everyone; but Tim was not going to force Liani to eat something she did not like, knowing fully well, later on she may find it less unpleasant, and grow accustomed to it or even like the blend of flavors.

All and all dinner went well, and everyone had enough to eat, and then it was back to reading for Liani and Kuri, while Tim took care of the kitchen clean up. After getting the kitchen taken care of and the ladies working on reading skills, Tim decided to go to his audio room and listen to some music. He had not really looked for any additional music to obtain as he had a good selection to choose from. Even though he had listened to all of them once, it was time to listen again. He spent two hours listening to blues type music, and then returned to the entertainment room to find the ladies were finishing up with reading for the night. It was time to watch a little something on the entertainment system. Once the selection was made, which was an animated movie for Liani, Tim went and performed his mediation routine, and was finished before the movie ended.

With the conclusion of the movie, it was time for Liani to get ready for some sleep time, and Tim and Kuri could have some time together as well. It was worth the wait as far as Tim was concerned. It was then that Kuri said it was getting near the time to consider a brother or sister for Liani. This did not bother Tim one bit, and simply inquired how close, and Kuri said probably around 3 month or so. Tim knew it would ultimately be decided by Kuri, when the exact time was right; but she already made it perfectly clear. Three children were too many for the majority of families in Japan that she would like at least three, maybe even four, but that would depend on how much work the others would be for her. Kuri had told him from the beginning that she wanted at least three children, and they should be around 3 years apart, so a 3 year and 3 or 4 month old child was the time frame for a second infant. The older would by Kuri's idea of schooling be in class, even though from home for a typical Japanese education, which was entirely the way she understood it to be. It was a little early for children in this country, but obviously Japan was ready earlier in life to start using the skills they learned, and with Liani being in a country that was not against women in positions of any type, she would have advantages Kuri did not.

Tim completed all his shopping for the holiday over the next two days, which included things for Kuri to be placed under the tree, as well as having everything wrapped either at the shop or at home for Liani. The more private items for Kuri would be given at a time without the whole family present. He also got all the food items for the holiday meal, including 25 pounds of red skin potatoes which he got so they did not need to be peeled to be made for the meal. His mother and grandmother were both doing the baking this year, as there were so many to serve, and each made two pies and a dozen and half biscuit rolls for the meal. Tim had obtained several types of vegetables for the holiday dinner, largely greens;

but also some cauliflower and broccoli with some nice white cheddar to make as a side serving. He got the wine and Asti as well as some good brandy, and a few other higher powered bottles just in case. He could find no Saki; but thought the wine and Asti would be something Kuri's parents could enjoy just as well. All of Tim's more personal item for Kuri were obtained from Victoria's Secret, a place long known for its sensual and pleasing women's garments, most were not items visually seen.

While in the shop, the first question they want to know was where she needed support or other enhancements. Tim told them she needed nothing of the sort, she was perfectly proportioned as far as he was concerned. They said, few women feel that way, what are her dimensions. When he told them, they all looked rather shocked especially with the waistline of 19 inches. They then asked whether she needed to help support her upper proportion, and Tim said not in the least, she was quite firm from her mediation routine, which was amazing to him as she could do things he could never possibly do. They asked how mediation helped in keeping fit. Tim had to inform them it was a martial arts routine, referred to as mediation, since it conditions physically and mentally to keep your mind in total serenity with your body and environment. They asked what specifically is so amazing. He related that part of her routine utilized every muscle in her body when she raised her leg one at a time to waist high, and then without any other body part to aid, raised her leg straight up in the air above her head and held it there for a period of time. Once done with one leg she then repeated the exercise with the other leg.

They asked what he had in mind finally, and he said he was looking for things that were extremely pleasurable for her to wear. She had to the point of childbirth never worn anything under her clothing, and outside of some skimpy panties still worn nothing else under her clothes. So it is especially important they have pleasing touch against the skin. They showed him a series of silk undergarments, which were exceptionally sensual to the touch, as far as most women were concerned. They came in a variety of colors; but Tim did not know if they would show under her outer clothing. They assured him they would not, especially since the upper portion garments were designed for very low cut dresses, and many had no straps to show around the neckline. Tim end up getting a dozen of those, and some lingerie for the late evening, they would be sensual to both of them.

Tim also found Victoria's Secret had evening gowns, unlike anything any other store had. His choice here was based upon whether they could do alterations afterwards, since his wife always had things of this nature more form fitting, to truly display just how well shaped she was. They said they did, and all that was required was her name, so no additional charges were applied to the alterations of a purchased item that included them. Tim provided Kuri's name, and got the evening gown which they said was more likely a size 3 with such a small waist line, and they wrapped it all for him and he paid them and headed for his next stop. His next stop was to see Toranaga, Tim had studied to the extent of his knowledge all the pieces to his samurai collection, and thought collectively they may all be from nearly the same era, and all of the pieces represented the Yolakawa shogunate. He was not certain of it, but wanted Toranaga to do an appraisal at his home, as opposed to bring all the piece in to him. He would be willing to pay for his time with the explicit condition that the collection was to be appraised, without Toranaga trying to acquire them for resale.

Once he arrived, he found Toranaga was not exceptionally busy for the time of year it was. He made his inquiry to Toranaga under the assumption that Toranaga would be busy for the next few days with Christmas coming. Toranaga assured him that it was a relatively slow time of year for his shop, as few people thought about artifacts for those gift items, and often his prices were in excess of what most considered for gifts. His best time came after the first of the year, when the true collectors were over the holiday expenses and gatherings. He told Tim if Tim had room for him, and could return him to his shop, he could do it right now, just as long as he put the window sign up and set the security system. Tim had no problem with that arrangement, and asked Toranaga what his fee would be. Toranaga said, since he had to trouble Tim for transportation to and from that would be sufficient, besides he would not mind seeing how his collection was arranged, and whether it was as meaningful as Toranaga thought it to be. Tim waited for Toranaga to take care of his shop for his being gone for a couple of hours, and then took him to the house. He let Liani and Toranaga meet for the first time, while Kuri and he also reacquainted themselves. Tim emptied out the transport, put the entertainment items into the appropriate location, and all the wrapped gift were safely set in the garage, until later. Tim then took Toranaga and the rest of them to the computer room, where all the samurai collection was kept. Toranaga remembered the sword, and forgot it had a sheath in such excellent condition but noticed the ring. Toranage asked, "Might I examine the ring, before moving on to the painting?" Tim disarmed the security case, and lifted it and held it up. Toranaga said, "Where did you acquire the ring, since it is also of the Yolakawa time and a most precious one at that? There were only maybe one dozen of these rings known to exist for the most honored of samurai." Tim explained, "When I proposed to Kuri in Tokyo, Japanese customs did not include rings of any type for the ladies. With Kuri, I needed to have a least a token to represent our engagement, and she chose this ring, since it has additional significance to her as a part of the Yolakawa samurai descendants. She also said, she had ancestry that were acknowledged as the most honored of samurai." Toranaga said he was done here, and went to examine the 5 rice paintings. Tim put the security case top back in placed and reset the code to activate. Toranaga spent 10 minutes looking at each of the paintings, and the last being over the security case. Toranaga said, "All excellently placed for the best overall story; but I had not realized you managed to obtain all five of the Yolakawa rice painting I had acquired, although not at the same time. There are only eight of this era known to exist, and although I know where the other three are, the owner has turned down all my offers to acquire them, the last being 200,000 WC for the remaining three, which was more than a fair price, since his collection is not so focused as this one. Since, I do know where the remaining three painting are located, I can give you the name and location; but it would be up to you as to how much it would take for you to complete the set. Your collection is quite valuable as a set. Individually the value is considerably less; but as a set currently your collection is worth between 1 and 1.5 million WC. Obtaining the other 3 rice painting would make it worth about 3 million, although once again individually not even 1 third of the value."

Tim wondered why Toranaga sold him his painting for so much less. Toranaga told him first he did not realize Tim had got all 5 of his painting, and since they were individually obtained they did not cost as much to obtain. Toranaga assured him he did not lose money in his resale to Tim, but since Tim was collecting works of art that went together as sets, they become far more valuable. Toranaga also said, he did not sell Tim the sword or ring, which was the two things that truly increased the value of all the rest. Toranaga said it was an honor to see so much meant to be together, actually within the same room. Tim was honest with Toranaga in telling him aside from one painting, and the ring going with the sword, he did not realize they were all Yolakawa era paintings, and chose them because they were specifically dealing with the samurai era. Toranaga said he was genuinely lucky to have obtained so many Japanese treasures including Kuri. Tim could not agree more.

With the appraisal complete, Tim returned Toranaga to his shop, and said if he got the time to try to get the other three paintings in the near future, he would get the information from Toranaga when the time came. Tim said he was sure that they were in Japan, if not in Tokyo; but at the moment his work required his presence more than his absence. Toranaga understood, and said if he happen to be heading to where they were, and he could convince the owner to part with them to complete the set under a single owner, how much Tim would be willing to get them for. Tim though about it a moment, and said including something for Toranaga's trouble, no more than 500,000 WC. Toranaga thought that was more than generous; but also understood how much more valuable the entire set would be reunited for the first time in 1200 years.

Tim thanked Toranaga, and returned to the house, and spent the remainder of the day with the rest of his family and made a dinner and everything, until Liani was put to bed. At which point, he went to the garage got the gifts that were to go to his mother house for under the tree, and took them over as well, cards with his gift to each member of both families, as he thought Kuri's parents might enjoy the idea behind Christmas for the youngsters in this country. All parents understood the joy of giving at certain important times in a child's younger years.

Once back, he got the other presents and brought them into the house and hid them in a closet that he was sure no one entered besides him. After that task was completed, he got to do his meditation routine, and then spend some time with just Kuri, which was exceptionally pleasant and erotic. She was exceptional at finding new ways to indulge into the pleasures they alone shared. They may have been new to Tim; but it was quite possible it was all a part of her own teaching into pleasures that seemed to be unique to the woman of Japanese ancestry. Two more days for the Christmas feast to be prepared, which Tim knew would need to start fairly early. It was becoming traditional for him, his mother and grandmother to all be involved in the preparations.

CHAPTER

11

C hristmas dinner preparations started promptly at 10 AM on Christmas morning with Tim, his mother and grandmother. Each had become accustomed to doing certain preparations, although, his mother and grandmother did go about the usual decision process, and how to best do certain ingredients to the stuffing, and the mashed potatoes. Tim already had a batch cooking up after cleaning them to use red potatoes with the skins. They did ask what made him think of doing it that way, as it had been years since they used red skin potatoes for the mashed potatoes. He said it just seemed like something to try again, and they gave him no additional comments, since they were the only option at this point. His mother found all the seasonings they wanted for the stuffing and mixed them into the mix that included of course bread cubes, warmed chicken broth, and a pound and a half of ground sausage. The sage and other herbs were reasonably fresh from one of the gardens, Tim had some growing and also his grandmother, so he did not know which garden it was from. The parsley was definitely from Tim's, as his grandmother seldom could use enough of it to have it growing. The turkey was prepared; but due to its size for so many people, it was a rather close fit to the computerized cooking compartment; but it did fit. The first batch of potatoes were done cooking, and the second and last batch were started. It would be awhile for the mashed potatoes to be all done; but since it was done it two batches, the first batch was run through the mixing device to get them all mashed up. They would need to be reheated for the other ingredients, and served later with the rest of dinner.

His mother and grandmother each brought two pies and a dozen and a half dinner rolls for the festive meal, and each had put their husbands, his father and grandfather in charge of bringing some over with them when they all arrived. That way, no one was too over laden with food to negotiate entering the house. With their arrival, the entertainment room was getting put to use, as the entertainment system was on for the normal sports of the day, which was usually dedicated to basketball instead of football.

The day before, his mother had asked Tim to bring over the ham, which was about an 8.5 pound boneless that was typical for the Christmas meal. Tim knew the principal concept; but his mother and grandmother were the only two people who had the medieval looking tool for injecting the ham with pineapple juice, which took a small can of 12 ounces. The ham was injected with the pineapple juice first, and then cooked for about two hours. After the glazing, which consisted of lemon juice, honey and brown sugar was normally basted and then injected; but it was basted about every five minutes to get the glaze to build up to a good thick coat. This part of the process was done at Tim's house, where the rest of the meal was prepared and cooking. The green bean casserole was something his grandmother did solo, as she would not divulge her secrets in the making of it. Tim knew it did not just have green beans, as there were pea pods, broccoli florets and cauliflower florets with snap peas and carrots that were shaved up julienne style. What the sauce consisted of was the biggest mystery, as his grandmother always had it prepared ahead of time, and simply mixed it all together into the casserole dish, which was rather large for tonight. Everything was set to be ready by 4 PM. A little early for dinner; but since everyone would have skipped lunch and some breakfast. It was imperative to have it ready a little bit earlier than a normal dinner hour.

At 1:30, everything was in its appropriate cooking compartment and set to be ready at 4 PM. aside from his mother starting with her basting and injecting process on the ham at 3 PM everything was set. His grandmother quickly left to her house to get the secret cranberry salad that was to remain chilled until served; but it was something else she would not let anyone else know how to make. Especially since it was something spectacular for even those who did not like cranberries. It was one of the dishes that would be empty before the night was over, usually before dinner was concluded.

At promptly 2 PM, Hiro and Lian showed up as they said. He surprised Tim by bringing a rather large bag with him once entering the house. Hiro procured three bottle of Sake, and a dozen sake cups for the festivities. Tim said, "I bet this is not from Seattle."

Hiro said, "Not a chance, they have no clue how to make a good sake, this is some of the very finest I can obtain for all my restaurants, and it was a very good year for it." Tim asked Hiro, "Is this one best at room temperature or warmed?" Hiro said, "You know about it being warmed? Well truly good sake is served at 95 to 96 degrees so it must be slightly warmed; but not hot." Tim asked, "How it is with turkey and ham?" Hiro stated, "Not sure, never had it with that particular food type; but this sake should go with anything warmed. By the way, the food smells wonderful, what all you got cooking in there?" Tim said, "Enough to make your restaurant proud, it took three of us to get it all prepared and into the computerized cooking system. There is turkey and glazed ham and quite a few side dishes. Although it may not be the typical Japanese style meal, I could not think of anything that would be bad for you or Lian. Although, there is no seafood in any of it, I think you will find it all enjoyable to try something a little different from your normal meals." Lian had remained perfectly quiet so just to bring her out of her shell Tim turn and gave her a kiss on the check and a hug and simply said, "You are in Seattle now, so it is more than okay to talk to anyone you wish." Lian who did not get overly embarrassed this time said, "I am fully aware of my surroundings, I just was waiting until Hiro was finished. I so like it much better here in that respect, I am allowed to speak my mind without too much repercussions from the men folk." Tim made sure that everyone got to meet one another, and let them all take up a seat. The third pot of coffee was brewing, but he suspected Hiro and Lian were more likely to want tea so he asked each of them, and it was tea, which he went and made for them to bring them each a cup. Tim announced he thought it might still be little early for other beverage types; but in the event it was desired, he ran down the list of what he had. Hiro said, "It may be early; but later do ask again, I hope that is the same Cognac. It was quite good."

At 3 PM his mother started the basting and injecting process for the ham to get a good glazing, and to also get all the flavor throughout the ham. It was a time practiced system, but the end result was something truly flavorful and quite delicious.

Once 4 PM arrived, Tim had the table all set and the counter space around the kitchen set up for the youngsters. Tim knew that Liani was capable of sitting there without too much difficulty; but was unsure about his brother's little one. He asked if she would be alright there or needed to use the high chair around the table. His brother and wife thought she would be fine there, and just wanted to be at the table close enough to keep an eye on her. The turkey and ham was carved and placed on platters for the table, and all the other dishes were there as well. Tim was the last to take a seat, which was nothing unusual to him and the dinner went without any problems. Hiro and Lian both seemed to enjoy everything they tasted, and as dinner was finishing up Tim got out the glasses and the wines to serve all the adults. Tim asked Hiro and Lian if they would like Sake or Asti, and surprisingly they both chose Asti, as they found from the wedding it was quite good. Sake would be served later if desired; but Tim already knew Hiro wanted to try Cognac and was unsure of Lian. With dinner concluded, and wine all around, Hiro raised his glass and loudly stated over noisy kids, "A toast from a Japanese master chef to all the master chefs here, the meal was a pure delight, and a most marvelous wonder in various flavors."

The kids were already back to the entertainment room with the entertainment system set to movies they all should have liked, and even with that the intellipads and games were still in reach.

Dinner lasted a little over an hour, and traditionally the pies would be served after everyone had the opportunity to relax from all the other food they consumed. Tim cleared the table, and as he suspected there was too much dinnerware and utensils to get into a single cleaning for the sanitizing unit. He got the first load started, which included the casserole and cranberry salad serving dishes, as they were as expected entirely consumed at the meal. He made sure all the initial utensils were sanitized, so there were enough for the pie later. 90 minutes after the meal was finished, everyone including Hiro and Lian went to his mother house, where the tree and gifts were placed.

Tim started the gifts by handing out his 13 cards, which he included Lian and Hiro into the gifts after confirming they would be present. The comment from the rest of the family was basically it was far too much. Tim simply said it was a gift, and for them to do with as it pleased them, so as not to cause any unnecessary hardships for them this year. His sister, Jackie told the kids that each of them would put half aside for their education fund, to insure they had advanced education, as in this lifetime, it was the only way to expect to ever get employed. She also made certain they each understood that their mother and father had no intentions of them being in their house forever. Although, the kids were young, they seemed to understand that as they got older they would need to go beyond high school in order to make their own mark in the real world, so they did not give any argument to their mother. They did not seem all that disappointed in still having 5,000 WC to get things they would like, not necessarily need. Tim then handed Kuri her gift, and the first to Liani, while everyone else started with their gifts to hand out. Hiro and Lian were fully in the mood of what was going on around them. Hiro asked Tim, "Is this how Christmas is always celebrated in this country?" Tim quietly told him, "As far as he knew, although it was still a matter of what families could afford, and it remains a holiday largely for the youngest, who get excited over having presents." Hiro said, "It is much different in Japan, it is a holiday for the family to reunite, maybe reminisce over times past. Good food and drink, but nothing quite like this. I can see the children are highly interested in what they find hidden within each box." Tim said, "I hope next year you can convince your son and his family to join us for this holiday, as it remains a time for family and everyone here seems to be getting along quite nicely." Hiro said, "I have never felt so welcome into another home in Japan, and I must say the food was exceptional, even for a master chef. So many different varieties of food used in different ways than in Japan. I would never have thought such food could be prepared so differently, and have such exquisite flavors." Tim said, "Every country has different ways to enhance the flavors of similar foods, which is what makes this country different, as people have ancestry from all over the globe, and have learned to live in relative harmony among others with entirely different origins."

Kuri had opened her gown with some surprise, and came over to Tim and said, "It is wonderful, where did you find such an exquisite gown?" Tim said, "Before I got it, I made certain that you could get any alteration done, since I have never known you to have anything like that without some. I will tell you later tonight where you can have that done after the other items I managed to find for you at home, but I did not think you would want to open them in front of the entire family." Kuri said, "You have been a sneak this year, how did you manage to hide things without my knowing?" Tim simply said he would never tell, otherwise he could not do it again." The time to present Tim with his gift had come around, and he knew it was largely going to be music, as it was the only thing his family knew he enjoyed that was affordable. Once again, Tim did not really expect anything from the rest of his family, and was gracious about each and every thing he received. He had obtained a dozen new blues albums, and to his surprise not a single one was a duplicate of something he already had. He was not familiar with all the artists; but that did not mean he would not enjoy the sounds they created. It amazed Tim how many people could play similar instruments, and still have something unique in the overall song. Whether it was the vocals, or the way they made the guitar seem alive, nothing sounded identical to each other, even when they played identical instruments.

Once back to the house, Tim first got the first load removed from the sanitizing device, and reloaded it with the remaining items needed to be cleaned. Since the two serving dishes from his grandmother were now thoroughly cleaned and sanitized, he set them aside for her and his grandfather to take back home. He then got all the kids some form of refreshments, and offered the adults something more to their liking. Lian decided on another glass of Asti, and Hiro wanted to try Cognac. His father and grandfather were in the mood for bourbon, and his mother and grandmother each had a glass of wine. Pie was offered, but everyone was still recovering from dinner and thought maybe in an hour they could do it. During the wait Hiro, his mother and grandmother all exchanged various cooking disaster stories. His grandmother, who had not very many to offer, offered her story of trying to make a peach pie for Christmas three years ago. "Since peaches are a seasonable fruit, and depending on supply from the southern states that grow them, I attempted to use synthesis peaches. As a fruit I had found that they were relatively close in flavor, and thought it might do for a pie. The baking process turned them more into pudding then fruit, and whatever they use for synthetic substitutes does not remain in the cooked state. It was the most awful pie I think I ever made. It was more like a soup, than a fruit pie, and no longer tasted in the least bit like peach. As a result, I will not use synthesized fruits for anything that required baking or cooking of any type."

Hiro had a few stories, largely from his younger days as he experimented with flavors to blend. He told the full story about using nuts in his wild rice mix before settling on the current version, which Tim helped him alter to its current blend. He mention how he got to be in the hospital for three days as a result of finding out he was allergic to peanuts. A horrific experience it was for a chef to find out he could not eat things he found to be quite tasty in his food blends. It was perhaps the single worst experience in his life short of having the restaurant explode shortly after opening. His grandmother and mother had no idea about that experience, and they inquired as to how it happened. It took Hiro nearly 30 minutes to explain the restaurant was targeted by criminal types, and set bombs in the restaurant to make an example for the other area businesses. He and Lian opened the restaurant as usual that morning, and within 10 minutes, the entire building erupted in an explosion sending the both of them out the front into the street, with severely broken bodies that took nearly 4 years to recover from. It was not a pleasant time for either of us, as the pain was so intense neither of them could even speak for over a year, and then only with sufficient pain medication. "Kuri made sure she was there as often as she possibly could, and even if I never mentioned it to her before, it was the one thing that gave Lian and myself the strength to continue to endure the long recovery and rehabilitation."

When the hour had passed, Tim started getting dinnerware and utensils out for everyone to have pie. His grandmother instead of a peach pie, made a banana cream pie which he knew between Kuri and Liani they would easily make disappear with just the two of them, but it appeared to be a favorite for all the other children as well. It was pretty much gone before another pie was even cut. The Dutch apple and pumpkin, were also made, and his mother managed to come up with a good cherry pie as well. Once everyone had a least one piece of pie of their choosing, except for banana cream, which went to the kids and Kuri, Tim got the kids another round of drinks, largely fruit juices. He then offered everyone else something to drink which consisted of everyone accepting the same as before except this time Tim got some cognac for himself. Tim had hardly had the chance to sit down since dinner, and that was not for a long period of time without having to get up for something else.

He found one of the lounge chair unoccupied. The entertainment system was on; but with everyone indulged in conversation with different groups, it was more or less just adding to the sounds of the room. Lian had been talking with Kuri, Jackie and Laura with the occasional input from his mother and grandmother. The men were largely talking sports, which Hiro was learning about and even found the local professional basketball team was interesting to watch, when on the entertainment system programs of the week. The kids were in kid's mode, and even though there was an age difference, they were all having fun together in some way or another. Something only kids could achieve was taking place in his entertainment room, he wished it would last forever; but he knew that was impossible, but he could hope. As the evening got a little longer, Hiro and Lian were the first to get started on heading home. As Hiro put it, the restaurant business never got to sleep for very long; but he and Lian both said that it was far more pleasurable than they would have ever expected, and were happy to be a part of the family gathering. Maybe with enough regaling of the great time we had they could convince their son and daughter-in-law to join next year.

Approximately 30 minutes later, his brother and Laura got Marie ready to go home as she was wearing out from a long day of activity. The next to show signs of a long day was Liani, who had not had a nap or anything all day, and surprisingly she lasted this late before indicating she was ready for some sleep. The remaining family members stayed about another hour, largely just relaxing a bit as even their vocal cords were tired from all the conversation. It was largely agreed that those presents that had been opened at his mother's house, could be picked up the following day, since no one had to leave town to get home any longer.

His grandfather had been kept busy with woodworking jobs by Toranaga, as he had orders for six more stands. Tim had no idea there were that many swords in Seattle. He knew they were not all samurai swords, but still it seemed there was a large number to keep his grandfather so busy. His grandfather even told him, he thought the last one he completed was for his friend, Trask. That stand was for a cutlass, he said was worn by George Washington during the crossing of the Delaware. It was considered to be quite valuable, both historically and financially.

Tim went to empty out the last of the dinnerware, and such items to put into its place before going to his secret hiding place for Kuri's remaining gifts. He got them into the bedroom unseen, and then found Kuri watching the late evening news and largely weather report to see what the next day might bring. He waited until she was finished with the weather, knowing after that she did not really care much. He gave her a kiss and said to follow him. She did as requested, and he then showed her the presents and said he did not know if she would like them, but he thought it might help a little with the colder weather. Kuri started with opening the first box, and found the first item and looked at Tim and asked, should I try each of these on here for your pleasure or see how they fit on my own. Tim replied it was entirely up to her, but she may find items that she has not used before, and might like to learn on her own how to make it work best. She took that as she should open them all, and then go into the other room to try them on, or have Tim leave as there was no full length mirror in the bathroom. Tim told her, 'it all came from the same shop including the evening gown. Since she will likely want to get alterations on the evening gown, it all came from Victoria's Secret, and all she had to do was give them her name to get the alterations completed, although that will likely mean a fitting to get it done correctly to her specifications. I did not expect to find an evening gown there when I went, but I did think you would like it as far as style was concerned. It also seemed to be something quite pleasant to wear from the feel of the material, almost like wearing nothing at all, which is how all these items are supposed to feel according to the people there." Kuri decided to use the bathroom to try the undergarment and once situated she reemerge to show Tim how it looked. Kuri said, "It is quite pleasant to wear which is not something I ever expected and the primary reason I never used them before. They were restrictive and harsh to my skin but these are like something I could enjoy wearing." She went back into the bathroom to try each and every one, and said all of them were absolute marvelous to wear and she thanked him for the gifts. Also saying she would not have thought to get any for herself, as she was willing to be cooler to avoid the scratching and irritation of those she previously tried.

She seemed quite pleased with her gifts, and gave him a rather long kiss to show her appreciation. She also said his gift would not be delivered until at least tomorrow, as they were having a difficult time keeping them in stock for the holiday. It was something she thought he would like, but also something for everyone to use, but did not say what it was exactly. Tim knew better than to try to pry information out of Kuri, who was a martial arts trained samurai. Kuri would say she learned it from him, but quite the opposite were the real truth. Which reminded Tim it was time to ask her something concerning her training.

Tim said, "Kuri I was wondering, since you often move through the house without so much as a sound, did your martial arts training include Ninja skills?" Kuri said, "Ninja class was totally separate from samurai, at least in the Yolakawa shogunate. Although there is a certain amount of skills shared between the two classes, the Yolakawa ninja's worn clothing that in no way associated them with Yolakawa. For all intents they were largely trained for stealth and skills for the purpose of assassination. Even though Yolakawa was honorable in respect to his people and surrounding neighbors as much as possible, some actions by other shogunates were too horrendous not to receive retribution from Yolakawa. Yolakawa never went after the entire shogunate and its people for the acts of a few. In those cases, it was handled by the ninja's who were as loyal as any samurai. First the ninja would infiltrate and remain hidden to discover who was most responsible. It was often only a small group of either samurai or sometimes the other shogun's ninja class warriors. Once the truth was discovered and Yolakawa was made aware of who was responsible, he dispatched his ninja team of sufficient number to work quickly and return without any losses. The ninja used a number of unique weapons. They called them throwing knives but none resembled a knife. Some were quite small, but had multiple pointed tips with such excellent balance they could be thrown 500 feet without missing their intended target. They also used poisoned darts with a blower piece they slipped into for the ninja to launch through blowing into the other end of the long slender tube. When done properly it launched the dart at relatively high velocity and the dart being quite small was often targeted to the neck of the target for quick action from the poisoned tip.

The Yolakawa samurai were renowned for the speed and grace they employed in times of combat. This is largely why the number of losses among the Yolakawa samurai were considerably small. There were some, but they usually were simply overwhelmingly outnumbered and often took

20 or more opponents down before falling themselves. The ninja class trained even more into the grace and speed aspect of the samurai training, creating a stealthy approach as a result of the years of training on grace and speed. The uniforms of ninja were often black with no identifying markings, this was in the case of one of the ninja being caught or killed in performing their required actions. Fortunately this never occurred with the Yolakawa ninja. No other shogunate was so fortunate and many learned never to send them at the Yolakawa fortress in which the samurai were always alert, and more than capable of taking care of the uninvited visitors. Most of the other shogunates learned this the hard way, after losing several ninja parties. History states that even among all the shogun's samurai and ninja class warriors, the Yolakawa were superior."

Tim was impressed, but surprised that she did not truly have ninja training, it was the method of her samurai training that made her so quick and quiet. He did not know how to practice such methods, as his training was not that of hers, even though he had incorporated some of her training into his own routine. It was at the base level that she learned that was so much different from his own training. After a good night in the pleasure department and a restful sleep. Tim arose for the normal breakfast routine, which after such a large meal the night before, he decided to make it a little lighter and easier for all to consume. Of course Liani was still more than happy to get fruit covered waffles, and never seemed to tire of it. Tim did not always use the same fruits to give her some variety. It was also because different fruits were not always available depending on the season. He knew he could use synthesized fruits as long as they were in no way cooked. They were one of the things that were quite close in texture and taste to the real ones as long as they were used as is. With breakfast nearly complete, he checked on the others and it seemed they were a good deal late on rising for the morning. Liani was still fast asleep, as the activity for her the day before had worn her out, but he did not think so much for her to still be asleep. Kuri was just moving around and had not even started her morning routine, which he figured she would do after she ate breakfast.

About the time that breakfast was ready and Kuri arrived, stirring could be heard from Liani's room to indicate she was now up. Tim heated up her waffle to get it warm again for her little breakfast, and Kuri went to make sure Liani was okay and ready to have breakfast. They arrived just as

Tim finished putting the topping on Liani's waffle, and the breakfast was consumed in relatively short order. Tim got Liani setup with her reading, while Kuri went to go perform her mediation routine. Tim got to clean up after breakfast, which did not take long, and then sit with his little girl while she read out loud. She was only having trouble with a few words, largely in whether it was soft or hard phonetically pronounced letters other than vowels. She had them pretty well figured out, and was doing pretty good with many of the words; but ones she sounded out that she was not really familiar with were her only hang up. Once she knew a word, it was locked into her memory, and simply seeing it in print helped her recognize the written form after trying to sound it out. She had become quite adept at turning the written word into the verbal word.

Kuri finished up her routine, and was finished with her sanitizing as well when she returned to the entertainment room where he and Liani were. She took over the reading assistant position, while Tim got himself ready and dressed. He had to go to his mother's house to retrieve the gifts for Liani and Kuri, although it was going to take more than one trip which he did not anticipate. The second trip, also included his new albums to put into the audio room collection, and listen to when he got the opportunity. With all the packages brought home, it was time to get out the remaining ones for Liani to open, and then pick from it something to wear for the day.

Liani like all young children, she started ripping and tearing at the wrapping paper to get to the box to open. While having an apparently good time she was making a bit of a mess, but it would not take long for the device just outside the rear door to turn into nothing more than fine particles of dust. Once all her gifts were opened and looked at, Liani was given the choice to pick out what she would like to wear for the day. She was actually trying to see how to best put the different items into sets before making a selection, which surprisingly was not too bad of a combination, and of course she pick out a new pair of panties and a and little ladies undershirt, since the weather was bit cooler this time of year. All the other clothes were put into her dresser in her bedroom, and Tim noticed it was probably time to put the bed up and take the padded crib into the other room for who would get it next. Tim put that on his list of things to do before the day was up, in all likelihood, once Kuri and Liani were back into the entertainment room and back to reading. Liani was if nothing else insatiable about learning to read, and soon started with printing the alphabet and words she knew. For a child under 2 and half years old, she was quite focused on the learning. The other thing to check today was the other house, he had not been there since making sure the updates had all been performed, and he would need to take an inventory of things needed largely nonperishable items, because without continual use, even with the latest and greatest environmental cooling system in the kitchen, nothing could stay forever without some spoilage.

Once Kuri and Liani were back in the entertainment room, which took a little longer, as it was time for Liani to go through her cleansing. She had learned quite well how to take care of her teeth, she was still not old or wise enough to be unsupervised with the rest of it. She was not shy, but preferred her mother for this type of supervision, largely because it was her mother. Tim did not mind, she knew her father was good for other things, and he felt that he and Kuri were doing a good job in raising her. As well as making her feel and understand she was indeed loved. With Kuri and Liani back into the entertainment room, he informed Kuri he was going to move the crib into the extra room to await its next occupant. He would put her other bed up and into place before cleaning up, and going to the other house for a checkup.

The crib took 10 minutes to move and the bed 20 minutes to setup, they already had the bedding, so it did not take long to do that and then Tim went to do his normal morning ritual, which included time in the sanitizing unit.

Once completed there, he dressed and gave Kuri and Liani kisses and went to check the other home they owned. His primary purpose was to insure that all the new robotic sweeper were running without a problem. which was easily accomplished by looking into every room to make sure none were still in it. They were all back into their nesting place recharging. The kitchen started with checking all the storage for amounts of nonperishable foods that would need to be restocked, but Tim found he was good on all of it. Nothing overly excessive, but nothing in dire need either. Next the environmental unit which had a few things that needed to be discarded, as they had been there too long, largely fruits and some vegetables. He had a couple containers of clutee that he thought would be better used at the other house, as well as some fish that should be used sooner then what he had in the house. The meats were holding up quite nicely, and he would leave them although, there was not an abundance of them if he needed to take them home at a later date, it would not be much of a problem. He took five storage containers and placed them in the transport, with something to cover them from exposure to light. He reset the alarm, and returned to the lake property where he found another vehicle there. He figured he should still get the containers into the kitchen and put away. He found once inside, the activity was in the entertainment room and he went about getting the five containers into the environmental cooling system. With that accomplished he went into the entertainment room. Kuri asked him if he liked his present which took him quite by surprise. The installers had just finished it up and brought up the picture from whatever setting the entertainment system had already selected.

Tim had never even considered that the technology he thought almost 13 years ago when first seeing the vidphone, was available for other uses. The screen was immensely thin with absolutely no visible edges. It was virtually translucent when off, and the wall and even the supports for it were visible. The supports would be the only indication something was there, although it would seem more like something was once there. The picture was even sharper than the original which surprised him also.

He said it was amazing and how did she even fathom the idea that the technology was available for something other than vidphone. She said she used the IG for ideas, and saw this and then looked to see who carried it locally. She and Liani had a good day out when he was at work that day. Before the installers left, Tim asked if the same type of technology was available residentially for vidphone, and they told it had been for about five years, like he was living in a cave somewhere. He then asked if they carried them as well, and the installers said they did not work for any single company, like many they were a home based business that did this for a number of companies. Tim thanked them just the same, and figured he could use the IG too. After they had left, Liani having been distracted from her learning, was now engaged in the animated movie that had started with the entertainment system being activated. It was a fairy tale story from none other than Disney, and like all of his movies, it captivated the young and some not so young. Tim let Kuri and Liani have the entertainment system to themselves, and he went to the computer room to do the research on the latest vidphones available. They were not as costly as he thought they would be, and they did like the new display on the entertainment system, have no visible edge lines and were quite thin. He checked to see how much he would need to transfer from his interest earning account to find he had received his weekly deposit, and would not need to move anything. He found out who had the vidphones locally, and went back up to the entertainment room. The movie was still playing, so Tim whispered to Kuri he was heading out for a bit to check on the vidphones for both houses.

He was not long getting to the local business that offered the latest vidphones, and found it including installation he could get both house taken care of for 300 WC. He took care of the charges, made sure the same installers were used for both homes, so that he did not have to be in two different places at the same time. And then it was set for two days later, starting at the lake property. Tim returned home having not been gone quite one hour, and the movie was not quite finished yet. Tim let Kuri know the vidphones were going to be upgraded in two days, and he did it here and the other house, which meant he would have to go over there when they were done here.

It was early enough for Tim to make lunch, and decided to use some of the ham and turkey for a luncheon bowl mixed with potatoes cubes and some eggs with Swiss cheese since it went with both meats. He considered adding some hot sauce; but thought Liani might not be ready for that yet, and declined to add it. It only took twenty minutes to have it prepared and ready at which time the movie concluded. Luncheon was served and it was simple, but rather good for a simple meal. The cheese actually made it tasty, and Tim was not sparse in its use for the meal. After lunch Kuri and Liani went back to reading while Tim cleaned up after the meal. He got everything in the sanitizer so as to be cleaned for dinner, which was likely going to be some more leftovers, but served in the conventional means it was already prepared.

From there he decided to pay his grandfather a visit, since he said something about having quite a few display-stands to be making. He went directly to the woodworking shop, which was exactly where his grandfather was. The room was far less congested, as his grandfather had replaced a large number of his old tools with newer less bulky versions, and obtained a tool chest for the hand tools that could never be overlooked, they simply allowed woodworking craftsman the flexibility to perform some arts with the wood that power tools simply did not do adequately. Carving intricate patterns into the wood, and making it appear seamless, his grandfather said could not be done with tools that were not used by hand. A small router and bit could make the original cuts; but to make it smooth and appear normal in the wood grain, the hand tools were the only true means to achieve it. It also allowed for more depth and intricate detail.

He found his grandfather in the process of doing some of the exact type of work using hand tools with sharp but shaped tips, and a small hammer to cut into the wood to a certain depth, and then tapping it forward to the point he desired, and the tip pushed the wood out from the piece he was carving into. It was rather fascinating to see how he worked the wood with these tools. He had a set of thirty different pieces, each with a different size and shaped tip. Placed next to one another they were each unique in shape, although the same material was used for the tip itself. They were quite sharp, and it appeared required some form of keeping them that way. Tim wondered if the tool had to be replaced when it had reach a point where sharpening them was no longer possible, or could the tips simply be replaced, assuming they could still be obtained. These particular tools, although in well-kept condition were quite old.

His grandfather spotted him and straightened back up with a little effort. Good you are here, I could use a little break from that position, and the old bones are not so flexible any more. Tim said he was watching and wondered since the tools like he was using appeared to need to be sharpen periodically to keep them in good cutting condition, what happens when it cannot be done anymore. His grandfather told him that it had replacement heads for each type he used, although he did not use all the cutting heads available. Primarily the ones for fine engraving for the larger variety of dimensional changes in a piece of wood. Power tools were much quicker, and the imperfections left could be sanded smooth with another power tool that had cylinder attachments for sanding. "For really large areas, good old fashioned sandpaper would be good. I keep a stock of replacement heads in one of the cabinets, and check regularly that I can still get them, but woodworking tools have not changed significantly in 300 years, and the ones I have are from a company still in operation," answered his grandfather. Tim said, "Since you were at the house for dinner, do you think I should have a few more chairs for the dining table made, since next year it is possible there will be two more to seat." His grandfather said, "You may get two more chair around that table with less wiggle room but not more than that, without an even larger table, and quite frankly you would need a bigger room for more table." Tim said, "There is enough room to have a second small table for say six people, largely children would that be a better approach?" His grandfather replied, "It might be better to get a small folding table available at many stores, so that you could set it for the times you need, and fold it up and store it and folding chairs somewhere else in the house, or even the garage. It would not necessarily match the regular dining table, but it is only going to be used once or twice at best each year. If it is for children, then it presents no real dilemma, since kids are oblivious to styles of furniture." His grandfather made a point that Tim never even considered, and it made perfect sense, they made a variety of folding tables with nicely padded chairs that also folded into more compact positions for storing until needed. He thanked his grandfather for the suggestion and said it made good sense.

His grandfather was curious about who the other two might be. Tim said Kuri had a brother and his family that now lived in Seattle, since he managed the Seattle based restaurant for her father's chain of restaurants. He also reminded his grandfather they were present at their wedding and reception afterwards. His grandfather did not remember half the people that were at that gathering, but did not realize that they were also in Seattle. He asked why they were not here on Christmas. Tim said they decided to have a more Japanese style Christmas of just family, and Hiro was going to remind him they were a part of a larger family now. Hiro was also going to make sure his son and daughter-in-law knew how welcome he and Lian felt, being at the house on Christmas. His grandfather thought they did alright.

Tim asked if he and Hiro had the chance to speak in Japanese. His grandfather said he forgot, since Hiro's English was so good he never even gave it a thought. His grandfather said his break was over, and Tim let him get back to his work and returned home.

The decision for New Year's Eve was made simply by Kuri as the options were all much too late for Liani. She was too young to leave unattended at home, so it was going to be a night in, and watch the festivities on the entertainment system. Tim still had some Asti for the two of them, so it would be simple. He always had shrimp in the computerized environmental cooling system so mixing a batch of cocktail sauce for shrimp cocktail would not take much, and they could enjoy each other's company as well.

Between now and New Year's Eve nothing out of the ordinary caused any problems. The vidphones were upgraded, and did not take all that long, as the trip to the other house was the longest part of it. They did replace the cables to the jack, saying that they could get brittle in time and cause problems, and it was done as part of all installations just to be sure. New Year's Eve arrived with Liani asleep by 10 PM, it was time for Tim and Kuri to get cozy and watch the festivities. At 11 PM, he got the shrimp cocktail out for them with a couple of good glasses of Asti, and they nursed them both until nearly the kissing hour. At least that is what Tim always considered the stroke of midnight to be. As the first second of the New Year came about, it seems every couple exchanged a kiss. Some were for long times, other just short little kisses, and for tonight Tim figured Kuri could dictate which direction they would go in. She chose a long passionate kiss that led to other pleasures after another glass of Asti. Tim knew the robotic sweeper came out at 2AM for the nightly cleaning but by that time Tim and Kuri were oblivious to anything other than the passions they were exchanging, which lasted until 3 AM. They were totally spent at that time, and had no difficulty in falling to sleep.

Tim was the first to rise; but much later than normal for him, and with the following day being his return to work, he could not duplicate the previous evening or morning depending on one's point of view. He started getting a breakfast for everyone, which today consisted of bacon, with hash browns with a bit of home grown clutee and eggs benedict for himself and Kuri. Liani had not quite got used to the idea of anything other than fruit topped waffles. She got along with some hash browns, and a single slice of bacon as she did like to try a little occasionally.

The smell of bacon gets them every time, as soon as the aroma hit the bedrooms it was like St. Nick had just arrived. Soon the sleeping beauties stirred and made their way to the kitchen, after taking care of the first stop after a night of sleep. Kuri still blurry eyed said, "It is so unfair you take advantage of our sense of smell to get us out of bed. It is like you only make bacon on mornings that everyone needed to sleep a little later than normal." Tim said, "It is just in your imagination, I never intentionally plan to cook bacon on days you sleep late, it just happens that way." Tim went about making sure everything was cooking to finish at the same time, since he lost track with the extra company. Liani was all ready to eat, but it was not ready just yet. He told them 5 more minutes, and got the dinnerware and utensils out and placed at the counter seats. That took care of 90 seconds, and soon the computerized cooking system announced everything was done. First went the waffles with fruit topping, a piece of bacon and the hash browns for Liani. Next the eggs benedict were set out for Kuri and Tim, and the sides soon after. Kuri had the chance to get in a couple bites before Tim got to take his seat. Breakfast went quite well with Kuri giving Liani a single bite of her eggs benedict which may have been a mistake, as Liani wanted more afterwards, and Tim and Kuri shared a little more with her. Tim asked Liani if the next time he made this, would she rather have it or the waffles with fruit topping. Liani thought for a moment and stated, since she could get the waffles most other days, she would like this on the days he made it.

The remainder of the day was for relaxing, except for the time Tim made the other meals. He got to perform his nightly meditation routine early for him, and spent some time listening to the new audio disks he got on Christmas. Then returned to the entertainment room, as it was time for Liani to be going to bed for the night, also a little earlier than she had for the last week. Tim and Kuri watched a new movie on the entertainment system, and then went off to bed themselves. Pleasures for the evening consisted of kisses and snuggling before falling asleep in each other's arms.

CHAPTER

12

Tim started out Monday with all his normal routines in the morning, followed by a quick breakfast, which did not disturb anyone else. Took his transport into the office, parked in his reserved spot, and said hello to Loretta asking if she missed him, which got a nonchalant wave, like did not know you were gone. Tim said his hello to each of the computers he dealt with regularly, and none jumped into to say much other than hello in response.

He was only in the office 10 minutes when the vidphone went active, and Nora announced it was Detective Marshall. Tim said hello and exchanged the typical how's the family, and if they all had a nice Christmas. It was followed with the same from Detective Marshall. Then to the point. Detective Marshall said, "Our primary suspects have been spotted several times, still in Hong Kong; but have managed to give the local authorities the slip in each sighting. Unfortunately, they have not been able to find where they are making residence. I suspect they have it under a name they only used for that specific purpose. Since Hong Kong has so many places to hide in plain sight, it would seem they did research where they wanted to get lost, after accomplishing what they set out to do. With the regularity that they have slipped through the authorities, I suppose it is possible they keep quick change disguises with them when they go out. The slightest change in appearance, could allow them to walk right past the authorities looking for them in the earlier appearance. Simple wigs and false facial hair of some type would be easy to use in a public facility, and in a very short time. It is impossible to have authorities check for these if they can't keep up with them to do such a search." Tim said, "At least it is known where they have decided to stay put, has anyone contacted the military to find out the process for missing inventory? Since we are not trying to get personnel records, or what I would think would be confidential information, it may provide some insight in how 12 or 13 or their laser light transmitting units got out into the public for nefarious uses."

Detective Marshall said, "I never considered inquiring, and would do so today to see what access one of these two needed to pull something off like this crime." Tim said, "I can do that if you think they will discuss it with me." Detective Marshall said, "I see no reason they would refuse to talk with you, as long as you do not mention it is to investigate a murder. As long as you do it in the fashion of trying to find out how they got used in a public setting, stick with that approach you should be fine, just let me know what you find out." With that the conversation was simple endings, and letting each to go about the daily duties.

Tim had Nora find the local military facility, and whom he might be able to speak to about the laser light units. She had the vidphone active in two minutes, and said he was speaking to the base commander General Robert York. The vidphone had a rather imposing figure at the other end, who looked like a smile would crack his face. Tim: "General, I hate to impose on you, but my name is Timothy Frantz, CEO of Global Security Corporation and I need your assistance, if it is not too much trouble." General: "That will truly depend on what you need, I cannot send troops into a public issue and many things in the military are rather sensitive." Tim: "I hope what I am trying to find out is not considered too sensitive, but I am trying to find out how approximately 13 of the military grade TRU's, I believe you call them laser light speed transmitting units, got to be in public usage?" General: "There are many ways they could have gotten to be used in public, but all of them would require some sort of military connection. First there is only one facility in the military that warehoused those particular items, and they keep computerized inventory records. A number that large would have registered as a theft and none have been reported, which leaves us to other means. Since these units are sent everywhere they are needed for communications, there is usually one or two spares sent out in the event of a unit being damaged, whether by natural or unnatural methods. The fact of the matter is most of our personnel do not get sent to resorts, they go into some of the least desirable areas of the world, and often with hostile forces nearby. Laser light units can be damage by hostile forces or several severe weather conditions. These units are usually discarded, as they are often too badly damaged to consider repair. Any unit once leaving the warehouse, is no longer tracked as inventory. No outfit would have 13 of them, as only one is required for setting up communications, as they can handle a large number of devices. Spares are sent in the event of damage and quickly can be replaced. Any unit that is returned for repair, goes to a single location and since they are no longer inventoried, could get fixed and removed easily without any questions, especially if the paperwork says scrap. This is the most likely possibility for your dilemma, and those units are repaired somewhere on the east coast. Not sure which facility specifically; but the Carolinas comes to mind. Does that help you any?"

Tim: "It helps more than you know as the units were found on the roof top of a casino resort in North Carolina, and were used for reasons other than military." General: "Could you further that information for me?" Tim: "They were used to acquire approximately 3 Billion in WC, from a long lost government covert agency that was disbanded some 85 years ago." General: "My, that is a lot of money that could have been put to better uses in the military." Tim: "My understanding of the covert group is they were completely off the radar within all the agencies, and got their funding through less than honorable means to fund their own operations." General: "I unlike many, really have no qualms about how the money was obtained, if it was put to good use like funding military or rebuilding public infrastructure, such as the roads we have to use these days." Tim: "As far as roads are concerned, a transport does not need the roads smooth, but wheels do." General: "Unfortunately, military vehicles all have wheels and although the bases have roads that are maintained, outside of the base leaves a bit to be desired these days, and many military vehicle are too large to have transports available. Although, some of the vehicles do not care much about terrain, but driving a tank through Seattle to go grocery shopping, is kind of frowned upon both by military hierarchy, as well as public authorities." Tim: "General, you sound as if you know this by personal experience." General actually had a bit of a smile, not much but a little one and said, "No, but have considered it lately." Tim thanked him for his time and appreciated his input, so he could fit it into finding the people behind the theft. The general said he was happy to be able to help.

Tim had Nora get Detective Marshall, and it took a few minutes because he was mobile, and when he answered he looked a bit upset. Tim apologized for disturbing him, but had the information about the rogue TRU's. Detective Marshall: "Give me what you learned." Tim: "I will give you the short version, there is only one facility that has them warehoused as inventory and it is a computerized inventory and no thefts were reported. Once a unit is shipped it is no longer inventoried and only one facility repairs them, it is located somewhere in the Carolinas, and can easily be repaired and then listed as scrap. This is the most likely facility to have the number we found to have been at the source locations. The General did not know the name of the exact facility; but it will likely show up as a location one of our suspects were working from." Detective Marshall: "That will help when I get the military records, which I understand are going to be sent to us this month sometime. Not much I can do to expedite them, as the government seems to feel the laws are for other people, not them." Tim: "I can see you're busy, but I wanted to get you the information as soon as I had it." Detective Marshall:" Thanks for that, but yes I am on another investigation, and need to get on with it." The vidphone was disconnected and Tim's went back to its position out of sight in the ceiling.

For nearly 200 years, information systems, regardless of the term applied to their function, always had multiple subareas to specialize in. This was largely because of the fact, no single person could possibly achieve everything involved from start to present. There was never an end. No matter how good things appeared to be, something always could be improved upon somewhere in the chain of events necessary to complete a day's worth of information. The Artificial Intelligent computer was successfully completed almost 25 years before the semi-intelligent system was produced. This stems from the fact the base code is from the AI model. The largest reason for taking twenty-five years was to limit the semi-intelligent computer sufficiently to appease the politicians responsible for restricting AI usage. Tim always thought it was the politicians' fear, they could be replaced by an AI system that made quicker and better decisions. They also feared the Artificial Intelligent computer would decide they were better off without human intervention. Since humans have emotions that can often come into play in the decision making process, it was something no technology could emulate.

The first hurdle in the process of Artificial Intelligent computer was accomplished 85 years ago when a material other than silicone was used to create a central brain rather than a processor. It allowed to overcome the binary system limitations that computers had used previously. Binary is a numbering system that operates in 2 numbers only. 0 and 1, as a result all computers were entirely limited to true and false answers to any given situation it encountered in the information it handled. Any gray areas would put the computer into an unrecoverable loop, requiring complete power off to stop the loop. Once the Artificial Intelligent brain was developed, it took over 50,000 thousand code people from hundreds of companies to find a coding system to base on Artificial Intelligence. It took five years for the team of top code people trading breakthroughs to fully develop a code for this type of system. Even then, the governments around the world wanted limitations incorporated, before it could be tested and tried under restricted conditions. Every subarea of information systems was largely a mental test as opposed to a physical one. In design, the constant need to improve and develop until the next level was accomplished in one's mental processes in deciphering information known and attempting to go beyond. In the various subareas of security, it was trying to think what the less moral persons might try to get into a system they had no authority to be in.

For a number of years, all systems have a single computer that acts as the interface between the communications methods to the internal system. This system is often not included into the overall system. It is the single largest factor in whether an intruder gets into a system or not. This system, usually has a dedicated team to monitor inbound information for attempts to induce a virus or malware of some sort to weaken the system to other types of attacks. Tim knew only a few things concerning this part of the systems group. He had no clue where their offices were, or who these specialists were. He did know that no outside intruders had penetrated the system. This was largely a result of the precautions coded into the system itself, to hold any attempt into the system that was not recognized as legitimate. The team could hold this information separate from the main system for days if necessary, to determine as much as possible from the possible intruder. If it was a new type of malware or virus, they could decipher it and inform the code people who created the constantly changing code. Like most every other type of information systems, security, they were one step behind the deviants. New means to intrude came faster than security people could predict or expect. Hackers on the other hand, could spend all the time they wanted devising new and unknown means to break a system. Tim wondered if those that thought of ways to illegally enter systems were using more of their brain. Or if the deviant portion was more developed than in those who tried to prevent it before it occurred.

Tim could relate to them in some fashions, as like analysts they were always one step behind the vast number of intruders, who if nothing else, were inventive. He came to the conclusion at the next board meeting he would inquire as to where these specialist were located so he at least introduced himself. Find out a little more about what they had to work with. Tim thought that they would have been the first to have received AI systems, simply because each was totally independent of the main systems. It would have been the system to determine if something should be allowed or disallowed to continue into the main system. It would require speed that semi-intelligent systems would not achieve. Tim wanted to know for sure and meet the people that protected their systems.

The next thing to interrupt his thought was Nora announcing that authorities had been dispatched to apprehend two money trails that had stopped. All trace information was being forwarded to them as it was the proof that provided them a concrete case for the legal system. The two intrusion were of more than minimum amounts for prosecution, and although they appeared originally as separate intrusions, the final point of money was in close proximity to each other, indicating a team intrusion. Tim asked how much was involved, and Nora informed him that the total was nearly 10 million WC. Nora stated," The funds would not be returned until the authorities were done with their process. All the current conditions of the funds were relayed to the financial customer we provide service for." Tim gave Nora his accolades for doing such a good job and then went about his other business for the morning.

His next point of business was to contact his directors at the other major offices, to see first off, that everyone was still there, and just to let them know he had not forgotten them. His next four hours were spent talking with the various directors, which at least he learned that Sven Noorlandur had returned to the Helsinki office, as he was now married and trying his best to keep it that way. He also learned that Sooni Hakawa was going to be leaving when the next renewal would be presented, as she had found someone who treated her well, and was going to be married and have children of her own. She also said she would give it all up for two hours with him in intimate surroundings, but did not think that was likely. This was the next best means to her own form of happiness. She said that the proposal and public display of love at Kuri's father's restaurant had brought about a little bit of change in the way men treat women in Japan. It is not every man; but the changes have finally started and that is something they as people owe to him and Kuri, for showing them a better way. Sooni finally said that the change may also be a result of the local news near the last day of the year, recapping the best news stories of the year. Since his proposal to Kuri, it has been shown each year, with new interviews, and this year someone sent in a photo of him on his knee presenting Kuri with a token of his love. As a result, for the first time in Japanese history, a jewelry shop near the restaurant, now offers engagement and wedding rings for women. There are also random acts of public affection, if you look hard enough. Tim only asked if her replacement had been selected, and Sooni said she had it narrowed down to three, but had not made a final decision as of yet.

With all the directors contacted in each major office, it was nearly time to head home. Nora then told him that another board meeting was on the schedule for the next afternoon. He thanked her and said good night as well as to Daisy and Anabelle.

When Tim arrived home, he found that Kuri and Liani had gone shopping at the grocers and restocked everything to maximum capacity. Tim asked Kuri if they were expecting a battalion for dinner in the next few days. With a bit of a laugh, she said no, but thought it was time to restock and got a bit carried away. Tim told her the number one rule to grocery shopping is never go hungry. Kuri agreed, as she learned today when it was time to put it all away. He gave Liani his nightly hug and kiss upon whatever part of her head he could reach, often the forehead or cheek. Occasionally the front of her nose or ear, if he felt like giving her a tickle.

It was then time to see if his new recipe for the evening meal was going to be something to keep or discard.

It called for stuffing mix, cream of mushroom soup, cubed chicken specifically broccoli florets; but Tim added a bit of his other favorites to it as well, and a good deal of Swiss cheese. It was a casserole type dish, which required no side dishes, and it sounded good even though it was simple. When dinner was ready and Tim set out the portions for everyone, it quickly disappeared. Liani was having fun with stringy cheese, but did not like it hanging off her chin or other parts of her face, but asked for more just the same. According to the serving sizes, they should have been able to get two meals from it, but it was all gone in one sitting. Tim found it was quite tasty as well, and figured although simple, it was a keeper for his recipe collection. Kuri said she wanted to know how to make it as well, since she found it quite good and might make it for a lunch.

It had been awhile since Kuri was asked to fill in at the restaurant; but informed Tim she would be needed the next evening at the restaurant. She would not need to leave until he got home, but would likely need to eat at the restaurant if she was not kept too busy.

Meanwhile, Detective Marshall had reached a point of exasperation with the lack of progress from the authorities in Hong Kong. He had to get authorization from higher up the chain to go to Hong Kong personally, and discussed it with his next higher member of the force. It was pointed out that such a trip would be costly for the department; but if he could get some type of outside assistance, it might be possible. Detective Marshall knew where to go for such assistance and had to develop a good explanation to get approval from both his superiors and the CEO of Global Security Corporation, although he figured that to be least of his concerns. He put together his proposal to his superiors and presented it to his captain to take it to the next level. He included in his proposal that he thought he could get some assistance from Timothy Frantz of Global Security Corporation, currently CEO. It would be good to get a quick response in order to find the people he believed were responsible for a murder that was now three years into the investigation and needed resolution. The suspects may be able to elude the local authorities far easier than a person they would not be familiar with. He did not have a specific time frame in mind, as he had to get the local authorities to act upon whatever he might discover. He hoped the suspects were not able to leave to another region prior to this occurring.

With his proposal submitted, Detective Marshall went home for the evening, hoping to have an answer before the next day came to an end. Once home, he informed his wife of what his potential plans were and went into detailed information about what he needed to accomplish during his absence. He insured her it was strictly work related, but saw no other alternative to bringing the case to closure. His wife was not overjoyed with this prospect of a lengthy absence of her mate, but understood his determination in finding answers to the problem he has long been dedicated to resolving. She was already accustomed to his long hours away from home, since this episode started. The two kids were a different story, as they were still young and not able to understand why their father was away so much, and not having time to spend with them.

First thing the next day, Detective Marshall made the call to Timothy Frantz at Global Security Corporation. Tim had only been in the office fifteen minutes when Nora announced that Detective Marshall was contacting him on the vidphone.

Tim had the vidphone go active and asked, "What do I owe the pleasure of this unexpected call?" Detective Marshall responded with, "I have made a proposal to my superiors to go to Hong Kong personally, to expedite the apprehension of those we suspect in the murder of your analyst. I will require a good deal of assistance from you and your organization, as we simply do not have the funds to pursue it without your assistance. I have not got the answer as of yet, but thought I should make the inquiry to you in advance to see if this is even possible."

Tim replied, "Your timing is quite good, as I have a board meeting this afternoon, where I can provide the proposal to the board members. I, unfortunately, do not have unlimited authority in this company, as those who own, prefer to be the decision makers when it comes to financial obligations. I can present the idea of providing a private jet and nice accommodations in Hong Kong while you are there, although I do not believe I can leave the jet in Hong Kong for the duration. We will likely be able to pick up the costs of meals, as it is common business practice for us. Refreshments of alcoholic nature will be your responsibility."

Detective Marshall said, "That would be far more than I would have expected, especially since I cannot give you a realistic time frame. It appears that Hong Kong prefers uniformed authorities for the visibility factor, and utilize few, if any, undercover personnel. That makes them easy for our suspects to spot and evade, so I plan to get some of their people to go plain clothes, while trying to apprehend our suspects. I believe, since I have little authority in Hong Kong, they will have to make the apprehension before bringing them back to Seattle for the legal process."

Tim replied with, "That sounds like a more reasonable approach, since you previously stated they seem to be able to change appearance quickly to avoid the local authorities, you may consider taking some such items for your trip. If you do not appear to be the same person all the time, it may help in a shorter stay in Hong Kong. Not being an authority on the subject of disguise, I cannot provide you much more, it would seem hairpieces and facial hair would be the quickest mean to change appearance."

Detective Marshall stated, "That is an excellent idea, I did not consider and I believe we have such kits already in place within our department. I will simple see about obtaining one, as I have been through a training procedure for the use of such items, although it has been quite a while since that took place. We have people who use them for their type of work, but I have not been involved heavily with them myself. As soon as I get an answer, I will let you know and thank you for any assistance you can provide." With that the vidphone was disconnected. Tim had gotten used to the detective being to the point and not wasting much time with his conversations.

The morning for Tim had no major issues, and then the board meeting time was upon him and he went to the meeting.

Trask opened the meeting by the usual means of anything new to be presented and Tim did not wait for everyone else to remain quiet this time. Tim opened with, "Detective Marshall has requested our assistance in trying to bring closure to the murder of our analyst, which is now nearly three years past. The plan is he will go to Hong Kong to find the suspects and expedite their apprehension, but the local authorities do not have the funds to conduct such an investigation. I propose using a company jet to get him to Hong Kong, although I did not guarantee him the plane could remain in Hong Kong for the duration, which could be a month or a year depending on how elusive the suspects can be. I also thought we could provide him hotel and meals as is customary for any of our own staff to be in a city outside of their own. I realize Detective Marshall is not one of our own, but this may be the only way to bring closure to this problem. It seems the authorities in Hong Kong, prefer the visibility of uniformed personnel over any other method, and this makes them easy to elude. I would require a quick reply to this request, as the proposal has already been made to the local authorities by Detective Marshall, and he was informed without outside assistance he would be denied."

Trask asked, "Tim, do you think this will help get this matter resolved, or is it simply going to prolong a dropped case by the authorities?" Tim replied, "I believe this is the only remaining alternative to bringing this to closure, but cannot predict the future as to the final outcome. I can honestly say, without doing this method, it will definitely remain unresolved, I have already had that experience, and it does not bring about good feelings in failures."

Trask concurred, remembering how Robin Torry managed to outsmart them; but he did not cause the death of anyone in the process. He made the decision to go ahead without asking the remaining board members, as it was obvious to him this was the only way to move forward.

Tim thanked him for his approval, and said there was one other thing he would like to know concerning the company, but it was not something he believe to be a cost item. Tim said, "Every company has a group of system specialists, solely for the purpose of monitoring inbound information for virus and malware being sent into the main system. Typically, this system is stand alone, and not considered a part of the main system, although every bit of information must go through it to be allowed to get beyond it to the main system. I am certain we have such a system, and people involved in that specific function, but I have never met a single one, and have no idea where their offices are located, or what type of system they employ. I would like to meet with them to see if we are providing them with everything they need, as they are the heart and soul of our system integrity."

Trask said, "My apologies for not having done such prior to now, as they do such a good job, I forget about them. I will take you there myself after the meeting is concluded, and introduce you to those present. We have a total of fifteen malware and virus specialists that work rotating shifts, to insure 7 day 24 hour coverage. They were the first to have AI systems, as they are stand alone, and all information must clear that portal prior to entering the main system complex. There are groups in each major office, as all satellite offices are also monitored from the majors, prior to being forwarded to the final location. I am uncertain as to the upgrades to the AI system they use, but normally they have the latest technology because they are the portal to all the main systems."

Tim had no other information to present to the board, and waited for the meeting to conclude. That took another 30 minutes as no other board members had new proposals, simply questions concerning those in place. Not a single member objected to Tim's proposal or questioned Trask's decision without consultation.

After the meeting, Trask took Tim to the offices of the virus and malware specialists who were all rather engaged in system monitoring. Trask made it a quick process with no names and introduction, largely because he could not remember all their names, and knew they were all the best in their line of security. Tim simply said, if they needed anything, not to hesitate in asking for it. One of the people stated, they did not get an overabundance of attack attempts, as they did not deal directly with money as investment and banking organizations did. Largely they got inexperienced hackers trying to see if they could get information from their system, and those attempts were typically discarded to make it appear as if the hackers got into a non-existent system. Occasionally, some were allowed in, but the main AI filtered them out, as it was more involved in that type of problem as opposed to virus or malware. They were not exempt, but virus and malware attempts were usually precursor to hacking on a weakened system. He was also happy to say no virus or malware had as of yet, entered their main systems, but with the ever evolving code for such attempts, it was still possible, they did not know every potential problem as they developed. Tim thanked them for their time and left with Trask.

On the way back to his office Tim said to Trask, "They seem perfectly content to be a forgotten, but vital part of this organization." Trask replied,

"They are a strange group of system people, although well paid, they know that if they do their job efficiently being forgotten is a good sign to them. Too much attention, indicates they are failing in their function. They also know more about their function and purpose than the rest of the company put together. They seem to enjoy being isolated to their own little world, and excel at what they do as a result. With being single minded in purpose, it allows them to perform better than also having to worry about system code, or analysis, or any other of the duties of system people. Hackers, for the vast majority still do not fully understand exactly what we do. As a result, they are confused with the fact that we deal with almost every financial business in the world, so they believe that money must pass through us at some point. These are the hackers that try to get into our systems, thinking it will be easier for them to get funds from the source, and since we have no funds, they are totally baffled. They usually find to break into our trace monitoring system it is a far more difficult task than to go directly to the financial organization they are considering targeting."

Tim was relatively aware of that fact, but confirmation was always looked upon with appreciation. They arrived back into Tim's office, and Trask went about his other business for the day. Tim decided it was time to hit the 35th floor break area for a little food and coffee, plus the view. He could get better coffee and food from his little area in the office, but the view was superior in the break area. He found three analysts also in the break area, which was rather unusual, and to his surprise they were all recent recruits, not just analysts.

Tim asked them if they were conspiring something, as it was usual for him to find others taking advantage of the facilities available to them. One replied, they were trying to collectively find a means to present the idea of a change in scenery in the offices. It was too pristine and getting to be burdensome to look at nothing but white. Tim said, he tried several times; but could find no supporting evidence to persuade them otherwise. At this point, the recruit said he did find some research on the IG that indicated white was a marvelous color for short time frames, such as hospital stays, and other facilities of a similar nature. He also found research that proved those who were to work in the environment often had offices that were richly appointed with high quality woods for desks and walls with pictures of whatever the occupant saw fit. The research also pointed out, that prolonged exposure to the sterile environment could create visual impairments as white was often a color to create blindness or color blindness. It is simply not the best method any longer. He understood the reasoning for creating such an environment, but with the robotic computers now in place even they are having a difficult time moving in an all-white environment where depth perception is lost. Tim told them to put together a proposal with the supporting evidence, and he would submit it to the board of director's for them. Hopefully they had better proof than he could derive early on in his career. Since he had the advantage of being in an assistant director's office, as well as director before CEO, his exposure to the serene white analyst's office was minimal.

The remainder of his lunchtime was spent looking at the ocean view and see if any of the sea life was going to make an appearance. It was not the time of year for an abundance of whales or dolphins, as they were in warmer waters for the time being, although it was possible for a stray or two to appear anytime of the year.

When Tim returned to his office, he found John Thompson waiting for him, which was not expected just yet, he thought. Tim asked, "How you doing John, and what tidings do you bring?" John said, "I am doing quite well, and it is time to present your renewal for next month. I may have another recruiting class for you to get to know by that time as well, but it is still in the negotiation portion to convince the majority, this is where they would be best served for their abilities and education." Tim said, "I hope you were not waiting long, but I needed to get something to eat and decided to get the break room view for a change in scenery." John said it was not too long, as he had waited far longer for Trask in the past.

John Thompson presented the contract for him to go over. John said, "The board has decided since the vast majority of people who were getting bonuses have left or gone up the ladder, that the bonus money would be dispersed through regular weekly payments. You will notice a rather nice increase to your current amount, this accounts for bonuses you may have received. Again this is a one year contract, and it includes a small increase also for your continued services to Global Security Corporation. Everything else is pretty much the same as any other contract you have reviewed."

Tim said, "Although it is not definite, I may need to go to Hong Kong for a week or two, and I only tell you this in the event it becomes necessary, I hope it does not coincide with one of your recruiting groups. I will have either Nora or more likely Loretta contact you, if this is to be the case."

John Thompson asked, "What is in Hong Kong that would require your presence?" Tim said, "That is where our potential murder suspects are, and if Detective Marshall finds it beneficial for another set of eyes unfamiliar to them, I may make myself available to finally put an end to this problem." John said he appreciated the advanced notice, and if it came to be, he would work around it, although the new recruits seem to get a more realistic idea about expectations from Tim. John then got up to leave saying Tim needed to have his renewal submitted to him within two weeks, so he could move forward with the matter. The day had also come to a close, and Tim departed for home, after his parting statements to his three systems, and Loretta who was also preparing to leave for the day. Since she was also going home, he decided to escort her to the parking area to insure she got to her vehicle without a problem.

The evening at home was largely routine, except Tim took a little bit of time to look over his renewal contract for another year as CEO. The only real change was they put his salary in weekly amounts of 250,000 WC, which Tim did the conversions to find it over 1,000,000 WC a month. He did not know if this was a result of not having received bonuses for the last two years, although he had not been able to submit any new technology or cost efficient methods. He had just figured his bonuses had run the course, and his monthly salary was more than enough. He found it fruitless to inquire from John, as it was normally a board decision on his salary each year, and it was not something to bring up in a board meeting. Since Trask had little reason to come in on a daily basis, there was no real means of obtaining the reason.

Dinner had been completed and he finished his meditation routine before looking over the contract, and with Liani in bed for the night, he let Kuri know his contract was provided for another year. Kuri was quite surprised by the increase, but did not look forward to another year without him around enough for his daughter, and soon a new arrival would be in the works. Tim also let her know he was considering going to Hong Kong for a week or two, to assist in finding the suspects in the murder of the analyst that has prevented him from returning to retirement, to help with raising a family. The hope and purpose would be for bringing this murder to closure so he could make this his last year as CEO. His potential retirement income would be nearly what he was getting currently, and they have had no shortages of funds at any point since he first went to work for Global Security, and it had been even better since they were married. It would be nice to plan a monthly trip to Tokyo, since they did have a home there that could use occupancy more frequently. Kuri asked whether the trip to Hong Kong was a family affair or Tim alone. Tim was honest, stating he did not know how much time he would be using in a day for finding the suspects, and could not believe he would be easily reachable for her if needed. He would love the companionship of Kuri and Liani; but it would not be a pleasure trip, where he could spend time site seeing and hitting the best restaurants and shops. Kuri understood, and figured it would be best for her and Liani to stay in Seattle with his family nearby, in the event something required help. The largest concern was always Liani staying in peak health and well-being, but children could have accidents that required immediate attention. It was something that was always paramount to Tim and Kuri that Liani could get into a situation that required a medical trip.

CHAPTER

13

The next day started with his usual greetings to Loretta and then Nora, Daisy and Anabelle. Shortly after, he got the vidphone from Detective Marshall to go active and he answered with Nora informing him who it was. Tim said, "Good morning, is this to inform me of your trip to Hong Kong?" Detective Marshall replied, "Yes, they have approved my departure, largely in thanks to your company's assistance in the expenses. I will be leaving in three days, if that is enough time for you to make arrangements. Tim said, "I believe that all the arrangements can be made by end of day, and wondered if my assistance in Hong Kong for a week or two would be useful to you." Detective Marshall said, "I honestly do not know at this time, I did not plan on it, and have no idea how much surveillance experience you might have."

Tim said, "Since I am not involved in your type of work the answer is simple, I have none, but as an unfamiliar face to the suspects, I might be able to help in locating them with a little bit of technique you provide. I would require a week notice, as I have to insure my absence can be worked around by those others in this organization." Detective Marshall answered with, "Facial recognition is the primary concern, if I forwarded a picture of each of our suspects, could you study the pictures to literally ingrain the features in your memory, so you could quickly determine with disguises in use, that you have spotted the suspect." Tim said, "I believe I can, since memory is largely something that I have always excelled with." Detective Marshall continued with, "There is no guarantee your assistance will be required, but I do see advantages to having more than one unknown

203

persons to our suspects. You are also likely more familiar with Hong Kong than I myself, and this could prove advantageous as well. As I said before, there is no guarantee your assistance will be necessary in Hong Kong, largely it will depend on the help I can get from the local authorities in becoming less conspicuous." Tim acknowledged the last statement and stated, "I simply need closure in this and am willing to offer whatever aid I can to expedite finality to this problem." Detective Marshall said he would keep it in mind and thanked him, and finished by saying he would send the pictures as soon as he could for Tim to use.

Tim's next small task consisted of asking Nora whether she could reach Trask outside of the office area. She said not since he left the CEO position, and remains only on the board of directors, and she added which should be board of owners. Tim could not argue that assessment, but told Nora it is more for outside influence that it is called the board of directors. It implies to the world of business that all real decisions must pass through the board of directors. Since Nora no longer had the means to contact Trask, he gave it a quick pause to consider who might have it. It did not take long to figure out that Trask would want regular updates on Tim's performance in the CEO position. After all, Trask would not stay away long if the company took a sudden downturn in some area of its expertise. That led to only one logical option, who better than Loretta to supply Trask with regular updates. With that in mind, Tim got up to go to the outer office where Loretta always was stationed. He approached the desk and said, "Loretta, knowing Trask well enough to know that he would not let his company operate without his own hand in the proceedings, I have come to the conclusion that you would be the best person to know how to reach him." Loretta looked up at Tim and said, "You are as smart as Trask said you were, how did you figure that out?" Tim said, "It was the most logical assessment I could surmise based on his former computer no longer having contact information for him. Who better than you to provide him with regular updates concerning the company he always considered his." Loretta replied, "I have informed him largely that the ship is running smoother than when he was here if that means anything to you." Tim said, "I do appreciate that, but mostly I need to get in touch with him, which was the reason for coming to you in the first place." Loretta asked, "Is this something I should be aware of?" Tim responded, "It is not definite, but I may need him to fill in here for a week or two in the near future and simply thought it wise to give him some advanced notice. If you do not mind reaching him and forward him to my vidphone, it would be highly appreciated." Loretta said she would do so immediately, and Tim returned to his office area, after telling Loretta he owed her another lunch soon.

Tim's vidphone was dropping out of it's hidden location about the same time he got back to his desk. Trask was present at the other end and said, "Loretta tells me you figured out whom might know how to reach me outside of those offices, I did not think I was that obvious. What do you need?" Tim stated, "This is mostly an advanced notice in the event I am away from the Seattle office for a week or two. It is not concrete, but I have offered Detective Marshall another set of eyes in Hong Kong to try to bring this issue that has been hanging over our heads to closure. He did not know if I would be needed for certain, but I believe it would be courteous to provide you the possibility of it happening. I also may not be in a reachable position, I feel you would like to be here at the headquarters in the event I do need to go to Hong Kong."

Trask asked, "Do you think you would be of any assistance to the authorities who have far more experience it this type of surveillance than you?" Tim replied, "I believe another unfamiliar face to the suspects would be very helpful in finding out where they have found refuge. Detective Marshall is forwarding me pictures of our suspects to engrain into my memory, which has always been exceptional, and I feel I can do it without too much difficulty, and maybe help locate the elusive people behind the death of one of our analysts."

Trask said, "I cannot argue with your logic, but this is far beyond what we would do in any other discretion committed under our monitoring services." Tim answered with, "True, unfortunately this whole affair is far beyond what we ever anticipated occurring as a result of our services. We never expected someone to kill an analyst with audio frequencies, or even considered the possibility of such actions. Also I do not believe it would be appropriate to put any of our personnel in jeopardy leaving this task squarely on my shoulders."

Trask said, "It could be extremely dangerous for you to follow-up with this type of investigation, but I see you are committed to doing it regardless. If the time comes, I will resume in your absence as CEO, but

I will not like it one single bit if any harm come to you over this form of investigation beyond our normal services we provide to our clients." Tim said, "Unfortunately in this case we are the client, as it was our analyst who was killed. I have to bring this to closure one way or another, and will not accept another failure, if I do not do everything possible to bring it to its proper conclusion. Also, I informed Detective Marshall I would need a week advanced notice to insure this company did not suffer in my absence, knowing fully well I may not be in a position to be reached or possibly even check in regularly."

Trask knew Tim's contract was ready for renewal and Tim had all the trump cards under the circumstances. Tim could simply not renew his contract and still be financially capable of acting entirely on his own to fulfill his determination on getting the suspects apprehended by authorities. There was no way to disapprove his request without Global Security Corporation being jeopardized in some fashion or another. His logic was sound, that he alone would be the best choice for such an endeavor, but Trask feared the worst and hoped he was incorrect in his assessment. There seemed to be no alternative to getting Tim to reconsider his decision on this problem. Therefore Trask ended with having Tim let him know if he would be needed. His best hope was that Detective Marshall would find no use for Tim to go to Hong Kong.

With that concluded Tim then made all the arrangements for Detective Marshall to go to Hong Kong using one of the private jets, and also the hotel that he had stayed in with the help of Loretta. He then asked Loretta which of the next two days she would prefer to have lunch with him. She chose the next day, saying she assumed they would be going to the same little restaurant they did before. Tim confirmed her assumption to find out that Loretta and her husband had been going regularly since Tim showed her where it was. She stated that the evening meals were even better than the luncheon menu and always changing the entrees made it so enjoyable. With everything completed for Detective Marshall, he returned to his office and Nora said she had a message to give him from Detective Marshall which had pictures.

Tim asked Nora if she could put the pictures up on the overhead display so he could view them for a long time. Nora did as asked and Tim studied the facial features of each of the two suspects. After engraining the features into his memory he tried to picture them with different colored hair or even hairpieces that included changes in length as well as for the male other facial hair. He spent the remainder of the day studying and committing to memory not only the facial feature, but the perceived alterations. He felt quite confident he could spot either one of them quickly, even in a crowd as large as Hong Kong. He then departed for the day for his residence.

Once home, the first thing he noticed was Kuri had gone to get her hair shortened considerably. It had reached a point of falling below her knees and he was told it was because it was becoming a bit too painful when sitting. If she chose to get her hair behind the seating, Liani who did get up and down frequently, would manage to step on it and pull it accidentally. It was also the same if she simply sat down with Liani. It was now trimmed to just waist level, and it was cut to a perfect line. It had been some time since she had done anything of the sort, and he wondered if she should become more American with much shorter hair, but decided she was still too Japanese for that. He gave Liani his normal evening hug and kiss on the forehead before heading to the kitchen for the evening meal preparations.

As soon as he started looking for what to make Kuri and Liani, both requested the chicken casserole meal he made last week. Kuri also wanted to be involved in the preparation, so she could make it for lunch for herself and Liani every now and then. It was first important for Liani to be occupied and remain seated, while her parents were busy in the kitchen, or else she would not get the meal she was expecting. With this concept of denial, Liani agreed to stay right where she was until dinner was ready. It took a little bit longer in the preparations, as he showed Kuri everything he did the first time, and let her do some of it with his instruction. Once prepared, he let Kuri go through the process of setting the times and everything on the cooking device. Since it was an all in one meal, only one compartment was needed for the food. Once that was set, they both returned to the entertainment room, to give Liani companionship until the cooking system informed them it was ready.

Dinner was exactly the way it was the last time, including it all being consumed in a single sitting instead of two, as the recipe indicated it would be. Tim had no real complaint concerning its disappearance, as it was a good indication that Kuri and Liani really liked his simple recipe. It was not a recipe of Asian style cooking as he would have made for the evening meal, since it had been some time for something in that nature of food.

Once the cleaning of the dinnerware and utensils was completed, Tim went to the computer room in the lower level to find how many shops in Seattle had disguises for him to employ while in Hong Kong. His first order of business would be to find shops that also provided some basic instruction on its application, since it was entirely new to him. He would go with the concept that he wanted it for his work as CEO to be able to go into various offices without recognition. This was to insure that procedures and functions were being properly performed on a daily occurrence. He could not do this without some sort of appearance alterations. Unfortunately out of 30 shops he found in Seattle, only one offered any type of instructional options. He made a note of the location which happen to be quite convenient to the office. As a matter of fact, it was located in the building adjacent to his own. He had never noticed it, but then he had no reason to look for such a shop prior to now.

With his research completed for the time being, he returned to the main level and went about his mediation routine which he was proud of not having missed but a single day since utilizing the techniques Kuri had him employ. He felt the exercise indeed developed muscle tone as well as peace of mind. He had had absolutely no mental lapses since employing the technique, and his stamina had definitely improved over the time he had been using it. He would never have thought this was possible from his previous method which was helpful, but not to the degree this technique had proven to be.

The one thing he did know as a result of his mediation exercise, it would become instinctive for him to employ the various moves as a means for self-defense, and he was not sure about from an offensive standpoint. All of his training concentrated on defense. He hoped he would not have a need to employ either, but that would only be determined in the event he indeed went to Hong Kong.

The time had arrived for Liani to be put to bed, so Tim went through the nightly process this evening instead of having Kuri perform it. It was not a long process; but Liani did need to go through the nightly hygiene ritual which she had learned to do quite well needing no assistance of any type. Tim watched until it was time for Liani to use the bathroom for other reasons, and she was not long in taking care of it. Tim put her to bed, gave her a hug and kiss goodnight, made sure she was complete tucked into her covers for the reason of the season more so then needing to keep her warm. It was still comforting to be toasty warm for the purpose of sleeping, as it was not easy to fall asleep when you were overly chilled. Liani was asleep in a few minutes, and Tim turned out the lights, and went back to the entertainment room where Kuri was. Tim had already decided it was time to give Kuri pleasures that would last for a couple of weeks of easy arousal, as it seemed like an eternity since he showed her his true affections. It was largely due to having a young child in the house, where too much activity could bring her out of her slumbers. She may then try to discover what woke her. It was a marvelous pleasures event for them both. And Kuri although too exhausted to do anything more that evening, decided the next evening would result in the expectation of a second child.

Liani was old enough to have a sibling, whether a brother or sister was not the concern, as much as having another young child to relate to. She was also smart enough to be a guiding force to whichever sibling she had to deal with. Kuri would like it to be a brother, but she had no control over that, and would be happy with whatever type of child she conceived. Whether male or female, was not as important as a healthy child to bring into the world. Since she had already had one bundle of joy, a second would be just as much of a blessing, and a welcomed member to the growing family. Kuri was determined to have at least three because in Japan. Although not law, two was considered the limit. In order to enforce it, Japan had so many penalties involved with a third child, only the wealthiest could even consider it. Although, it was far more common for the less than prosperous to have such an error in the household for a short period of time, as the third child they could not afford to keep, was put up for adoption. Kuri was well aware of the fact that they could afford such a luxury in Japan, but it was far more important to be here where there was no consequences to consider. Since all education has costs associated with it, she could easily afford her children following a Japanese educational program from home. Soon it would be time for Liani to be enrolled for the start of semester that most suited her third birth date.

They were both taken by sleep shortly after the pleasure activities concluded; but even then the mind would go through the nightly process over concerns or similar such thoughts to complete prior to slumber winning out.

The following morning, Tim arose at his normal time but felt like he needed another three or four hours of sleep. He never felt like he was short on sleep after his standard 6 hours; but today was different and he did not understand why. He slowly went through his morning routine and recovery was not taking place. He continued with having breakfast and getting ready to head into the office, but still felt run down. He had too much expected of him to stay home, so he trudged on and left for the office.

He greeted Loretta on his arrival telling her lunch would be around noon if that was good for her. She did not indicate it would be problem so he continued to his office. He said hello to Nora, Daisy and Anabelle without out any problems needing his attention. He had Nora bring up the pictures again, and spent the next hour refreshing his memory, although, he did not really loose anything from the day before. He felt he should continue to refresh daily, considering the importance of these pictures to his reason for going to Hong Kong and wanted no question of identification.

Next instead of calling a meeting, he wandered back to the offices of his technology people and found Jonathan Trask. Tim saw he was working with another robotic humanoid system and tried not to be an interruption. Tim asked, "Jonathan, how far along in the robotics are we at this point?" Jonathan did not stop his work on the robotic system and answered with, "We have all of them in place here in Seattle and are working on a dozen for each satellite office under our umbrella. We have shipped six offices the first dozen. A dozen was the number selected, as some of the small satellite offices only need twelve. After all the satellites are done that fall under our control, we will start with the other major offices to completion at each, since none of them have the number of analyst they have here. Once that is done, then satellite offices under each major will be done before returning to our own satellite offices that need more than a dozen. It will take us likely another year before every single unit is in place, but we have progressed rather well." Tim thanked him for his input and left to his office not wanting to be too much of a bother to the technology people.

He did get the progress report from that area and his next check would be for the medical staff to see if a notable improvement had been realized in the stress factor among analysts.

Once he returned to his office, Nora stated that the director had called to inform him that he was presented with a proposal from three analysts concerning the overabundance of white in the office space. Tim knew there was a director in place after a long absence, but had no idea what his name was, only that he came from one of two California satellite offices. Tim asked Nora if the director left his name or if she was aware of his name. Nora checked her memory as the director did not state in his message and found his name was Alberto Rodriguez. He told Nora to let Alberto know that he would be up to see him in the next fifteen minutes, as he also intended to go to the medical staff for some progress reports from them. Nora complied with Tim's request. Tim still had time before fulfilling his luncheon obligation with Loretta and got himself a nice cup of coffee before departing for the 35th floor.

His arrival was relatively precise, and he knock quietly upon the door of the director's office to keep from startling him. Alberto rose and motioned Tim in where Tim started with, "I apologize for not having met sooner, and unfortunately I have been rather preoccupied with a problem that has existed since becoming CEO. I am Tim Frantz. Alberto replied, "Pleasure to meet you, you may call me Al." Tim said, "That makes things simple, we could use a lot more of that around here. Nora, my computer said you had a proposal for me, am I to assume this is from the three recruits I met in the break area last week?" Al said, "I do not know if they are the same three you met, but it is a joint effort from three of our more recent recruits. They told me they all had equal parts in the proposal, and did not believe it was a proposal worthy of any of them to get a promotion or even a bonus, but they feel it would vastly improve the environment of the offices. I have looked over the proposal and it appears to have been well researched and presented."

Tim took the proposal and said, "I will look it over extensively prior to submitting it to the board, which is going to be nearly a month since we just had a meeting. As I informed the recruits, there is no guarantee, but if the research information is sound, it may prove to finally get the board to rethink their position on the white environment." Al responded with, "That is all we can hope for, I have noticed with robotic computers system allowed to traverse between offices, that there is a lot of bumping and banging occurring from the inability to differentiate between wall and door." Tim got up to leave and said, "Do not feel at any time you cannot present proposals to me to get to the board for a decision. I hope to see more to indicate the analysts have ideas that improve business in whatever way possible."

Tim walked down the hall a short distance to medical staff, to find a single individual at the reception desk. "Tim said, "I was expecting more people here is everyone that busy?" The person at the desk said, "Hardly, they are all in the monitoring room keeping an eye on analysts, I can take you back there if you like." Tim said that would be fine and she took him back where the other eight people were. Even the acupuncture specialist was in the monitoring room.

Tim said, "I hope I am not disturbing you, I was trying to get an update since the robotic systems have been put into operation." There was no reply, so much as every single head making a motion to indicate he was not disturbing anyone. He started with the acupuncture specialist asking how often he was required to perform his craft. He said seldom and it was a good thing he was handsomely paid. He would be in big trouble if he were still independent and had so few clients. The only other person he talked with was the department leader who stated that they only had a 5 percent stress related problem among the analysts, and 3 percent of them had stress from outside of work. First with the Artificial Intelligent system doing the majority of the work the analysts have not been overburdened, but with the robotic systems every analyst has taken to learning what the technology can do for them. Although, they do not have audio from the rooms, it was obvious that all of the analysts were now conversing with their computer systems. Many of them even go to the break area with their robotic system, either for conversation or to make sure nothing requiring their immediate attention occurs while on break. "It would appear from my view point, unless something drastic occurs, stress level are well under control in this office and no longer any more excessive than any other work environment." Tim thanked them for their time in giving him an update and he would go back to his office to put together his findings and present the board with a new concept towards the retirement program.

It will have taken 14 years to get the stress levels to level equivalent to the rest of the working world, but it seemed it was going to be no different than any other position companies offered. The fact they were the only ones in this type of business, would remain its most unique quality and attraction for qualified people. Tim returned to his office approximately fifteen minutes ahead of his luncheon with Loretta. He decided to put the proposal on his desk and wait out at Loretta's station for her to be ready to go.

Seeing Tim arrive and take a seat Loretta said, "You are early, but I have nothing currently that requires immediate action so if you like, I can be ready in five minutes, but need to go to the ladies room first. Tim said, "Take all the time you need, I am in no hurry at the moment." Loretta got up from her station and disappeared down a hall and returned exactly five minutes later. It was off to the local restaurant that Tim had found to have exceptional food for all the meals they served.

Once seated and menu's brought to the table Tim asked Loretta if she would like a glass of wine with her meal or cognac afterwards. Loretta was rather surprised and asked, "What would Trask make of us having such a beverage with our lunch?" Tim responded with, "While I have been coming to this establishment for 13 years, if I recollect correctly, Trask is the one who started this luxury." Loretta then replied, "I have no idea about Cognac, so a little wine with the meal will be perfect." Once they made the choices, Tim asked the server to suggest a wine that would go best with their selections. The server suggest a Chablis that was good for both of their choices and Tim request a glass for each of them. The server asked if they would prefer a bottle and Tim replied that just a glass for each would be sufficient.

The conversation before and during the meal was largely family oriented as to children and such. The meals were absolutely delightful and the wine was perfect for it. Tim took care of the charges for the luncheon, and they returned to the office for the remainder of the day.

Tim once back to his office went over the proposal the new recruits had presented. It was exceptionally well-conceived. It started out with the basis of the current environment research being over 15 years past was outdated by more recent research into the serene surrounding of the analyst's office space. More recent research was fully documented, it showed that the all-white environment was best utilized in places the person's being subjected to it, were temporary and limited to two weeks in such an environment. The places most likely to use this were hospitals for patients required to stay for a short period of time, whether for diagnostic or recovery procedures. Operating rooms were still largely using this environment, but seldom did any person remain within the room for more than 8 hours. Those people who worked in such facilities, normally had offices or other rooms that were not so sterile. Often rich wood desks whether real wood or synthetic materials were used was not important. Those that had offices, usually had family photos and other types of pictures within the room. Extended exposure to an all-white environment led to depth perception difficulties and other sight issues similar to snow blindness. This reference is used extensively throughout the research, as it is the most known problem in climates that are often snow covered. Tim concluded it was very well documented with research references including where and what group did the research. It also referenced how to get the entire research results and documentation from the IG. Tim also made a mental note to inform the board they may have to start replacing walls, if the robotic systems continued to run into them as the director had mentioned, there was a lot of banging and bumping heard throughout the day from his office.

His next chore was to put together his own proposal to changes in the current retirement program. Tim started out with, since Global already committed to a number of ten year contracts, they should not be altered in anyway shape or form as these people were subjected to higher stress levels prior to the changes that have made their jobs much easier. Once every last robotic computer system was in place, his findings were from the medical staff here in Seattle, where the stress levels were always the most significant in the company. The robotic systems in Seattle have made it so every analyst is now fully engaged in learning what the system can do for them. With the AI also performing 95% of all the required work, the Seattle headquarters was experiencing a mere 5 percent stress related issues. Of this 3 percent bring the stress with them from outside of the work environment. It means from our medical staff's experience that the stress levels in Seattle, are no different than any other position in the working environment. Whether an initial 10 year contract is still to be utilized is the Company's option, but Tim did not believe it would be necessary to change that. The company could still offer retirement options after the completion of 10 years, but Tim would suggest the amount be reduced to 40% from its current 75%. This would be a good reduction in expenses. Whether additional extensions be done annually or in five year increments only to analysts once 15 years is reached, retirement could be incremented to 50% with 65% after 20 and 75% after 25 years. It would still be advantageous for people to want to work here a full 25 years, with the prospect of being able to retire on an extremely nice monthly amount, 20 or more years ahead of this country's normal retirement age of 70.

Additionally, with longer terms to reach full retirement potential, the company should not have the number of analyst's in life long care facilities, or the number of positions to fill as a result of stress overload syndrome. Tim believed he had covered all the basics for his proposal, which he believed would be accepted by the board as it meant a significant cost reduction in the way they currently did business. It was not like a company with between 125 and 150 billion WC in assets would require more, but it would allow them to retain it for far longer periods. He did not know; but assumed they also had some of the more liquid assets invested for additional profits to be used towards retirement and long term care.

He had completed his proposal with at least two hours left in the work day, so he decided he could leave the building for a short time to go to the shop that was nearby for his disguise materials, and a quick training he hoped.

It only took a few minutes once out of the building to locate the shop, and he entered with some apprehension. The salesperson was more than helpful, as Tim explained he was entirely new to the use of such items, but felt to achieve his objective he needed to change his appearance. In order to visit various offices under his company, to insure all procedures were being performed correctly and accurately. The salesperson understood his dilemma, and showed him some of the things most useful for what he had described. Tim further explained, he had no previous experience in employing these items, and wondered how long it would take to learn it. The salesperson said it would only take a few minutes, as it really was quite simple. Tim selected three different hairpieces with matching facial hairs, some only mustache others both beard and mustache. The salesperson also suggested a makeup kit, which would allow him to change his feature subtlety if the surrounding required it. It included several shades of tanning makeup as well as colors for his eyebrows, since they should match the color of the hairpiece. This was something Tim did not consider, but thought it a wise suggestion. The makeup kit he obtained, also had places to keep the hairpieces and facial hair from becoming overly disturbed. The salesperson explained that Tim did not want to have the hairpiece looking like he just got out bed. The cost was not exceedingly large, although it was higher than he anticipated, but once again never having used such materials before, he had no idea how costly they should be. The salesperson said that some of the cost was a result of the hairpieces and facial hair being made of real hair, instead of synthetic material, which was cheaper, but often easily damaged making them unusable. If you spend a little more to start with, you actually save in the long run as the items do not have to be replaced unless something catastrophic occurred. Fire was the one thing that nothing could hold up to including real hairpieces. Tim did not think he could hold up to fire either, but he did not think his suspect would have a flamethrower strapped on either. It would be awfully conspicuous to wander around Hong Kong with such an item.

The salesperson showed him he only need to apply an adhesive material to his face for the facial hair to stay in place, and also showed him that in the makeup kit a bottle of alcohol that was used to remove the adhesive, when he removed the facial hair. It was necessary to make sure it was removed from both his face and the facial hair backing for a next use. It was not water soluble for the simple fact he could get caught out in the rain. It would not be a good idea to have his facial hair fall off as a result.

The whole process took 30 minutes, and Tim returned to the office with his newly acquired makeup kit to take home that evening. At the end of day, Tim got his makeup kit and departed for home.

***

The next three weeks were completely routine with the exception of a long pleasures session that evening. Based on how Kuri behaved during the session, Tim got the distinct impression that Kuri was trying for child number two in the household during the next nine months. It was not like she had not given him ample warning. Tim was fully aware it was entirely in her control, as to the timing of the next event that would result in less sleep at night for a little while. It was still a marvelous night with Kuri and he sleep quite well afterwards.

On the start of the fourth week at the office, Tim received the vidphone contact of Detective Marshall. Detective Marshall asked, "How well have you studied the pictures I forwarded to you?" Tim replied, "The day I received them, I spent five hours first concentrating on the facial features, then picturing them with different hair colors and lengths as well as potential facial hair. I then have spent one hour each day since refreshing those images. I feel I can spot either one of them easily, even in a crowd as large as Hong Kong has for pedestrian traffic." Detective Marshall said, "Good, although you could have warned me just how congested this place is, when it comes to people on foot." Tim said, "I do not believe unless you see for yourself, that any amount of words could do that justification." Detective Marshall, "Yes, I believe that assessment it quite accurate. At any rate, I have found with all the people coming and going, another set of eyes unfamiliar to our suspect might prove useful, so consider this your one week notice. I will expect you in Hong Kong next Monday, and assume you will be staying in the same hotel, which is quite luxurious for the likes of myself. I am far more accustomed to some real dives for accommodations, largely because that is what the department can afford. I am typically content with walls that do not flex with a simple touch, much less any type of force." Tim said, "That sounds much too shabby for my liking, I much prefer the accommodations this company has found for traveling to other countries." Detective Marshall said, "No doubt, you could get spoiled by your company, only good thing for me is I do not get to spend large amounts of time here to be spoiled too badly, although the restaurant is a whole different matter. They do not know how to serve a mediocre meal in any strength of the imagination." Tim stated, "No, being associated with Global Security Corporation does have its perks." Detective Marshall said, "You call them perks, I would love to see what castle you live in." Tim said, "My homes are relatively modest." Detective Marshall replied, "You said homes as in plural, how many do you have?" Tim said, "I have two in Seattle and Kuri, my wife, and I have one in Tokyo. The first house had been in the family since I was born, and could not see it changing families, so I keep it as guest home. It did get some use while her brother and his family got acclimated to Seattle, and found a home of their own. Just in time for her parents to take up residence, while they decided whether to stay in Seattle or Tokyo, where he has five other restaurants to oversee."

Detective Marshall, "I must be in the wrong line of work to miss out on so many luxuries, although I am a rich man, if I view it from a family point of view. Three children all of school ages and a lovely wife. My oldest son is quite the football star, and even though he is only in his first year of high school, he already has had a dozen college recruiters keeping an eye on him. It would be quite marvelous if he got a full scholarship for his football skills as a pass receiver. This year, I saw him climb the ladder as they say, to get one finger on a ball that he slowed down enough to get his hands on, before it came close to touching the ground, and race toward the end zone for a touchdown. It was quite spectacular from my viewpoint." Tim said, "That does take some kind of talent, I played sports as a youngster and preferred football, but I broke my wrist. and during the six month's it took for the doctor's to decide it had healed sufficiently not to cause any more problems, my mother decided I was not going to play football any more. The sad truth of it though is, I was not good enough at any sport to be a highly paid professional, and had to take a different path."

Detective Marshall, "Much the same for me, except I did not break anything, I simply could see far better players than myself, even within my own team, but I still love the sport and fantasize about being that guy who did everything it took to win. So I try to apply that to what I can do. At any rate, I need to get back to surveillance, maybe I can get a handle on these peoples location before you get here." With that the vidphone disconnected, and Tim was looking at a blank screen retracting into the ceiling. He no longer considered Detective Marshall rude for his abrupt endings, he just figured the detective had too much to do with the hours he had to work with. This was the first time Tim had discussed anything other business. The board meeting was scheduled for tomorrow, so he thought he could wait until the meeting to inform Trask he would be needed starting next Monday, while Tim's was in Hong Kong.

Tim was not much longer off the vidphone when Nora announced that Sooni Hakawa from Tokyo was calling into him specifically. Tim told Nora to put it through and the vidphone dropped out of the ceiling with Sooni already waiting. Tim asked, "What do I owe the pleasure of your company today?" Sooni said, "I told you I would let you know who my replacement was to be, and the decision has been made for Soo Kawasaki, she was considered for the position when I first got it. Since, she has been with the company only a year less than myself, I decided it was her time to advance up the ladder. I believe I told Kuri about the wedding date being next week, but since you are so busy with this problem of a murder, I did not think you would be able to attend if I sent invitations to you. It is not like I do not want you and especially my dear friend Kuri to be here for it. Considering the conversation with Kuri that you have been so involved with this problem, she and I decided it best not to send an invitation and have it alter your plans." Tim said," It is short notice for me, since I did not even know you had this planned so far along. I just made the arrangement to be in Hong Kong next week starting Monday, to see if we could find out where the suspects for the murder of our analyst might be residing. I will be working directly with the authorities, one of whom is from Seattle, and decided he could use my assistance. Anything you need as a wedding gift although, it would likely be too late for the wedding from me?" Sooni replied, "I informed Kuri of the options, and did not realize she did not tell you anything before, but I am not getting any younger. If I am going to have a family, I best get started before I dry up and turn to dust."

Tim responded with, "I do not believe that is possible from any female of your origins, I can see other women with that issue long before a woman from Japan. You know too much in the ways of preventing that type of problem." Sooni said, "I see Kuri has trained you well in the chemistry of our women, although she likely knows far more than many women from Japan, considering her ancestry." Tim said, "She told me how most Japanese women teach their young women in the ways of pleasure, based on the knowledge they acquired from their mother so on so forth. She said something to the effect that at some point, all women had an ancestor who was at some point in time a geisha, and from that they learned to pass it down from one generation to the next." Sooni said, "Yes this is true, but not all geisha houses were equally trained in those arts. I believe Kuri had an ancestor in one of the finest ever known in Japanese history, and it was far superior to all of the others. Some of poorer houses had inadequate training, and as a result failed to stay in business. Some also failed to provide better training over time and failed for that reason. As I said, not all houses had equally trained geisha girls. I will be leaving the

Tokyo office in two days, and enter the next phase of life as a woman of Japan. You and Kuri stay in touch, I will let Kuri know how to reach me after the wedding, and we have a suitable residence." Tim bid her good fortune in her endeavors as a wife to some lucky guy, whom Tim did not hear who it was.

The following day had the board meeting in the morning, where Tim opened up by saying he was expected in Hong Kong come next Monday, which the majority of board did not understand why he was, but Trask did, and he shook his head in acknowledgement. Tim stated, "I have a proposal, which I believe to be quite profound from a group of three of the newer recruits, and they claim to all have an equal part in it. Tim went through fifteen minutes of explanation and the current research which he would give to Trask at the conclusion for them to go through for an answer to the proposal. He also made it a point to state that the current 35th floor director is being continually interrupted by the constant bumping and banging of robotic systems unable to judge where door or wall is, have insufficient depth perception in the sterile environment. He then spent another 30 minutes going over the details of his proposal for analysts hired after the last robotic system was put into operation. Tim could tell from the faces of the board members, this proposal would have no problem going through, as the dollar signs lit up in everyone eyes that were board members. Trask asked if Tim expected another bonus on top of his already large salary, to which Tim replied he never expected bonuses, and he felt he was already paid quite beyond his duties as it was. Trask stated that was not possible, as he had been instrumental in so many of the changes that got the company to this point already. Trask said as Tim already knew, that bonuses for the most part to those who had earned them in the past, were now included into their monthly salary. New proposals, such as that of the new recruits, if a bonus were deemed appropriate would still be issued. Tim also included in his proposal that since the current medical staff is likely a bit bored with lack of practicing their skills, which although he saw no reason to induce cut backs, should anyone leave, it might be best to discuss with the head of the staff, if a replacement will be needed. Tim added he suspected that if there is not much practice for these types of specialist, they may leave of their own accord, to go somewhere they can better utilize their training and grow from experiences elsewhere. Tim did have to entertain a number of questions from the board members concerning his proposal, which he felt he answered properly to remove any haze from the picture of where he was going. He did repeat that they were committed to fulfill all the current contracts already in place, and it would be damaging to the corporate image, if it were altered after a signed contract was in effect. Every one of the board members seemed to fully understand the possible damage such would cause.

Once all the questions were satisfied, and Trask called and end to the meeting, Tim presented Trask with both proposals. Trask asked, "Since I am expected to be here next Monday for up to two weeks, is there anything I should be aware of that is pending over your head, aside from the investigation. Tim told him there was nothing that he was aware of at the moment. He did not know how up to date he was on the robotic systems, and told him where they stood on that issue, but suspected he got more up to date input from his son far more frequently. He did ask Trask one question, "In all the time you were sitting in the CEO desk, why did you not ever take Loretta to lunch?" Trask looked at him funny and pondered the question, trying to remember when he did take her to lunch, and came to the conclusion he never did. Finally he said, "I guess it just never occurred to me, she has always been just out of sight most of the day, and it was not often I went past her desk outside of coming and going for the day. I usually arrived before she did, and left afterwards, although not terribly much longer. Do you think I should do that while you're in Hong Kong?" Tim said that was not for him to say, but it might be nice if he did. Tim added, "Beside if you want her to give you good input when I am back in this office, it might sway her some to know she is not underappreciated and forgotten by you." Trask said, "Duly noted. Have you had Loretta to lunch?" Tim said, "Twice since finding out her name that last time being three weeks ago, where she enjoyed her meal and the Chablis." Trask said, "What no cognac?" Tim replied, "It was offered, but she never had it before, and decided not to try something new she might dislike." Trask said, "I have not met a single person who dislikes cognac, so maybe we get her to try some soon. And how did you figure out I was getting updates from Loretta?" Tim said, "Since you have always looked at Global Security Corporation as yours, it made perfect sense you would not stay away for extended periods of time, without some feedback from someone. Since none of the computers had any means to reach you, Loretta was the most logical choice."

Trask said, "You are definitely too darned smart for your own good sometimes, and the really bad thing about it is she keeps telling me you run a better ship than I did." Tim said, "See what a couple of lunches will get you in return." He then gave a rather short evil laugh to emphasize the point. Trask said, "That reminds me, how do you change gears from playing hardball to subtle persuasion?" Tim said, "I have no idea what you're talking about." Trask said, "I heard from a certain government specialist that you persuaded the military to rapidly release records to the Seattle authorities concerning our suspected murderers and used hardball tactics. Shortly after you got some other information from a local general concerning laser light transmitters, and offered him a rather lucrative numbered account long not used. It was also brought up that the agreement would be half the money for infrastructure repairs, which by the way if you have not noticed, road repairs are being done all over Seattle, and who knows how many other places."

Tim said, "Sorry, I had not noticed since my transport never touches the road, and I have not seen any vehicles or signs to indicate such activity." Trask replied, "That is likely because the synthetic materials they use requires little drying time, and will last many years beyond the older materials. You still did not answer the question though" Tim said, "I tried to be subtle with the military records people, but they were uncooperative, until I pointed out as a part of the national government it was likely that all their funding was funneled through us, and it would be terribly unfortunate if it got diverted for some other purpose. I do not consider that to be truly hardball, as it was only suggestive." Trask said, "You do play hardball, you just do more gracefully than I do, and I have no subtle nature to change gears to. So at least I understand how Loretta can say you run the ship better, you have better moves than I did or do, whichever is most applicable." Tim said, "I did learn from one of the best, but some qualities are all my own and I do not believe they can be taught." Trask said, "No they cannot, it is one of those qualities you either have or you don't, although it might be possibly to teach at a young age; but your parents have to have those qualities, and mine did not."

The conversation concluded, and Tim returned to his office and had Nora call his house just to make sure that he told Kuri he was going to be needed in Hong Kong next Monday, but for how much of the two weeks he did not know. She said he did bring it up the previous evening, and wondered why he thought he might have forgot, as it was not like him to forget anything. He said to Kuri he thought he had, but the last two days have been a bit of a blur with everything happening so quickly, he just wanted to make sure it was not something he intended to do, and did not. She assured him he did remember and then Tim said he would see her when he got home, and ended the vidphone connection.

Tim had to concur with Kuri's observation that it was not like him to forget anything, and he tried to retrace his actions from the night before once he was home, as a mental exercise. His little exercise was rather precise, and he indeed remembered the moment when he told Kuri about his being requested in Hong Kong, but it was so quick that he put it out of his thoughts as a done deal. That at least explained why he could not remember having completed the task. He also went through his makeup kit, and found a rather extensive bit of information in a pamphlet concerning the use and application of the various components, including ones he did not obtain. He did find he had the moisturizing cleanser for removing any makeup. It was also suggested that if harsher cleansing tool were used, to consider using this moisturizing cleaner after to prevent any effect from the other, such as alcohol, which dried the skin considerably for many.

CHAPTER

14

With all the arrangements made and making certain that Kuri knew who to contact in the event of any problems while he was away, he departed to the airfield where the private jets were kept. He had two weeks of clothing packed, and his makeup kit and had no difficulty finding a place to leave his transport for the up to two weeks he might be away. As a result of the time zone difference to Seattle, he left on Saturday evening instead of Monday morning, expecting to arrive in Hong Kong early enough to be able to go to the hotel. He anticipated enough time to get his clothes unpacked and hung, although this time he had far more casual clothes than a business trip would permit. Before getting into the hotel transportation, he asked the crew to stay in Hong Kong for the duration of his stay, as long as it was not required to be somewhere else for business. The crew said they would, but it was possible that Global Security Corporation might have need of them elsewhere, and if that was the case, they would leave a message for him at the hotel. If they did need to leave for any reason, they would make sure they could return to Hong Kong upon completion. With that Tim asked how the company was taking care of their meals and room while away from Seattle. Global Security Corporation had arranged all crew members a bank access card to an expense account for travel purposes of all jet personnel, and they were well taken care of with the use of the card. They also said that certain restrictions applied as far as alcoholic beverage and personal expenses, which was more than acceptable to all of them. It was not uncommon for crew members to pick up keep sakes for family members when visiting other countries, this expense was out of their own pocket. They each had their own limit on what they felt was acceptable spending amounts.

Tim arrived at the hotel at approximately 5:30 PM Hong Kong time Sunday, which was plenty of time to get unpacked and hit the hotel restaurant for a good meal. Hong Kong like many other large cities never seemed to sleep. It was a 24 hour a day city, so the restaurant was always open for business, although in the early hours of the morning, food preparations were done more slowly as the cleaning process was also a necessity. Once he had dinner, and returned to his room, he performed his meditation routine to get in harmony for some sleep. He wanted to get up early enough to do what he planned.

He was successful in being in harmony within himself and his surroundings, and was able to sleep quite well. He arose 20 minutes ahead of his wake up call for 6 AM. He cancelled the wake up which was done simply through voice to the room system involved in wakeup, time of day and appointments to make. Not as much as an in home system; but quite sufficient for most all temporary living facilities. He quickly got cleaned up completely, and it was time to try out his makeup kit to become someone else that even Detective Marshall might not spot easily.

He selected one of the hairpieces that had only a mustache, and trying not to get too much adhesive on his face, he placed the mustache over his upper lip and made sure it was equally displaced. Once satisfied with the way the mustache laid, he fitted the hairpiece on, making sure it completely covered his own hair. He had initially selected this particular hair and facial hair combination, because it would require no additional makeup for his eyebrows or facial features. He select casual clothing that would give people of Hong Kong the impression he was a first time visitor to their piece of the world. A tourist was not out of place in the city of Hong Kong. Most natives of the city were not surprised by the tourists, but could easily make the decision they were indeed tourists. He had time for breakfast, and made it to the restaurant with more than enough time for his favorite breakfast in Hong Kong, consisting of the Hong Kong omelet, hash browns, and a muffin with preserves. The coffee was fresh, so he got that as well, knowing it would still only be acceptable. It was all taken care of including the charges to his room with 15 to 20 minutes before he expected to meet Detective Marshall in the lobby.

Tim did not have a means to contact Detective Marshall as of yet, only a time to meet him in the lobby. Since the detective was staying in the same hotel, it was nearing the 8 AM meeting time and Tim left his room for the lobby area. He was relatively sure he could spot the detective long before the detective would locate him. He was only in the lobby 10 minutes, when he spotted the detective who was not in any type of disguise, but wearing clothing less conspicuous than that of a law enforcement person. Tim saw him looking around and right at him several times before Tim approached him. Tim asked, "You looking for anybody in particular?" The detective immediately recognized the voice, but was taken by surprise of Tim appearance. Detective Marshall said, "I must say, you do look quite different than on vidphone. Where did you get the stuff to alter your appearance so much, good job by the way?" Tim explained there was a shop close to his office in Seattle, and they were the only location in Seattle that provided any type of training in the use of this stuff. Tim was not accustomed to either the adhesive or the mustache, and hoped that he could ignore them enough not be blatantly obvious it was new to him. The detective handed him a rather small ear piece and said this is to keep in contact with the group, who are in on this surveillance project. He continued with, "The group uses code names as opposed to true identification, since this is my operation I am papa bear, we have one female from the local authorities she is mama bear, the other four members are wolf, and piggy 1 through 3 you will be baby bear as you are the newest to this type of work. This small earpiece is both send and receive and is extremely sensitive, so you only need to whisper to let the group know what you may have found. I will still be your primary contact, and I have a location for you to sort of maintain, but you cannot sit in one place extensively to keep from being spotted by those we seek.

The hotel was located about one block east of the local office that was leased by Global Security Corporation. The major apartment complexes were all located farther west, and the detective was placing Tim approximately half way between the hotel and the start of the apartment complexes. The apartment complexes were all high rise buildings, some having multiple levels underground as well as mezzanine levels before getting to the numbered floors that went from 1 to 99 for several and the other were just short of 90. They were very tall buildings regardless, and most elevator systems were limited to two digit numbering. All the apartment complexes had mezzanine levels, where various shops and restaurants were located, largely for the residence of the buildings. Residents could also go into other apartment complexes mezzanine levels in order to have a little more variety, and not every apartment had the identical shops or restaurants. Most all the apartment complexes cover a wide range of apartments, some of the smallest did not have kitchens, and those residents needed to visit the restaurants for the meals they required. It was not a problem to many of them, as they had no cooking experience anyway, so they already were delegated to purchasing meals. Every apartment complex had one restaurant for the budget conscious resident. The meals here were inexpensive and simple, but accomplished the need for meals.

The apartment complexes also had penthouse apartments for the business executives that had no financial issues to be concerned with. The largest was 10,000 square feet and these were rented at 1 million WC per year. Only annual contracts were available on penthouse apartments, with the entire year being paid in advance. There were smaller penthouse apartments that were available for less currency; but the one year advanced payment was required on all penthouse apartment. Since occupancy was never an issue for the apartment complexes, one penthouse apartment normally belonged to the building owner. The owner had the pick of the entire penthouse selection at one time, and since ownership did not normally leave the family, it was based on when the apartment was first built. Most of the owners were able to relocate to higher and larger penthouse apartment as the buildings reached higher altitudes. Many of the apartment complexes were at the maximum building height allowed in Hong Kong, the few that were not, were not far from it, and with at the most had room for 10 additional floors. The owners to this point determined the expense was greater than the potential rents received.

As Tim and Detective Marshall were heading farther east of the hotel, it was near time for many people to be heading into the work space they were required to be in. Half way to the destination Tim was expected to be placed, Tim spotted an anomaly that caught his attention. He did a quick study and the facial features matched his one suspect and the dark wig and mustache were not in conjunction with the lighter colored eyebrows. He was also heading west, which put Tim into an unknown alarm mode for the quick sighting. He told Detective Marshall he needed to check the person out a little better to be sure it was whom he thought it to be, and did an about face back toward the hotel. Tim tried to maintain a fair distance from his suspect; but not lose sight of him in the large work crowd in Hong Kong.

He almost lost him twice; but managed to reacquire his target who was now past the hotel and heading in the direction of what concerned Tim most. He saw the suspect enter the building of Global Security Corporation, and that was his biggest concern. He remained away from the door long enough to have allowed him to enter an elevator, but Tim could not get close enough to see which one. He entered the lobby area and headed to the security desk where he inquired from the guard where the person he thought to be an old acquaintance might be heading to. The guard was rather inclined not to give a perfect stranger any kind of information concerning those people who were allowed into this building. Tim asked more politely if he was heading to Global Security offices where he knew a fair amount of people, and suggested to his acquaintance that they might have use for his particular skill set. The guard did confirm he was going into the Global Security offices, but would not divulge any more information. He was somewhat relieved that the guard was prone to security more than giving away information that was nobody's business, except those who worked within the offices. Tim left the building and went back to the hotel, where once in the elevator he said quietly to his communication equipment "Papa bear I am following up a lead so forgive me, this may take longer than I anticipated." It was acknowledge quickly, and Tim got to his room and immediately called Global Security Corporation to get in touch with his longtime associate if not friend, Cho Ling. It took a few minutes to get connected between the hotel and the Global's security functions, but finally Cho was at the other end and the first thing Cho said, "How did you get this number?" Tim had almost forgotten he was incognito and said, "Cho this is Tim, even if I may look a little different it is imperative we meet very soon." Cho going from concerned to surprised, said, "How do I know it is you?" Tim thought about it for a second and said, "How is the wife doing since leaving her college for a more mundane life?" Cho smiled and said, "She is doing fine, taking care of the child who is not yet a year old and what is with that new look?" Tim said, "I would prefer to make explanations face to face, but I need you and whoever is involved in your most recent hiring, to meet me in the lobby where we can get a seat at the restaurant, and be little less conspicuous, if you do not mind." Cho said, "Is there something I need to be aware of." Tim said, "Only that if the person I saw enter your building not long ago is a communication technician, then we have a problem. I do not know what name he might be using, but his area of expertise would be communications, most like the TRU's we employ." Cho said, "That is not much to go on, but I will find out who did the most recent hiring of any such type of person and try to be there in 30 minutes." Tim thanked him and stated in the lobby to start with.

Tim waited in the lobby nearly 45 minutes before Cho and another person entered the lobby area. Cho, still rather unaccustomed to Tim's appearance did not spot him until Tim started walking towards them. Cho said, "I still cannot get over how different you look." Tim did not reply as much as motion them to follow him to the restaurant, where they got a slightly secluded table so they could talk. Tim asked if any of them wanted coffee or anything else while they were here. The Human Resource person whom Tim did not know by name, asked if he was allowed to get some breakfast as he had to rush out this morning without it. Tim told him to order whatever he wanted he would put it on his room charges without any problem. Tim then asked, "Have there been any recent hires in the communications group?" The Human Resource representative said, "Strange thing is that our former communications technician had not shown up for work for several days, and did not call in with an explanation. He is an older individual with health problems that have kept him from making it to work from time to time; but he always called to let us know. He has a position that is not overly demanding, so we have always given him the time to recover from his health issues. We checked all the locations where he could have been taken in the event of a medical emergency and got nothing from any of them. After five days without hearing from him and having no idea where he may have disappeared, a walk in, looking for work who had all the qualifications for that position was brought in with the knowledge that it may not be permanent. He started three days ago, although two of those days were weekend. He had a nice, but unverifiable resume, since he was a self-employed government contractor involved largely in laser light transmitters and satellite positioning technology. Governments do not track the contract employees, and since they are typically term related, outside of access to what they need done, there is no real paperwork to follow up with. Also being his own boss, there was no means to contact anyone to vouch for him. He did have the qualification and we had the need it seemed, so he was brought on in Hong Kong."

The Human Resource representative placed his order in the slight pause and Tim ordered coffee and Cho ordered tea. Tim asked what name this person was going by and this got a strange look; but the answer was James Hodgkins. Tim said, "Since the communication systems is not accessible through the main computer system, has the previous technician's access been suspended or revoked?" Cho answered for both of them, "Unless the other technician was explicitly told to do so, it is unlikely, but only the head technician in communication has that ability, much like all the other offices including your own." Tim replied, "I need this James Hodgkins to have zero access to the TRU's, also I need your head technician to suspend the former persons access; but prior to that, to check the TRU logs to see if during his absence, he manage to access it."

Cho said, "What is going on here, we do not normally do these types of things that I am aware of, although no new employee is given immediate access to any equipment, except analyst only to their very own computer system?" Tim responded, "I believe this person you call James Hodgkins is really one of the people behind the death of an analyst in Seattle three years ago. This is largely why I appear the way I do, as this morning was my first step in Hong Kong in quite some time. This is where the trail has led, and I do so want this murder to see closure for this company. I do not take defeat well as I can testify from the Robin Torry incident when I was still AD in Seattle." Cho said, "Would it not be a little too blatant for a person responsible for the death of an analyst to go to work for the same organization he is trying to avoid?" Tim said, "It was once said the best place to hide was in plain sight, and he may be bored with little to do over the last three years. It also seems rather convenient for a person to show up for a position five days after the original holder vanishes. I hope no harm has come to your other technician who went missing, but I will bet James has a hand in it."

With that said, Cho got his intellipad out and made the call to the office to be directed to the head technician who answered almost immediately. Cho asked, "Are you alone?" The technician said, "Currently I am as I have James on the roof for TRU test procedures that usually take an hour or more. He has been gone 15 minutes, why do you ask?" Cho said, "This is directly from the CEO, first has the missing technician accessed the TRU system since disappearing?" The technician stated, "That is a rather unusual thing to ask of a missing person, but I will check, give me a few seconds." He was not long but answered "This is quite unusual, it has been accessed twice, the first time it appears only long enough to verify access, and the second appears to have been long enough to check the configuration; but no alteration were made." Cho said, "That access code needs to be suspended or revoked, whichever can be done from your end, since I am not knowledgeable enough to know which." The technician said, "Okay, that is done, I can only revoke. Now can I ask why this is being done?" Cho said, "I am going to pass you over to Tim your CEO, although you may not recognize him I sure didn't." He handed the intellipad over to Tim and Tim said, "I believe your latest addition to the staff is a murder suspect we have searched for three years, but I need to try to keep him in your company until his sister can be located, and apprehended as well." The technician said, "Do you not think suspending the access will give him the hint." Tim said, "Just say it is standard company procedure when an employee leaves and that should suffice, although he really should have no reason to ask, unless he is the one using it." The technician said, "I will do so, and hope I do not give it away that he may have been discovered, I have no past experience for this sort of thing." Tim said, "Just try to act as business as usually, it normally works." Tim then handed the intellipad back to Cho, who checked to make sure his connection was ended before putting it away.

Cho stated, "This is definitely stepping out of the box for us." Tim said, "We have been in uncharted territory from the very beginning of this problem, so why change it now?" Cho said, "Maybe for you, but this is a new experience for me, next you'll be asking me to get out my old decoder ring and give you encrypted messages." Tim said, "I do not think we have reached that point just yet, but I will keep it in mind." That at least got chuckles from the three of them. Breakfast, coffee and tea had arrived, and did not take exceptionally long for it to all disappear. Tim did ask if the human resources person had a photo of each employee taken during the hiring practice. It was company procedure and he always followed the practices of the company. Tim asked if he could get the most recent photos of both James, and the previous technician that James replaced.

The Human Resource person said he would get them off the computer system and asked where to send it. Tim had him send it to his intellipad that he had in his room, but he knew the address it responded to from out of his memory banks. With breakfast done for one, Tim let the two of them return to their normal daily activities while he took care of the charges to his room. He returned to his room, and waited for the photos to be sent and also gave papa bear a heads up on what he believed he had found. Since, James Hodgkins was not likely to depart from work until five PM Hong Kong time, Tim tried to figure out what he could do to follow him to his residence, if possible. It would have been nice to have a way to place people on the way between the Global Security Corporation offices to the apartment complexes but he could not provide the pictures for them to use.

After a 45 minute wait for the photos to show up on his intellipad, he noticed the features were indeed those he was looking for, and now he had to find a way to get this information to the authorities. His best possible means was to use the communications gear provided him and he spoke a little louder being in the room. Tim said, "Papa bear, need to meet in lobby have something you need." Papa bear acknowledged and said 20 minutes. Tim went to the lobby and waited for Detective Marshall. He was quite accurate with his 20 minutes, and he took the detective up to his room in the hotel to get the photos on the intellipad. The detective asked, "What is this for?" Tim said. "Look at this picture and tell me it is not our suspect?" The detective studied the picture and denied that he could say any such thing. Detective Marshall then said, "How is it that a person with no surveillance experience is on the street 30 minutes, and spots the suspect when all of Hong Kong, and myself have only spotted to lose again." Tim said, "Good memory skills is all I can say." Detective Marshall said, "You're not one of those rare people with a photographic memory are you?" Tim said, "No, all the testing I went through as a youth proved I did not, but I had a very high retention level for what I read or looked at and only took a few more looks to retain it all."

"What is this other picture for?" asked Detective Marshall. Tim said, "The best way to do this is to start at the beginning from leaving you earlier. I spotted an anomaly as we were heading to where you wanted me to go. It was the person in the other picture, which I believe is the suspect we have been wanting to apprehend. In following him I found him going into a building that greatly concerned me, and I was correct to be concerned, as it appears he is working under an alias in the Global Security Corporation office here in Hong Kong. I had to get confirmation from the security desk guard, and he was reluctant to provide me with any more information than the person was going to the offices of Global Security. He is using the alias of James Hodgkins, so it is unlikely that same name is being used for the residence they are using. Most likely one of the apartment complexes, as this island has very few homes and they use all the space they can for apartments. Once he was inside, I returned to the hotel and contacted my Hong Kong director requesting a meeting with him and whoever was involved in hiring a recent communications employee. At that time I had no name to go by and it took my director 45 minutes before meeting me in the hotel lobby with the appropriate Human Resource representative for the company. During the meeting, we confirmed that first the suspect had indeed started working there because of the disappearance of this person on the second photo. I got the second photo mostly to confirm he was not a John Doe in a morgue on this island. I hope for the best, but have to fear the worst for this individual. Much of what I did during the meeting was for my companies benefit, but I can go into details if you like."

Detective Marshall was intrigued by Tim ingenuity in this so he asked for Tim to go into the details. Tim continued, "The meeting first came to the person who was previously performing the same function as our suspect. It seems he went missing, he apparently has a number of health issues that prevented him from always going into work, but he always called to let the company know of his issues. His position is not as taxing as many others in the organization, so the local personnel worked with this particular individual for his health issues. They checked all the emergency medical facilities for any sign of the missing person, thinking he could have had a medical emergency that prevented him from calling in. They got no such response and after the fifth day he was missing a walk in, who is our suspect, conveniently was hired into his position under the temporary category. This still raised other concerns for me concerning Global Security Corporation on what type of access he was given to our communications system, so I had restriction placed on his abilities to jeopardize our systems. I have made it so the person calling himself James Hodgkins can remain employed there as a means to track him to his location for his sister to be found as well. I did not try to prevent him from returning home, as I believe we want the pair not just the one." Detective Marshall agreed and asked how he accomplished all this in such a short time.

Tim's reply was simple dumb luck as best as he could figure. Tim then went on to say that as an employee of Global Security Corporation the person calling himself James Hodgkins was going to be at Global until 5 PM Hong Kong time. He wonder whether the photo he had of how the suspect looked, as of now, and unlikely to change as long as he was at Global, could be distributed to all those involved in the surveillance team. Detective Marshall did not have a means to send them a photo, but could distribute it the following morning, when he got together with the team. Tim was hoping for better; but knew it would have to do. He said it was then up to him to follow him from Global Security Corporation's offices to see which complex he considered to be safe haven. It also explained why the sighting of the suspects were rare, as they could easily get everything they needed within the apartment complexes. He also said they were far too young to want to remain reclusive, which is likely part of the reason one is working to cope with boredom, or worse planning to cripple Global's communications. Tim said he had to retract to an earlier point as far as the offices were concerned. Tim then stated, "The person who had the job and is missing, has signed into the system twice even though missing. As far as I know the only way to do that is from within the communications area, as this system is not accessible from the main system or remote entry. It leads me to believe that the suspect is involved in the disappearance of the person to hold that position prior to James Hodgkins." Detective Marshall said, "That puts a different twist on this altogether. If he had harmed the person or committed a second murder, that falls under the local authorities jurisdiction. Even kidnapping and holding him captive, is within their jurisdiction, and they are likely far less restricted in interrogation than we are in our country."

Detective Marshall continued with, "It seems in our country, suspected criminals have ten time the rights of any victim. I understand to some degree the precautions of insuring the wrong person is not penalized for something they were not responsible for, but it does make the job far more difficult and prolonged." Tim had nothing to say as he was in an area he had no experience or knowledge of. Tim did say, "I really do not care who gets to take credit for resolving this problem, I simple want it to be resolved, so I can go forward." Detective Marshall completely understood, as three years was a long time to have a murder hanging over the heads of anybody.

Detective Marshall said, "If you are going to try to follow this person to his place of residence, it is imperative you keep a very safe distance. With all the foot traffic in this city, that presents all kinds of obstacles and you could lose him. If that happens do not become overly alarmed as long, as we know what we know now, it is only a matter of time before we can apprehend him and hopefully his sister. I would also prefer the pair; but I will accept either, with the idea we can get some information from the one we bring in. Most likely it will be this person calling himself James Hodgkins, in the meantime, I will double check all the records of the apartment complexes for that last name being the renter. All the apartments must keep records of their residence up to date with the authorities that keep those type of records. They usually are not law enforcement, but we would have access to that information from the local government officials responsible for it."

Detective Marshall said, "I will leave the team in place for now, with the possibility the second suspect might be spotted, and in the event you get into trouble with your following Hodgkins this evening. Do you have a plan in the event you are spotted and confronted?" Tim said, "I simply plan to act like a tourist, who is returning to the place the travel organization arranged, which is the apartment complexes, after a day of seeing the sites." Detective Marshall said, "That seems quite feasible, good thinking."

With that said, Detective Marshall said he should get back to his area for surveillance, not truly expecting to spot the other probable suspect. Tim had no idea what he should do until closer to 4:30 PM where he would wander to the west side of the office entrance, and watched for his known suspect to leave the building. Tim was sure there was more than a single exit to the building; but the elevators were closest to the front exit with the security guard posted there. The other entrances, were largely for service people for the building, and other offices that had no need of the elevator bank. The vast majority required the elevator, and the closest street exit, which was the small lobby area. He decided to go to the restaurant for a decent lunch as his amount of time in the jet and already acting like a spy, was adding up to some time. He was afraid if he did nothing he might nod off and miss his window of opportunity. He spent a long time after getting coffee deciding on what to eat, there were too many selections that peaked his interest to only decide on one. After eliminating many, he still had to decide between three and it came down to two were too heavy for his lack of sleep, so he went with a stew selection that intrigued him. It was Hungarian goulash which he had never had before but it sounded good. The restaurant had become rather busy while he made up his mind on what he would have, and as a result it took longer before his meal was served. It was not like he was in a big hurry; but an hour and a half in the restaurant was excessive to him.

The meal however was quite delightful, even though Tim could not identify what spices were used to generate such a marvelous taste. He was not overly full having just enough to sustain him until dinner, and keep him alert. He decided with only an hour to go for his suspect to emerge, he would go and find a good position to keep track of him leaving the office building. He had hoped to find a good place on the opposite side of the street so he could follow without appearing to be following him.

Unfortunately, there were far too many street vendors with equipment he could not see past for that purpose. That left him on the same side of the street where he found a spot to station himself, approximately a quarter of a block west of the office building. It took him nearly forty minutes, and it was in front of a large shop. Tim acted like he was window shopping to decide if he wanted to enter for a better look at the wares. His suspect exited the office building at 5:05 PM, which meant he was pretty quick to get to the elevator after his work day expired. Once out of the building and his target heading west, Tim began to follow, but the amount of foot traffic was making it difficult to keep track of the suspect. He closed the gap, and followed for nearly half the distance to the apartment complexes when his suspect did an about face. Tim did not panic but continue on his path now heading towards his suspect, and the distance was closing. Tim had merely though he would pass him and find another location to visit farther up the road. Instead, his suspect veered directly into his path and push him toward the building and asked, "What are you following me for?" Tim said, "I did not realize I was, as a tourist to this city and a day of seeing the sights I was trying to make my way back to the place the travel agency arranged for me." The person calling himself James Hodgkins was not expecting the answer but viciously said, "I catch you following me again and you will regret it." Tim said, "Not knowing your schedule, I will try, but cannot promise anything." With that his suspect turned and went once again toward the apartment complexes. Tim feigned fear and went to the other side of the street to continue toward the apartment complexes.

Tim managed to keep track of Hodgkins on the opposite side of the street without being spotted a second time. The apartment complexes were on his side of the street and he knew his target would need to cross near the complexes. Tim maintained reasonable distance and saw the complex that Hodgkins entered. Tim hastened his pace to get to the glass door entry quick enough to see how many got into the elevator with him. He got the doors just as the elevator doors opened, and Hodgkins and two other entered. Tim got inside to watch the floor position that the elevator stopped at. First stop was the eleventh floor where it pause long enough for someone to exit, before repeating the process on floor 26 and finally the 40th floor. Tim whispered into his communications equipment, "Papa bear, the target has enter apartment complex closest to the main street, and the elevator stopped at floors 11, 26 and 40 and there were two others in the elevator when it ascended." Detective Marshall, "You got some courage to keep following after being confronted, what if he had a weapon?" Tim slyly replied, "What if I do?" Detective Marshall replied, excellent work for a professional much less a rookie, meet you where?" Tim replied, "My room will be fine it has been a long day."

Tim hastened his pace to get back to the hotel, and arrived at his room to find Detective Marshall waiting for him outside the door. Detective Marshall said, "I had less than half the distance and no street to cross, so I figured I would get here quicker than you. Tim enter his retina scan to open the door, and as soon as the door was closed he removed the hairpiece went to get a wash linen and removed his mustache with a little bit of pain from hair being pulled. He use the wash linen with some alcohol to remove any adhesive. He now felt like he was going to crack, so he used a bit of moisturizing cleanser and immediately felt better. Tim looked at Detective Marshall and said, "First things first, I been in that all day, and it was beginning to be irritating." The detective agreed with him especially for someone who had never done it before. Tim asked, "What is the plan now that we have discovered the apartment complex being used by these people?" Detective Marshall, "First, I must commend you on your accomplishments for a single day. The local authorities had nearly six months, and did not locate this and for an additional month, neither I nor my team of local people were able to locate them. After tomorrow morning, I can get the photos distributed to the team and after five tomorrow we can have the three little pigs stationed in the hallway of each floor to pinpoint exactly where they are. I am not sure what you need to do at this point but you have gained us more progress in a single day then seven months prior surveillance accomplished."

Tim said, "Since I was confronted, it is unlikely wise to use the same disguise as today and think none at all for the time being." Detective Marshall, "You realize that it takes some people months to figure our variety is a useful tool. You have the makings of an excellent undercover agent, if you ever decide you want to change professions, although I doubt seriously we can afford to pay you what you are accustomed to." Tim said, "Since I have no real assignment for tomorrow, and due to the lack of sleep I have planned on sleeping until I am done to get back to my old self. After that I can check to see if Hodgkins has raised any flags at Global Security Corporation as a result of the restriction I imposed upon him this morning. If he is involved in the disappearance of the previous technician, I see no reason for it to be otherwise, then he may find he no longer can gain access to the communications equipment with the former employee's access codes. Any questions concerning procedure in that arena would be an indication he knows more than he is saying. The only way to truly find out is keep asking about what he is doing while in their offices. It is also important to find the head technician alone to talk with him on the subject. It would be a problem to discuss Hodgkins with his presence with the head technician." Detective Marshall, "You have access to something we do not, so I will let you deal with that as you see fit. I am completely out my league when it comes to your company's procedures and protocols. Being in your position, I am sure you can deviate from them more than others." Tim said, "For three years now, I have been in uncharted territory concerning this problem, so I have had to become a little relaxed in normal process and tread into the unknown. Having my analysts all over the country do interviews with people whose sons or daughters were once employed, was far beyond what we provide in services. Since in this case we are our own client, I have gone outside of the box. I have had to continue to do so throughout this whole affair and hope once concluded, I can remember what is normal."

Detective Marshall stated, "Yes, I would imagine having all the lines erased makes it a little more challenging than chasing other people's money around the globe." Since you are here in the same hotel, what plans you have for dinner tonight?" Tim said, "Due to lack of sleep and needing to perform my meditation program tonight, I was thinking of room service instead of restaurant hopping. Tomorrow might be a better idea for us to dine together, and I would imagine you would like to eat somewhere other than the hotel restaurant." Detective Marshall said, "I am not sure about that, the food here is quite excellent and they change the menu nightly. So there is always something new to try, although, I am a little turned off by the heat levels of the local cuisine, much too spicy hot for me. It keeps me up most of the night with heartburn, and I have no idea where a local drug store is or even if they have what I know to help." Tim said, "You might be rather surprise with the locals on the things they use for medicinal purposes, but then you might also be surprise with the results. The long practiced art of herbs is a Chinese tradition, and even though some taste horrible, they provide very rapid relief in comparison to their chemical counterparts."

The detective said, "Maybe tomorrow you can take me to one these places, and at this point, I would be willing to try anything that might work. Hong Kong seems to like to put a spicy flare to everything they serve, as far as meals are concerned." Tim said, "I believe that is true of the hotel restaurant, but I do know places that serve food not so spicy although it is more Japanese style food than Chinese, but still very tasty. I personally enjoy the hot spicy foods, and have never experience your problem, but understand it can be rather intensely uncomfortable." The detective said, "That is an understatement, it is quite miserable as far as I can tell. Since tomorrow is the soonest we can get a dinner together, I guess I shall hit the restaurant for something to eat, and let you get your activities completed." Tim let the detective out, checked the room service menu for what he might order, and made his selection, called for an expected time which would be enough for a short, but not complete exercise. Tim decided to start with the most beneficial portion of the exercise and be limited to a 20 minute routine as opposed to an hour and 10 minutes.

Tim's dinner was a combination plate consisting of General Tso's Chicken, some Hunan Beef, with fried rice and two egg rolls and fried won ton. As was expected the main entrees were quite spicy, and he had two drinks included in his order one being a mixed alcohol drink and the other Chinese tea. Tim was not the biggest tea drinker, but this restaurant did tea quite well. They were also not real good with coffee. After savoring every bite of his food, he consumed his drinks, although much of the tea was already done with the meal. It was only eight PM; but Tim was exceptionally tired not knowing if it was the travelling or the excitement of the day's activities. He turned down the light after putting the serving dishes and platter in the hall by his door for pickup, and went to bed and was asleep in no time. It was eight AM before his kidneys screamed it was time to dispose of all the liquid he consumed the evening before. Tim was not fully rested, so he went back to bed after responding to his nature call. He slept two more hours and felt far better than two hours earlier.

CHAPTER

15

Tim arose and performed the morning hygiene ritual he had done for as long as he could remember being able to for himself. His memory still had some images where his mother had to help him as a toddler. After that was complete, he decided to give Cho a call to see if there had been any follow up with James Hodgkins. Cho answered with, "Now there's a familiar face, no make believe today?" with the question far more in his voice than in grammar. Tim replied, "Not today, according to the detective, I accomplished far too much so I got the day off." Cho responded with, "That is not unfamiliar territory for you, you have always gotten more done in eight hours than most can do in 24, if my memory has not failed me. I have not heard anything from the communications area today, and find it may not be wise to call without an alternative reason should the lead technician not be alone." Tim said, "That's easy, you are the director it cannot be unheard of you asking someone to report to your office." Cho replied, "That's easy for you to say, you have been at it much longer than I, and I have never asked anyone to report to my office, including myself. I will take your lead though and go with it. Hope he does not need directions, not sure I can tell him how to get here." Tim engage his memory and asked if it was in the same location as last time he was in the offices. Cho replied they did not move it for my benefit. Tim said, "Then you are in the southwest corner as long as it is the same as before. Do you still have the monitoring duties in that office?" Cho said, "Yes, but with the AI doing most of the heavy lifting there is nothing interesting to watch. I remember when Zi was here talking about analyst banging their heads on any surface they could, and other raving at an empty room. Hong Kong has never had the highest stress related problems as other but Zi did say we had some." Tim said, "You may get even more bored when the robotic computer systems start going into your offices." Cho said, "Then you better get me a bed when they show up, there are days now I find it difficult to keep the eyes open." Tim said, "That sounds more like the result of a baby in the house, than work related." Cho said, "Guess I do not need to tell you then, if you can already guess that. Should I ask you if we have a girl or a boy to be certain?" Tim replied, "My guess is a boy, little girls calm down much sooner and acclimate to sleep time sooner also."

Cho said, "Well you guess incorrectly, the girl is nearly 6 months old and still wants to be awake for an hour, sleep for an hour, and we have not found any way to change it. I suspect being in Hong Kong has as much to do with it as anything else, since this city never sleeps. We have not figured out how to make all the noise on this little island to have quiet times, so the baby can sleep in longer increments. I have at least discovered it is usually some loud noise that rouses her, but how to prevent it I do not know. It takes time to adjust, and so many sounds are still relatively new to a 6 month old, it wakes them and they having been startled from sleep do not go immediately return back to slumber land. Yo-Li's doctor said it would eventually become something children would put out of their minds in order to get a good night's sleep, but the time frame varied from child to child." Tim replied, "I guess living in Seattle, I do not have that problem to be concerned about, and never would have thought about the environment being the issue. Hong Kong is undoubtedly populated far beyond the state I live in." Cho said, "Having been there once, I can say from a sleep standpoint, I have never slept so soundly, here it requires putting yourself into the correct mind set to block out the noises you don't want, but then there is still some you do. I do want to hear the wakeup call, but not the sirens or other noises of the night that can pierce the night air."

Tim said, "By the way dad, what is the girl's name?" Cho said, "Did I not tell you already?" Tim replied, "Would I have asked if you did." Cho thought a second, "Likely not, we named her Shoo, it was actually the name of Yo-Li's great-great grandmother, and we Chinese are if nothing else, traditional about names. It is considered a great honor to have the same name as one of your ancestors, who are no longer around to use it. If you want a history lesson I am not the best source for that sort of dribble, but I do follow orders when they are given by the little woman." Tim said, "Funny how that works, isn't it?" Cho simply nodded in agreement. Tim continued on by saying to contact him at the hotel once he got the update from the head communications technician. Tim said he was particularly interested in whether he made any inquiry concerning past employee access codes and procedures. With that the vidphone connection was broken, and Tim got completely dressed for something to eat in the hotel restaurant.

An hour later Cho returned the call with an update. Cho went right into his report by saying, "I did have to request the lead technician to report to my office, as it was the only way to get him alone. As you suspected, Hodgkins asked him about company procedure concerning past employees. The lead technician explained to him and I quote. 'I probably did not get it done within the time frame the company requires as it took me 3 days to find the procedure for a departing employee. Since it did not provide information concerning more than people retiring or leaving of their own accord, it took another day to get clarification from Human Resources on the person you have replaced temporarily. Having never had to deal with this before, I needed to review additional information on how to accomplish it, and finally got it done yesterday in accordance with company policies.' Cho continued with, Hodgkins did inquire which I believe means to you that he is the person who used the access codes to look into our system, since the person went missing." Tim confirmed this to be his suspicion, and thanked Cho for the quick response. Cho said, "I also had to inform the lead technician of where my offices were as he seldom went anywhere within the analyst's office space. He has no equipment there to be concerned with, and only knew how to get to the break area when he had the time. It is a good thing we covered that little detail earlier or you might still be waiting."

Tim said, "You did a good job, and I thank you for this information. Keep an eye out for Hodgkins to prevent him from disappearing before the week is up, please." Cho said he would do his best; but since he was not ordinarily in the area where communications is located, he could make no promises. Tim acknowledged the dilemma and hoped for the best." He got his communication gear and put it in place to see if any activity was occurring and found all quiet. He spoke, "Papa bear is the plan in motions?" Detective Marshall replied, "All is in place, it is a simple matter now of quitting time arriving." Tim acknowledged and kept an ear on the activity, which was little at this time. It was too late for breakfast, so Tim decided an early lunch would help pass some time, and went to the restaurant with his communication gear still in place. Tim guessed that those on the other end were going to know what he ordered for lunch.

Tim chose something relatively simple, but nourishing and to his surprise he only had to give the server a number for his selection, as opposed to descriptive details. It was a roast beef sandwich on rye with Swiss cheese, and bowl of soup for the day, which Tim could not identify from it ingredients, but was tasty just the same. And a small side dish of roasted potatoes with bacon bits, with some sort of mild garlic sauce and sprinkled with a sharp cheese that Tim had never had. Since he could only identify the potatoes and bacon bits, and having already gone down this road in obtaining recipes, he simply enjoyed the delightful tastes of the meal. It accomplished the intended purpose of having food to satisfy his hunger, and he finished it off with tea as opposed to the coffee they made here. He then had the charges put against his room and returned to his room.

During the entire time there was nothing said in the communications gear. Tim figured he had another 4 plus hours to wait for anything to truly become necessary to listen to, so he removed his earpiece and went on to his computer device to see if anything had been sent to him from the Seattle office. He had nothing new there, so Tim decided to take the earpiece with him and go see about the local pharmacy offerings for Detective Marshall and his issues. He did some inquiring and the specialist told him there were 12 degrees of the condition he was seeking to resolve, and without input from the afflicted, he could not be of much assistance without the other party. Tim had no idea there was so many levels of heartburn, as far as what was offered in Seattle. He only knew there was a large variety to choose from and never having needed such an aid, his knowledge of the products was none. Tim told the pharmacologist he would return later with the person requiring the solution, and made sure this business would be open still. He was assured it would be, as the evening produced a much brisker business.

Tim returned to his room at the hotel having spent two hours away from it, and was closer to the time he anticipated any activity from the surveillance team. Time seemed to stand still for the next two and a half hours. Tim felt like it took 48 hours instead of 2 and a half hours, but finally there was activity on the communications equipment provided by the detective. The person calling himself James Hodgkins was spotted leaving the office building, and since his destination was known there was no need to follow him. The next spotting was approximately half way to the apartment complex and the third as he entered the complex. The three little pigs were stationed on each of the three floors Tim provided the day before, and piggy number 2 spotted him exiting the 26th floor elevator. Since people in the hallways of the apartment complex were quite common, Hodgkins did fail to notice he was being watched, and went directly to the apartment he was using as safe haven. Piggy number 2 made sure of the apartment number, and reported it through the communications equipment where he asked for further instructions. He was told he was dismissed for the day, and the other two pigs were to be on the 26th floor no later than 7 AM the following morning. Once the male had departed for the day at the Global Security Corporations offices, they could then take the female suspect into custody. Papa bear was signing off for the evening and returning to the hotel.

Tim pulled his earpiece out and awaited the Detective to arrive as was the plan the night before. Fifteen minutes later Detective Marshall knocked upon his door, and Tim let him into the room. Tim said, "It was good progress for one day. How do we proceed for tomorrow?" Detective Marshall said, "The first thing we need to accomplish is having the female in custody, if that occurs early enough, it may be easiest to get you involved in entering the Global Security Corporation's offices, assuming you can without an escort, and try to take the other suspect into custody." Tim said, "I believe the male suspect may have information concerning the whereabouts of the missing technician, so it is vital we get that information from him. I cannot say if the missing technician is dead or being held captive, but only Hodgkins would know for sure."

Detective Marshall said, "I believe in this country with a kidnapping, the local authorities can involve the military for questioning. The military is not bound by the restriction of law enforcement here, and would likely get the information far quicker than law enforcement. We must first take him into custody, without a fatality to obtain that information. Once cornered, I have no idea what reaction he may have or take as a result."

Tim said, "I can access any building in the company so I was informed, but have never attempted it to this point. It would be best if I and you as well as another member of your team, enter the offices for the purpose of apprehension of Hodgkins. Not having ever been to the area where the communication equipment personnel are located, I cannot provide you with any type of advanced layout to that area of the building." Detective Marshall said, "We will just have to go with it and react in accordance to our suspect." Let us plan on a 9 AM time frame, and I will have mama bear meet us there. This way we will have time to make the other arrest, and have a better opportunity in apprehending the pair. How long it will take after that is accomplished, will truly depend on which country is going to take primary lead on this case. If your missing technician had indeed been killed after being kidnapped, it will likely fall under Hong Kong's authority, and we add the original murder into the equation. There are distinct advantages to Hong Kong getting the arrest as primary. The law here has far more severe penalties for a convicted murderer." Tim said, "Again, I simply want closure to this problem that has gone on for three years, and not truly concerned about whom does it."

Tim changed gears and said, "I did have the opportunity to visit the pharmacy of the locals earlier, and it was made quite apparent that for your problem you must provide better input to the pharmacologist for the best treatment." Detective Marshall said, "I supposed that means we should go there quickly before doing dinner. Did you have any place in particular in mind for dinner?" Tim answered with, "There is a nearby restaurant that serves relatively good Japanese cuisine, which is much more in the milder food types than the locals serve. Having eaten there before, it is not bad food, although having a master Japanese chef for a father in law, I can honestly say his is the absolute best in the world."

The detective said, "Is it as good as the one in Seattle that opened about a year and half ago, it is located at the very edge of little Tokyo in Seattle, and it is absolutely superb. I remember one time we went, the hostess who greeted the guests was an absolute goddess with a body to die for. I do not know how she poured herself into the dress, but it gave away every gorgeous curve of her body." Tim said, "Careful now that is the mother of my child and my wife." Detective Marshall, "I think I should be jealous, she is a sight to behold and with all your money, why is she working there?" Tim said, "She simply fills in to help her brother out from time to time, as so many of his employees are college students, and there are times when classes get in the way of work schedules. She accepts no payment, and usually does not get called until that day she is needed. Her brother is the master chef of that restaurant, taught by his father and it has become the franchise restaurant of the chain of six. The other five are in Tokyo, where her father originally started the restaurant. My father in law has gone from restaurant owner to the overseer of his entire chain. He now lives in Seattle, and once a month goes to Tokyo to insure all the other restaurants are following his processes to the letter. He has grown considerably in the last four years, from a single restaurant to a chain of six, and his reputation is renowned as a master sushi chef. We should probably continue this on the way to the pharmacy, so you can see if the locals have a better and quicker relief for your heartburn."

It was agreed, and they exited the room and left the hotel to go to the pharmacy not terribly far away. Tim said, "They said something about 12 degrees of heartburn, so it will likely be necessary for you to answer questions to obtain the most effective remedy." The detective asked if they could go by the normal over the counter remedy he currently used. Tim did not know and did not inquire when he visited. They arrived at the local pharmacy in ten minutes, and Tim saw there was a much larger number of people inside than previously. The only recourse they had was to wait in the line for assistance from the single pharmacologist, who was the same person he spoke with earlier. It took another twenty minutes; but the pharmacologists recognized Tim and asked, "Is this the person who requires treatment?" Tim nodded in a positive manner and told the detective it was necessary to determine the severity of his heartburn as there are twelve degrees of the symptoms, and equal amounts of remedy. Detective Marshall asked if he gave him the name of the normal remedy if he could work with that. The pharmacologist said he could not, as he was unfamiliar with any other form of remedy than the ones he uses. After answering questions over the exact symptoms the detective experienced, it was decide he was level 9, just short of the acid reflux condition that had been described in other parts of the world. The pharmacologist dispensed 20 pills, which were compress herb combinations specifically targeted to his ailment. They were placed in a small bottle with a label affixed that was largely Chinese characters, with very small English print underneath the characters. He then said, "You may want to wash it down with water, but do not let it dissolve on your tongue as it is highly unlikely you will find the taste pleasant. Take the remedy only at the onset of the symptoms, as it takes only 3 minutes to dissolve in the stomach, and only five to counteract the acid that causes the heartburn. The charges were only about half of what his normal remedy cost, and the detective was quite pleased. Once he had his remedy, he asked one last question, "Since I am from Seattle, and I know we have a Chinese population there, will this label tell another what to provide should I find it more beneficial than my current remedy?" The pharmacologist said, "As long as your pharmacy is fluent in Chinese, and follows the same practices it should be identical."

With that completed, it was time to get dinner. The restaurant was only a couple minute farther east and the detective said, "I have passed this place every day for over a month, and never looked to see what it was." Tim replied, "Now it is time for you to actually enter it, so that you can decide if it was worth it or not. I do not promise you it is as good as Seattle, but quite acceptable."

The restaurant had a fair crowd, but not to the likes of any of Hiro's restaurants. Tim was surprised to see that it was truly owned by Japanese, which was rare in Hong Kong. The server brought menus, and Tim and the detective looked it over and both decided the best thing on the menu was likely the teriyaki steak meal. It included a carafe of sake with the main entree, a rice side dish as well as three teriyaki sticks and some soup. Tim was not familiar with the soup, but that did not deter him from trying it. Before placing the orders, Tim inquired about the origins of the sake, as he knew there were good and bad variations, and he was not too fond of the bad ones. The server said with some pride, "It is our own recipe, and the sake it made by us, I believe it to be quite good, but from my days in Japan, I know of only one that is better. We cannot get that one because of some long standing feud between the maker, and the Chinese that is over 1000 years old." Tim told him since he believed he had had the best, he was willing to try theirs.

The server first brought the sake to the table requesting Tim to sample it. Tim complied and said, "This is quite good, but I agree my father in law serves the best in his restaurants." This got the server a bit suspicious and he asked, "Who might be your father in law?" Tim said, "He is quite renowned in Japan as a sushi master chef that is known as Hiro in Tokyo." The server was quite taken, "It has been quite some time since I have been in Tokyo, and last I knew his restaurant was severely damaged and he was badly injured, has he recovered?" Tim replied, "It took nearly four years for Hiro and his wife to recover from the injuries they sustained in the explosion, and it was touch and go for over the first year they were in the hospital, but they were strong and determined to overcome their injuries. The original restaurant was deemed unrepairable and could only be torn down. He opened a new location, which I do believe is not terribly far from the original. His reputation allowed for the business to return and with a few additions to his menu, the restaurant had long lines awaiting to get in to have his marvelous meals. As a result, he has been able to quickly expand to five restaurant in Japan, and his flagship restaurant in Seattle, where he now lives." The server said, "Then I have been honored with your patronage, I know my food is not nearly as good as Hiro's; but I hope you enjoy what I do offer, and hopefully this business will allow me to get back to Tokyo for a long overdue visit. If I can get there, maybe I can visit his restaurant for a taste of heaven."

20 minutes later the food was brought out to them and they both went about consuming the meal. The soup was quite flavorful being a seafood base stock, which was not overly filling. They both thought the teriyaki steak was acceptable, but would prefer Hiro's, and it was especially true of the rice dish, as it had nowhere near the flavors of the dish that had become so popular for Hiro. Tim knew how it could be improved, but was not going to give away any trade secrets for his father in law. Since he knew he had a hand in Hiro latest entrée that made him so very popular in two countries, he would keep it that way for him. The detective did enjoy the sake, and had never had it before, so it was unlikely he had the best that was discussed. He also found the teriyaki stick quite enjoyable, but was not a big seafood person, even though he lived in Seattle. After the meal was completed, Tim took care of the charges and they made their way back to the hotel. Detective Marshall had no reason to try his remedy, as Tim did at least find a milder food for him to indulge in, and he was not suffering any heartburn issues.

Upon entering the lobby area, Detective Marshall said he would meet Tim at 8:30 AM in the lobby, and should know by then, whether the female was in fact in custody for them to go to the offices. Tim once again felt he did not need to go in disguise, so his preparation time would be entirely normal. The detective said since he had been busy for so long with this case, he was going to his room to retire for the evening, and hopefully be fully rested for the event to unfold. They both got in the elevator, and went to their respective rooms, and detective Marshall was on the floor below his, so Tim still had no idea which room he was in, but he really did not need to know.

Upon returning to his room and doing a short cleanup from the day, he went through his complete meditation routine, which afterwards felt far more in unison with mind and body than the last day. After completion of his routine, he checked to see if there was any world news broadcast on the entertain system, and found one that was actually one of British origins, and far more likely to provide a better outlook on the world events. There was nothing to be concerned mentioned about Seattle or any other major office location so after viewing it, he shut it down. He went to go through his nighty ritual, which included his hygiene as well as a long hot shower, as he believe it was only Tokyo that had the sanitizing units in the rooms. Once dried and feeling much cleaner, he also retired for the evening as his sleep schedule was still a little out of focus for normal. He made sure he would be up by 6:30 AM, and went to sleep within a few minutes.

He was awake 15 minutes earlier than his wake up, and did something he almost never did. He stayed in bed for the fifteen minutes longer to insure the wakeup was taken care of. Once it occurred, he immediately got out of bed feeling far more refreshed, and back to normal, and went directly to take care of his morning hygiene routine. Once completed he selected his attire for the day, which was much more businesslike than before, and after the 30 minutes of taking care of all the morning rituals he departed for a breakfast in the restaurant. He knew exactly what he was in the mood for, and it included those hash browns that took him so long to discover the secrets of. His breakfast consisted of the Hong Version of a Spanish omelet, the hash browns, with three slices of bacon and an English muffin. He chose coffee, and hoped it was not too awful. The restaurant had improved in the coffee department, it was still hardly the best he ever tasted. He was done at 8:15, after taking care of the charges and went to the lobby to await the detective.

He only waited five minutes when the detective appeared from the direction of the restaurant, which was not the same as the elevators. Detective Marshall said, "I do have to say this restaurant offers some really good breakfast menu." Tim agreed and said since he just left the restaurant, how was it they did not spot one another. The detective replied, "Too busy eating to pay any attention most likely." Tim asked if he tried the hash browns with any of his breakfasts. Detective Marshall said, "It is one of the best I ever tasted, so since the first time, I will get them every time I can, while in this city." Tim said, "Agreed, I was so taken by the marvelous flavor the first time I had them in Hong Kong, I tried to find out what the recipes was without any success. The restaurant refuses to provide recipes to any in order to maintain a strong business flow. I can understand that to some degree, but some things should be shared. It took me a good long time to discover the secret ingredients to duplicate them at home." The detective asked, "You mean to tell me that you can make those same hash browns at home in Seattle. Tim said he could, and even give them some more unique ingredients that blend marvelously to create an even better version." Detective Marshall said, "I have no such talents for cooking, so the wife takes care of it, good thing too, if it were up to me we would either be broke from eating out or starve. Neither of which would be acceptable."

Tim said, "When I first started with Global Security Corporation, I do think I had been in my position for a year when my parents offered to sell the family home to me so they could build a place around the family lake property. At the time, I had never done a thing in the kitchen, or any other such dealings with a house. I asked how I was supposed to do it when I had not the first clue about cooking or taking care of a home. My mother showed me all the basics she felt I needed to know, and it grew from there. What I learned from my mother and grandmother, is cooking is forever an experiment. Any recipe can be improved and refined, and there is always something new to consider for any type of food recipe. Some experiments are quite successful in taste and appeal, while others can have horrible results. Simply put if you do not try, you cannot have either, but with failure comes excellence with different ingredients. The kitchen devices do the majority of the work, cooking is preparing the ingredients. All the best recipes use spices and herbs and you as a cook, decide how to put them together for the best taste. It is also important to cook to your own tastes, as you must be pleased with the results before you can expect anyone else to have the same response."

The detective said, "I will keep that in mind when I get back to Seattle, and see if I can be a little more help in the kitchen first." Detective Marshall then said, "The operation at the apartment complex has been successful, the female suspect known as Rebecca Robins is in custody and gave them no resistance. So we are indeed going to the Global Security Corporation's Hong Kong office to try for the same results. I do not believe the male suspect will be nearly as cooperative, so be wary."

They made the short trip to the Global Security Corporation office building and mama bear whom Tim had not met, was also just arriving, and Detective Marshall gave her a wave to indicate they were here. It was only a couple minutes before 9 AM and the three of them entered the office complex. Tim simply stated to the security guard the other two were with him and expected to continue on but the security guard inquired, "And just who are you?" Tim looked directly at the guard and said, "As your CEO I have the power to insure you are not here after today, if you continue with this action." The guard was taken by surprise and said, "I am sorry, I do not see you often enough to recognize you on sight. Is there something I need to be aware of happening here today, as it is not often you enter this office?" Tim said, "You may watch the elevator in the event the person known as James Hodgkins manages to elude us and tries to leave. Since I believe you are unarmed, make no attempt to detain him just make sure of the direction he heads after leaving the building." The security guard acknowledge Tim's requirements and let them continue on to the elevator.

Tim and the law enforcement pair entered the elevator and Tim said, "Here goes nothing, I cannot guarantee this will work as prescribed." He then looked into the retina scanner and the correct floor lit up and the elevator started its ascent. Tim said, "Guess it works, that might come in handy." Once they arrived on the floor that had the offices of his company, he went directly to the director's office and knocked quietly. Cho simply said, "Come in, not having raised his head from the desk that had his attention." Tim said, "This a fine how do you do, I expected better from you", with a short chuckle.

Cho immediately rose from his desk and stated, "Sorry, I was not expecting you since you did not call." Tim said, "We needed to keep a certain element of surprise concerning James Hodgkins, so I thought it best to arrive quietly. Would you like to take us to the area where communications is located, since I have never seen that area of the building?" Cho said, "Immediately, is there anything I should do when we get there?" Tim said, "It would be best that you stay out in the hallway once we arrive, I have no idea what to expect from a cornered rat."

It took almost 10 minutes to negotiate the halls and stairways, as the offices were on multiple floors, but only an elevator to the main. There were elevators specifically for travel within the floors of the Global Security Corporations Hong Kong offices, but they were not convenient for this purpose. Stairways were also much quieter for the purpose they had to perform. Once at the door to the communications area, Cho said, "It is not locked so you may enter at your will." Before entering Tim asked, "Are there any other exits or doors to this area?" Cho said, "None that I am aware of, but you know how they like to camouflage certain things within the offices." Tim was fully aware of that possibility, and making sure that Cho was in position not to get pushed into the room and the authorities ready to take up positions upon seeing the layout, Tim opened the door. The three entered with Cho remaining just outside the doorway, mama bear took an immediate position near the door, in the event the suspect made a hasty attempt to exit.

The room was quite large; but considerably congested as it appear to be the stock room for spare parts for all the equipment utilized by the company. It left narrow passageways between shelving and equipment which was advantageous to them as it would restrict the suspect's mobility considerable. Tim and the detective advanced forward trying to spot where the technicians were most likely to be within the room, visibility was hardly excellent as some of the shelves that were fully stocked with almost no visibility. Tim was as much foreign to this room as the law enforcement officials, but he move onward with the detective close behind. Tim finally located a pair of technician rather well concealed, largely because they were seated as opposed to standing, and performing any activity. They were simply monitoring the conditions of the communications equipment with a specialized diagnostic piece of equipment that Tim was unfamiliar with. He approached quietly and from about five feet away the detective announced, "Artimus Robbins, you are under arrest for theft, murder and possibly kidnapping." James Hodgkin made a quick movement and went after Tim with a vicious looking knife.

Tim's instinctive reaction was to lean back and thrust his leg upward duplicating his exercise he had been performing for several years. The impact to Hodgkins was far greater than Tim considered himself capable of, it also flashed back into his memory all the vulnerable locations of the human body for optimum results. Some points were lethal, while other were debilitating and he caught Robbins directly under his outstretch arm with such a forceful impact that Robbins not only dropped the knife to the floor, he was partial paralyzed on one side of his body. The paralysis was only a temporary condition. Robbins fell to the floor, having lost the use of one side of his body with an impact great enough to dislodge his hairpiece. It did not fall off completely; but was now obvious his hair underneath was not the same color as the hairpiece.

Detective Marshall asked since it happened so fast he did not even have time to get his weapon out completely, "How did you do that, even I cannot react that quickly in times of assault distress?" Tim said, years of martial arts training and daily exercise becomes instinctive I guess, since I did not think, it just happened." The suspect was restrained, and it took an hour for the paralysis to reduce to a point that Robbins could move with some assistance.

The detective careful not to leave any of his own fingerprints or other material on the knife, picked it up from the floor and deposited it in to an evidence container he had upon his person. He examined it and Tim asked, "How is it that he was able to get that through the elevator system with all of its security sensors?" Detective Marshall replied, "It appears to be a ceramic composition, very difficult to obtain, but can get through virtually all weapons sensors, since metal content is what most of them are triggered by. This is a nasty looking blade, it appears capable of removing limbs with a single motion. An 8 inch blade is not easy to hide, difficult if not impossible to detect."

With the suspect in restraints, and he was then escorted out of the room and this time, Cho took them to an elevator that would take them to the main floor. They departed the building fifteen minutes later with Art Robbins in tow, and Detective Marshall said, "This is where we part ways for now, I have to assist mama bear in taking him for questioning, but I believe the military personnel will get him shortly after. It has been decided that initially the Hong Kong authorities will proceed, and hopefully we can find out if the missing technician is dead or alive, and what condition he may be in if the latter is the case."

With the detective and mama bear departing, Tim returned to the office complex to have a sit down chat with Cho, as it had been awhile since they had the opportunity to exchange pleasantries. It was closing in on lunchtime and although a little earlier than normal, Tim had convinced Cho he was due for a nice lunch outside of the offices. Tim said as they were exiting the office building, "Cho you may pick anywhere you like, take as long as you like, but keep in mind with the events that have unfolded wherever we go, I could use a good stiff drink or two." Cho replied, "Considering the danger you put yourself in that does not come as a surprise, but I am glad it was you and not me, as I would be laying in a pool of my own blood, likely deceased if it were me. I do not know where you learned to do that maneuver, but I have no such talents. As children in Hong Kong, parents, usually the father, teaches their children self-defense, but it order for you be effective it must be practiced ritualistically you're entire life. I have not done so and have never needed to."

Tim said, "I should thank Kuri for saving my life, if she did not take the time to alter my routine with moves she thought to be more beneficial to my meditation process, I would not likely have reacted in the same manner as earlier. Surprisingly, I reacted instinctively, without any thought about it, I simply did what was needed at the time. Defense is obviously a wonderful experience, although, I hope never to be in such a situation again." Cho said, "You call that defense, it looked a lot more offensive than defensive to me." Tim said, "My early martial arts instruction taught me defense only, but as they continually emphasized, defense can be as debilitating as offense when used correctly. Most fatalities in the martial arts are a result of planned offensive moves. Those that practice those methods are shunned by most of the true martial arts experts the world over. At the same time, they must teach ways to defend against such an offensive maneuver. At least that is the way they explained it to me when I was young. I have tried to use the martial arts as an exercise for meditation purposes ever since, although I had become a bit relaxed after starting work with this company. Kuri set me straight, and I have been doing it daily without fail." Cho said, "Maybe I should get lessons from Kuri, she certainly seemed to know what you needed, but then I do not practice like I should have, and probably just need to get back into a program to be more involved on a daily basis." Tim said, "It has definitely got its benefits when you get into a daily routine, and it becomes instinctive when the training is called upon. I had no idea I could react so fast, and with such force in a split second of time."

Cho had selected the restaurant he wanted to have lunch at and as Tim expected, the place was entirely local cuisine with spice levels to maximum for the full effect of hot spiced foods." The restaurant was an establishment that Cho had taken Tim to before, and if he remembered correctly Cho told him to go with medium specifically and unless told on taking the order, it would be very spicy. He also remember Cho saying this place prided itself on the amount of alcohol that was sold with the meals. Cho then said, "I specifically chose this restaurant for your request, as they get their stiffer refreshment from around the globe. If they do not have what you want here, it cannot be found in Hong Kong. Once menus were brought Tim asked what type of brandies they offered, the server replied with a list of brands they had, and of them Tim recognized three brands which he knew of and two were quite good the third was considered more potent than most others in that category of liquor. He selected that and a relatively large snifter preferably. He also made the decision he would forego a heat level and see what Hong Kong really was in foods. Tim asked Cho if he cared for anything to drink, and Cho asked if it would get him into trouble, although he knew from a past luncheon a drink or two was not in violation of any company policies. Tim asked in return who was going to get him in trouble within the companionship of the CEO. Cho fully understood the retort, and selected his own drink before the server left to get the drinks. With the server gone Tim asked Cho, "Do they serve any type of bread or unsalted crackers here." Cho not truly understanding the question asked why Tim would want any such items. Tim explained in his experience they deaden the effects of highly spicy food quicker than anything else. Cho then understood and replied "I do not believe so, as they want to sell more alcohol." Tim knew what his alternative was and when the server returned with the drink, the orders were placed and Tim asked for a separate side dish of plain white rice. The server responded with, "You have been trained well for a westerner."

Cho asked what that was all about, and Tim explained the white rice would serve as a substitute for the bread or unsalted crackers. Salt intensifies the heat of the spice while starchy foods reduce the effects significantly. Now Cho was learning something that no person ever explained to him in the consumption of this type of food.

The meals were brought, and Tim asked for a refill on his brandy, and Cho was still nursing his drink and passed on a refill. The food was wonderful in flavor; but the heat level gave Tim all the side effects he could have expected in having such a hot spicy food type. He was not used to the intensity of the spice, but it was not like he could not endure the effects, and even at such intense burning, the flavors were quite delectable. He managed to get it all done before using the plain white rice to dull the burning effects. Additionally, the brandy had relaxed him substantially from the adrenaline flow from the earlier action of defending himself. He felt much more like his normal self with the exception of the lessening burning effect of the meal. Once the meals were consumed Tim requested tea for afterward and Cho did the same. The short lunch excursion lasted an hour and 45 minutes, including the time to return to the offices. At this point Tim bid Cho goodbye and returned to his hotel for the purpose of calling Kuri to thank her.

He started by saying, "Kuri, I owe you my life for teaching me the changes in my mediation routine, without which we would not be having this conversation." Kuri broke in, "Why, what happened?" Tim told her all about the encounter with the suspected murderer and how his instinctive reaction was to defend himself with the kick exercise that she had taught him, and he had practice for the last 3 plus years every day. She was much more relieved that he was not harmed in any way, and inquired as to what happen to the person who made the attack. Tim said all his martial arts training flashed into his mind, and his kick connected with a highly vulnerable spot that left him paralyzed on half his body for over an hour. Even then, he had to be assisted to exit the building, but as of today, both the suspects were in custody of law enforcement or worse. Kuri wanted to know what was worse, and Tim explained with the disappearance of a technician in the Hong Kong office that if kidnapping were indeed involved, that local military would get him for obtaining the information. The military does not have the same restrictions as law enforcement, so Tim did not envy the person's position. Kuri said that was true, and they could use some extreme measures to get the truth from the person of interest. He spoke to Kuri for about an hour, but told her he was going to stay in Hong Kong until he knew what happened with the missing employee. He did not think he would be in Hong Kong for the full two weeks, and he would let her know when to expect him.

Around five PM Tim's vidphone went active in the room, and it was Detective Marshall. The detective inquired, "Where have you been, I have tried to reach for half a day through the communications gear I gave you, and had no reply?" Tim said, "Sorry, did not think about it this morning, it has been in the room all day since I met you in the lobby and went together to the offices, I did not think about bringing it." Detective Marshall said, "No harm then, I will be up to your room soon to get you up to date on what has unfolded since this morning." The vidphone went dead, and best Tim could tell it was from somewhere else in the hotel that the call originated from.

10 minutes later he was letting Detective Marshall into his room. Tim still did not know where the detective was on the floor below, but did not really want to know at this point. The detective started out by saying, "The female suspect really known as Rebecca Robbins, and did not fully know what her brother had done. She admitted she was the person responsible for obtaining the high frequency signal program, but told her brother to use levels that incapacitated the listener, no more than that. She was not even aware of the analyst being killed by the frequency her brother used. She had been quite cooperative, but is still involved in a criminal activity that resulted in at least one death. I suspect she will not get the severest penalty for her involvement, but the theft time alone would keep her incarcerated for a fairly long time. As to the male known as Artimus Robbins, he is in the hands of the local military personnel to extract information concerning the whereabouts of the missing technician. He, to this stage of the interrogations, has not uttered a single sound, much less word. The military will get the information that I can assure you, it is a matter of how timely to effectively locate the missing technician. If he is

still alive, and unattended for too long a time period, he may still end up a fatality as well." Tim said, "I hope it does not take too long to crack that nut, as I intend to stay around until I know for sure. Regardless, if we find the missing technician alive or dead, I feel it is the company's responsibility to see to his needs at our expense. He should not be penalized for going above and beyond his required duties, and he certainly has done that."

The detective said, "You sure do take this personal don't you?" Tim said, "I believe it is part of my responsibility to see to the needs of the people who work so hard for us, would you have it any other way in your line of work?" Detective Marshall said, "I guess I have not looked at it from your viewpoint, but that is accurate in your question. If I did not feel my family would be taken care of with the event of being killed in the line of duty, no I would not be here." Tim then said, "It appears if our positions were reversed you would be taking this personal as well." The detective nodded in agreement.

"On the lighter side, I have called and thanked my wife for her training in keep myself out of harm's way, and what do you want to do about dinner?" Tim asked.

Detective Marshall said, "I need something substantial, as I have had nothing since breakfast, today's activity did not allow for me to consider a lunch. I know the hotel restaurant has menu items that would suffice, but since it seems to change daily I cannot recall what they offer today." Tim said, "The nice thing about the restaurant on the lobby floor is the daily menu is posted near the entrance for those who are undecided." Detective Marshall replied, "Really, I did not know that, it cannot be too obvious of a location. " Tim said, "It is easy, if you know where to look." With that said, they left Tim's room to go to the lobby level restaurant, where Tim walked up to a display about ten feet in front of the restaurant. Tim asked, "What do you see?" The detective said, "It looks like an ad for some other location in the hotel." Tim asked what was on the back side of the display, and the detective maneuvered to the rear of the display and found the menu of the day. He said, "I'll be damned, I never thought to look here for the daily menu." Tim said, "They actually change it three times a day for breakfast, lunch and the dinner menu, since there is not enough room to place all three at the same time. The dinner menu is typically the largest of the three, and always posted here in case you ever need to use it before entering. Tim had managed to move to the menu side and said, "It looks like you in luck they are offering German cuisine tonight, and they cannot spice up that food type to please too many people, although with your problem it may still be an issue. German food usually had a good deal of vinegar based sauces and that is an acidic liquid of its own."

The detective said, "I should have you around for all my meals to determine if it will cause a problem, even my wife does not know that about vinegar or other spices, she just knows if it works with the meal or it doesn't. She knows not to use sage in Italian foods, but that was by mistake." Tim answered with, "As I said, cooking is forever an experiment, some thing's work quite well and others a total disaster, but until you try, you do not truly know. That is unless you are familiar with the flavor of every herb and spice available, if you have that unique quality, then you may not produce any disastrous results."

They entered the restaurant, and were shown to a table that was slightly secluded but not overly so. It allowed them the opportunity to discuss the proceeding that would occur with the suspects in custody. Detective Marshall could not provide an estimate to the time of the full closure, as even the Hong Kong's legal system could be excessively time consuming. The detective also went on to say that since the murder was committed outside of Chinese soils, they were not likely to impose a death penalty. With that said, he also concluded that it was unlikely he would survive a lifetime in a Hong Kong facility, as the Chinese criminals do not take kindly to any infringement from westerners upon their territory, even if it is a detention facility. They take it personal and will use extreme prejudice towards any outsider.

Over all, Tim got the impression that once the penalty was imposed upon Art Robbins his days were largely numbered. With that in mind, it would prove to Robbin's benefit, to withhold information for as long as he possibly could. Tim hoped the military process would loosen his tongue quickly, instead of the other option. Tim was now officially in Hong Kong for three full days, and considered they had made a great deal of progress in the short amount of time. He still wanted the matter fully closed, prior to returning to his retirement to spend a good deal of family time with his family, which if Kuri had her way was going to be larger soon.

During their conversation, they placed their respective food orders and by the time the majority of the conversation was had, the food arrived. They each made selections they consider pleasing to their own palates, and conversation during the meal was non-existent. Tim also ordered a nice Rhineland wine, specifically for the type of food they were about to have.

Once the meals were done, and there was still some wine to partake in, the conversation resumed on a different track. Detective Marshall stated, "As to Rebecca Robbins she has completed her interrogation with full cooperation, and was totally unaware of the missing technician. As a result, she had no idea what had become of him, or where he could possibly be located, although she said it would need to be somewhere in the nearby area that was not easily accessible to outside persons intruding. The detective made it perfectly clear he did not know enough about Hong Kong to be able to provide an assistance to the local authorities in finding him. It was also apparent from Rebecca that in many ways she was glad this was over with for her. She did not feel she could continue to live a life of total seclusion, as she had already been far too reclusive over the last three years. She said it seemed every time she left the apartment with her brother they were observed, and had to quickly dawn disguises. She said it was far beyond what she thought it would be, and eventually refused to so much as leave the apartment. She was also going stir crazy as a side effect of so much time being alone. It was also the primary reason of Art going back to some form of work, but was much more accustomed to long terms in his disguise. Tim asked, if there was any way that he could talk with Rebecca Robbins, since she seemed not to be any type of threat to his wellbeing. Detective Marshall could see no harm in it, and stated he would take him to where she was being detained in the morning.

Once they finished the bottle of wine, and Tim had all the charges and gratuity added to his room costs, they returned to Tim's room at the hotel. Tim asked what he should do with the earpiece, since he could not see with both suspects in custody any additional reasons to keep it. Detective Marshall was fully in agreement with his assessment and took it back, saying it needed to be returned to Seattle where it came from. It was time to part for the evening, with the detective saying he would meet Tim by the restaurant at 8 AM. Tim acknowledged, and let him leave for his own room or the hotel bar, not knowing which was more likely.

CHAPTER

16

Tim had done all of his evening routines and even checked the nightly news cast that he found earlier to be more inclined to provide him information pertinent to outside of Hong Kong. By 11 PM he was ready to get some sleep, figuring he would wake no later than 6 AM and did not use the wakeup system.

He was correct as he was awake and rising at 5:45 AM. He proceeded to answer nature's call, and then go into his normal morning hygiene routine. His selection of attire was less business like and much more casual, as he did not feel he required business clothing to go to the place where Rebecca Robbins was being held. He did want to hear for himself just how much detail she could provide, concerning the incident that took place at the Seattle offices just over three years ago. His best guess is she did not think her brother was going to commit murder without her being informed of his intentions. If that were correct, he doubted she would have provided the means to perform such a heinous act. Once dressed, and still having time to get to the restaurant, Tim decided he best check his computer for any messages from headquarter.

He got out the computer and checked to find all was quiet on the western front, although in reality Seattle was east of Hong Kong. At least as far as the closest means of direct travel it was far quicker to go east than west. It was something to inquire from Kuri when he got back home to Seattle. At 7:45 AM, Tim left his room to meet Detective Marshall around the restaurant, which Tim assumed was going to be by the display that held the menu.

Tim arrived in the hotel lobby and walked towards the restaurant to see no sign of Detective Marshall, so he choose a seat near the restaurant entrance. 10 minutes later the detective came into view and spotted Tim by the entrance and headed directly toward him. Tim got up and they went into the restaurant, where they were immediately taken to a table and the menus were already in the hands of the server, who set them down and said he would be back shortly to take their orders. Tim already knew what he wanted and it seem the detective was knowledgeable of his selection. Tim said, "I do enjoy the Hong Kong version of a Spanish omelet with hash browns and an English muffin, although I wished they served a better grade of coffee, although it had improved." The detective asked if the Hong Kong version included some form of hot spicy additives, and Tim said "Of course it does, this is Hong Kong." The detective decided although an omelet sounded good, he would wait until he could identify all the ingredients. He stayed with what he knew he could eat, without any unwanted after effects. He did tell Tim he had to use his pill from the local pharmacy last night after the German food last night, and it was the fastest relief he ever experienced. The pharmacologist told him five minutes and it was just like it had its own clock with a second counter. Detective Marshall proceeded to say, "I get back to Seattle, I may find it necessary to locate a similar location in little China in the Seattle area. I hope that label does all it needs to do to get the same stuff."

Tim replied, "Being in your line of work and having such frequent bouts of heartburn, when you get back to Seattle, I would suggest seeing a doctor to be sure you do not have the beginning stages of an ulcer. It is not uncommon in some professions, and with laser surgery it is quick and easily resolved, with an absolute minimum of recovery time. I am not trying to be overly troublesome; but it is something you should consider." Detective Marshall said, "Yes, you are probable correct, it just seems I always have something else to keep me from getting that done." Tim said, "Well if it were me, knowing I have paid time off, I would make the appointment and then schedule that day off to insure it got done." Detective Marshall replied, "I never considered that option, thanks for the advice, I will do it that way after a talk with the wife, to insure it does not interfere with her plans with paid time off. I usually have a honey do list longer than a year's worth of paid time off would finish." Tim said, In that case, delicately imply that if you did not get it done, it could lead to far more severe issues, and no honey do lists would ever be done." The detective said, "You surely have a wisdom about you that does not go with your youthful appearance."

Breakfast orders were given and the food was at the table like they were spotted at the entrance and totally predictable. Tim knew for the most part when it came to food he was anything but predictable, although he had to admit he did have a favorite breakfast when in Hong Kong. Once they had eaten their breakfast, and Tim had taken care of the charges to his room, they were off to where Rebecca Robbins was being detained. Since the restaurant coffee was not too horrible this morning, he did get a cup to go. On the way, Tim asked Detective Marshall if he had learned his way around Hong Kong since he arrived. The detective replied he had been delegated to only a few streets, largely the main one that went between the hotel and the apartment complexes. He said he did get to go past the apartment complex to the street the police was located, in a rather non-descript building, in comparison to most of Hong Kong that he had gotten to see. It took nearly 30 minutes to walk to where the authorities called home, and Tim agreed, it was quite out of place for Hong Kong. It was only a five story dingy building that was literally a waste of space in Hong Kong. It could easily have a 75 floor structure in its place, but Tim assumed it was owned by the government, and they did as they pleased when it came to structures and budgets. It was obvious the building had seen a few years of neglect, since it was way over due for some sort of exterior cleaning or renovating.

Before entering the building, Tim asked, "Do you think they will let me speak to Rebecca alone?" Detective Marshall said, "It is an unusual request, but given the fact she has already completed interrogation, I see no reason why they would refuse. It would be best to see if mama bear can assist in this." They entered the building, Tim remained in the rear this time, he did not know where they were going and did not want to appear to be in charge of this little trip. The detective located mama bear proposed Tim's request, and she went back inside to get the upper staff to give the final approval before saying it would be acceptable. It came down to mama bear informing the upper folks, the person who wanted to see the suspect alone, was the same person who single handedly disabled the other suspect before a single weapon could be fully drawn. With that bit of information, he was approved to see the female alone, as it was apparent to them under no circumstance could she prove to be a threat to such a skilled person.

Mama bear reappeared and said it was acceptable, and took them to where she would be brought to have a conversation. Tim was shown to a fairly good size room, with a long table, which appeared to be quite stout in construction. There were two chairs on opposite sides of the long table, Tim was pointed to one, and the other he notice had a rather large ring of very thick metal embedded into the floor surface, which was likely some form of concrete, considering the age of the building. Rebecca was brought in with hand and leg restraints, and then was locked into the ring to restrict her movement from the chair near it. Tim asked if it was necessary, and he was told it was procedure, and more to protect him than her comfort. Once she was returned to her holding area she would be free of all restraints.

Tim started out by asking Rebecca if she was doing okay since yesterday. She gave a positive nod, but did not speak. Tim said, "I am sure you do not know who I am so let me introduce myself. I am Timothy Frantz, currently CEO at the company Global Security Corporation. I am here to see what you might be able to tell me as to your part in the murder of my analyst, that we have attributed to you and your brother. Personally from what I was told of you after yesterday, I believe your brother made you as much a victim in this as any other."

She looked at him with a slight tear rolling down her cheek, and said, "I did not know what he did to your analyst. I am responsible for obtaining the research that made it happen, but when I agreed with Art to help him, it was for the money I found, and only to incapacitate anyone listening to our transactions. The program I got is not modifiable, but has many different levels, and I specifically told Art not to use the last 4 as they were potentially fatal. He told me he used a lower level, he lied to me, and apparently he lied to me about a lot of things over the last four years. It would seem he wanted revenge for my oldest brother, who worked for your company until his breakdown. I never held your company responsible for my oldest brother's actions. He knew from the very beginning, it was a highly demanding and stressful position, but the pay was ten times what he could make anywhere else straight out of college, with no real experience.

He was stubborn about believing he could not handle it, and spent so long convincing himself he did not need help, he drove himself to a breakdown. Even at that, your company went above and beyond what any other employer would do, and made sure he received the best care available at their own expense. Art did not accept that his older brother was not driven to his state by your company. Apparently, he was going to get his revenge one way or another, and he took me down his path by misleading me into believing we were harming no one, and just get the money and disappear. I could not understand why we were still so high on the list of people to find after taking money no one knew about for 90 years. I grant you that 3 billion in WC is a rather large amount, but all this running and moving and pretending to be somebody other than ourselves, has already cost 1 billion of it. It might have been worth it if Art did what he was asked, I am pretty sure when the money disappeared, so would the hunting."

Tim said, "It certainly would have from my company's perspective, what has kept us in the hunt, was the death of the analyst for simply doing his job. It is my company's job to track and follow the movement of money that has been appropriated in less than legal fashion. Normally, when the money trail stops, the affected financial institution is notified for them to proceed in the fashion they deem necessary. My computer system forwarded all the pertinent information accrued in the trace for the purposes of legal proof, but the job is over for my company at that point. We are not law enforcement authorities, and do not want to be under any circumstance. Having been with Global Security Corporation from the first day they went in to operation, I am quite familiar with how the job stress affected different individuals. Those who were not cut out for the type of security we did, were the most vulnerable. Unlike most financial companies, we concern ourselves with virtual all the money that is moved around the world every day of every week. Most financial organizations, only concern themselves with their little piece of the pie and they do it inadequately, which is what made my company such a necessity in a world where the only crime that was considered acceptable, was steal other people's money through the use of computer systems. Largely it is hackers, but occasionally a wiser figure shows up to present a serious problem. The death of the analyst, was one such problem, and it took me way out of the parameters of what my company does for a business. In this case we were the victims, and I personally was not going to let it come to a close without a proper conclusion. I am sorry for what happened to your oldest brother, the company did try to offer all types of assistance to prevent it, but at that time it was still an individual must want it system, as opposed to mandatory periodically stress testing, and if necessary dismissal before becoming a breakdown victim.

In some ways, we created the monster by offering a substantial retirement plan with the completion of 10 years of service. Along the way, we have continually improved the ways to reduce stress for the analysts, and find additional medical staff members offering other services to aid in reducing stress. We have been so diligent in this effort that the highest stress office being Seattle, since it did the largest portion of the work, is now no higher than any other job available. All stress cannot be removed, that is unattainable by any company, largely because people have other stress related issues outside of the work environment."

Rebecca said, "It sounds like your company genuinely cares about those who work for them." Tim said, "The original CEO, who is also one of the owners, believes everyone who worked for him was like family. I have tried to continue that tradition, although I have had to do things far outside of the company procedures with this particular incident." Rebecca said, "If it means anything, I am sorry for what my brother did to cause your analyst's death, I am partially responsible, since I obtained the program that did it, but I never wanted it used that way."

Tim said, "I believe you, you do not seem to be the vindictive type of person. Maybe you can help me fill in the gaps from the beginning, if you do not mind." Rebecca said, "I see no harm in that. Five years ago, shortly after I entered the military to further my medical education, my brother Art, was already in the communication part of the military. My oldest brother, who prior to my going into the military was out of control, would not have a conversation with reason involved, and was always mad about something all the time. I needed to leave that because I could not take it any longer. My oldest brother had changed into someone I no longer recognized, and was unsure if he was even safe to be around." Tim said, "That is the final stage of stress overload syndrome, unfortunately, it is typically a result of an individual who needs some sort of stress relief assistance, denying to himself or herself he or she has a problem. Self-denial is the reason breakdowns becomes eminent."

Rebecca continued, "My brother's breakdown occurred before I had completed my first year in the medical research area in the military medical program. I was sort of surprised that what I was doing was not for the purpose of healing, but incapacitating or worse to potential enemy forces. The research was geared largely at communication systems, utilized by military forces, specifically considered hostile forces. It was assumed that to affect a hostile force's primary communication center, the whole would become extremely vulnerable. I continued working in the research department for my entire time in the military, but I was in contact with Art throughout my time in the military. He became upset with the news of our oldest brother being in a long term treatment facility for mentally broken people. I know there is better terminology for my brother's condition, but his mind was breaking when I was last around him, so it seemed it became complete broke when he was put in that facility. I know for a fact that Global Security Corporation took care of all the expense, and did not create a financial burden to my parents, they had endured plenty from my oldest brother's behavioral changes over the last two or so years he was still capable of working.

When my mother called to say that my oldest brother was showing sign of improvement, I thought maybe he could be fixed, but I did not think he would ever return to his former self. Shortly afterward my mother called again, to say that he had committed suicide by overdose from medication. He broke into the medical facility area that contained all the medications. Maybe you can explain that to me, because I do not understand how you can start to improve and then commit suicide."

Tim said, "The facility cannot repair something that has been broken, in the case of a mind, so what they try to achieve is preparing a person to life in a less confining environment, where they can do some things for themselves, but still need assistance for other things. For instance, they can dress themselves, typically feed themselves and perform some simple tasks. They cannot be trusted to cook for themselves, or use a good deal of complicated equipment without becoming frustrated. Once the mind is broke, many parts are dormant and will never return. Some people know enough that as a person they were capable of far greater things prior to being in such a facility. They become so depressed by what they will be able to do, compared to what they once were, they chose the easy way out."

Rebecca then asked, "How can this happen though?" Tim replied, "The method employed for people with damaged minds is to set up a routine for them to follow. Repetition is the only learning method found to be successful with such patients. Lights out routine is identical for all the patients, and that is to signify bedtime and sleep. It is possible a medical staff member forget to lock the entry door to the medication room, but highly unlikely. Typically a patient will figure out something to use to pick a lock, and grab a bottle of pills and take them all. A bottle of pills in a place like that consists of 25 to 30 pills, and the medications used for people in such a medical facility are highly potent. All of them would produce a quick overdose death with the entire bottle being consumed, unless the person is found in 15 minutes, it is too late. Also because of sleep time being a time where the absolute minimum personnel are within the facility, it can easily go unnoticed."

Rebecca thanked him for giving her an explanation she thought she understood now, how it happened and why. She said, "So that means, primarily his last decision was of his own doing. I can actually understand my brother making that decision now, since he really brought it all upon himself by not seeking help, when it would have helped. I suppose I should continue, Art called more frequently after my oldest brother was gone, and started making inquiries about what I was working on. I did not think much about it at the time, it was not a top secret program, and he was also military, so I told him. After about a year longer of the research getting closer to its expected completion, he asked if I could get a copy of the program, and told me what he was planning on a use for it. I told him it was not ready yet. At the same time, I was doing some computer research into archive files on previous attempts and failures, concerning the type of research we were performing at the request of my superior. I had mistyped an entry to bring up another archive record, and got something totally unexpected. The record I got, which since I was in government archives, was a financial statement of a very large amount of world currency. I looked through page after page of investment earning entries and found no entries for deposit or withdrawal. So I continued going back and it went back 90 years before I got an entry other than investment earnings. It was a rather large deposit, and prior to that were a number of smaller withdrawal, but all the activity after the deposit was investment earnings. Since I did not leave the government archives, this account had to belong to the government, but for what purpose I could not find out. I originally thought I had found a means to continue to fund our research project for a very long time. That changed when my superior denied using monies not allotted to them. At no point in this period did Art give me any idea what he was truly doing other than he had a plan in the works.

It was another six months that my brother kept in touch, but did not really give me any more idea about his true plan, only that he would have everything ready by the time the both of us had completed our time in the military. Due to the type of job and training he entered, for he had more time to complete his commitment than I, but it would be only a week or two difference, since I entered later than he did. Just before the date of release for myself, with him shortly behind, I told him about the government account I found, and suggested we try to get some of those funds. I could bring the account information to take advantage of it. My thought was by getting a good amount of money from under your nose and disappearing with it, that would make him happy, but apparently I was incorrect in that. The rest, you pretty much know and in reality you know more than I, because I was not aware of your analyst being killed until yesterday. I had insisted it was unnecessary to go to that extreme, and if he did that, they would not give up so easily."

Tim said, "You are correct there, it is specifically that death associated with the program you obtained that pursuit had continued, even after you had successfully acquired 3 billion in world currency. From my company's standpoint, if you had just simply taken the money, you would likely have been able to do whatever you pleased within 6 months from getting it. The financial firm that handled the account, was not going to pursue you, since they got a large portion of it still in the account. Although that is likely untrue anymore, as I informed a helpful military commander, who provided a good deal of help in figuring out just what your brother was capable of doing in the communication and technology area about the funds. He also explained how your brother Art was able to obtain most of it, without raising a theft flag. Ultimately, the commander was to use no more than half of the funds for military acquisitions, the rest for infrastructure repairs. Roads were being repaired for the first time in a good long while, so I feel he has started using those other funds.

I feel from our conversation today that your brother Art has made you almost as much of victim in this plan of his, as the analyst that died from it. I will try, but can't promise anything to have your portion of the case moved to Seattle, where with your cooperation, your penalty for your part in this will not be as severe. At this point, I am not even sure the theft is going to be pursued by the investment firm who had earned a good deal over the last 90 years they had the money in their control."

Rebecca asked, "Why would you want to do that for me?" Tim said, "You have been misled, and had some part in the plan, but you seem to have a good heart and just by being a good family member to your brother, you are being dragged down with him. It seems he did not share enough of the details to give you the opportunity to decline."

"Thank you for trying, whether successful or not is not as important as making the effort, and you do not owe me anything. I would image you are a person who genuinely cares about the people who work for you, and your company, and under better circumstance, I might have tried to work there myself, if I had not followed my brother's lead."

Tim had to knock on the door to be let out, but he stayed long enough to insure Rebecca was not treated poorly. The authorities who came to get her were considerate concerning her treatment, and removed the leg restraints entirely, to allow her to walk less troublesome. The arms would not be freed until she was back in the holding area. Tim made his way back to the area where Detective Marshall and mama bear were last seen.

He did find the detective, but mama bear was nowhere around, but then she did normally work out of the location. Tim asked if mama bear was anywhere nearby, and he was informed she was out on another case, having this one in the books. Detective Marshall said, "You were in there quite a long time, did you get all the information you needed?" Tim replied, "Probably more than I needed, and I would like you to make every effort in having her returned to Seattle for her part in this, she has been misled quite severely by her brother Artimus. Granted, she did have some part in it, but her only involvement is in our country. She knows nothing about what has occurred here other than trying to stay secluded to let things pass." Detective Marshall said, "You think she had nothing at all to do with the missing technician or his kidnapping, and whatever else it turns out to be." Tim said "Exactly, she is not that vindictive or that hostile, honestly, she seems to have a good heart and put her trust in the wrong brother."

Detective Marshall replied, "It is a good thing I already put that in motion then, although it will not be instantaneous. She will likely be in Seattle within a month, and she is not being treated too poorly here, due to her degree of cooperation." Tim said, "It seems a pity her own brother would involve her in something and not give her enough details to decline participating." Detective Marshall said, "It is all a part of the deviant mind, but then you would have to have some psychology training to understand that." Tim did have a fairly good idea of how to judge people as far as behavior was concerned. Detective Marshall had no other plans for the day with both of the Robbins' in custody. Rebecca had only some information that was helpful, as she was giving full details. Artimus was under military interrogation techniques, and from what the detective had heard, he did not envy the suspect in the slightest. According to the locals who have dealt with the military under these conditions, no person has withheld information as long as a week over the last fifteen years. They are not as concerned with the treatment of prisoners as the authorities need to be. As a result, anytime the military can be legally used, they are. Tim was now playing the waiting game, it was something he really was not experienced with, as his duties at Global Security Corporation there was always something to do, even if it was until something else completed. They had returned to the hotel, grabbed lunch in the hotel restaurant and returned to their respective rooms.

Tim felt like a caged animal, pacing back and forth, just waiting for the chance to escape. On the fifth day after the apprehension of Artimus Robbins, he had broken. Detective Marshall had called him on the room vidphone to have him in the lobby as soon as possible, so they could go to the location they were told the missing technician would be. As quick as he could, Tim made it to the lobby, and the detective had also just arrived. Detective Marshall explained on the way, "Robbins found out about a major building renovation between the hotel and apartment complex. The plan was to work from the top 50th floor down, one floor at a time. There was a vacant floor for the temporary location of those displaced on the floor under renovation. The project was expected to take 2 years to complete, and they were only one month into the work. The building has two lower levels, and the technician is supposed to be in lowest level, which was not going to be visited for nearly two years." They arrived by foot at the building he was told about and entered, to find the elevators to the basement levels. The local authorities were supposed to already be there, but there was no medical vehicle in the front of the building. When they arrived at the lowest level, it was quite dark, there was a single source of illumination in the whole floor, and it was quite inadequate. They could see other lights moving around a bit, largely on a wall then down out of sight, so they headed toward them. The technician was still in restraints of some type. A large steel girder was used as a support system, and it had a hole recently cut in, which a chain was placed through and used to restrain the technician. There were three empty water containers laying near him that if used in ration, one would last for a day. There was no knowing how long ago they were given, but at least five days had passed, since he had any attention. The technician's restraints did allow him some movement, but not terribly much. From a seated position he could raise his hands high enough to partake in food or water with little slack for much more. It was also enough to stand or lay down right next to the girder.

The technician was unconscious, and medically not in good condition. First he was severely dehydrated, which was the first thing medical personnel would need to address. The emergency medical team was already in route, and should be there any moment, he heard said. The authorities were being cautious about the restraints for two reasons, first they did not want to harm any further the hostage, and second, there were no trigger devices being used to set off an explosion or some other devious trap. The authorities had been there fifteen minutes before Tim and Detective Marshall had arrived, and after another 7 minutes, they started to remove the restraints by old fashioned methods of picking locks. They were not highly practiced in this any longer, since everything these days was computerized, and electronic methods are far more commonplace. It took another 10 minutes to remove the restraints, to free the technician, and have the medical team give him a quick diagnostic to determine if he could be safely moved.

His vital signs were poor, but they were present, and this told them his dehydration was likely more severe than initially thought. Tim asked the medical team if he could go with the technician, since he did not believe he had any living family members left. They said normally not, but without any family someone needed to take responsibility. Five minutes later they were in the medical emergency vehicle with the technician strapped down, and safe to transport to the nearest facility, which took only three minutes. Once inside, Tim reported to the desk that the patient just arriving would be taken care of by Global Security Corporation. Not knowing if he had medical coverage or not, Tim said as CEO he was authorized to insure his recovery. If he had medical coverage, we will take care of all that is not covered, as the technician should have not a single WC out of his pocket for all he has been through. Tim also made it a point as an employer, his company was well aware of all cost concerning medical testing and procedures, and would need to be kept abreast of the charges instead of simply a final bill. This was to insure they were not being overcharged by anyone involved. This was all perfectly acceptable to them, and Tim made a final check on the technician, who was still unconscious but receiving care for dehydration, as well as lack of nourishment for an extended period of time. He also noticed another person looking in and he inquired if he was a member of the surveillance team working with Detective Marshall. He said he was piggy 2 on the team and asked who Tim was. Tim said he was baby bear, but he is really Timothy Frantz CEO of Global Security Corporation. Piggy 2 was impressed that a business person was able to subdue an assailant so quickly. He was here to get the technician's side of the kidnapping once he was able to talk. He was unsure how soon that would be, and Tim said he would not expect much for at least the rest of today and all of tomorrow, the technician was in pretty poor condition when he was brought out.

Piggy 2 agreed, and would return Wednesday morning to see if he was able to talk then. He left, Tim made another look in to see everything was pretty much the same, and there was no emergency response team needed. He left the medical facility and had no idea where he was in respect to the hotel, but figured it was not too far to walk. His first thought was to look up to see if he could identify anything that way, and scanning about he saw the apartment complexes, which he could get to in short order, and go to the hotel from that point. He arrived at the corner of intersecting streets, and needed to turn right to keep the apartment complexes in view. After another 10 minutes on foot and getting to the intersecting streets at the apartment complexes, he realized he was on the opposite side on them and had to turn right again. This street was much longer than he realized, with the way the complexes were positioned and they were massive buildings.

It took another twenty minutes to negotiate the distance from one intersection to the other where the apartment buildings started and ended. Although Tim was sure they did not have a single owner, the design of the buildings, a total of 10, all appeared similar. Likely they were all built through the same firm that designed them. Tim had to cross the main intersection to get to the side of the street the hotel was on; but Hong Kong's intersecting streets were designed for far more foot traffic than vehicular. Lights made wheeled traffic wait for pedestrians to cross, as opposed to the vehicles having more time going through intersections. Still it took another 25 minutes to get to the other side and back to the hotel lobby. Tim knew if he understood the ways of using smaller foot paths between his starting and ending location, he likely would have cut his time in half. Getting on the wrong path though, would have taken longer and he simply did not know it well enough to take the chance.

Once returning to the hotel, he decided he used sufficient amounts of energy to have lunch at the restaurant. First he asked at the main desk how many rooms were occupied by his company. His assumption was the jet crew was also staying at the hotel under the company travel arrangements. He found there were a total of 8 rooms assigned, one his, one the detective, and the rest the crew for the private jet. He asked if he could get a message sent to each room to reply to his. The request was granted, as they were not interested in jeopardizing all the business they had from Global Security Corporation, but it was normally against hotel policy for security reasons. His message was simply morning departure to return to Seattle approximately 8 AM. He included the detective in the event he also wanted to return to Seattle, since he had to wait for any further development in Hong Kong. With that complete, he went to get some lunch.

His lunch was local cuisine which he enjoyed even though the spicy level had its affects. Once he finished lunch, and had the charges put on his room, he return to his room. He had six messages from all the crew members saying they would be at the airfield promptly at 8 AM for departure preparations. Tim knew from experience that usually took them and hour of checking to insure the jet was safe for takeoff. It was a mandatory pre-flight inspection for all planes. Even small planes, had to perform the inspection, although it likely did not require as much time to complete. He did not hear from Detective Marshall until just after 5 PM, it was not a message. The detective had returned from the authority's location and went immediately to Tim's room to see about dinner. He, like Tim, was not overly fond of eating alone in a public location. Some conversation was far more appreciated, then complete silence outside of placing a food order.

Tim asked the detective if he had been to his room, and received Tim's message. The detective had not, so Tim explained what the message was, and when he would be leaving the hotel for the airfield in the morning. The detective agreed, he had run his course for now in Hong Kong, although he would likely need to return once the legal proceeding were started. It was most likely as the team leader of the operation, his testimony would be required in order to complete the process. He said he would certainly take the lift home, so he could see his family again, as he had been away for quite some time. Dinner was decided to be at the hotel restaurant, since they both would need to get ready for a morning departure time.

Once the meals were served and Tim took care of the charges, they would return to their respective rooms to pack their belongings. Conversation at the table was light, largely family oriented, and little was said concerning the case, because it was already said. The only thing brought up during the dinner conversation was the detective said he would keep Tim apprised of the progress of the pair in custody. With dinner concluded, and the detective taking his heartburn remedy, Tim decide to hit the local shops in the hotel complex, to obtain mementos for Liani and Kuri. For Liani he found a fairly good sized stuffed Panda, an animal that was found in China. Although there were none in Hong Kong, the island was included in China, so he felt it was appropriate. Kuri got a unique piece of jewelry that represented the island. He took care of the charges from his own account, and went to his room to pack and have almost everything ready before morning. Something's would still need to wait until morning, but that was normal for hygiene items, and a set of clothes to wear the next day.

Prior to starting the packing, since the time difference allowed him to reach the offices in Seattle, he used the vidphone to inform Trask of his return. Tim stated, "I have also authorized the medical facility to cover all charges concerning the technician who was held captive that were not covered by his medical insurance, if he had any. A decision had to be made immediately, and there was no time to wait for a board meeting to get approval, so if I overstep my authority, the company could deduct it from my own salary." Trask said, "That will not be necessary, I would have done the same thing, since the technician did nothing to cause his need for attention." Tim told him that both of the Robbins were in custody in Hong Kong, and it was now a matter of how long the legal proceeding would take for complete closure over the loss of their analyst. He then said, "I would not like to experience ever again the reaction to an armed assailant, it was most harrowing, and if it were not for the alterations to my martial arts meditation routine, I would not likely be making this call." Trask was alarmed by this, asking, "How did he even get a weapon through the security systems in the elevators?" Tim said, "The 8 inch blade was of a ceramic composition, and the detective explained to me most security systems are triggered by metal content. The composition of this particular blade had none, and therefore went undetected." Trask asked, "Is there any way to modify our security systems to detect such items?" Tim said, "I am not aware of any, as so many other items that pose no threat, may also trigger alarms." Trask asked, "Should I expect you to be in tomorrow?" Tim said, "Unlikely, I would like to have a little time with the family I have not seen lately, but you can expect me the following morning. It is a little ahead of the original time frame I said it might be."

Trask asked, "How is it the authorities were able to spot the people once you arrived and could not before that?" Tim said, "They did not, I spotted Artimus Robbins in the first 30 minutes I was involved, and was with Detective Marshall as well, He did not see the anomaly that got my attention, and I left the detective to follow to be sure I was correct. Would you believe he had taken a communications' technician position in the Hong Kong office? Since this truly alarmed me, I returned to the hotel and contacted Cho to see how exactly this could have happened. Since Cho is not involved with the hiring of personnel, I had him also find out who did, and had both of them meet me in the hotel restaurant. That is where I found out the technician who was doing the job had gone missing, and although he had some health problems that caused him to miss work from time to time, he always called to let them know. He did not on this occasion, and after checking that the technician was not under medical emergency care anywhere in Hong Kong. They found nothing to explain his missing, but after the fifth day of his disappearance, Robbins walked in for a position if one was available. He had an untraceable work history, and used another name to get hired on. I found his timing to be highly suspicious, and spent the next five hours insuring certain precaution were taken, and try not to alarm him at the same time. First we managed to contact the lead technician who happened to be running tests that had Robbins on the roof for the process. With the lead technician alone, we were able to confirm the missing technician had accessed the equipment after having gone missing. To insure the system could not be compromised, I had the lead technician revoke the missing technician's access to the communications system. Also had the technician take the stance if Robbins had inquired to company policy, it was standard operating procedure to remove former employees from the system for security reasons.

I also arranged for the human resources representative to forward Robbins photo, which he was using a disguise, and the missing technician's photo as well. Since he would not depart the building until a little after 5 PM. After finishing up with Cho, I made sure the detective understood what I planned to do next. I was going to try to follow Robbins from the office building to the place he was using as safe haven.

As that was taking place and Detective Marshall had already said the photos could not be distributed to the team until the following morning, after Robbins would have left the apartment, I manage to spot him leaving the building. Since so many people are on foot in Hong Kong, apparently I had gotten too close to Robbins in my attempt to follow him. Around half way between the office and apartment complexes, he did an abrupt 180 degree change of direction, and was now heading toward me. Not panicking, I continue my course and expected to pass him and then find another location to resume what I wanted to accomplish. Instead he jumped directly in front of me, and shoved me against the building inquiring why I was following him. My reply was as a first time visitor to Hong Kong, and an entire day of seeing the sights, I was merely trying to find my way back to where the travel agency had me staying. If he thought I was following him it was certainly not intentional. He accepted my response but warned if he caught me following him again, I would regret it. I responded by telling him since I had no idea what his schedule was, I could not make any promises, but would certainly try to avoid him. I crossed to the other side of the street and continued to follow him from that viewpoint, knowing he would need to cross at the intersection to get to the apartment complex side of the street.

Fortunately, he did not spot me again and after seeing from a distance which apartment complex he entered, I rushed to the glass entry doors in hopes of seeing how many others got into the elevator when he did. I was quite lucky, as I got there in time for him and two others to enter the elevator and the doors closed, when I got to watch the floor level indicator to tell me the three floors instead of over 100 to watch him from. At that, I returned to the hotel after informing the team though the gear they gave me, which of the three floors he might be using.

With the photos not being distributed until after he would leave in the morning, the plan was to have a team member on each floor to observe which apartment he occupied." Trask said, "One thing is painfully obvious to me, that we should incorporate employees leaving us having their system accesses removed, to prevent any other such intrusions in the future. I will have to bring it up at the next board meeting; but I see no logical reasons to have it declined."

Tim continued, "On the following evening after work hours, team members were in place on each of the three floors to observe which floor, and apartment Artimus Robbins occupied. Instead of reassembling a team to make an arrest that evening, it was decided to have a pair on the floor he used the following morning early enough to see him leave. At that point, the team members were to attempt to apprehend the female, Rebecca Robbins, hopefully without too much resistance. If that took place as planned, myself and Detective Marshall with an additional member of the local team would enter the Global Security Corporation's Hong Kong offices, and with Cho's assistance. I had no clue where the communication area was in the office complex, to make the second apprehension. Everything went according to plan, except for the large knife, but it was resolved and took Robbins over an hour to have his temporary paralysis subside to a point where he could be assisted from the building. The rest of the time has been spent concerning the missing technician, but since this was committed on Chinese soil, the military was involved in getting that information from Robbins, and he held out five days before breaking."

With the conversation concluded, Tim and Trask disconnected, and Tim made a final quick vidphone call to the front desk, as much as a courtesy as to having everything ready to make a hasty departure. He informed them, that in the morning all 8 of the rooms occupied by Global Security Corporation would be checking out in the morning from about 7 AM, until shortly after 8 AM. The desk appreciated the advanced notice, and indicated that all the room bills would be ready, although they were largely directly charged to Global Security Corporation, there may be some incidentals the company did not cover. Tim informed them for this one occasion, to put all of them on his room charges, as the company would indeed pick up his costs, even if not normally covered.

Tim then went ahead and got everything he could packed, although the stuffed Panda was too large to fit in his luggage. He was glad it came in a bag to carry easily. Everything was ready except the clothes he would wear the next day, and his hygiene materials that were in a small travel case that matched his other luggage. He still had five days of clothes that had not been needed, but that was not so much a problem as it was nice to know he was ahead of schedule. Tomorrow would be his 9th day out of the planned 14 days, and his arrival in Seattle tomorrow would be likely at a different time than his departure time, when time zones were taken into consideration. It was still six hours of flight time largely over water. Over the last 100 or so years, jets had become fuel efficient to the point of 10 hours of flight without refueling. Tim did not know the same of single engine aircraft, but by the same token they were never intended for intercontinental flights. Tim decided for his last little excursion before going to bed, he would indulge in a nightcap in the hotel bar. He went to the bar, got a good sized glass of the Cognac that Trask has favored for as long as Tim knew him, and after sipping at it an hour before finished, he return to his room for sleep. He did already complete his mediation routine just after finishing his packing.

The next morning at precisely 8 AM, he met the detective at the front desk and went over all the charges to his room. He was surprised to see very few incidentals from the crew and none from the detective. He gave the front desk his approval to forward all the cost for the group to Global, and they went to get into the hotel shuttle vehicle, which already had their luggage loaded. They left for the airfield, which was not terribly far in a vehicle, but to walk it towing luggage, was simply not practical. They were unloaded and in the lobby by 8:20 AM, where crew members got their luggage loaded onto the plane and then continued with the preflight inspection they were accountable for. The detective and Tim waited in the lobby, where Tim got a good cup of coffee for the first time in a good while. Although the hotel had improved, it still could use a good deal more improvement to be considered good coffee. The detective asked if it was any good, and after Tim said it was the best on the entire island, the detective also got a cup. Detective Marshall said, "It seems like forever since I had a decent cup of coffee, I almost forgot what it really tasted like, this is rather good by the way." Tim said, "Hong Kong knows far more about tea than coffee, but I do not always think tea is a suitable substitute for coffee. I will usually take tea with most of the local cuisine, because some of the coffee is so horrible, it was a waste to even ask."

Detective Marshall said, "I am not overly excited by tea, so I find some other type of drink I can tolerate, although a good stiff bourbon is usually good the world over. So seldom during the time we were in surveillance for the suspects, did lunch even get to be a consideration. Which reminds me, since I was with you when you spotted the suspect and I did not, what gave him away to you?" Tim said, "His eyebrows were not the same color as his hair and facial hair." Detective Marshall said, "How did I miss that? Well just in case you have not been made aware of it, you were instrumental in locating and apprehending our suspects. Without you observant abilities, we would likely still be looking for them." Tim said, "Maybe, but keep in mind with your instruction, and the fact I had an entire month to concentrate on the suspects, I had the upper hand. You mostly like had a day or less, as with the rest of your team to study the facial structure of the suspects. Also, I had sufficient time to visualize what they may appear like with different hair color, and possible facial hair for the male, I did not picture a bearded woman at any time."

Detective Marshall said, "Duly noted, but just the same, without your assistance we would not have advanced so far, so quickly. I believe I owe you some thanks for allowing me to go back and see my own family, before they forget about me."

The crew had finished the preflight inspections, and Tim and the detective had finished their coffee. They got to board the plane, where Tim inquired from the crew if that had enjoyed the stay in Hong Kong, as he got no call or message for their need elsewhere. This brought smiles from every single member of the crew. The attendant who took them to their seats said, "It was truly remarkable for all of us, as often as we have been to various cities, rarely do we stay on the ground to see the sights. We had two days as a group excursion to see what Hong Kong was all about, and had to offer. I believe we may have covered every square inch of Hong Kong, and it is remarkable how they keep so many people in such a small area. We even got to learn a little history, did you know that the only two single family residence on the entire island, belong to the two English family ancestors, consider most instrumental in the development and bringing commerce to this island?" Tim did not know there were only two single family residences on the small island, but knew there were very few, and had no idea they belonged to British ancestors. The attendant continued, "The original two English shippers, although arriving at separate times, were both considered more pirates than commercial shippers in England. They were tolerated for their abilities to bring to England otherwise unattainable goods. They also were rivals in the beginning days, and always trying to put an end to the others business dealings, if not the end of the other family, to have complete control of Hong Kong under a single family. It is quite a good history on the ingenuity of both to survive and flourish on an island, considered largely uninhabitable, at the time they first arrived on Chinese lands. You might find it quite interesting to get the entire story first hand yourself." Tim asked if this information was available on the Information Gateway. The attendant said only bits and pieces, as the true historical documentation is largely kept at the small museum, at one of the two properties for the revenue it generates. The people who operate the museum, are extremely knowledgeable of the actual documents accrued by the families, over several hundred years.

Although it was relatively early in the day, after the plane was at its normal flight altitude, the attendant return asking if anyone wished to have drinks. Tim felt it might be a good idea, and the detective asked him what he might suggest. Tim said, "If it were not for Trask insisting on the planes having his favorite brand of Cognac, he would not consider a drink this early. The Cognac is superb, and if you are unfamiliar with it, this would be an excellent time to make the discovery." The detective had never had it before, and was willing to make the exception as well. They still had at least 5 and half hours of flight time remaining. On the private jet, the glasses for brandy and cognac were identical, but in other establishments, they differed only slightly in the width of the bowl. Tim was unsure if the cognac glass was also consider a snifter, although you normal went through the same process prior to taking a sip. When the cognac was brought, Tim took a moment to explain the process of having such a drink, and also provided a visual demonstration. The detective did as instructed and exclaimed, "This is some really smooth stuff, and do all brands taste this good?" Tim said, "Like any such beverage, there are variations from good to poor, and this is the best. Unfortunately so is the price, but for me it is well worth it." The detective then said, "So you are telling me that if I like it, I can't afford it, should I acquire a taste for it." Tim said, "That is debatable, but if such is the case, I will get you a bottle once a month, just to keep you happy." The detective responded with, "I may hold you to that if I find out how much it is." The detective had consumed his cognac, and it was enough to relax him to the point of nodding off. Tim inquired before he truly feel asleep, if he wished to be awaken for the inflight meal, which the detective said he would, should he actually fall asleep. He did, and Tim figured he had been far more sleep deprived it his time in Hong Kong than Tim had been, and did nothing to disturb him.

Approximately 3 and half hours into the flight, the attendant asked Tim if they would like the inflight meal served in five minutes, it was a nice cut of steak, with mashed potatoes and a vegetable mix that had a fairly tasty sauce. Tim said it would be fine and waited three more minutes to disturb the detective from his slumbers by saying he hoped steak was not something that set off his heartburn issues. The detective roused from his nap was still getting more in tune with being awake, than the arrival of the meal.

He saw the food and asked if the private jet always served such exquisite meals for the people onboard. Tim said that although there was not a menu selection to make, they usually had a fairly good meal for passengers and crew. Tim also said that unlike commercial planes, the meals were actually prepared and cooked on board, since they did not have hundreds to serve. It made it a much better meal than premade meals delivered to the plane, by a specific food service organization, which was in the business to make money. The detective inquired as to one of the crew being a chef or at least cook status. Tim confirmed that to be the case. He said there was for all flights, six crew members regardless of a single passenger or two dozen, the maximum passenger capabilities of the private jets, although it allowed for a great deal of room for passenger to maneuver about. Also for long flights, the seating could be converted into full length beds for most people. The detective now understood the distance between the seats.

The inflight meal was more pleasing than some; but they never served anything that was terrible. It seemed to Tim he had missed out on a good steak dinner for longer than he thought, and made a mental note to include some in his next grocer excursion. It might also explain why he considered the meal so exceptional. The detective had no difficulties making his disappear, and the vegetables were in a sweetened sour cream type sauce that Tim considered quite excellent. The meal was cleaned up with over an hour before they would be in range of Seattle, and the attendant inquired about after dinner drinks, which made the detective perk up enough for another glass of cognac. Tim agreed it was good choice for the meal, and two were brought to their seats.

The remainder of the flight had little more conversation as they anticipated getting to see their families once again, and the detective had been away far longer than Tim. In all truth, Tim had been away longer on some of his previous business related trips, but had no family at that point in his career with Global Security Corporation. Just before touchdown during the descent, Tim asked Detective Marshall if he had a vehicle at the airfield or needed a ride home. The detective said he had his company issue vehicle at the airfield, and providing it had not deteriorated to dust during his absence, he should be okay to go. Tim asked for clarification about his vehicle, where the detective informed him the authorities with limited resources these days, were not too quick to replace vehicles, and his had certainly seen better days. It was still usable by their standards, and they did do all the regular maintenance, which he did not have to do out of his pocket.

Once on the ground, and all the luggage brought out so it could be taken to their respective vehicles, Tim made certain the detective was able to depart the airfield before he actually made his way home.

CHAPTER

17

Tim arrived home when it occurred to him, Kuri was not expecting him as he had gotten too involved in getting everything prepared for a quick departure. He had neglected to call home to inform her to expect him. He was going to see how the family took to surprises, so instead of gathering his luggage and getting it to enter the house, he left it all in place and entered through the front door. Liani and Kuri appeared to like the surprise, as first they were not alarmed by someone entering unannounced, as only a few people could do it; but he got a good welcome. Kuri then asked how it was he was home so much sooner than he had led her to believe. Tim explained the only hold up, and said the male responsible for the kidnapping of the Hong Kong technician having committed a crime on Chinese soil, could not hold out more than five days in the hands of military interrogators. Hence, with everything completed other than the legal process he had accomplished all he could and returned home. He finished his details pertaining to the last week in 30 minutes, with Kuri and Liani listening intently. After that he retrieved his luggage, which include a hardly used make up kit. and two full piece of luggage with a travel case and large bag. It did take him two trips, since he had no cart or other wheeled item to move it all in a single trip. The first thing he did was remove his items for Liani and Kuri to present them with their mementos from Hong Kong. He did not have to explain anything to Liani about her gift. He explained to Kuri that the item was merely a keepsake, nothing he truly expected her to wear daily; but it was a unique item to Hong Kong. Someday, hopefully in the not too distant future they could visit Hong Kong as a short get away from Seattle.

He did let Kuri know that due to the length of time he had already been up with Hong Kong's time zone difference to Seattle, he would likely be ready for some sleep before Liani was tonight. Kuri having remembered the experience from her stay in Seattle and return to Tokyo fully understood, and said as much.

It was too early to make them a light lunch, and his meal on the plane was still sustaining him quite well. As a result, he went to unpack all his clothes and whether used or not, they were too crumpled to not go into the laundry equipment for a cleaning and just to appear more presentable. Once taking them to the lower level, and getting what was more than a single load going, although in this case, they were not the type to try to separate into like cycle types. Since he was in the lower level, he stopped in the computer room took a good long look at the Japanese décor he had, wondering if he had anymore samurai painting coming his way. He brought the computer desk display active with a single touch, and decided he should check his account balance even though he did not spend excessively in Hong Kong. When he got the balance up it was obvious to him he had far more available, as the last deposit the week before was at his new salary. He was not interesting in making another call to the investment people to alter his deposits and did nothing at all today. He would likely transfer fund to his other interest account rather than keep it all in the monthly spending account, which rarely had half of it used. What he did do, was look for the nearest provider of the cognac to order a case for Detective Marshall. At 500 WC per bottle, he doubted it was something the detective would willingly spend on a single bottle of any type of alcohol. At 10 times the cost of a good bourbon, he had the case sent to his own house, as he did not know how to get it to the detective. Once that was completed, he returned to the main level and spent time with his family.

Kuri wanted to hear every detail of his trip, and especially his full recount of reaction to a knife wielding assailant, because she was uncertain of her own reaction. He had already told her of the encounter once; but not to the degree of questions she had as he explained it. She was well aware the martial arts after years of practice would become instinctive to the correct means of defending one's self. Tim made it perfectly clear if it were 4 years earlier, his instinctive reaction would not have included the reaction he used to disarm and temporarily paralyze the other person. It was like his foot knew before he did, the precise place to do the most effective means of disabling his offensive counterpart. He had not even thought about points of vulnerability since his days in martial arts training. They did go over them repeatedly, as a means to counter those who used the arts for offensive purposes. Although, those persons were highly shunned by true martial arts masters, the masters knowing they did such, meant the means to defend from such an encounter had to be included into training, and someone had to act out the offensive only person. For demonstration purposes, they never did this in a full speed, full contact exercise. It was always intended to show the means of each move, and how to counter the offensive moves through good defense. The masters emphasized that with practice of the defensive countermoves, the mind would know exactly what the body should do in the case of a real encounter at full speed. The masters said, with continual and daily practice through an exercise routine, the mind would literally slow everything down for you to properly defend yourself from any attacker with the correct countermove. Often with the most vulnerable point for the precise countermeasure employed. Tim having never experienced a real encounter, never believed such things were true until it happened in a split second.

Kuri said she had never heard such an explanation; but believed it were fully possible, with untold years of a good meditation routine. The exercise is for mind and body in harmony point of view, also a means of incorporating the most used defensive moves. The mind is the most powerful tool used in the martial arts, at least in Japan.

Tim explained for many years in Seattle, and most of the countries, the most common martial arts instruction was largely of Korean tactics. In the middle of the 20th century a particular martial arts expert who was also in the movies, had a different approach. Not sure what his name for the techniques he developed was called. As a youth he learned from many different styles and techniques from various Chinese Masters. Although this person was born in the United States, he had spent so few years in the country, he had poor English skills, and was shunned for it in the US movie industry. I believe the martial arts instruction I received, may have been of this nature, and it was called Hido (pronounced Heedough) and it was made of a mix of martial arts skills, considered to be of the most effective combinations of different Chinese techniques. No single technique was more effective than this method, although the Japanese methods were never available in the United States, or anywhere outside of Japan.

Kuri said that is because it is only taught by one family member to the next generation, and there is no single name for it. Each family, depending on ancestry, had literally its own unique skill set. The samurai methods, largely sound much like your Hido as it was a combination of the best techniques found among the original samurai of the various Shoguns at the time. Keep in mind, that during the time of the Samurai, the skills were superior to any from the Chinese, who invaded the little island for the purpose of owning it for China. The samurai repeatedly defeated any such attempts, and occasionally made a strike of their own on Chinese soils, but the sheer number of Chinese warriors usually prevented the success of the invading samurai, although the casualties were far fewer than when the Chinese invaded Japan. Normally with a Chinese invasion, no member returned to his lands, whereas the samurai seldom returned with less the 75% of those who went.

Kuri went on to say that she believed history proved that skills in the martial arts used by the samurai, were superior to those of the Chinese. Like all martial arts, specific weapons were included in the training methods, and the samurai favored the sword as the weapon of choice. During the time of the Yolakawa Shogunate, besides having the best samurai, the shogun also had expert archers. They were often perched in high places like trees and some taller buildings with difficult viewpoint from the ground level. Having the high location allowed them to see attacking forces well in advance and eliminate many of the attackers before they ever got to draw blades with the samurai of Yolakawa. Most other shoguns only used a few archers, but Yolakawa had many, seeing the value they provided in repelling attacking forces from either another Shogun or the Chinese.

Tim remembering his mental note while in Hong Kong asked Kuri. Tim asked, "Kuri, consider me ignorant in this matter but why do most Asian countries including Japan, refer to us as westerners, when in fact we are east of all of those countries?" Kuri said, "I suppose that might be confusing to someone in Seattle. It is a term from before your country truly existed as the United States. In the late 1500's and early 1600, those first people to arrive in China and Japan were from western European countries.

England, Portugal and some Spanish were all from countries west of China and Japan when the term was first put into use by Japan and China. It was never truly updated as the terminology was simple too long into practice."

Tim said, "I guess that makes some sense, I never considered how long other countries histories would be taken into account to our own." Kuri said, "It is the only way it could be considered from our viewpoint, considering we have an ancient culture even to most European countries. For over 1000 years the largest concern for the people of Japan was the sheer numbers of persons on the Chinese lands. We had limited resources on our island, and the primary interest was to remain outside of Chinese control. Although we were successful, during that same time beyond China which was never in our interests, the nation's west had advanced remarkably fast and gone from being tribal groups, to civilizations with tremendous industrial growth. Japan as well as China were largely stagnant in those advancements. As a result, the European nations that showed up in large ships, had weapons we were unprepared to deal with. We had always used swords, and they had firearms as well as large cannons that were too much for sword or bow and arrow. It became immediately apparent some type of accord had to be made, quickly. The ultimate accord was over commerce in the exchange of goods unique to each country. The downside, was the English who arrived first, wanted exclusivity in the exchange of Japanese goods to England, as well as English goods brought to Japan. It took months for ships to travel between the countries, at the time they were sailed by wind power, so they were at the mercy of the weather. Those conditions often extended the amount of time sailing between the two countries. There was also the problem of pirating while at sea. This often resulted in a ship being overpowered and the cargo stolen, with the end result of a ship being sunk. It did work both ways, as sometime the ship with the cargo, was able to defend and sink the other ship. As I understand how this worked initially, it involved rival countries. As the English became the primary country on the seas while defeating other country's ships, it turned into rival English traders, many considered pirates by the English government, trying to become the sole traders to Japan or China."

Tim marveled at the knowledge Kuri had concerning the history of her country in the relationship to the arrival of British traders, also deemed pirates. The time frame she was using was before his country was anything more than the new world, to those who had made the attempts to explore small portions of it. Tim was not that big of a history scholar, he had specific topics he researched and paid attention to. Other than that, he was not overly concerned with who did what 600 to 700 hundred years ago, only glad he was not there at that time. It was far too hostile and lethal for him. Besides if someone else did not harm, maim or kill you, disease easily could.

After a good long time with Kuri and Liani, it became apparent to Tim that dinner was in order. He excused himself to see what was available for the evening meal. He checked the environmental kitchen cooling systems for what was most plentiful, and found a good deal of seafood items and chicken. It seemed he would need to replenish a good portion of the other meats he usually kept in stock. He would need to put the list on his intellipad to give to Kuri to get what was needed, since he was expected to be in the office in the morning.

He decided from what he did have was to add some chicken to the three type of seafood in the wild rice dish he served with teriyaki steak. Instead of it being a side dish, it would be a single course meal. It also meant he could not be overly frugal about the amount of chicken he added into it, since seafood was seldom filling unless eaten in very large quantities. As an additional bonus to the meal, he added one of the other teriyaki sauces not used for the steak. He selected the blend mostly used in stews and soups.

While preparing everything for dinner Tim's thoughts were on a brewing idea he thought might be a means to increase the services offered by Global Security Corporation. Increased services often meant increased profits, but he would need to inquire with a different group employed at the offices than he normally dealt with. He did not want to present a half-baked idea to the board, without finding out if the logistics of his concept were feasible. He would be outside of his realm of expertise, and felt his idea could be presented if it meant somebody else had to do the frosting. So first thing he would do the next day, was have Trask show him where the communications group was in the Seattle complex. As Tim understood it, they did own the building now, and he was sure other areas of it might be used for their own purposes. Other tenants on other floors simply had a new location to send lease payments to. A building such as the one in downtown Seattle would not have month to month rentals, only one or more year's leases, to keep occupancy at a profitable level. He would still need to involve others once the idea was presented, as to how many businesses would think it would benefit them with this service available.

He had prepared everything while in thought, except for the wild rice which he blended the selected teriyaki sauce into prior to the steaming, to allow the flavor to more fully penetrate the wild rice. Once that was completed, all the separate portions were put into the compartmental cooking device to be blended upon completion. He would then add the compliment of vegetables used for the wild rice upon occasion.

The main dinner components were ready in 30 minutes, and with a larger serving dish he added room temperature clutee, the Helsinki vegetable, small pea pods and some shaved carrots and mixed it all together. Since the main components were quite hot, the vegetables were simply mixed in to maintain some of its crispness.

Tim explained to Kuri and Liani this was a bit of an experiment, as it seemed in his absence, the stocks had been depleted, and this was what we had the most of to make into a meal. It should be satisfying, but it may require refinement for later meals like this. They both ate every morsel they could get, and they were quite pleased with it just the way it was. Kuri inquired about the sauce, as she could definitely tell it was not the same as the steak; but it went marvelously with the food combination he served. He told her it was one most suitable for stews and soups and one of the four they got from Japan. He had not used much of it since getting it, but now he would need to order more. She also said she had intended to restock the kitchen in the next day or two, since that was when she had expected him to be home from Hong Kong. Tim was satisfied with the results of his little cooking experiment, and could not determine where any improvement was needed. Cooking was still an experiment, and he was sure something would come along to add into it.

After dinner, he took care of cleaning up and starting the sanitizing system to have all the utensils cleaned for their next use. He then put together the list on his intellipad for the items needed for restocking, and it was largely meats other than chicken in various cuts. Steaks were the first thing that entered his IntelliPad, some others were prepared for stir fry and Chinese meals as well. Vegetable and fruits were also running low, but not nearly as depleted as the meats. Once completed he asked Kuri if she wanted to take his intellipad or send it to hers. In this case she said she would take his, as hers was fairly full with Liani's reading material, which she was going through rather quickly. Liani was becoming quite adept in reading skills, and going through most books quickly. Kuri was getting ready to upgrade the difficulty level well ahead of when she originally thought.

From there, Tim went to go through his meditation routine, he had since his encounter with the knife wielding Artimus Robbins, become prone to making certain he did it daily, regardless of his desire. Although he hoped never to be in a similar situation again, he could not overlook the fact it saved him from serious harm or worse. Kuri had Liani promise her she would not leave the seating area of the entertainment center and spent forty minutes observing Tim's routine. At the conclusion, Kuri said, "You have become quite good with that meditation routine, it is no wonder it became instinctive to you. It is also amazing how fast and hard you can kick when adrenaline flows." Tim replied, "That is an understatement, I had no idea I was capable of such force from instinctive reaction, and even though it occurred in a split second, it seemed like a much longer time frame."

Kuri went over and just hugged him saying, "I am just glad you were not harmed, it would be difficult for me not to have you around anymore. It would be especially difficult to have the number of children I would like around here without your participation." Tim said, "That is true, but you would be well taken care of and could have any other man you ever wanted, if something were to happen to me." Kuri said, "I do not want any other man, you have no idea how long I had to wait to find one like you, that made me feel cared for and loved, besides you have never denied me the ability to speak what I thought. That simply does not happen in Japan."

They both returned to the entertainment room where Liani was busy reading, and as promised did not move from her seat. Tim asked her if she would mind reading aloud so he could hear how good she has gotten. Liani read like it was merely talk, she had no long pauses or stops to the pronunciation of a single word. When she was done, Tim said it was definitely time for the next level for her. Tim decided it was time for Liani to quit reading and change over to watching the entertainment system where he found an excellent children's program for her to watch. It was one of the all-time classic Disney movies with Mickey Mouse as the sorcerer's apprentice, which ran for over an hour and half. It had extended commentary from the master himself, which had been given more up to date enhancements in video and sound quality, as well as remastered for better color. Since Walt Disney had been gone for a very long time, it was even interesting to Tim to hear from him in his own words. Tim found it even more fascinating when the master of children's animation showed how many drawings it took to create simple movements in the characters to appear in film to be moving. This was done before any such thing as computer generated graphics existed, this was all done by cartoon artists, who would spend hundreds of hours drawing the same character in mild variations of the same picture to create movement through the use of filming. It also showed how if the film was not fluid in movement, they would have to add additional drawings to create the fluidity desired.

For as many times as Tim had seen this particular Disney classic, this version was one he had never encountered. It was quite remarkable the artists could perform such masterful film creations with colored drawings. To think of all the hours it took to draw so many pictures with only the slightest variation from one to the next. And turn all those thousands of drawings into an animated movie. He himself thought the task daunting with computer generated graphics, but to do it from paper drawings, he could not even consider that something he could do. Aside from the fact he had poor artistic skills, he could not even duplicate stickmen to indicate such motion when put into sequence. With the movie over and Tim's bit of revelation over the techniques used, it was time for Liani to be put to bed. Since this involved nightly hygiene, Liani preferred her mother to oversee this routine. Tim had no issues with it, simply assuming Liani rather have someone of the same gender present. He did not think it was unusual for a young girl of Liani's age, being a little shy about some things that needed to be done.

Once Liani was in bed and given time to fall asleep, Kuri decided to give Tim a geisha style welcome back to the bedroom. This was not a multi-hour session; but it entailed a little more teasing for arousal purposes of both of them. Kuri said it was something explained to her from the geisha viewpoint, as it was also their job to be profitable. Since profit meant more partners to entertain, time was a valuable commodity to the geisha house proprietors. Needless to say it was quite erotic, pleasurable and intriguing for both Tim and Kuri. It was also, Kuri told him, to insure that Liani was not an only child. Tim took this as Kuri was no longer taking precautions, and was planning the second child arriving within the year. It would fall in line with what she originally said about children at three year intervals.

They slept within each other's embrace until morning arrived. Tim tried to release from his embrace to get out of bed for his workday without disturbing Kuri. He was unsuccessful, as Kuri told him she loved him and liked him being home. He returned to the bed and gave her a kiss, and said he liked being with her no matter where they were. Unfortunately he had to live up to other commitments, which meant being CEO of Global Security Corporation. They did provide an exceptional incentive at 250,000 WC per week. Tim was made aware by his sister that was as much as she and her husband made together in ten years. He let Kuri try to return to sleep; but it was likely she would not stay in bed much longer than Tim leaving the house. He made a simple breakfast, something more like what Liani would want every morning. Kuri already said she would be going to the grocer to restock, and with no bacon most of the shredded potatoes gone, and very little peanut oil, his breakfast choices were few. It had been a long time it seemed that he had fruit covered waffles with a drizzle of blueberry syrup.

He did is normal cleanup of the kitchen and then his morning ritual to go to work. Kuri was performing her meditation routine before he was ready to leave. He told Kuri it was not one bit fair to have her looking like that when he was trying to leave for work. It was difficult enough leaving most mornings without seeing her perfectly proportioned form in its natural state. She smiled and said she was hoping it would keep him home one more day. Tim regretted leaving that morning, but he was a man that lived up to his commitments.

He put the transport on auto pilot just so he could keep the vision in his head, knowing it was too much of a distraction to drive in manual mode. He did not come out of his revelries until the transport had announced they were in the parking space assigned to him in the parking garage. He thanked the transport for a pleasant drive and went to the office. He greeted Loretta, she welcomed him back, and he entered the main office. He had arrived a little early expecting Trask to come in about 5 to 10 minutes later, but he was already there.

Trask said, "Welcome back, I guess I missed this place more than I thought, since you have held the office. It did not take long to get back into the hours I once kept being here half an hour before everyone else. What do you need before I return to the old age home where I belong?" Tim said, "You are not that old, and the only thing I believe I need from you before you get to return to semi-retirement, is to be taken to the communication group office." Trask asked, "Why would you want to go there, they do a marvelous job and they like their privacy or so I am told?" Tim said, "It's just something I had to do in Hong Kong, and it made me realize I had no idea where our own group was at, and I need to ask some questions." Trask said, "This sounds like another idea brewing should I inquire into it further?" Tim said, "It is far too early to say it is an idea until I know it is feasible, and I am in the questions need answers stage. That does not amount to an idea until I know it is possible. Should it prove possible, then we can see whether it is something to move forward on, but in this particular case far more will need to be done by others, I simply do not have the expertise to do it."

Trask said, "You realize although you were only away 10 days, in that time I got the preliminary annual report from the accountants group. Global Security Corporation is now in excess of 160 Billion WC in assets. 50 billion are in real estate, all the office buildings and properties we own. That leave 110 Billion WC in liquid assets. Although a large portion are invested for earnings, all of them can easily be turned to use the way we have arranged it. You are responsible for this success far more than any other person associated with this company, including myself. None of these assets include the funds invested for retirement or long term care that is kept entirely separate for those specific uses. Every owner, all 10 of us have at least 10 Billion WC for our ownership, aside from the salaries we receive like every other person in the organization. I do not know how much we all owe to you for having made this company formed into more your image than any of ours."

Tim said, "You pay me quite well, and I am not that responsible for the company's assets. I could have never put together a group to lay the ground work, or have the insight to acquire properties that we did not out grow. You performed all that with the help of the others that only you knew how to contact. I know nobody in professions aside from this one. I do not believe Detective Marshall would have been able to assist in putting together this organization of experts. I only know information security and technology to make it work for this profession. Lately, I have had little time to look into new technology that would make this job easier for all, or improve what we currently use. I hope that will change now that the two suspects are in custody. I do not believe I have to follow those processes that took so much of my time. I may need to go for the legal proceedings for the suspect who will be brought to Seattle, but I no longer have to spend months and years looking for them. In all honesty, all I ever did was present ideas that resulted in you obtaining your original goals quicker than if I did not."

Trask responded with, "Some are true to that assessment, but other ideas would never have developed if you did not provide them. Even as a means of humor, which by the way has been one of the most effective means we have in bringing stress levels in line with other companies. That would have never happened in the way the rest of us thought out the company plans."

Tim said, "On the robotic systems I did not provide you with much to go on and you moved it forward in your own office first, before deciding the benefits were too great to overlook. I truly cannot take credit for that technology advancement. I provided no means of incorporating it, you took that to other people to move forward."

Trask said, "I see it differently, but your own humility will not let you still see your full potential. That is probably a good thing, cannot have too many people like me around. Anyway I shall take you to the communications group. You do realize they have been moved down to the 34th floor for the amount of space needed for their equipment."

Tim said, "How could I realize that, when I never knew where they were to start with, but it does make sense after seeing Hong Kong's group. They also stocked all the spare parts for all the equipment in the building. I do not see that being advantageous to this location though."

Trask stated, "Since you have likely not been to the 34th floor since your initial interview when we did a mass hiring for analysts, things have changed a little bit. There is no longer 34th floor access from the lobby elevator. It only allows entrance to the 35th floor and those who have offices on the 34th use a secondary elevator from the 35th floor. That elevator only allows access between the 30th to 35th floors, although we hold the other floors, they are not leased. Other floors above 35 are planned, but nothing has started. Below are accessible from the lobby elevators and require no special authorization at this time. So are you ready for the roundabout trip to go up 4 floors?"

Tim said he was, and Trask started off toward the elevator that went to 35, the concealed elevator. Once on the 35th floor they exited and made one quick turn to get to the 34th elevator. Tim did not remember it being there when he was in the director and assistant director's office prior to the CEO position on the 30th floor. He asked Trask how long ago this was put into place. Trask said, "It had been there from the beginning, but it was temporarily covered during the hiring event. Since it took nearly a year to get all the positioned filled and we had not expanded to the 34th floor, it remained covered until the first 34th floor expansion took place. At that time, the security procedure was changed in the lobby security for 35th floor only access to insure only authorized personnel utilized the elevator. That would have been about 9 years ago give or take."

Tim said, "I never even noticed, while I spent all that time of the 35th floor, suppose it was simply I was not looking over every inch of office space after the first year. It did all look the same." Trask said, "That reminds me, the 3 analysts have presented some fairly sound research, and having gone back to the original consultants, I have been informed that the newer research presented by them, is more accurate. It has not been long enough to get with the other members for the next board meeting, but it looks like changes will be in order."

"That would be good," replied Tim. "It might also be a good time to expand the analyst's office spaces, since they all now have a robotic computer systems to take up space. If I remember correctly there was barely room for two people in mine." Trask said, "I never considered that, but you are likely correct, it would mean moving a number of offices to the 34th floor to accommodate the change in office size. I would need to see how much room we have left on the 34th floor for that type of expansion, and whether it will require moving communication again."

They were on the 34th floor and the communication group was the closest area in proximity to the elevator. A good bit of the 34th floor was still unoccupied, and the dozen analyst's offices were at the far end of the room. It left a good deal of expansion, but Tim did not know if it was enough or not. Trask entered the communications area with Tim right behind and found the lead technician. Trask asked Tim if he could find his way back without an escort. Tim replied he saw no difficulty in it and Trask excused himself to go hold down the fort until Tim returned to the CEO's office.

Tim introduced himself to the lead technician and the technician introduced himself as Jack Korvin. Jack then asked what he could do for Tim. Tim said, "I just need some questions answered if you have the time." Jack indicated he had nothing but time since the AI system did almost all the work. Tim asked, "Since light speed has become the means of communications, I highly doubt system to system can be done directly in the Information Gateway, but is there a way to do such a connection?"

Jack Korvin answered with, "It has been done occasionally from here usually a result of a business moving to a larger location. It requires contacting the Satellite Company to set up the specific TRU addresses involved to redirect until further notice. That process can take them anywhere from a day to a week, why do you ask?"

Tim said, "In my time in Hong Kong, I got the impression that although your group was invaluable to the processes we use, they majority are quite bored, does the same hold true here?" Jack replied, most times, yes. We do testing, which is really a way to kill time, because the TRU's are mounted so stable there is little chance of them getting knocked out of position. As far as I know, Global Security Corporation is the only business that requires upgrades from the TRU manufacturer to be examined prior to installation. This is a security precaution implemented by the board, due to the large turnover in analysts. It has never produced anything other than acceptable code changes, but to insure a disgruntled former employee happen to be involved with the TRU code, it must be checked first. Have to make sure someone does not find a means to cripple our system or worse, because we did not check the code first. This largely is my responsibility, but updates only occur two or three times annually."

Tim asked, "What if we came up with a plan to get you more people, and keep you a little busier, would that be something you would have interest in?" Jack said, "I am all ears, I do love my work here; but it can be a bit boring when you so seldom need to perform any type of action or reaction. We have had the occasional attempt to place a virus into our system to cripple it, but that is not often enough to keep us busy. What do you have in mind?" Tim said, "This is strictly in the conception stage, but there are a number of companies with restricted access systems. It is a costly procedure to those businesses. At this point in time, I do not know if there is enough of these systems for a means to make it profitable to us. Since, it is unlikely that any company will give us free and unlimited access to their information, it would likely require a contact to each company that thinks it might be good for a monitoring service. My initial thought is that all transmissions intended for the company are filtered through our communications network, which you and your people do the monitoring. Do you follow me so far?" Jack said, "It sound like a plan, but it will take contact with the satellite company as well to divert all transmissions to one TRU to our TRU's, to filter for impurities in the information sent. It would certainly give us something more to do and feel more productive in this organization. What you describe would not involve analysts, would it?"

Tim said, "No, it is a bit out of my area of expertise, but it would be a valuable service to add to those we already offer. It would fall largely on the lead technicians in the offices to insure it is done properly. I would certainly include incentives to make it worth everyone's effort as a part of taking on a new service." Jack asked, "What kind of incentives?" Tim said, "Since the largest responsibility would fall on lead technicians, if the profitability of this service proved out, I would insist on bonuses be divided among lead technicians. In addition, not knowing if this will lead to stress issues like analysts first encountered, being included in the retirement program for all communications technicians. The stress levels would determine percentage, and timeframe for retirement. Currently for analysts hired after all the robotic systems are in place, it is 40 percent of your salary in 10 years, 60 percent in 20 and 75% in 25 years. For original analysts it was 75% for 10 years of service, but most have left before they made it to exactly 10 years. With the AI system doing the majority of the work, I do not see stress levels being that high for communications technicians. Even after 25 years for many, that is well before they could retire anywhere else, with far less retirement money to work with."

Jack Korvin said, "Those are some mighty good incentives, makes me wish I was an analyst instead of a communications technician." Tim said, "Considering 95 percent of the analysts that started with the opening of this company failed, and most are in care facilities for being incapable of anything mentally taxing, you might think differently on that." Jack said, "Point taken, I did not realize it was that stressful."

Tim said, "Does this concept seem like a service we could offer?" Jack said, "Knowing a good deal of companies are in home businesses that require restricted access, it may not have the potential of the other services. I know almost every home based business that created something unique without having started out with precautions, learned the hard way when a bigger fish got it into production before the home based business owner was able to get it to a potential buying interest. Most of them now use a separate computer for their product, and another for IG access. Some build a prototype, kept secure for demonstration purposes, and do not allow it out of their sight during that time. Again, most of them learned this after being the victim of idea theft. Large companies employ a number of people for the specific purpose of stealing some small business's design concepts. Do not know about all military, but this country has already spent the money for the additional technology unique to their systems, and are unlikely to want any part of it." I cannot say how many larger companies and government groups may think it a benefit, which you will need from someone else. I do see the potential advantages, and if it comes to a service you can count me in."

Tim was in the communications area for a little more than 45 minutes and got the most important information for the idea he was forming. It took another 7 minutes to get the two elevators to get to the 30th floor and return to the office.

Trask was waiting for him and said, "You know, I have missed coming here every day since I have no longer needed to. Now that I am here every day for the last 10 days, I found myself wishing I were home with the wife, or running about town doing what I like. It is a quandary to me, why it is so much different now than the 10 years I was here every day. Never thought much about what the other family members were up to, just assumed they had their ways to keep busy. There are times though, where I see too much of my wife, and I do not want to start taking her for granted. So I am thinking, since she has something to do once a week, I spend that day here with you to see if I am still a viable part in this company. I would not need Loretta to fill me in every week, if I can see it for myself."

Tim said, "It is your company, you certainly do not need my permission for doing that. It will cause me no problems as I do what is needed when it is needed. Although, I might have a little more time now, to look into the technology changes that have occurred over the last four years." Trask said, "That would be a good thing to learn from you, since you seemed far more adept at it than anyone else here, including myself. Should I ask what you did in communications for nearly an hour?"

Tim said, "Largely the lead technician has given me the information needed to see if the idea I have brewing is feasible. It is, now someone else will need to tell me on what scale, as I do not know and neither did Jack Korvin." Trask said, "Fill me in coach, what are you thinking?"

Tim said, "Fine, but keep in mind this is far more a concept than a real plan. Since there are a large number of businesses with restricted access systems and they are not inexpensive to keep in that mode. I was looking into the possibility of offering a service utilizing our communication groups to divert all the transmissions to the restricted access systems to look for problems. The AI systems handles the largest portion of that function, but transgressions are displayed on their monitoring equipment. This type of service would not involve a single analyst, and be done solely through our communications groups. If the fee is not too excessive it might be something to offer to small in home businesses, who rely on their designs to sell to larger companies. Many learn the hard way, they have had their idea stolen by the larger companies, and put into production before they can react to the theft. I simply do not know how big of demand a service such as this would have. Additionally, I have no real means to find out. I believe it has potential, and now knowing it can be done with the aid of the satellite companies, I would like to have it further investigated as a potential service we can offer. It may mean additional communications technicians, and additional monitoring equipment. I do not see this as being anywhere near as stressful as the first 10 years of analysts. I do believe it would mean a little more salary to those involved, and if a bonus were to come as result, it should be divided between the lead technicians as the biggest responsibility will rest squarely on their shoulders. Also, I believe if we were to offer this as a service, the communications technicians be included in the retirement plan; but at what time frame will be determined by whatever stress levels it might create."

Trask said, "You are taking us into new frontiers with this type of service. You do realize that no member of the board or ourselves for that matter have extensive expertise in this area, what makes you think it will work?" Tim said, "You have not had to watch every move by every analyst hired for the functions of those people. I seriously doubt with the company's penchant for getting the best possible employees, it is any different in the communications group. The lead technicians I have met, are all quite good in the area they have the expertise. It will be the lead technicians, who would have the biggest part in this service being successful, if it becomes an offering. First, I would think by whatever means you have at your disposal, to find out how many businesses would consider this a viable option for them. Without that type of input, I cannot fathom a way to determine if we could offer a service reasonable priced, without some idea of how many companies might have use for it. It will require information and business contacts we have never needed before according to the lead technician. Since we are targeting restricted access systems, they are not going to give us a free run at the information they have in order to determine if it is authorized. The AI will need some guidelines, likely differing with each business, to determine if an unauthorized attempt is being made at the business. As to the monitoring that is flagged by the AI for review, it would require a contact within the business to make that determination, with that contact having more extensive knowledge, than they would allow us to have. It would still be approved or disapproved by that business the service is for. Since I do not believe many of these types of businesses operate in 24/7 mode. I believe the largest part of this service would fall in a Monday through Friday normal work week time frame. We being the company with 24/7 coverage, would still have people present during other hours as is normal for us; but should not need increased staff outside of the normal work week. I will leave you time to digest as much of this concept as I can give you at the moment to determine if you wish to move forward or leave things as they are."

CHAPTER

18

Trask had started the ball rolling on the number of restricted access systems in use around the globe with the other board members, and the teams they had around the globe. He was given the impression it would take 3 to 6 months to get the final results, before he left that day. He would be in every Wednesday for the next year at least.

For the next three weeks, everything went pretty much to routine at both work and home. There were no major issues to deal with and in that time, Tim had only found one technology improvement and he was uncertain of whether it was truly needed.

On the Wednesday, Trask was in the office, he had Nora bring up the information he discovered. To see if Trask thought it would be something he might consider utilizing. It was no major profit maker, or even something to help further reduce the stress level of analysts. It was a newly developed synthetic skin for the robotic humanoids around the entire Seattle office, and many of the satellite offices under their control. It presented a more human touch to the robotic systems currently operating in the offices. Tim was not looking to create a more realistic type person, but for the ability to do simple handshakes, or the sound deadening of running into walls and such. Although the board had not met just yet, to give feedback on the proposal last submitted by the three recruits. There was no cost prediction for the synthetic skin to make it difficult to make a firm decision on utilizing it. Tim simply let Trask decide if it was something he would consider putting to use. If it was to be a trial run, Tim was sure Nora would not mind having a more realistic appearance. Tim jokingly said, it may mean a make-up room for Nora to look her best. Trask thought it humorous as well. Tim got no real read on Trask as to whether he was considering it, but left it at that.

Another Wednesday was spent with Trask to show him just what technology research was. Largely, it started with looking into a number of articles on the Information Gateway to see what had been in the works. Many of the articles were once again detailing robotic functions that were major improvements, or new to the use of robotics in the manufacturing environment. This was not an area Global Security Corporation had become active in for their own needs. That same day, Tim, Trask and Loretta went to lunch together for the first time since Tim had been at the company. He had separate lunches with each before, and never both at the same time. It was on this luncheon, which Trask proved to Loretta the Cognac he preferred was at this restaurant, largely due to his insistence. He also made certain that he was not the only one to partake in it. Trask provided Loretta with the proper technique demonstration before she duplicated it. Loretta found Cognac to be quite a bit better than wine.

In the third week, the board meeting was called for and Tim offered one additional proposal he felt should be incorporated into the standard procedures of the entire company. Tim said, due to the problems he encountered in Hong Kong and although it may be rare enough. Having a former employee still having access to systems and entry should be revoked upon the exit of the employee. Should a former employee return to the company at a later date, then access can be reestablished, already having records of the person. Since in the case of Hong Kong, and an employee had gone missing, somebody else used that access to look into the system. He did not think it impossible for former employees to do so remotely, if they felt they had been wronged by the company in some fashion or another. As a precaution and security measure, he strongly suggested the procedure remove people no longer with GSC, to prevent such incidents from occurring once again.

This got an overwhelming approval at the meeting by all the board members without any long and drawn out discussion. It would be the responsible of the security guard for the elevators and the HR people for all the analysts, to have the name forwarded to the code group to revoke the name on the list from system access. Tim also added that communication and virus malware groups being somewhat private would have to have any former employees access revoked from within their own little groups. No one else had access to their systems, although he did not believe there was much turnover in those areas. Procedures should be forwarded to them for this purpose.

On Friday of the third week, Nora announced the vidphone connection from Detective Marshall of the Seattle Police Department. Tim greeted the detective and asked what was going on. Detective Marshall called to inform Tim that Rebecca Robbins was coming to Seattle over the weekend, being escorted by mama bear and wolf although, the only reason two were doing it was, it was their policy. Rebecca was not a major threat to either one of them, but Hong Kong had a few more dealings with more vicious persons, so two were always required. Did not have the date for her trial just yet. Tim would be needed for that, to give his information to the legal system concerning her participation in the criminal activity that took place.

Tim acknowledge that and told the detective he had a gift for him at his own house; but did not know how to get to him. He did tell the detective he would need to acquire his own number of proper glasses for the consumption of it, and if he did not want to share it then he only needed one. The detective asked if it was Cognac, and Tim said it was the same brand he had on the plane from Hong Kong. The detective said he would only need one, since his wife hardly ever drank anything of that type of beverage. He said she might drink a glass of wine once a year, except she was fond of something for New Year's Eve at the turn of midnight, but that was bubbly. The detective said he would likely be at the station on Monday morning, if Tim wanted to bring it to him there. The arrangements were made and the police station was not all that far from his office. This time it would be with his own transportation though.

The end of day and start of the weekend led to having as much of the family over for dinner as was willing to attend. It turned out to not be the best weekend for it. Both his brother and sister with their families, were going out for visiting the other sides of their families, while Kuri's parents were in Tokyo for the monthly check on all the restaurants. That left only his parents and grandparents to join them. With the Seattle restaurant, always busy, Kuri's brother and his family seldom could get the opportunity to attend a family get together. After making a dinner for the ladies for the evening, Tim asked what Kuri would think a good dish to serve that was not teriyaki steak for the next evening with the guests coming over. Tim was thinking a good pork or chicken type stir fry, which was not too spicy, more in the Japanese style than Chinese. Kuri said that would be good, but instead of white or brown rice have a bed of fried rice. Also needed a pie or two for desert. Tim asked if she ever had coconut cream pie, it was similar to banana cream; but less filling. Kuri said she never had it but she would try it, not sure if Liani would like it, but would not know until she tried it. With that in mind, Tim checked the stocks and needed to get a few things in the morning to insure all would go as planned for the evening meal.

The evening routine was still Liani pouring through all the reading material she could. She had become quite adept at the reading skills, and Tim suggested to Kuri maybe it was time to get her over to printing, and then writing, or she would be reading high school books by the time she started school. Kuri laughed; but said it would probably be a good idea to keep her in the learning mood, and to change gears a little bit. Next would be basic math skills, which usually was not started until near school age for kids in this country. Japan starting ahead of the curve, Tim did not know where it fell into their schooling. Liani was reading until nearly 10 PM, having finished yet another book which was at about the 3rd grade level from Tim's recollection. With the book finished, it was time for Liani to go through her bedtime preparations with Kuri, and then to bed. Tim went to the lower level and performed his meditation routine, he learned firsthand the importance this routine was in keeping himself from harm from another. He would not get lazy in his performance, considering how little time one had when a threat could become reality. He performed his routine with a new found determination to keep in the best condition he could.

After he completed his routine and returned to the main level, he went through his normal nighttime ritual. It was time for him and Kuri to do some relaxing in front of the entertainment system, with something they could enjoy which was not animated. The movie chosen was an action film with a mix of martial arts, in addition to other more common weapons. Kuri noted that the particular martial arts expert, was not truly likely to move fast enough to avoid speeding projectiles; but the concept was intriguing. She explained what see saw as far as technique was concerned. First, the expert determined which hand was used for the handgun. Facing his opponent, he would twist his torso for a smaller target area, and always lean back in the same direction, to match the hand. Allowing the projectile to speed harmlessly past. The expert's weapon was referred to as throwing darts; but none resembled what many considered to be darts. These were relative flat, with multiple pointed tip from 3 to six with the center being quite flat and easy to grip in two fingers. It took many hours of practice to be accurate with such a weapon. They were deadly accurate when properly used, which was no farther than 50 feet and shorter preferred. Over 50 feet, took too much time to make a good throwing motion, which was done from one side of the body to front release, with a wrist action to achieve velocity. At the completion of the movie Kuri informed Tim she had a doctor's appointment set for Tuesday.

Tim knowing Kuri did not tell him of most of her normal checkup appointment nor Liani's for that matter. It left him with having to ask why she was telling him this. She said it was to find out if Liani was going to have a brother or sister in less than 8 months. Kuri said she was going to insist on not seeing the scan, so she would not know which, if in fact there was one on the way. It would mean, approximately 9 weeks after Liani started her schooling, she would be in the hospital for a couple of days to bring home her baby brother or sister. It may be necessary to see if his grandmother or mother could insure she did her schooling during her absence and likely his, as he would want to be there also. Tim said he could check after it was confirmed, but he saw no reason it would be out of the question for either his mother or grandmother. Both loved having new family members to spoil. Kuri said it would not be a new family member they get to spoil, but one they already have had the opportunity with, and that Tim made it difficult for anybody to spoil a child, who already had life pretty easy. Although, they both could dote over her quite well, whenever they came over during the day, while Tim was at work.

Once again Tim is the last to know, because he did not know his mother or grandmother just popped in to see their little Liani. They probably know how smart she is too. It was not like Liani was a bragger; but her interest in reading was rather relentless. She could not get enough it seemed.

The night was simple cuddling and light affections, and that lasted throughout the night until they fell asleep. It was a pleasant sleep and Tim awoke first, which was hardly unusual. He was able to get out of bed without disturbing Kuri, and went about his morning hygiene ritual before making a breakfast. He decided no bacon, since it was the one thing that roused the ladies out of their sleep. He could not make hash browns without bacon, so he decided on a breakfast sandwich using an English muffin with an egg and some ham and some cheese. He made enough for all three of them, and this would be right up Liani's alley, as she could use her hands to eat a sandwich.

Even though no bacon or hash browns were made, the ladies of the house managed to rouse themselves from bed to arrive in the kitchen in time for breakfast to be served. Tim said to Kuri, "See no bacon, and yet you're still here." She said she could still smell something cooking enough to wake her. She was also a little bit hungry to add to her ability to get out of the bed. Liani, now having a bed, she could easily get out of on her own, took care of her initial needs to get to the kitchen.

Breakfast was served, and although it was not as much as some breakfasts, it was sufficient to get to lunchtime. Cleanup duties fell into Tim's responsibility, and Kuri started Liani on her latest skill of printing the alphabet, after a quick set of instructions. Liani got right to the work at hand, and Kuri went to perform her meditation routine, while Liani promised not to move from the seating area in the entertainment room. Tim completed the cleanup and checked to see how Liani was doing. It was not pretty; but practice would allow her to improve, but it could be identified and considering she never held any type of instrument to produce print, she was doing fairly well with the stylus used on the intellipad.

Tim went off to perform his morning hygiene ritual, and dress so he could go to the grocer as soon as Kuri had finished her routines. He was finished, before Kuri had completed her meditation routine, so he went back to keep an eye on Liani. She was making her way through the last half of the alphabet, but would need to go through it several more times to clean up her printing for straighter lines, and circles as well. Still she was well ahead of most children her age. In 2 weeks, she would reach the half way point to year three. He wondered if Kuri had asked her about having a brother or sister to keep her company, and occupied as well. It was not his place to ask until it was confirmed, and that may be what Kuri would wait on.

It was another 40 minutes when Kuri made it back to the entertainment area, and Tim let her know he needed to go the grocer to get things for the dinner for the evening. Asked what time everyone would be expected, and Kuri said 6 PM for dinner. They usually arrive a little earlier for conversation, and to see their granddaughter or great granddaughter depending on whom it was. Tim told Kuri he did not expect to be gone too awfully long, but he had not been to the grocer on a weekend for some time, and it was usually a little busier that time of week.

When Tim got to the grocer, he was surprised by the number of people who chose today to get food, he tried to get the things he needed quickly, but there simply were too many people to get it done quick. He had to wait for everything it seemed. The checkout line was even longer than the lines to get to the items he needed, although he was able to get all he needed, it took over an hour and half for what normally would have taken 10 to 15 minutes. Tim vowed to himself, never wait until Saturday again for groceries. When he returned home, and Kuri saw how little he really had she asked what took so long. He said it seemed the entire area had decided to go get groceries today, and he largely had to wait in a line for everything he got and then longer to check out. As a result, he will never go on Saturday again for groceries. He was gone too long as far as he was concerned, and he discovered he was not too patient when it came to shopping of any sort. He liked very much going and getting what was required, and being able to leave promptly.

He would need to start something for lunch in an hour, and he did not want anything too heavy for a big dinner planned for the evening. He thought out his options and decided a julienne type salad with chicken and ham thinly sliced, some cheese and the standard vegetable mix of his salads. He had a rather sweet honey mustard dressing that should blend nicely.

Since everything was already prepared in containers in the environmental kitchen cooling system, all he had to do was place the correct amount of each item in a serving dish, and top with the dressing to mix into the salad. Until that time arrived, he spent it with Kuri and

Liani in the entertainment room. With Liani busy learning to print, there was not much conversation, it was sufficient to just be together as a family. They each took turns trying to improve Liani's technique in printing, but it took time with a new writing implement to learn the coordination to have it move exactly the way you want it. Getting Liani to keep practicing would not be an issue, she had the thirst to learn as much as she could as fast as she could. Tim and Kuri both decided, it would be better to learn to write than how to use the computer for the same purpose. At some point, she would need to have a signature, which was still necessary for certain documents. Although those documents may be digitally stored, the signature was used as proof of almost any form of contract.

The time for lunch had arrived, and Tim took all of 5 minutes to have it ready for everyone to enjoy. Kuri and Tim did have to help Liani with her salad, she was better with a spoon than a fork, and still preferred fingers first. This was something that required practice as well, but it would come in time. After lunch, which everyone enjoyed, Tim took care of the kitchen cleanup and it was not extensive. He took the opportunity to go to the audio room to listen to one album, since he had not heard most of the ones he got the last Christmas. He found it had the wonderful guitar that got his interest to start with. He discovered the person playing was Hubert Sumlin, who was an excellent guitar player, but spent most of his career in other people's bands, as a member. He was quite good with making it sound emotional with feeling, but felt he never had the voice to go on his own. Tim was sure he could make that guitar sing for certain. After listening to the audio disk, he went to the computer to find his normal spending account had too much money in it, and transferred a good amount to the interest earning account. He still left 300,000 WC in his normal account, which was largely more than the family spent in a month. Kuri had increased the food trips to the grocers, but other than that, expenses were nominal for upkeep on 3 homes.

He returned to the entertainment room, and stayed with the lovely ladies until around 4 PM in order to get all the dinner preparation done, to have the meal ready at 6 PM. It took Tim roughly one hour to get all the food prepared completely, and into the compartmentalized cooking device. Fifteen minutes later his parents and grandparents arrived, a little earlier than expected; but not too early that it was an issue. With their arrival,

Liani put down her intellipad without being asked, to give them a welcome that only children can accomplish. Liani always enjoyed the company of other family members, and was now to the point where she could converse with them to a good degree. She understood all the questions asked of her, and although she did not vocalize a large vocabulary just yet, she answered them. Knowing the family would usually indulge in coffee before and during most meals, he had the coffee ready. Kuri preferred tea, and Liani some juice. He started the next pot of coffee after serving out the first pot. Dinner was ready at precisely 6 PM, where Tim had set the table and set out a large serving dish of the pork and chicken stir fry in a teriyaki and soy blend sauce, with fried rice, which included several additional vegetables, in small little pieces. It blended into the rice better that way, but still created the extra flavors.

Everyone put their rice down using the stir fry combination over the top. It was intended to be an all in one meal. The flavor was perfect from Tim's perspective, but he was not the only judge at the table. It was something different from what most of them normally ate. Since all the food disappeared, Tim made the assumption everyone enjoyed their food. With all the dinner plates cleared from the table Tim offered the coconut cream pie as desert, and refilled all the coffee cups. Also got Kuri more tea and Liani more juice, she had really taken a fancy to grape juice. Tim offered other drinks, but tonight everyone was sticking to coffee, so he made another pot for those who would want more. With the dinner and desert served, everyone headed to the entertainment area to decide after the nightly news broadcast, what to watch. Tim took care of getting all the items used for dinner and desert into the sanitizing unit, and started the device. Everything from lunch through dinner was now being sanitized and when completed, Tim could put them back into the proper places. He joined them in the entertainment room. These days, Kuri and Tim were not the attention of his parents and grandparents, Liani was soaking up the attention. It was quite acceptable to Tim and Kuri for that matter, but occasionally they would have to respond to a question. The latest question was asked of Kuri like somebody had foresight wanting to know when Liani would have another sibling to keep her company.

Kuri did not give them any clue she was going to see the doctor in three days, and just said she hoped it would be soon. Of course, Liani wanted to know what a sibling was, and Kuri, his mother and grandmother all gave her similar responses. Of course, that led to other questions, like where do you get them from, is there a store for them too, was how Liani phrased it. Tim had to say since she was a smart girl she would know when her mother started to change a little, that she would be able to expect another brother or sister. Tim was not about to explain to a child of less than three years of age more in depth. Kuri decided it was the best approach for now until she was older, and it would be a part of her other learning from mother to daughter as was Japanese custom.

The nightly news had come to closure with no major events to address. The movie choices were varied; but none of the ones available were movies Tim was interested in seeing. The alternative was sports programming, which none of the ladies much cared for, so the movie selection was one the ladies agreed they would enjoy seeing. Tim found it a rather dull film, and his grandfather must have felt the same, as he was asleep after 15 minutes into the movie. His grandmother commented he had spent too much time in his workshop getting the pieces done for Toranaga, although he never had a problem sleeping through movies he found boring. The movie lasted 90 minute longer than it should have in Tim's opinion, but after it was over it was time for everyone to head to their own homes. All and all, Tim thought the evening meal went well and Kuri told him she thought so too, since there was nothing but empty plates in the end. Liani was ready for some sleep as well, and she did not quite make it to the end of the movie.

Kuri got Liani roused enough to go take care of her nightly routines before going to bed, and Tim went to the computer room to perform his meditation routine. Kuri had Liani all taken care of and back to sleep, and came down to watch Tim's routine. In particular she wanted to make sure of his five minutes per each leg hold. When Tim was completed, Kuri only said he appeared not to have any problems holding the position for the correct endurance. She could see nothing he needed to improve in his routine, it was as complete as her own, even under different styles.

The night was fairly well spent, and they were content with just holding each other until sleep came to them both. It was a peaceful night and they both slept quite well.

Kuri awoke a couple minutes before Tim for a change, and got out of bed to go right into her meditation routine. Tim remained in bed; but opened his eyes just enough to watch her every move. Even in the buff the grace she moved with was captivating. He watched until the very end, something he almost never got to do, but the leg move was something that he could never achieve, and it was amazing to watch her perform those moves. She did not notice him watching her, and then he moved enough to show he was awake. She asked how long he had been awake, and Tim told her long enough to see every move she made and was still amazed by it. She called him a sneaky husband if she did not know he was awake from the beginning. He simply said it was so seldom he got to see every move she made that it seemed like the best opportunity he would get for a while. She told him it was time for him to start breakfast, and to make it the good one with bacon, hash browns and eggs benedict. She was hungry this morning but did not understand for what reason. It was not like she and he had a long night of pleasures to work up an appetite. Tim just said, maybe she was eating for more than one. It was one of the signs the last time when she carried Liani. She had to think back on that to recall if it was, and she could not be sure about his observation. She did not know for sure just yet, but the doctor would confirm it, although she could not think of anything in recent months to have cause her to skip a month.

Tim went to get the requested breakfast started, and Kuri considered it time to check on Liani to find her just waking from a long night's sleep. It took just about an hour from preparation to serving and the line was already formed and seats taken. Tim was glad he did not put out the cups and utensils, thinking they would have pounded on the countertop to display their impatience. As far as Kuri and Liani were concerned, it was about time when breakfast was served, and they did not wait even a second for Tim to get the breakfast drinks. That was before he even got to the seating side of the counter top to take his seat. Liani was well into eating her muffin type sandwich of course with her hands, which would require a little bit of cleaning afterwards. She found she could do the bacon that way also; but used a spoon to hold her hash browns to get to her mouth. For a girl who only wanted fruited top waffles, she was enjoying her breakfast with no fruit.

Tim got to do the kitchen cleanup, and start the sanitizing unit before getting to the point to get his morning ritual completed and dressed. The weather although a bit chilly, was not too awful for this time of year, and Tim though a family stroll through the woods would be good exercise for Liani. Kuri agreed that Liani spent far too much time with an intellipad in her hands. They spent an hour and half walking through the wooded area on the properties. While out, Tim was checking for various limbs that may have broken off and in general the condition of the trees. He came to the conclusion the best way to get his wood for the grill would be to have tree experts go through the forest area without taking any trees down. He would want them to trim the parts necessary to improve the growth and take care of branches not doing well. He did not think the time of year would be advantageous to trimming only what was needed. Thinking the time to determine that would be when they started budding. Once back to the house and coats removed and hung, Liani was back to the intellipad, working on her printing skills. The day was for relaxing and outside of Tim making a light lunch and later a fair dinner all was pretty calm around the house. Tim got to perform his meditation routine several hours earlier than normal.

The evening was considered over with Liani getting ready for bed, and being tucked in for the night by her parents. Once asleep, Tim and Kuri retired to their own room for some affection time before going to sleep themselves.

Monday morning arrived with Tim getting up a little early to make his delivery trip to the Seattle Police department, where Detective Marshall was working from. The Cognac was kept in the garage until he arranged a means to get it to him, and took only a moment to place in the transport. His trip was no more eventful than any other to the downtown area. He had to wait for the detective to make it to the front desk, longer than he planned. Detective Marshall also asked since Rebecca Robbins was in their protection, whether he needed to talk with her anymore. Tim had all the information he needed from Hong Kong and had no additional reasons to converse with her at this time. He did not want to really sway his opinion formed from the first conversation in Hong Kong. He took the detective to his transport, and presented him with a full case of 12 bottles of Cognac as promised. Not truly knowing which vehicle was the detective's, he left it to the detective of where he would keep it until he went home that evening. It seemed Tim found a good place to park as the detective took it two vehicles, to place inside the vehicle where it would not be noticed. Outside of a few pleasantries exchanged, they both had other duties to perform and went their separate ways.

Tim arrived approximately 15 minutes later than normal, and Loretta asked if he had a rough weekend. Tim said nothing of the sort, he had a delivery this morning that took longer than he anticipated; but he was not excessively late. He got to the office and the week was about to begin. He said hello to Nora, Daisy and Anabelle with greetings returned and nothing major to report.

CHAPTER

19

Tim's major hurdles in the death of a Global Security Corporation analyst were largely behind him, except for the legal proceedings, and he had no option but to wait until he was told otherwise. One thing he had put off due to all his time spent pursuing the Robbins in Hong Kong and the search prior, was to call General Robert York to inform him he might be able to obtain more funds, but it would need research on his part. While it was fresh in his thoughts he said, "Nora, can you place a videophone call to General Robert York when you can please?" Nora replied, "You know I cannot resist when you say please." With the completion of her statement the videophone came out of hiding and the general was staring back at him. Tim: "General I hope I am not disturbing you." General Robert York: "Not at all, I was able to acquire a large number of tires from your last call, and I believe the roads have improved a bit in the time as well." Tim: "I was told by others, the roads were being repaired, but I have driven a transport for years, and never contacted them, and never travelled while repairs were in progress apparently, but that is the precise reason I called. Since Clean Sweep was into multiple means of methods to obtain funds, and not seemly concerned about just how they went about it, I find it difficult to believe they would put all of it into a single account. Since I do not have access to government archives, I thought you might be able to dig deeper into it for other accounts, which may not have been accessed for at least 85 years. The file name given to you previously was discovered entirely by accident, but the person who found it, had to go back nearly 90 years into the investment earnings before finding a transaction other than investment earnings.

Truly not knowing how file names were developed by the government 90 to 100 years ago, I cannot tell you how to go about your search. If the names were chosen by the Vice President at the time, I truly doubt he was that inventive about naming files to insure he did not forget about them when needed. If the file names were assigned by another government agency, that could lead to problems. Although, I do believe that all the accounts would have been started at nearly the same time as the first account you already accessed."

General York: "I see, this is very enlightening. I will look into it and let you know what I discover, although I cannot promise it will be in the next 48 hours. This could be a wild goose chase, but I see where you may have some logic in you line of thinking. It never occurred to me they would not want to keep all of it in a single account, but I am no finance wizard. It seems logical that when you obtain money from means less than lawful, to keep it from becoming seized, and you would not want it all to be in a single bundle."

Tim: "I just thought it might prove beneficial to find all of it possible, instead of letting some investment firm making large earnings from money that could be used for better purposes. I have no idea how much you might find, but if it is substantial, I believe you already have a good idea how to put it to its best possible usage. I wish I could be more helpful for you than a vague concept, but without the archive files available to anyone other than the government, I must let you do as you wish with this information."

General York: "I will assume the Vice president created the file names and in all likelihood they will be sequential to keep from getting confused over other files he may have had to deal with at that time in our history. Even then, computers played a large part in the workings of government in this country. I believe there were still some people not that computer savvy, and did not always trust them. Even then, they would not have been in the majority of the populace of any government."

Tim and the general made their parting statements and the vidphone disconnected, and retracted into the ceiling location to keep it out of sight until needed. Tim had no real pending issues that required his immediate attention. The AI network was continuing to keep up to date on 95% of all tracing issues and with audio trace back into the plan, the analysts were quickly able to resolve the other 5% of issues needing their intervention. He did not anticipate any additional input this quickly from the search over companies interested in the restricted systems support proposal recently submitted. So he went about some research into new technology available, to see if anything would benefit the security business. Before getting started with research he made contact with JP and Loretta to see if they would like to join him for lunch today.

It was accepted by both and he had a luncheon date set before getting into his research. He did research time up until his lunchtime appointment which proved entirely fruitless. Once again, he was not finding anything that would achieve better results in the security of the Information Gateway than what they already had incorporated into their procedures already.

JP arrived in Tim's office just as he finished up with his research attempt, and he greeted JP. JP asked, "Are you about ready for lunch?" Tim replied, "Just finished up here, and we just need to get Loretta and we can go." From there the two went to the front desk where Loretta was just getting up for her trip to the ladies room to be ready in five minutes. Tim and JP waited for her to arrive before they went to the elevator, to exit the building. In the elevator JP asked Tim if he knew of any design consultant by any chance, as the people from properties were looking for one for expanding this building. Tim inquired as to how they were going to be expanding. JP said the plan was to add 10 floors above the 35th floor for executive office suites. The idea was for prestigious office space for those companies and businesses that wanted to be seen as highly successful, and the space would not be used by Global Security Corporation but as a means for increasing property revenues. Tim said he could check with his brother who worked for a San Francisco based firm that were design consultants, and had a good deal of experience in the type of expansion he was talking about. Tim did not know if his brother would be the consultant involved, not knowing his specific area of expertise in design.

They arrived at the restaurant, and business was rather brisk today and they had to wait about five minutes for a table to be ready. Conversation at the restaurant was entirely family oriented, and Tim was in a waiting pattern to find out if a second addition to his family was going to be confirmed the following evening. As far as his input to the conversation it was largely how well Liani was doing in her reading and writing skills at such a young age. Not quite being three years old, she was remarkably determined in learning. Tim thought she already had the reading skills of a school age child in fourth grade; but was just now starting with writing. JP and Loretta could not believe at her age she was already so far ahead of children her own age. Tim told them it was from her Japanese heritage, and her mother insisted she start her schooling at the age of 3, like all other Japanese children. Even Kuri found her learning intensity far beyond most at her age. JP admitted his were grown enough to be on their own, but none were to the point of giving him grandchildren, but it was a possibility now that his daughter had recently married.

Tim asked why he was not aware of that. JP told him they were sneaky about it and nobody knew until after the fact, and it was a little late to have a ceremony and all the normal process of a wedding. Apparently, the two decided to keep it as simple as they possibly could and made the decision without consulting either of their parents.

Tim said his mother said the same about both his brother and sister, and his parents were rather disappointed in how they found out. Loretta only added a little to the conversation and enjoyed her meal. Tim took care of the charges for the luncheon and they all returned to their office area. Tim spent a little time conversing with Nora and she really had nothing for him to do while he waited for any responses from his proposal, the time for his jury deposition or any other issues on hold.

Surprisingly enough, near the end of his workday, his vidphone went active with Nora announcing it was General Robert York. He had the general in his view as soon as the vidphone came into full view. Tim: "I certainly did not expect to hear from you so soon, what's up?"

General Robert York: "Got lucky I guess, you were correct in assuming Clean Sweep did not put all the funds into a single investment account. By doing a search with the original archive file name, I found they had a total of six accounts. One being the one we already knew about. What took so much time was going back through all of the accounts to find the last activity other than investment earnings. One account was used to pay out all the members of Clean Sweep, with a rather large amount to live off of for two or three centuries. Many were for 500,000,000.00 each, but I believe it was prior to world currency and most likely US dollars at that time. I believe the exchange rate was relatively close to one to one at that time. That account was only at 5 billion left with investment earning as of today. Two other accounts had about the same as what was already found. I am thinking these were largely expense accounts to cover the cost of whatever business each account was set up for. The remaining two accounts however, were rather massive. Each well in excess of 100 Billion WC. One account would be sufficient to cover the entire cost of updating our current major road surfaces throughout the entire country. I will be sending that along to those who can put it to the best possible use. Although the government department contracts all the work out, no longer having people in the government to perform the jobs. On the other hand, with the work contracted out, it gets done much quicker and efficiently. Still, it would mean new road surfaces for all of the country, at least with major roads. The other account I need to see from farther up the chain how to best go about it, but I suspect it would allow us to revamp the entire military from where we are currently. So I do thank you for providing me this bit of information."

Tim: "It was government funds, I felt it would be best utilized by the government than obtaining the funds for other uses. I am glad it will be used for the major thoroughfares to allow for better surfaces to use with wheeled vehicles."

Tim and the general continued to talk about items not pertaining to the funds found for about 15 minutes. At which point the vidphone connection was terminated and Tim prepared to leave for the night. Tim left for home for another uneventful trip. He greeted his lovely ladies upon arrival and said he had one more thing to do prior to starting dinner, and told Kuri he was heading to his brother's home to see about a project Global was considering undertaking quite soon.

He arrived and his brother answered before he had to knock, apparently he had more security than Tim had on his home. Tim started out the conversation with, "Since you are a design consultant, do you have a specific area of design you are mostly involved with?" His brother, George, said he did whatever the concept covered so no particular area, he just did not get involved with estimated costs for the project. "Why do you ask?" Tim said, "Global Security Corporation has decided they want to add an additional 10 stories to the current building for executive suites, for the primary purpose of leasing to those who want more prestige in their business appearance. I was asked today on the way for a luncheon, whether I knew anybody who was a design consultant, and you were the obvious person to come to mind. I did not know what process you might need to follow through with your company, so I came to ask you."

George: "I believe being the only consultant in Seattle that I am aware of, I would be the one to initiate the process. That would mean a meeting with whoever you have in charge of that particular function within your company. It would be a rare thing for me to have a face to face meeting with a potential client, but that would be the best way to go about it. I usually get projects sent to me, and work from the particular requirements provided to come up with a design concept that meets the needs of the client. It is not always a fast process, truly depending on what is needed. Some companies we do business with are also the construction company, and only want a design, whereas others want the whole package to include every phase of the construction process. As a design consultant firm, we have people outside of our company capable of performing virtually any type of procedure involved in the construction process, right down to finishing details as simple as window coverings."

Tim: "The person who asked me would not be the person for you to meet; but should I give him this vidphone routing to start the ball rolling, or does it need to be arranged through your home office?" George: "I can do the initial contact and just inform the home office about the potential business. Until there is a firm commitment, and often companies want design plans from several before committing to any single one."

Tim: "I do not think they are looking for multiple designs, although they would be relatively new at additions to existing properties they own. I believe this would be the first of all the properties they own around the globe, which last I heard was every building except for Hong Kong and Tokyo and St. Petersburg, where the purchase price was too steep considering the demand, those cities have for space. St. Petersburg was simply against government policies for anyone not Russian to own property in the country. To be perfectly honest, I do not have any idea how many locations they have with all of the satellite offices. I have never visited. Not that I would want to visit every single one of them, but there should be at least 50 or 60 in this country alone, and that does not include our northern or southern neighbors. I was told all the properties were selected because they had room to expand as a part of the purchase process. Leased properties did not all get that same consideration, although many had purchase options including the office in Seattle."

George: "Interesting, does that open the possibilities of other expansions in the future?" Tim: "I cannot say one way or another, although with additional services offered there is usually a need for additional employees, depending on the type of service. As I see things currently from the offices I have been able to visit, those have already used all the space they have, but also keep in mind two of them are leased properties." George: "I will keep it in the back of my mind that a potential exists. It will effectively work in Global's benefit as your best works comes from potential of more business at a later date." Tim told George to expect a call from James Preston once he got back with him, likely the next day, Tim was not sure how quickly he will make contact with you, but he will not likely be who you would meet with." With that Tim returned home to get dinner started for the family and he had no idea what he was going to make.

He returned to the house and immediately stated he was open to suggestion for the evening meal. The ladies made it quite easy by requesting the rice dish with teriyaki and fish with all the vegetables that more resembled a stir fry than the side dish to the steak. With this input he went about preparing the single dish meal. Tim learned from previous usage of this recipe it would not get as many servings as it suggested, and the meal would be entirely gone tonight.

The good thing about the evening meal was it had a shorter preparation time than most, and in 45 minutes dinner was served to everyone's satisfaction. Liani was particularly pleased as she tried to eat far more than she normally had for any meal. It left quite empty dinnerware everywhere. Kuri reminded Tim she had a doctor's appointment the following day, and Tim had not forgotten simply did not anticipate hearing the outcome until he returned home the next evening from work. Tim went through his nightly routines and after Liani was put to bed he and Kuri retired for the night as well. Kuri's conversation was short and primarily concentrated upon the doctor's findings, but she did not feel like she did with Liani, and wondered if it was a false reading for her. Tim responded with that was the purpose of going to the doctor as much as anything else the following afternoon.

Tim rose the following morning at his normal time, and prepared a quick breakfast instead of something to arouse the others. Once finished with everything in the kitchen, he went to take care of his morning hygiene process and dress for work. Kuri and Liani were both asleep when he left for the office.

Upon his arrival, he greeted Loretta first, then his computers once he got to his desk. Nora and Daisy had nothing new to report and he seldom expected anything from Anabelle, although he made it a habit to acknowledge her presence as well. Tim thought it funny that he no longer thought of computers in the office as objects of technology. Since the voice package made them so much more realistic in verbal communication, he considered them more like people. The day was fairly routine with no new issues and none of his pending issues making any fast headway. Late afternoon Kuri had called, and Nora announced her and positioned the vidphone for his short conversation. Kuri said the doctor confirmed she was indeed going to be bringing their second child into the world. She had no real answer about why it felt different, but Kuri did not want to know if the child was a boy or girl, and wanted to find out when the time came. She said it was largely because until the baby was born, nothing could really be done until they had a weight, and size to determine the needs in clothing and diapers. Tim was happy to know he was going to be a father once again, and with Liani nearing 3 years of age, Kuri should be capable of attending to one with Liani involved in her schooling by then. Tim was given an expected date of arrival by Kuri, based on the doctor's findings, and knew he would need to arrange time off for the event, but it would still be a matter of when she was ready, and setting a date for time off was not practical.

With his vidphone call completed, he went to find JP to give him a little advanced notice. Tim told him as before he would require 5 days from the day Kuri went into the hospital, and had some recovery time, before he would return. JP gave Tim his congratulations and fully understood it was not an exact science to the date that Kuri would go into labor. He did say from experience, that after the first the next ones were a little quicker to arrive into the world, as far as labor time was concerned.

***

Tim's next three weeks were entirely routine until he got the call from Detective Marshall. It was a Friday, relatively late in the afternoon when his vidphone went active with Nora announcing it was the detective. Tim: "Detective Marshall, I do hope this is not for another case of Cognac." He said with much humor in his voice. Detective Marshall: "Not at all, still have most of it left, but the wife seems intent on helping me consume it. For someone who seldom had much more than a glass of wine or two in a year, he assumed incorrectly she would not enjoy Cognac. Just calling to say come Monday, your presence will be required concerning your testimony for Rebecca Robbins legal proceedings. They did not provide an exact time, but you will need to go to the courthouse building for the process. I hope you know where that is, as I do not believe it is too far from your offices, but the courthouse is not by the department here. I cannot believe you will need to be present more than that day, as the case is pretty simple. I cannot give you details, but Artimus Robbins who is still in Hong Kong, had provided all the details we need to proceed here. Once he was broke by the military personnel, he was easily persuaded to provide the rest of the details in the plan that brought about the 3 billion WC obtained, and the death of your analyst."

Tim: "So you cannot give me anything from Artimus admissions to know how to prepare for Rebecca's part of this legal procedure." Detective Marshall: "Sorry, but no, it might be considered that I helped prepare you for your statements involving Rebecca in this affair." Tim: "I understand, but it will depend on when I get to be involved in the proceeding as to what I might have to say in this." Detective Marshall: "You will likely be expected to wait outside the chambers, until you are called upon, they will not allow you to overhear what took place in the courtroom prior to your deposition in this case, it is simply the way the legal system has worked for many years." Tim: "I guess all I can say then, is thank you for at least some notice in advance. What is the wait time for Artimus Robbins to go through the legal process?"

Detective Marshall: "I do not anticipate your presence being required in Hong Kong, merely a vidphone deposition, although I will likely need to be present for it. I would not expect anything for another six to nine months for the Hong Kong proceedings to start. They have a little more backlog than we have, and it takes time to get the process into the courtrooms to finalize." Tim acknowledge the detective's information and ended the vidphone connection after a short parting statement.

Tim went to the other offices, knowing JP was usually present with his talent search, although the needs for analysts had diminished considerably, but people were still on the 10 year plan for retirement, and would be for at least another 9 to 10 years. He found JP in his office to inform him he was expected on Monday to appear in the courtroom for his testimony concerning the death of the analyst, and did not anticipate it taking more than the day, but while he was away, to keep track of the daily proceeding which Tim did feel would not be too great. The AI system was performing most of the daily work, and he had not had anything to deal with directly for the last month or more. JP said to consider it done, and hoped all went well in his courtroom appearance.

Within the next hour, the day at work had come to an end, and Tim told Nora as well as Daisy he might not be in Monday, due to a courtroom appearance concerning the death of the analyst over 3 years ago. He did not expect to be gone beyond Monday, and did not even know if he would be gone all day Monday. He was expecting the legal process to be longer than an hour, and most likely they would waste his entire day, or close enough to just head home from there.

His weekend was arriving with an exemplary meal planned for the evening. He did prepare for a rather wonderful Stir fry of the sweet and sour variety and he used both pork and chicken for this occasion. The meal was superb by everyone's comments on the food he chose to serve that evening. Liani was so happy about the flavor she decided to even lick the plate for every bit she was proportioned. It did not go over too well with her mother, but Tim found humor in the whole event. Which also got Kuri's temper to show a bit, with his chuckling while Liani performed in a less than lady like manner.

The weekend provided no real excitement as it was intended to be largely relaxing, with the exception for two additional dinners that were anything but routine. He did one Chinese meal that was rather spicy, and although Kuri was able to handle the spice of peppers, Liani was less than pleased with her mouth on fire and could not understand why liquids would not make it go away, even though Tim expressed she needed to eat the bread to make it better, she did not believe him until as a last resort adhered to his suggestion. Tim did learn it would be best not to give Liani anything too hotly spiced until she was a little older, although he fully understood some people could never acclimate to the sensation of hot spicy foods. He did not know if Liani had zero tolerance yet, it would be a learning experience for them both. Sunday was his best teriyaki steak and side dishes that although had been served in the past, it was not a weekly or monthly meal. Liani was much more content with the Sunday meal than Saturday's. Tim also made a trip to the audio store to see about obtaining or ordering additional audio disks for his growing collection of blues and classic rock, slanted towards blues. He had found one artist who played the Stratocaster and ironically they were Native American. Tim thought with all that was involved in the treatment of the natives in the past history, it seemed like this band had more right to play the blues than most. He unfortunately had to order all dozen discs he had found in his research, and they would call his home when they were all in, as opposed to having him make multiple trips. Tim hoped it would be less than a month, but he had no real options but to wait until he got the call.

Kuri decided during the weekend, since she was very early into her pregnancy term that some pleasure time was in order, although it did not include any unfathomable moves on either of their part in the participation of the activity. Much to Tim's disappointment the weekend had come to its conclusion, and he had to go to the courtroom building instead of the office. He did find through the Information Gateway it was very close to the office, and he could walk there after putting the transport in the normal parking garage. He made a breakfast with some scrambled eggs and muffins with preserves, thinking it was not to aromatic to awaken the house ladies. He was correct in his assumption, and after checking to make sure, he completed all his morning routine without disturbing either Kuri or Liani, and left for the office parking garage. He felt a bit strange about parking there, and not going into the office building. He had to make a concentrated effort to walk away from the office building.

His arrival at the courthouse was entirely without anybody to meet him in the nearby area. Entry was anything but normal to any building he ever passed through the doors of in the past; but Tim had never had a reason to enter a legal system building in his lifetime. First, he had to pass not one but two detector systems, after emptying his pockets of everything he carried. These items were placed into a tray and passed through a conveyor type detector, like he was going to hide a handgun in his wallet or use his emergency transport entry keys to hide an explosive. Even after passing through two detectors, a security person for the courthouse had a hand held detector that was an even more sensitive than the two walk through units. After several passes which were triggered by his belt buckle. They finally decided he could pass into the building, and the directory was at the top of the steps to the elevator bank. Detective Marshall did not provide him with a name to the judge involved in the proceedings, but he only found one floor for criminal trials. He went to that floor, to find the detective awaiting the courtroom doors to be opened for the first to enter. He acknowledge the detective; but provided his name to the courtroom attendant in the hallway. The attendant merely told Tim to take a seat and wait until he was called.

Five minutes later, the doors opened to those allowed to enter, and then were closed once again. Tim had to wait four hours before someone came out and asked Tim to enter the courtroom. Tim was never in one, and did not have the first idea what he was expected to do once inside. He stood momentarily when the prosecuting attorney called his name to take the stand. The attorney motioned him forward, and pointed to the enclosure next to the judge's station. Tim entered the box, was asked whether he would tell the whole truth, which he said he would and was told to take a seat.

The legal system no longer used the bible to swear people in, as it did not coincide with separation of state and church. It was deemed foolish for the legal system to hide behind the bible in getting to the truth, which still seemed largely a matter of who was seeking what to be considered the truth.

The prosecuting attorney had Tim give his full name for the record of the court and immediately afterward asked Tim what events took place on the date of the analyst's death. Tim explained that after over a week of investigating the theft they finally had enough information to utilize a reverse trace process, rather unique to Global Security Corporation's internal capabilities. They already knew where eight of the eleven transmitters were, but the intruder behind the theft left a time release virus on the satellite that was needed to pinpoint the last three transmitters. Upon initiation of the reverse trace with analysts from three different offices tracking one each, the computer system at the Seattle headquarters set off the alarm that something had gone badly wrong in the analyst's office in Seattle. Tim said he immediately went to the office doors, and activated his voice command to release the lock for entry, and he found the analyst slumped over his desk surface still with headsets in place. Tim removed the headset to be alarmed by a blood trickle from the ear from the side Tim could see. He immediately checked for any signs of life, and there were none, and had the computer system contact authorities.

The prosecutor asked what happened next. The authorities arrived in quick fashion and Detective Marshall after a quick check on the scene, took me to their station to be detained there until more information was discovered. The prosecuting attorney changed gears by first stating that he had heard the demands from the job at Tim's company were rather excessive, and whether Tim could provide some insight into the reasons. Tim stated from the very startup of business, all the hiring representatives went through extreme precautions concerning how much more stress was going to be involved in a position with Global as an analyst. It was even put into the hiring document that was signed by each and every analyst that ever went to work in any of the offices around the globe. As a direct result of the rigors of this position, the compensation package was excessively larger than any similar position anywhere else on the planet. The original group that assembled the organization even went through having psychological staff in each office, to assist analysts with recognizing and coping with the stress the position would cause for most analysts. Global Security Corporation tried to take every safeguard they could to allow analysts to obtain 10 years of service, where they could retire at 75 % of the highest pay they achieved as employees.

"Tim does your company really compensate everyone fairly in this position?" was the following question from the prosecuting attorney. Tim said based upon his parents reaction from his announcement after being first hired, he believed they were far better than what other companies were willing to start analysts, straight out of school with absolutely no proven abilities. Tim was asked if he had any previous analyst experience prior to Global and Tim replied he just completed his degree program at MIT and this was his very his first paying job. The prosecuting attorney asked for starting figures, and wondered if they had changed since the startup. Tim told him that all analysts started at 20,000 WC per month with payments weekly, and as far as he knew it had not changed, even though they have substantially reduced stress rates through numerous means since the original startup. The prosecuting attorney agreed that the compensation was considerable for a fresh out of school employee, and even for many long time employees.

"How soon were you released by the detective first on the scene?" Tim said he was there approximately five hours, with not a single question asked of him and released with the autopsy results, which confirmed he was not involved in the analyst's death. The attorney asked, "The detective in charge of this investigation also says you were instrumental in bringing the entire case to its current point, can you detail this?" Tim said, it started over three years ago, how much detail is necessary will be up to the courts; but first it took over a month for my computer system to locate and categorize all former employees of Global, as I felt with the events that took place, somebody knew too much about our internal operations. The computer had to categorize over half a million former employees, and find last known whereabouts. The categories were former employees leaving on their own decision, those asked to leave, and those who were in long term care. The names list consisted of over a half a million names, and I could not see the authorities being able to investigate that many within a reasonable amount of time, and also figured Global did not have as many restrictions imposed on finding a potential answer internally. So having Global analysts worldwide take portions closest to their offices, the questioning process which I developed for all analysts was first used to determine if any employees who left of their own accord, felt they were cheated or any other reason to take vengeance against Global.

To shorten the process it took over a year to eliminate all the names on the list except for the list of deceased former employees. "That list would require the completion of more extensive information, that I had already had the computer compiling. The names from this list had to go to the authorities to further investigate as I could not put Global employees into a situation that could have deadly consequences. Shortly after providing the list to Detective Marshall I talked it over with my wife and decided since I could not put another analyst in harm's way, I could hope my own martial arts training would be sufficient to let myself do some of the ground work for the authorities in Seattle. First two dozen were done in person, and my findings were nothing like I would have anticipated. All the family members I talked with largely parents of the deceased employee, felt no ill will towards Global Security Corporation. They said in each and every interview that the company did far more than any other company in first trying not have the mental breakdown problem, and then subsequent care after. It was done at no cost to any family whose son or daughter was employed at Global. After the first two dozen, I was able to conduct the interviews over vidphone which allowed a speedier process, and led me to the two people in question, which was immediately given to the detective in charge in Seattle."

The prosecuting attorney asked, "Why would you ever take upon yourself such a daunting task, knowing fully well this was something for the authorities?" Tim told them for two reasons; first the authorities did not have the personnel to perform a task this large in a fashion that would not go into decades, at which point it may have gone unsolved. "Second, was more personal, but in this case, Global was in fact its own client with the loss of one of its own employees. As to the personal part having lost once it was discovered I do not like being beat, and I did not want the death of a Global employee to go unresolved."

The prosecuting attorney then stated, this is all good information, but Rebecca Rollins is not on trial for murder, merely an accessory. "At what point did you first meet Rebecca Robbins?" Tim replied, "I did not meet Rebecca until after she had already been apprehended and the Hong Kong authorities had finished questioning her. My conversation with Rebecca was merely to fill in the missing pieces to the death of an analyst, and believe she was unaware of it until her arrest."

"What make you think that?" Tim: "Over the last 14 years I have had to learn to deal extensively with people, many times in a very short time frame, and must be able to get a good read on the other person. Rebecca in our conversation, after the Hong Kong police had all the information they felt she could provide, seem to have a good heart. I do not believe she would have ever planned anything that would lead to someone else dying as a result. As a medically trained person, there is a need for compassion toward people, to be good at what you are involved within any area of the medical profession. Rebecca has such a demeanor."

"Tim you realize you are making it difficult to prosecute this person to the fullest in this courtroom." Tim said, "I cannot completely exonerate her, she did obtain the program that ultimately killed the analyst, but I do not believe she ever had that intended use in mind when providing it to her brother. Her only other part in this whole affair was the acquisition of some 3 billion in world currency, which is from an account that has no one watching it for 90 years. My company did not go after her for that portion of the activity, as we have no authority to do so, and I do not believe the investment group in control of the funds has any authority in it either. In hindsight considering all the funds that were truly available, she only got a small piggy bank."

"No further questions, this is not going the way I was expecting; but I reserve the right to recall later today if necessary." Ended the prosecuting attorney. Tim was told to go back out and wait. Tim complied with the request, and a few minutes later Detective Marshall came out to see him. Detective Marshall said, "You realize you have probably made it so Rebecca will get a very light sentence, which may even be probation, in her part of this criminal activity." Tim said, "So be it, her brother was the one who was responsible for the worst part of the entire crime. You realize if they just took the money and nothing more, they would be have been free and clear more than two years ago, with nobody to authorize prosecuting them for the theft." Detective Marshall: "I believe you at least touched on that during your deposition. You may not have come out and said it directly, but you certainly implied it, and it seemed that your only reason was for justice over the murder, which is not what she is really on trial for, just her part in it as an accessory." Tim: "Do you think the attorney will recall me?" Detective Marshall: "I know I would not, if I were in his position, but he may decide to go for a reduced sentence more in line with what you have said, to at least justify his being in his position for the department."

Detective Marshall returned to the courtroom, and 45 minutes later the doors opened, and everybody which was not that terribly many, started to exit. The last two people to exit were Detective Marshall and Rebecca Robbins. She did not say a word to start with, but simply put her arms around his neck and gave him a big hug and a kiss on the cheek. Tim said,

"Excuse me, but I am a married man!" She said she did not know how else to thank him, and did not believe words would do it justice, all the charge were dropped as the real murderer being her brother, was still incarcerated in Hong Kong. Rebecca said, "Nobody has told me what to do with the money that is left from what was taken." Tim said, "If your brother still has access to it, I would move it somewhere only you can access it, but there is nobody left alive to request it returned to them. That for all intents and purposes means it is yours to keep. With that, Tim asked simply, "What did you take in your schooling in the medical profession?" Rebecca said she only had a bachelor's degree in psychological behavior, and to truly go far in the profession, a PhD was mandatory. Tim said, "Knowing at this point you really do not need money, you might be able to work in our medical group, and still continue to advance your education. I do not know that the pay is going to be great, but it is experience while you advance in your education, and some pocket money for a billionaire." Rebecca said, "Really, you would let me work there after all that has happened." Tim said, "I did not see you to be the reason behind the loss of life, as I said in Hong Kong, you appear to have a good heart, I give you the chance to prove it, as some people still need help, although things have improved dramatically with the aid of technology. I cannot make you any promises, since I have no say in the medical staff hiring or company for that matter, but the office is not far and it is not quite quitting time. I can take you over if you so desire."

Rebecca said she did not bring anything for such an opportunity and fully expected to be in jail by the end of day. If Tim thought it would do any good, she would go with him, just to find out.

Her parents were there as well and they all walked over to the Global Security building, and Tim said her parents would have to wait in the lobby area on this floor, as the security in the building was rather stiff to go where they were going. He asked the security guard whether he could escort Rebecca to the 35th floor medical offices, and the guard said as long as he was cleared to use the elevator, he could escort one other person only. Tim thanked him and went to the elevator, was scanned and went to the 35th floor of the building. It was not far from the elevator to the medical offices, and he introduced her to Doctor Ward, who was still the person in charge of the medical staff. Tim said he did not know if the staff was fully up to personnel with all the latest changes, and the Doctor said she had a number of people leave for more challenging opportunities, and said to see if Rebecca was someone she might find useful in her daily work schedule. He would let Rebecca speak for herself after that and to call him, if it was not too short, but he would go check on JP and be right back. Doctor Ward and Rebecca went to a room where the two could talk, and Tim to the 30th floor to see how JP was holding up.

Tim arrived, said hello to Loretta and went directly to his office expecting JP to be there, he was not. It was not early enough to go home yet, so he headed back to JP's normal office location and he was there. Tim said, "Too boring out by my desk for you?"

JP chuckled, and said he thought he could do it all from his office, and still keep his normal duties running, he just had Nora come along to let him know if anything required his attention. Tim said he did not even notice Nora was not in his own office, which got a little feedback from Nora. That got JP's attention, and after he finished laughing, he said, "I see what you mean about Nora being a little different from other computers, I do not think I have ever got anything like that from my own." Tim told him he was done with the courtroom, but had a person in the medical staff to see about working here, and needed to get back to escort her out. He would be back to his desk in the morning like nothing had ever happened. JP said he could manage until the morning and Tim returned to the 35th Floor medical office area and simply waited.

Tim waited for another 30 minutes before Doctor Ward and Rebecca Robbins reappeared from the office area they occupied for the 45 minute interview. Rebecca was smiling, and Tim was soon to discover she was indeed going to be working in the medical staff office. She would start the following Monday morning, where Doctor Ward would meet her in the security lobby for the retina scan procedure, to allow Rebecca access to the 35th floor. Tim found out that Doctor Ward did all the hiring of the medical staff, unlike the rest of Global Security Corporation that went through the Human Resources department. The reason was simple, Doctor Ward was far more familiar with what the medical staff needed than the HR group, who concentrated on Information Systems personnel. That included analysts, code experts, technical personnel and communication. The largest area had been analysts, but that had slowed considerably with the reduced stress problems. Rebecca said she was not going to get rich by any means at 4,000 WC a month, but considering her education level, it was comparable to any other position she could obtain without more advancement in school. Doctor Ward said, the possibility existed where after the first three months of making sure she had a better grasp on her duties at GSC, she may be required to work a different shift. Since the medical staff had to have people for all the shifts, and with the stress levels being lowered, people in her group were looking for more challenging opportunities to advance in their chosen profession. Rebecca said she could continue her education from home at whatever time she was not required to work at the medical offices, although it may take a little longer by having employment and schooling.

She then asked if Tim was serious about her keeping all the money. Tim confirmed he was indeed serious, and reiterated there was simply nobody remaining alive to request the funds returned, and neither the investment group nor GSC were authorized to do so on anyone's behalf.

It was nearly end of day for the first shift of Global, so Tim escorted Rebecca to the lobby to get her parents, and leave the building just ahead of the departing members of the Global Security Corporation, largely analysts. Tim left a little early also heading from the security lobby to the parking garage.

When Tim arrived home, Kuri said his brother George wanted to talk with him. Tim asked if he should do it before or after dinner preparations. Kuri said he might as well do it first, and Tim headed over to George's house not all that far away.

His brother told him that Global Security Corporation had recently hired into their property group a person specifically for property expansion. "That person reported to Zi Chang, who was whom he talked with today. He wanted design plans to expand the current Seattle office ten addition floors, with the elevator to be an addition from the side of the existing building to eliminate any other floor modification to accommodate the additional elevator. Apparently they will be expanding a large number of office buildings, with some other office enlargement process that will be taking place. Based upon what I can put together for them on the first project, may result in additional projects. They know for certain it will be largely satellite offices in the US that are largely capable of outward expansion, instead of upward. They did not know at this time about global offices, but would, well before the first plans were completed. As a result, I will be drawing up plans based upon the building layout already on record. This will allow me to find dimensions and not need to go to the office to take measurements and essentially speed up the process. They did not know about office dimensions for each floor, and thought it would be best to build to suit for the tenants once an agreement was made. Seems they have thought it out rather thoroughly, and I will be able to draw up plans for the basics in about two weeks. Largely because I do not need to do anything beyond support structure, and open floor space in the beginning." Tim was happy for him and hoped it all worked out to his brother's benefit.

Tim returned home to get dinner started, which was going to be the chicken casserole type meal that never seemed to have anything left at the end of the meal. It was pretty tasty and not too difficult to make. Liani was always happy to get this meal, which seemed to be one of her favorites.

The evening was rather quiet, Liani was no longer doing her ABC's, but working on printing entire words, and improving her writing skills. It would not be long before she would be learning to sign her name in script, instead of print. Tim thought she might have that completed before she started her formal schooling, which was only a couple month away. She certainly seem ahead of the curve when it came to starting school, and Tim had no idea if the Japanese schooling system advanced students like this country, to get them into the higher grades where learning was achieved in line with the level of the student. He asked Kuri, and she did not know as she did not remember it occurring anytime during her school years, but she also was attending classes from home and did not have very much interaction with many other students.

Tim's next day was a bit of a surprise as he entered the outer office, Loretta informed him the board was gathering in the conference room for the monthly meeting. Tim inquired why he did not have any advanced warning like usual, and Loretta simply told JP the day before and it would seem he failed to mention it to Tim in his short visit. Tim decided he would still go to his office and get a mug of coffee from there, before entering the conference room.

Surprisingly enough he was the last to arrive, but not by too much as another member was just getting seated. Trask opened up the meeting with details from the previous meeting. First the office expansion and redecorating had been approved, and would be started soon. Next the building expansion was noted and the plans according to the design consultant based on the requirement given, would be ready in approximately two weeks. Since tenant acquisition had not begun, the expansion floors would be entirely open space until suitable tenants were found, and then the office size and interior design would be according to the new tenant. Since some companies had specific ideas concerning the interior space they occupied, this was the board's decision on how to best go about the expansion. Nothing could be done until all ten floors were added with elevator service to the addition. Trask thanked JP and Tim for locating the design consultant, and said the company had an outstanding record concerning the buildings and designs they had done previously. The company specifically was hardly the least expensive to use, but had never in their history had a building or expansion not exceed building codes and had zero defects in the construction process. Trask went on to say that Global Security Corporation owned all the properties worldwide with the exception of three buildings. Hong Kong and Tokyo largely because it was not cost effective, and the third being St. Petersburg, where the Russian government simply did not allow anybody other than Russian to own property within their borders. As a result, all satellite offices were selected just outside of the Russian borders, to accommodate neighboring areas, as well as those within Russia, but St. Petersburg accounted for 90% of all Russian business that GSC handled.

Trask then turned the update over to another board member, none other than Redfurd Waters. Tim had not seen Redfurd too frequently since he no longer was in Sierra, but he was the negotiator of the company. Redfurd started by saying over the last month I have been researching the proposal from Timothy Frantz concerning a possible business service to add to the services we already provide. I have found there are 535,000 restricted access systems in major businesses around the world, and many would welcome the concept of a less expensive means to continue restrictions needed by their particular organizations. Since almost every company does restrictions uniquely, it has been determined to perform this service for major businesses it would need to be rather customized for each business.

Also the monthly cost would be customized based entirely on how much we cannot perform without full access, and this we determined we do not want to have. I have not even started with in home businesses and would like additional input from everyone in how to go about this.

Tim said, "Most in home businesses are operated by a single person, possibly two or three at the most. Still it would all be housed in a single location. In home businesses would need to be an inexpensive service to those interested. My thoughts on this are quite simple, all in home businesses be offered the identical package meaning little customizing of the systems to these type businesses. At say the cost of 100 WC per month we restrict access to all. Only with a call from the home business to the communication group to let us know in advance, to expect and permit an incoming request to his system. Without advanced notice, it would being denied to keep the home based business safely protected. I believe we are only going to be diverting inbound access to any of the systems we add to this service. As a result they can send information anyway they like to whoever they like unencumbered. This is actually the preferred method for all businesses, as they will only send sufficient information to describe their product, without so much detail as to have someone steal their idea. I was informed that small in home businesses were susceptible to large companies getting into their system to steal ideas, and get to market before the home base business could react. Large companies have departments for this very purpose, as it is easier to steal than create from concept to detailed products. We may cost some larger businesses income, but theft is not a very honorable means to conduct business for any company.

Redfurd said, "I was unaware of this, it would make an excellent marketing approach to in home businesses, but should not be brought into the conversation for larger businesses that have done this type of theft in the past. Redfurd asked why only 100 WC for home based businesses. Tim responded the cost had to be reasonable to them in order to take on this type of service. If it was overpriced, the home base business would continue to operate an at risk business system. Redford understood, and Tim added, "If they provided this service to just 200,000 home based businesses it would equate to 20 Million revenue each month. There are far more home based businesses in the world and protection to all is our goal. I am certain large businesses will be the higher income bracket for this endeavor, but we will need to expand the communications group and AI configuration with those additions. For home based business we could easily operate with just additional personnel in the communication groups in our offices to handle potential inbound notifications for permission to access their system. We cannot control the amount of access once permission is granted for a single event; this still puts in home businesses at some risk if they are dealing with less than honorable organizations. Should such an incident occur, the home based business would have our record of the access permission for legal action, whereas there would have been no record in the past."

Redfurd stated from what he had learned and his research, he saw no reason this service could not be offered. There was more than enough business available to make it profitable, and even if we simply concentrated on home businesses there were far more of them than large restricted access systems. He did find in his research among the major businesses, it included governments outside of this country, which would need to protect itself from sensitive information getting into the wrong hands. They currently could not afford the type of protection they desired, as it was highly expensive and rather limited in the number of companies that provided the code and specialized equipment.

With Redfurd's concluding statement, Trask put it to a vote among the board members as whether to proceed forward with the new service or cancel it entirely. Tim was not eligible to vote, as he was not a board member. The board determined by majority, not unanimously, to go forward with the proposed additional service. Two members did not see the need to add the additional service, but had no foundation other than the company was large enough. The remaining members saw it differently and thought there were always ways to expand the profit margins. Tim added one last statement after the vote, and said the lead communication technician would need to be involved with setting up the parameters of such a service; as he would need to make the code changes necessary to the communications system to divert inbound transmissions for other companies. He only knew the need of all TRU addresses to contact the satellite companies to divert inbound transmissions to GSC communication systems. It was a service previously provided to companies already serviced, who were changing locations for the main offices. Apparently something done by banking on a regular basis to provide a more prestigious look or simply outgrew one location.

There was quite a bit accomplished in this meeting of the board, especially considering there was nothing new to be presented. Tim was asked with the meeting being closed to introduce Redfurd to the communication technician who would be involved in detailing the requirements of the new service. Before GSC could begin marketing the new service for clients, all the parameters of the service had to be formulated to determine how to best approach the potential clients. Tim took Redfurd to the communications area one floor below, and first informed Jack Korvin that the new service would be offered, and introduced Redfurd to work out the particular parameters to move forward. It was a heads up to Jack to be ready to acquire more technicians as well as his workload would start to increase. Tim asked Redfurd if he could find his way back without any problems, and Redfurd assured Tim he could. Tim returned to his office to finally say hello to his computer systems for the day. They all made comments about his tardiness, which Tim simply defended himself by saying a meeting was called for first thing and he was just now getting here from that meeting.

There still was nothing new that required his immediate attention from any of the three systems, and he least expected anything from Anabelle. He decide to use the Information Gateway to research new hacker codes that may have come about in recent months. To his surprise he found two articles dealing with a dozen new codes, specifically generated for light speed information transfers. It was truly the first time his codes were solely for light speed transmissions, and also a first for a quantity exceeding a single code. He transferred the information to his intellipad and decided first to take it to the systems people, essentially the twins to test in their system. He had Nora contact Tim Topeki first to arrange a time he could see the Celini twins to determine if the new codes could break through their own systems, before having them added to the AI systems.

Tim Topeki told him if he knew where they were, he could go see them anytime he needed. Tim thanked him and headed to the office of the security code testers of GSC. They were busy making use of their skills, but nothing so important that a little interruption would cause any issues for them. They were in the process of testing client systems to see if they could breach them. Tim took out his intellipad and stated he thought since this was their specialty, that testing the waters before adding them to the AI system might prove beneficial. They quickly added the new codes to their own systems and started immediately trying it on client systems for the more likely result being positive. They asked where Tim had got the new codes, and he state he found them in an IG article from a MIT site that always had the latest information for security people such as himself. Being a MIT graduate provided him with access to this particular information site managed within MIT. That told the twins they would likely not have found them in any fashion quicker than Timothy Frantz.

As soon as they started testing the new codes, they got almost every single one to breach client's systems. Of the dozen, only two did not breach the client's system being tested. They changed gears to their own system, and six of the dozen were able to break Global's systems and with that they said it was imperative to get these into the AI since they never gained access once in all the past attempts. They got on the vidphone to the system code specialist and told him a dozen new codes were required to be entered in the AI code and borrowed Tim's intellipad to forward it directly to the specialist. This prevented Tim from doing it personally or via inputting them through the aid of Nora. Tim was looking forward to having some additional items to do for the day, but from the twins reaction it was probably more proper to get it done immediately. After the twins gave him their thanks for two reasons, first making them aware of the new codes, but more importantly a reminder that even their own system could be breached with the right tools, and they would try to be more vigilant in finding new codes.

Tim returned to his office with much less to do than he had hoped for the remainder of the day.

Tim decided to give General York a follow up call. He had Nora reach the general through the vidphone which this time was in position prior to the connection being completed. General Robert York: "I certainly was not expecting to hear from you again so soon, I have not even figured out how to disperse all these funds. Tim: Exactly what I had hoped to hear. I know you had two rather large funds, which I will let you deal with as you see fit. I was calling to see how much was actually left in the three smaller funds." General York: "I have not even considered them at this point, do you have a use in mind?"

Tim: "I did not know if what I have in mind is possible, but I thought I would ask, but first is there more than 20 billion WC in the accounts combined?" The general said that it was about 10 Billion more. Tim said: "Sierra is a location for one of our major offices, but is largely a poor and undeveloped country. I know they were trying to achieve building schools in order to address the needs of the people, who have long been unable to advance. I believe the government was working on the fundamental schools for the education deemed appropriate for all people, and was hoping to build advanced centers for education to bring them into this century. The way it was described, was to building the schools in order to have a volunteer staff of educators to teach in subject areas that they had experience in. It was by no means equivalent to a program such as college level in many countries, but at least a step to move forward. I was wondering if a fund of 20 Billion from your findings, would get them farther along in this process, although I do not know who in Sierra specifically would be the best person to reach."

General York: "That is an excellent idea, it would give Sierra a friend in this government and the means to advance their own people in entering a more current job market in the world. Since I spent a few years in that area, I believe I know exactly who could make this possible, and insure the funds are used for exactly the purpose you have in mind. It will also leave more than enough funds in the other accounts to use in areas this government needs to address. I will let you know before day's end if my contact is still in a position to help, I do not want to just send money to the country's government, as they have a tendency to misappropriate funds for other uses to address larger regions of the continent. That area in Sierra is long overdue for something positive to happen to move them forward. When I was there, I was surprised at how little most people had to work with in many factors, education being foremost, but some of the shacks they called a home, were in serious need of improvement, but without solid job opportunities, they appeared stuck in a rut they could not overcome."

CHAPTER

20

Tim arrived home at the regular time to find both Kuri and Liani watching the first news broadcast of the evening on the entertainment system. It was a bit different, since the normal was Liani with her mother making sure of her reading and printing, or at least doing some form of learning. Tim said hello before getting close enough to give them both his evening hello kiss and hug for Liani. Tim had to ask why the interest in the news so early. Kuri told him her brother called to say the news was doing a piece on the restaurant, and did not know what broadcast it would be on for the night. Tim asked whether the news indicated if it was definitely to air this evening, or was it just a filler piece in case the news was too dull tonight. Kuri did not know, so she and Liani were watching to see her brother and Liani's uncle. Tim said to call him in if it did come on while he went to get dinner ready.

Tim had dinner fully prepared and in the process of cooking, and the first nightly broadcast ended with nothing about Hiro's Authentic Japanese Restaurant. Tim knew the next broadcast would not occur for a couple more hours and dinner would be ready, served and cleaned up after, by the time it started.

Dinner was served and consumed, and Kuri and Liani went back to see if the next news broadcast was started up. Tim cleaned everything in the kitchen, and started the sanitizing unit before taking a seat next to his darling women, although one was not quite three years old. She did get Kuri's good looks though, and Tim knew she would be a real heart breaker coming into her teen years in the future. He hoped she stay a little girl forever, but that just was not possible, and he did not look forward to what it might lead into. She was also proving to be too smart for most boys, which would present additional problems he had no answers for either.

The second news broadcast of the evening, which was usually longer than the first had started, and at the very start it had her brother and the restaurant news piece. Largely few questions were asked of her brother, but the piece was realistically a taste test for what would be a very good review of the restaurant, in the quality and variety of dishes served at Hiro's Authentic Japanese Restaurant. The biggest hits being the teriyaki steak dinner and the sushi which was cut to pure perfection. Several sweet and tangy dishes and one soup made honorable mention, as some of the best food found in all of Seattle, regardless of the style of food any particular folks were accustomed to having. It would be a shame to pass up an opportunity to visit this restaurant, and once done people continue to come back. That was how the news piece concluded. Liani was happy to see her uncle on the entertainment system, and asked if she would at least see him this year at Christmas. Tim could not answer the question, and Kuri had not followed up with her father concerning it. She told Liani she would ask her grandfather about that the very next day, after her father went to work. The remainder of the evening was entirely routine, except for Kuri who was being tired out quicker than any time before from the pregnancy. She had told Tim already that this child did affect her far more than Liani. Due to all these factors from how different this pregnancy was from the first, even though she did not have the doctor tell her the sex of the child inside, she felt it had to be a boy. Tim considered this as a mother's knowledge that only she could have. He would be happy with whatever they had when the time arrived, but he did notice Kuri did not have the energy she always seemed to have. She was still able to perform her morning meditation routine, and take care of Liani most of the day, but her endurance was shorter than previously. Tim and Kuri went to bed a little early and simply held each close until sleep took over.

The following day at Global was with Trask at the helm for his weekly day in the office. Loretta had informed him the number of calls to Tim the previous day were rather excessive from all the time she had been there. Trask got to do the vidphone detail to hear from two dozen investment firms. The calls were not so close together to have them holding while five were on the vidphone display. He did have a few times with multiple people. After the lull from the two dozen, Trask asked Tim, "What is going on with all these calls of thanks anyway? What did you do to create this, since they do mention you by name?"

Tim told him of his code find the day before, and instead of putting it directly into the AI system, he took them to the Celini brothers to test first. "They were happy in some ways, considering they breached our own system for the first time since they began testing. After they breached it with six of the twelve codes I found, they called to the systems people to have them immediately entered, and then started testing client systems. The new codes were breaching almost every system they tested, and I left them to their fun. An hour after I was back in the office, the calls started pouring in from clients. I thought we had a big problem, and wondered what we could have done to have so many clients calling at the same time. The Celini brother followed the unwritten code of security people, and shared the codes with client systems which I found no problem with."

Trask said, "A dozen new codes, all at once, that has never happened before, what was so unique about these codes?" Tim: "These codes were specifically for light speed transmissions, I did not check them for what exactly they did, the Celini brothers would likely tell you more than I in that area. Considering the large number and all for light speed only, I thought it best to let them test the codes for effectiveness. Apparently they work quite well." Trask: "That would seem to be a bit of an understatement considering the response we received. As for the Celini brothers, they follow the same methods most security people do when it comes to code discoveries, I know I have instilled into many, and although we do it as profession courtesy, it had been a tradition among security specialist, since long before I entered the profession. In past experience, some security professions only share that type of information with their closest associates, while other share with everyone they know personally. Since we operate on a global platform, my code testers, share it with all our clients at my request. It was done this way for the simple reason, the more we can prevent from occurring the less work we create for our analysts. If we kept these codes to ourselves, I cannot fathom how many breaches and transgressions we would need to uncover. Where did you manage to get all these codes without the Celini brothers already aware of them, they are rather good at what they do?"

Tim: "One of the advantages of being a MIT graduate, they have an Information Gateway site available to past and present information security enrollees for that type of information. One of the ways an education provider manages to remain a leader in that profession. You have to be either a graduate or presently attending school for that specific profession to have access to this site. They have people who like the Celini brothers scour the information world for new codes. Once found and proven, they enter them into the site for all who have access to put to use."

Trask: "You telling me this is a restricted access system in an educational facility?" Tim: "Not so much restricted access, as having a rather complicated authorization code to access. It is not a public site, but if you somehow acquired my access authorization, you could look yourself. I do not share this code with anybody though."

Trask: "Understandable, it keeps you on top of the game, and once again you step to the plate and hit a home run." Tim: "You also have to sign an agreement with MIT for access, which specifically states the information you obtain from this particular site will not be used for anything other than legal and honorable purposes. I cannot say every program offered by MIT is without any legal event, but as far as information security there has never been a single breach in that contract. Also the school has a highly regarded legal team, which insures the schools integrity remains unblemished. Although law is not considered a technical field and the school does not offer a program, they have managed to acquire some of the best in the country to hold a position at MIT."

Trask: "Well that is some accomplishment for an educational facility, I assume it would be foolish to try to go up against them in a legal battle." Tim: "They usually win, if that is what you want to know." Tim then said, "How about lunch, you up for it?" Trask said, Is it that time already? I believe it is my turn to cover the meals and drinks, should we ask anyone else?" Tim said, "It is up to you, I had Loretta and JP out less than a week ago, but I am sure they would not be disappointed with another invite." Trask called JP to see if he was interested in lunch, and JP agreed and said he would meet them in the area where Loretta was. With that Trask and Tim went to the front desk area and Trask inquired if Loretta would like lunch, as she accepted, but needed to make her 5 minute trip before leaving.

Precisely five minutes later they were all assembled for the short trip to what had become everyone's favorite downtown restaurant. Tim himself knew of several excellent restaurants, as he assumed the others did as well, but this was by far the best in downtown Seattle of the restaurants in the area. Tim, if given the opportunity would still go to Hiro's restaurant before this one, but it was an entirely different style of cuisine. Trask decided to start everyone off with the first of two glasses of Cognac, for and after the meal choices. Menus were distributed and it did not take too long for everyone to make up their minds on their particular selection. Tim noted that none of them ordered the exact same entrée. The closest was his and Loretta's choices, he had ordered a grilled tuna steak whereas Loretta selected a salmon steak. Tim also decided instead of a baked potato he would try the restaurant's version of sour cream mashed potatoes to see how they competed with the family recipe, made largely during holiday meals.

Conversation while waiting was varied but not business related, and when everyone had been served, all went quiet. With the conclusion of the meal, Trask had the second round of Cognac brought to the table, and everyone thought the meal was excellent. Tim found the mashed potatoes although quite good, they had a considerable amount less sour cream than the family recipe, which were much better. Tim also realized the family recipe was for everyone's enjoyment, not to produce a profit from. All in all, they were good enough to have again with a meal when he came to this restaurant. Trask covered all the charges for the meal, and they returned to the office with each Loretta and JP going to their own stations on the 30th floor. Trask and Tim returned to the CEO's office, which Tim thought was much too large for any one individual, but he did not have anything to do with the planning, as it was before his time at Global Security Corporation. The remainder of the afternoon was relatively quiet and only one additional call came into Trask concerning the new codes. Tim had asked Trask if things were always so quiet in the CEO seat. Trask said it was only since implementing most of Tim's stress reducing proposals, that it had become a bit boring. His days were spent with far more clients to contact, as a result of analysts not observing a problem and the computer was told if any issues went without resolve by GSC within two hours he was to be notified.

That meant either the analyst and JP either missed the transgression, or JP was too far out of his area of expertise to provide the customer with a reasonable explanation, and therefore let it hold until Trask took care of it. Since JP was the best people person Trask knew, his knowledge in the analyst profession was very limited, and it was not uncommon for it to get to Trask in order to receive its proper explanation and recourse for the client. Trask said in hindsight, it was a fair trade off with JP as director as he did take all the more mundane projects in the director's position and even handle a fair percentage of the client calls.

Just as Trask finished the vidphone went active and Nora said it was General York again. Tim asked for clarification on again and she said, "He called earlier when Trask was taking client calls and I did not get the chance to tell you. Sorry about that." General York was seen on the vidphone and he went right into, "As I said yesterday, I hoped to get back with you later in the day, but I could not get through, I assumed you must have been rather busy. I tried earlier and your computer, Nora I believe, she said she would let you know but it has been a couple hours and I had not heard back. At any rate my contact in Sierra is now in charge of multiple department of that area, including the one we discussed. He said with those funds the program would be in full operation within six months, and he was truly grateful to have those funds to get the advancement of people moving forward."

Tim: "That is wonderful news, I guess I should give the director a call and let him know his intentions to become a volunteer can move forward. He will be trying to teach in the information security profession, as his education is in that field. He really is pretty good at it, although he does not step outside of his area of expertise too much."

General Robert York: "It was a good thing we did for them, and the repercussion from this single deed will not go unnoticed by two governments. Got to keep this short got things to do over infrastructure."

The vidphone connection terminated, and the vidphone display retract into the ceiling. Trask asked if there was anything he needed to know about what Tim has been up to as of late with all his spare time. Tim explained to Trask, that after finally getting to the bottom of the murdered analyst, he contacted the general to inform him that since the covert group the stolen funds came from, was out of business some 90 years ago, there was a good chance they were not all in a single fund. "The general found them and two were rather massive is all I was told. One of the massive funds was sufficient to take care of all the major roads in the country, I believe this entails more than simple repair. He made it sound like the roads would be entirely resurfaced with more current material to last for a very long time. The second massive fund he thought was sufficient to revamp the entire military structure of this country. I do not really know what that means, but it sounded good from the general. There were 3 smaller funds that he had not done anything with and we decided to see if it could be used in Sierra, to finally help bring that underdeveloped country more in line with the needs of today. Chaka had made mention of education for the masses, and they had made some progress, but not to the point of more advanced education beyond academics. The money was sent by the general for that very purpose."

Trask: "And you think I am a humanitarian, what about you?" Tim: "Not a single cent belonged to GSC, and I had no way to access it or even find it in government archive files. If anyone gets the humanitarian label it will be General Robert York."

Trask: "It amazes me that you will never take credit due you for the good things you have done as a member of this organization. If it were me, I would have made it a public announcement in some fashion that with General Robert York, this achievement was made possible." Tim: "All I did was make a suggestion to the general. The general had access to the funds, and spending time in Sierra knew who to contact. He followed through with the suggestion, so I feel I had very little to do with it and should not be given undue credit. I could not even access the funds to make any of it possible."

Trask sort of saw Tim's point, but still could not understand entirely what in Tim would not let him accept credit for his good deeds. He would not delve farther into it because he knew he would never understand, as he was simply not a humble person in any sense of the description listed in any source of the definition. Not being exceptionally humble, he could not comprehend the quality, so it would remain an unsolved mystery to Trask.

Tim, after his conversation with Trask, had Nora reach Chaka Toukee in the Sierra office. The conversation took about an hour, since Tim had not been in touch with him since the beginning of the problem that occupied him for over three years. Chaka was happy to hear he might soon get to be an educational instructor to help people in Sierra move forward in job skills needed all over the globe. He also informed Tim that his original idea of remaining director and being involved in education would work out quite well.

The remainder of the day with Trask was more or less uneventful, although some activity occurred it was not sufficient to keep either of them fully occupied for the entire day. The rest of week went by with no incidents to keep Tim busy like he was as an analyst. In many ways Tim never considered himself anything more than a good information security analyst. He sometimes wished, he still was nothing more than that. Although he did appreciate the salary his title had brought with it.

When Monday morning arrived and he entered the lobby area, he saw Rebecca Robbins awaiting Doctor Ward, to get her into the security process, so she could enter the building without an escort, although she had not really seen much other than the medical facilities. She smiled at Tim as he entered when she saw him. He stopped long enough to find out if she spent all of her money already. She laughed lightly and said she had not, although her parents were helping her find a home in the area that was not overly excessive, but one she could call her own. Tim also made sure that Doctor Ward had been told her newest employee was waiting in the security lobby. The guard confirmed he had called and was told she would be arriving as soon as she finished up with some paperwork for security to go forward with the retina scan. It would not be much longer since Rebecca had been there ten minutes already.

Tim only waited long enough to insure that Doctor Ward made it to the lobby, and he entered the elevator to the 30th floor to get to his own office. He greeted Loretta as he entered the outer office area, and bid good morning to all three of the computer systems he stayed in contact with daily. Everything was pretty much running without need of human intervention for the artificially intelligent computer network. Tim was bored, not something he would have ever anticipated while being a part Global Security Corporation. He started performing his meditation routine regularly around 10 AM each day, believing he would not achieve oblivion from anything that required his immediate attention.

***

Five months had passed with him performing his routine both at work, and in the evening at home. He saw Rebecca Robbin about once a week in the security lobby as they entered at nearly the same time. He did not make visits to the medical location on the 35th floor for the sole purpose of checking on her progress. He entered his office on this day and shortly after he arrived Detective Marshall had called via the vidphone to say the Hong Kong proceeding were to start the following morning Hong Kong time, and he should expect to be contacted for his testimony over the other suspect involved in the murder of the GSC analyst. Detective Marshall did say he hoped he was not going to exonerate this one as well. Tim assured he would not, and felt this one was the person entirely responsible for all the problems to his company, and himself as well. Detective did not know what time this would take place, or even if it would be at the start of the proceedings, but since there was a time zone difference, he would not expect it to take place until afternoon arrived. Tim thanked the detective for his advanced notice and said he would be expecting the call. From there he went to Loretta to inform her he would likely be receiving a Hong Kong vidphone call concerning the legal proceeding that will be taking place starting tomorrow. He did not get a definite time or day for it to happen, but it was crucial he got the call. Loretta asked what it was concerning specifically to insure he got it immediately. Tim said due to the trial being in Hong Kong, his testimony which was important to the case, was going to be done by vidphone as opposed to his having to be in Hong Kong in person. Loretta said she would make sure the call got to him when it came.

Back in his office, he informed Nora of what was going to occur and once it started he would not be able to give anything else his attention until it had been completed. Nora said she completely understood and would make certain, he would not be disturbed when the call arrived.

The day went by slowly; but when Tim got home, he was happy to report after over 5 months of Kuri being pregnant, she was starting to show physically she was with child. Liani had been officially in school for 2 months, and Kuri said the school sent her a message over the IG to her intellipad indicating Liani was too advanced for the school year she was enrolled in, and wanted to advance her two grades to third year of schooling. Kuri said that Tim was correct in thinking she was too advanced even for the Japanese school system, and she told them they could do that and starting tomorrow she will be in the third grade. Tim went over to Liani and gave her a big hug and kiss and congratulated her on her good schooling habits. It called for a bit of a special occasion meal, and if Tim had known before arriving home, he would have got a banana cream pie for the occasion. Kuri said she already did and it was in the kitchen environmental cooling system awaiting dinner to be ready.

Tim asked Liani what she would like to celebrate her advancement in school, which she did entirely on her own abilities and desire to learn. She asked her father to give her some choices. Tim providing her with teriyaki steak, the chicken casserole dish she loved so much and the teriyaki seafood with chicken, pork and vegetables with brown rice. Liani said her dad was making it a difficult decision because she like them all quite a lot. She took five minutes to decide, she wanted the teriyaki rice seafood dish, and only because her mother made the chicken one for lunch. With Liani's decision, Tim went about preparing dinner. In this case with almost everything already in containers the preparation time was minimal, and once everything was prepared he set the cooking device for the two items requiring different cooking methods.

Dinner was ready and Liani was anticipating food five minute ahead of the announcement, by already having gotten to her seat and ready to be served. She had a glass of grape juice with her meal being served, and Tim dished out Kuri's, and his dinner and got Kuri her tea and he had some coffee. It was a quiet dinner, with both Kuri and Tim keeping a close watch on Liani, as she was eating like it was her last meal. Tim had to say something, "Liani, just because this is a celebration dinner for you, does not mean you will never get this menu item again." Kuri laughed slightly, before chastising him for saying that to his own daughter. Which Tim replied with, "Yes, but when she is older and even more beautiful than her mother I fear I will not own a big enough club to beat the boys away from her." Kuri raised her voice a bit saying, "Tim that is awful, what would make you say something like that, she is only a little over three year old!" Tim said, "Maybe, but telling the truth has never been the wrong approach before for me." That got no reply but a good punch to his arm, and Kuri was much stronger than she looked because it hurt.

With that, Tim got out the banana cream pie, cut a good sized portion for both Liani and Kuri as they both had an affection towards this type of desert, and he took a smaller piece to insure they had some for lunch the next day. While cutting the pie he noticed his arm still hurt, and he tried to put it out of his mind, but it was determined to keep coming back to get his attention. He set the pie in front of the two waiting longingly for the sweet creamy pie, and Tim brought his around to retake his seat. He decided to simply eat his pie in silence. Once desert was finished, Tim went about the kitchen clean up and started the sanitizing unit. Once done he went to join Kuri and Liani in the entertainment room, where Liani was looking to see if she had a new curriculum for her schooling. It had not been updated yet, and would likely be updated by the time she started in the morning. Tim inquired with Kuri if she was mad, and she said she was not. Tim said since his arm still hurt he just wanted to make sure, and told her she was far stronger than she looked. Kuri said, "Strength comes from within and martial art training does not deter it one bit." Tim said, he never wanted to be the recipient of one of her kicks because he never wanted to see that part of China. Kuri wanted him to be more specific, and he told her the force would likely send somebody flying and they would not touch ground again until well into mainland China. He was content with simply seeing Hong Kong. Kuri said that it was not likely that anyone could generate that much power from a single kick, even if it felt like it to the receiver. He just said he hoped to never find out for sure.

The entertainment system was active and with Liani between grades it was decided she could choose what they watched. Liani picked a movie that was far from what Tim would have expected, it was not animated or even a children's program. It was a movie about space exploration and battles with alien species in an attempt to conquer planets near earth. From the alien viewpoint, it was to achieve a base to conquer the inhabited planet in the same solar system. The space warriors of earth were determined to prevent it. It was not a terribly bad movie, a little farfetched from Tim's viewpoint, but the story had plot and decent acting. When the movie concluded nearing Liani's bedtime she ask if aliens really did exist. Trying to explain to a 3 year old about the limitation our planet had in reaching just the planets in our own solar system was largely futile, with every statement receiving another question. She had not had any schooling detailing our own solar system, and in the end all Tim could really get her to understand is that no other beings have proven to exist. There was a whole lot of space never seen. If such aliens existed they had not advanced enough to make it here, and we had not advanced enough to venture too far from our own planet earth. With that Liani was put to bed, fortunately she did not watch a movie to give her nightmares like some of the really old horror classics could produce. Tim went right to doing his routine from Liani going to bed. He decided to do this exercise at least shirtless, to see why his arm still hurt. Looking in the mirror he had some mild discoloration where Kuri hit him. He could not ever remember having had a bruise before, and wondered just how strong she really was.

Tim finished his routine, performed his nightly hygiene, and then Kuri went about her nightly routine which including her 100 strokes on her hair. Tim was still without his shirt when she came out and noticed his arm and she asked what he did to get the bruise. Tim looked at her sort a funny and sarcastically said, "I wonder?" Kuri took it exactly correctly, and said she could not have hit him that hard. It sure did not feel that bad when I did it. Tim continuing in his sarcastic mood, asked if she ever saw any tools anywhere in this house. She said she did not remember seeing any. He then asked if she saw him leave the house to go to the only place nearby being his grandfather workshop. She said no again. Then how else could it have happened? Kuri decided she would give him a small apology, and really did not mean to hit him so hard to leave a bruise. Tim was not really mad about it and forgave her, but did tell her he never remembered ever having a bruise before even as a youth involved in sports. Even his broken wrist from football, did not leave bruising that he remembered.

They decide to get some sleep for the next hectic day in life of having a three year old at home and in school. Kuri was made aware of one thing upon Liani starting third grade so soon into her formal schooling. The intellipad although it could be used for the first day, was not going to work exceptional well after today. The grade required better visual display than an intellipad could offer, especially true in split screen mode where an instructor would be discussing the material on the other half of the screen. Liani was going into subjects that Tim and Kuri has not given her any start in. She could count but did no math as of yet, and she would be now, also some history, geography and basic science. These were all new subjects to Liani and Kuri was happy that reading was still the main means to learn it, but she felt she should have better prepared Liani for these subjects. Kuri simply did not expect the Japanese school system to advance a 3 year old girl so quickly to third grade. Tim spent the whole day outside of his 10 AM meditation routine waiting for the call that never came. At the end of the work day he went home.

Kuri immediately said that Liani was going to need the computer to do her advance in school, and did not know if he wanted to let Liani do that from his computer desk, or if he preferred to get her one of her own. Tim saw no reason to get her another computer, and she and Kuri could use the computer desk. Liani had not had much time on it so Kuri might need to stay with her to make sure she can use it properly. Kuri agreed, and said since it was in the lower level, and Liani was not all that good on stairs, she would likely stay with her the majority of the day.

The evening went much like every other day. Tim asked Kuri if he should take Liani down to the computer for some basic use practice. She said it was not necessary, she would do it the next morning with Liani's start of class.

Tim's call from Hong Kong came near 2 PM that following afternoon.

CHAPTER

21

Tim arrived at the office saying his usual hello to Loretta and three computer systems. Over the previous five months in his waiting for the Hong Kong trial. His brother's firm, largely a result of George, had received the contract to expand the Seattle headquarters building 10 floors upward. Construction had begun three months prior, with the first part being to set up the temporary elevator, which would later be fully converted into the elevator to reach the 36th to 45th floors. The temporary portion was for external use of the construction people to get to the area where the work would be performed. The first five floors of the addition were in place for the very basic framing of girders and support structure, with five more to go, before a roof could be laid to support the equipment that would be required for the building, as well as moving existing equipment on the 35th floor to the top of the building. Also during that time, the new service from communications had been started, and the marketing plan was first to go after home based businesses with a need to protect their system. This approach did not require excessive additional personnel, as the marketing plan was quite simple and direct. Home based business would all be protected under the same parameters for 100 WC per month. In its simplest form, no access would be granted to the client system without advanced notification to expect the event. The only difficulty this presented was the incoming data had to be reviewed for the name of the sending person, as most home based businesses had no idea how to obtain TRU address information, other than their own. It slowed things slightly, but for the majority of companies, it was highly preferred for information to go to potential clients or buyers of a particular invention or technological advancement, it would be sent by the client to insure only what was intended had been sent. Global Security Corporation was already performing this service globally to 400,000 home based businesses, and per individual they thought the service was far less expensive than they would have thought.

The major reason for marketing to small business first, was the pure simplicity of the service. For large businesses, which would have to be customized to each business and priced accordingly, had too many unresolved details that needed answers before going forward. It was largely due to equipment needs, and additionally communications people required for that portion of the service. One additional alteration was included into the small business contract. Notification to allow access came with a 10 WC per use charge, and this was to keep the service from being abused and trying to keep the clients completely safe, by only sending to those they wanted to. Without the service, if the home based business did not have any safeguards, they could be breached at any time. These safeguards were far more costly than the service. The one thing never considered by Tim in his proposal for the service, was it opened up a market to independent marketing people that would offer GSC service, performed by GSC; but they would charge 150 WC per month, and provide GSC with the details. This allowed the independent marketer a 50% profit per client, still keep the service reasonable and located home based businesses that they did not know about. The independent marketers were not employed by Global Security Corporation, but created a larger percentage of new business. With the independent marketing people business was expanding in home based business at a much more rapid pace than Global had anticipated.

Tim's call from Hong Kong came at precisely 2 PM. Nora was immediately active in her do not disturb mode. She was actually moving between entries, and made sure no other person attempted to enter the office, until at which Tim had completely his testimony.

The legal representative for Hong Kong asked Tim to give his full name for the record. Tim complied with the request. The prosecutor then said, "Since you were not present from the start, I will give a quick overview of prior events. First Hong Kong has been granted the authority from Seattle to prosecute on both kidnapping and murder, even though the murder did not take place on Hong Kong soil. This agreement was made with the Seattle authorities to expedite the trial. Your testimony is required, because you were directly involved with bringing this to the attention of the courts."

"When were you first made aware of this problem?" Tim stated, "The first problem was made known to me on the very first day I was made CEO of Global Security Corporation, and it started with a large theft of funds from a client we provided service for." Prosecutor: "Can you provide more detail into the theft?" Tim: "As soon as I arrived to the office my computer system, which has a human voice package, was screaming for attention to the transgression she had been made aware of. My computer who is known as Nora, had been doing this for three hours prior to my arrival, and after informing her I was present, we started to analyze the transgression. It was a very complicated theft, that entailed using nearly a dozen computer systems and rogue TRU's to keep the identity of the intruder secret." Prosecutor: "Did this lead immediately to the mishap that has brought us here today?" Tim: "No, it did not occur immediately, I called a meeting of all the major office directors, to quickly pinpoint the origins of the equipment believed used. The intruder had planted too many deterrents in the process to resolve it quickly. It took about a week to locate how most of the items were used, and none of them led to anything beyond a general location. The intruder also planted a time release virus on one satellite used for three of the locations. It caused the satellite to be down for several days until the satellite company could remove the virus and since it entailed going back in saved backup data, they did not know if the information we needed could be provided. That brought about another meeting with the other directors to select candidates for a reverse trace procedure to locate the three devices we could not pinpoint. That procedure was initiated with three different offices tracing one piece of equipment through audio trace. 15 second into the trace, the Seattle computer systems went into alarm state, and informed me of a situation involving the analyst from that office, which is where I am located. I went to his office as quickly as I could, found him slumped over his desk platform with headsets still in place. In removing his headsets to check for vital signs, I saw blood trickles from the ear I could see, and there was no pulse. He was dead. I had my computer Nora immediate contact authorities who arrived in short order."

Prosecutor: 'What happened once the authorities were on the scene?"
Tim: I answered a few questions was told I had contaminated a crime scene and was taken to police headquarters and detained until they investigated further. Apparently, I was considered a suspect for simply trying to check on the welfare of an employee. I was there for five hours without a single additional question from any of them. Once the autopsy results were in, I was released and on my way out of the building, the detective in charge confirmed I could not have been the cause of the analyst death and he was dead 15 seconds after the audio analysis started." I was returned to the office by the police since they took me to their own location."

Prosecutor: "At what point did you get involved in trying to determine who was behind the death of one of the employees at your organization?"
Tim: "I believe it took about a month of analyzing the information we were able to obtain to have it lead to nowhere outside of the equipment locations, which local authorities were monitoring after insuring it was safe. I made the offer to Detective Marshall in order to speed up the process, since the authorities did not have the resources to investigate in a timely manner. The offer was accepted and I had determined the best place to start was within our own organization as too many things from the information we had gathered pointed to somebody having information to our operation, that would not have been publicly known. I had my computer system start doing a research and categorization of all past employees. I assumed, and it seemed to be a correct analysis that somebody felt they had a grudge against GSC.

It took nearly 3 months for the computer systems to generate all the names of over 500,000 former employees. Once this was completed, I had it categorized into former employees leaving of their choice, those who were institutionalize for stress related breakdowns, and those who were asked to leave to keep them from the stress related breakdowns. It took nearly a year and a half of interviewing to eliminate those who left by their own choosing and those asked to leave. During the time the computers were also checking for last known whereabouts of all the people of the list. This allowed interviews largely with the parents to determine if anyone had the skill set determined to have accomplished both the theft and death of the analyst. The last list of institutionalized former employees was separated into two categories, and there was a percent of deceased, which I selected to leave to last thinking, it would not result in finding those responsible. It did not take terribly long to find the vast majority who were under lifelong care were still in the facility, and incapable of performing the acts that brought us to this point in the investigation, largely performed by Global Security Corporation analysts worldwide"

Tim: "With the list of deceased members encompassing the globe, it was broken into regions and sent to authorities locally, and dispersed to the most appropriate authority group to get investigations done a little quicker. It was also apparent to me, I could not put analysts into a potentially hostile situation, and had to rely on authorities. Having martial arts training, after discussing it with my wife, I offered to assist in the investigation further in the Seattle area to help speed up the process, and having fewer restriction in going about the investigation, felt I could accomplish it in a quicker fashion. I made the offer to the lead detective and it was accepted. I conducted the first 2 dozen interviews face to face with the parents of the deceased former employees. My findings were not at all, what I had anticipated, as none of the parents or families of those interviewed had any ill will toward the organization I head. I was sympathetic to their loss and offered my condolences, but at the same time the parents were all entirely grateful for everything Global Security Corporation had done in both attempting to prevent the breakdown, and absorbing the expense entirely of the care of the former employee. From there I went to vidphone interviews to finally get to the pair of people thought to have been responsible for the death of an analyst."

Prosecutor: "Once you had identified the suspect persons responsible, what did you do next?" Tim: "The names were given to Detective Marshall, and together we determined with a two year head start, the suspects were likely anywhere except the last known whereabouts. It took about a month of the authorities looking into various records to pinpoint them in Hong Kong, where they had been for at least six months. They originally used hotels and short term locations to stay, but then fell off the grid. No records were found to indicate they had left Hong Kong. The Hong Kong authorities were provided a description and photos, of the brother and sister being sought. After four months of only spotting and losing them again. Detective Marshall contacted me, requesting financial support to go to Hong Kong personally, to see if he could expedite the matter being an unseen person to the suspects. I offered my assistance as well, to give him another set of unknown eyes to look but he did not immediately accept, instead asked how I was in recognizing people's features. I told him I had an exceptional memory and he forwarded the photos to me, to study. I had them for a month and all the while I studied them, and also tried to picture them with different hair colors and possible facial hairs not in the photo. I was also informed that a large reason the suspects were able to easily elude authorities, was the local authorities were too visible and had no undercover personnel."

Prosecutor: "Did you ever go to Hong Kong personally and if so, why?" Tim: "Yes approximately one month later Detective Marshall asked if I could be in Hong Kong the following week, as another set of unfamiliar eyes would be helpful. They had made almost no progress after he got a small team of local police willing to work in regular street clothes instead of a uniform. I arrived in time to get a hotel arranged and meeting the Detective early Monday morning, in the hotel lobby as Global had him staying in the same hotel. I had acquired during the previous month a makeup kit to allow for appearance changes in the event, I had been spotted by the suspects. In my changed appearance the Detective did not recognize me, and I had to let him know it was me he was looking for. Once that issue was resolved, we departed the hotel to a place he wanted me to remain in order to spot the suspect if at all possible. Before arriving at the location the detective had in mind, I spotted an anomaly and informed the detective I was going to follow it up. He had given me in the hotel an ear piece used for communications with the group of authorities involved in the search for the suspects. My worst fears were that the person I thought might be the male suspect was heading to the local Hong Kong offices of Global Security Corporation. My fears were realized as I watched him enter the building. I tried to get the security guard to tell me where he was heading and what his name was, by saying I thought I spotted a friend who I suggested try this company for a position. The guard would give no information beyond he was going to the floor our offices were located. I was greatly concerned, contacted the Detective through the earpiece and went to the hotel to arrange a meeting with the director and the HR representative who might have hired the individual I thought to be the suspect."

Prosecutor: "What happened at this meeting?" Tim: "The first part was by vidphone to my director who I had known for several years. In my disguise he did not recognize me and almost refused to converse with me. This hurdle was overcome and we arranged for him to bring the HR representative that may have hired the individual in question, and I also requested a company photo, but that did not come until later. An hour later I met the two in the hotel lobby and took them to the restaurant for a more private discussion."

Prosecutor: "I need to interrupt a moment to clarify what anomaly you saw to get on this track of investigation." Tim: The possible suspect was in a disguise with dark hair and facial hair, but his eyebrows did not match the rest of his hair coloring." Prosecutor: "And you were able to spot this in a pedestrian crowd as large as Hong Kong?" Tim: "After a month of studying his features, and imagining his appearance with various colors of hair and with or without facial hair, I did, Yes." Prosecutor: "That is hard to believe, you are on the ground in Hong Kong less than 30 minutes and spot the suspect that authorities, who are trained specifically for this type of work could not do over 5 months. How is that possible?" Tim: "As I previously stated, I have a very good memory, to further that information as a youth my memory was so good, I went through testing for a photographic memory, the results were that although I retained 75 to 80% of something I saw once, a photographic memory retained 100 %. I had a full month to study the features of the suspects, and practiced in one hour every day until I was called upon to put it to use. It has served me well over the years, and one or two months before I turned 20 years of age, I had a master's degree from MIT in Information Security. That is publicly documented."

Prosecutor: "I guess that means we should not question your memory, which is quite an accomplishment by the way. Continue with you meeting please."

"In the meeting, I was made aware that the suspect was hired temporary as the previous person did not show up, and could not be found anywhere including hospitals and morgues. It was unlike the person who had health issues, not to call and let the company know. His position allowed for some flexibility in his continued employment, and those he worked with were willing to give him that flexibility. At that point, to safeguard my own company, I put into effect procedures to do just that. Part of that involved contacting the lead communications technician to find if he was alone and able to have a conversation. As it happened, he was running a scheduled equipment test and the suspect was on the roof for a two man test procedure. I had the lead technician verify if the former employee had been removed from the system and he had not. Then had the lead technician check the logs of the equipment to determine if since the former employee disappeared, he had attempted to get into the system. It was confirmed that it had been done twice which the technician found rather odd. He was asked to remove or revoke the former employee's access rights, as a precaution and informed the person temporary was not who he seemed. The technician had never revoked an employee before and had to find out how to comply, but it would be done. With that part of the meeting concluded, I continued with the pair in the restaurant to keep an eye out for potential issues to arise concerning the suspect, and knowing that the company keeps relatively up to date photos of all employee on record, requested the photos of the suspect who was using an alias, and the missing employee, and dismissed them to return to their duties. I received the photos around 2 PM in the afternoon Hong Kong time.

When I received the photos on my intellipad, I knew I had the suspect and his precise whereabouts. He would not be leaving until at least 5 PM Hong Kong time, and using the earpiece I asked the lead detective to meet with me. It was determined he could not distribute the photos until the next morning and we put into plan, I would try to follow the suspect to his place of sanctuary, if at all possible.

At just before 5 PM, I tried to find a way to spot the suspect from the other side of the street, but visibility from vending carts and other obstacles prohibited it. I took up station farther past the hotel, assuming his most likely destination was one of the large apartment complexes in the opposite direction.

The suspect exited the building shortly after 5 and heading in the direction I thought he would. Unfortunately, there was just too many people to keep the distance I wanted, and I had to close the gap some to keep him in sight better. Half way to the assumed destination the suspect did a full 180 degrees turn, and was heading directly at me instead of the same direction. I did not panic and maintained the direction I was going to find a place farther down, to take up station to continue following him. Instead of walking past me, as he closed, he jumped in front of me and pushed me against the wall and asked why I was following him. Sticking with my first time tourist approach, I apologized but did not intend at all for him to think I was, after a full day of seeing the sites in Hong Kong, I was merely trying to find my way back to where the travel agency arranged my stay. From there, I went to other side of the street to continue to follow as after his threatening retort, he returned to his original direction. I managed to keep him in sight, without being spotted a second time. Saw which of the apartment complexes he entered and rushed to the glass doors with the hopes of seeing how many went in the elevator with him. I arrived just in time to see only he and two others entered and once the doors closed. I entered the lobby area to view the floor information to see which floors were being stopped at. I then provided the surveillance team with the three floors used."

Prosecutor: "You had a busy day from the sounds of it. And yet you accomplished what authorities could not. Where did this lead to?"

Tim: "Since photos could not be distributed to the team until the following morning, the next day really did not start until 5 PM. The detective in charge had people placed on the three floors of the apartment complex to determine the exact apartment the suspect was using. Since it was previously discovered they had acquired a number of false identities, they were not using the same alias for the rental, as they had for hotel room or employment. It meant the only way to confirm, was visually and that was accomplished that evening by 5:30 PM Hong Kong time. The detective dismissed the team members for the night, with the intention of a pair be there in the morning after the male suspect had left for the day. Once that occurred, the two team members would apprehend the female, assuming she would be in the apartment. Since that occurred as planned, part two was to enter the Global Security Corporation Hong Kong office to apprehend the male suspect. This all hinged on me being able to access the elevator without an escort, which I was told as CEO, my retina scan was sent to all offices for access, but I had never tested that until we entered GSC offices and it worked. We went first to the director's office, since I had no idea where the communication department resided in that or any other building. It took about 30 minutes into the building before we were at the door to the communication department. As a precaution to the Hong Kong director, I insisted he remain outside the door, because I had no idea how the male suspect might respond.

The group consisted of myself, Detective Marshal and the local member I only knew by her code name of mama bear. Once opening the door and insuring the director remained outside, mama bear took up station immediately inside near the exit door, believed to be the only one. The detective followed me as we tried to find the area the technicians were physically located. It was a very large room with an abundance of equipment and shelving stacked with everything used technologically by the company. Vision was largely obscured and having never been inside the room previously, we slowly made our way toward the rear of the room, where we finally saw the technicians seated around specialized monitoring equipment.

Even from the back, the suspect was recognizable now that everyone had his photo and the detective announce by name, the suspect was under arrest for murder and possible kidnapping charges. The next thing happened literally in the blink of an eye, but was in slow motion for me, at least in my mind. The suspect produced a rather vicious look blade type implement, and charge directly toward me. My martial arts routine instinctively took over and I positioned myself for a defense maneuver which was a very powerful kick beyond anything I thought I was capable of. Simultaneously my early training flashed of points of vulnerability of human weakness points. I managed to make contact under the extended arm holding the weapon and the nerve bundle I connected with left the suspect temporarily paralyzed for a little over an hour. After that, both detectives stated that it occurred so fast, they did not even have time to fully draw their weapons. The suspect was restrained, and we had to wait until he had regained some mobility to move him out of the building. Once in the lobby, I was told I was no longer needed for the procedures at the police department building, and we went separate way for the day."

Prosecutor: "Is that person in this room?" As he said this, the vidphone at the Hong Kong end panned the room and Tim identified the defendant as Artimus Robbins. Prosecutor: "You are telling me he tried to murder you also?" Tim: "I cannot say if his intention was to murder or merely escape, I only know for certain he produced a weapon that I could not understand how it got past all the building security."

Prosecutor: "I would like to add to the charges of attempted murder, in light of the fact, this action was witnessed by at least three other people at this time." The judge of the proceeding although unseen, stated the charges would be added to the case. Prosecutor: "Since your actions were the sole reason for still being here, why did you remain in Hong Kong?" Tim: "I remained because there was still a missing employee of my company whose status was unknown. Whether this person was dead or alive and if alive what condition was he in with the lack of care he was receiving? I felt it was my responsibility to see this person had been taken care of by my organization, depending on the outcome, but he went above and beyond what his job duties would normally entail. I felt he deserved at least that."

Prosecutor: "The detective has already stated for the record, due to the crimes committed on Chinese soil, the suspect was turned over to military interrogator to get a quicker resolve to the missing person. I believe he said it was the fifth day when information became available. What happened then?

Tim: "The detective contacted me and took me to a building between the hotel and apartment complexes, that had been schedule not long before for a major renovation. The building renovation was in progress, but it was going to be at least 2 years until it was completed, and the suspect used the lowest level to keep the missing person. When I arrived with the detective, the very large floor space of that lower level had a single light, insufficient to illuminate much beyond a small radius of where the light was at. It took about five minutes to locate where the missing person was, and other local authorities were already present and determining the best way to take care of the missing person. It had been at least five days, this person had not had food or water while being chained to a support girder. He was not conscious, and did not appear to be in too good of physical condition. Medical crews did not arrive for another five minutes, during that time the authorities were only able to pick the lock in order to remove the restraints. It was old school, and quite some time since any of them had to unlock anything that was not electronic in nature. When the medical team arrived, the outlook was not good, he was badly dehydrated and needed better care facilities to determine the extent of his issues. I went to the hospital with the medical crew to insure that this individual's treatment would be covered by my company, not knowing if he had medical insurance or not, I made sure that any costs he could not cover, were covered by GSC to insure his recovery."

Prosecutor: "I assume with the apprehension and finding the missing person you were done in Hong Kong?" Tim; "Yes, I left the very next morning and the detective hitched a ride home as well." Prosecutor: "I have no further questions to the witness." Again although unseen the judge asked if the defense wished to cross examine the witness. They declined seeing that the case was lost. Tim was excused, and would not be needed again. The entire process took almost 4 hours. Tim was an hour late leaving for home and Kuri did not know why. He had Nora call Kuri and speak on his behalf and let Kuri know he just left to get home. Nora said, "Consider it done and good night."

Tim apologized to his ladies for being so late, but Hong Kong trial procedures were not quick by any means, he had spent nearly four hours providing testimony to the person responsible for the death of the analyst. He made dinner and spent the evening seeing how Liani did in her first day of third grade. She said she was learning quite a bit more than reading and writing, but thought she was doing okay with it. Kuri confirmed she picked it up pretty quickly, even with the quick advance in grades. She did not do too bad learning how to use the computer either, and would be able to do it entirely on her own once she got the hang of going up and down stairs. It seemed to be harder for Liani than all the other things combined. Tim also announced he would know in a few days if he would be able to go back into retirement, and spend more time with his lovely women. Liani did not know what to make of that, but Kuri was quite pleased to hear it. He did say he would still need to finish out his contract time; but would not renew it, and hoped Global Security Corporation had no further need of him. Kuri said she hoped so also, but did not believe that would ever truly happen. GSC would find a reason to ask Tim back and in all likelihood, offer him something she would be hard pressed to say no to.

From there, Tim went through his second daily mediation routine, which normally occurred after Liani was put to bed, but tonight he started early, to see if it would help him relax from the time he was giving his testimony. He was still perturbed about the prosecuting attorney questioning his memory, although he understood why, it still bothered him more than it should have. His mediation routine had worked its magic and he felt much more like he should with mind and body once again in unison with one another. He returned to the entertainment area, where the women of the house were engrossed in the last news broadcast of the night. According to Kuri, Japan's criminal network once again made the news, but this time instead of it being a result of some mishap they were responsible for, it was the authorities putting an end to one of the major networks with large scale arrests. Kuri in her excitement over the event rapidly explained to Tim that over two and half year of surveillance had the entire puzzle fall into place, and over 300 hundred arrests had been made over the last two days. She further explained and for the first time since Tim had known her, she was mixing Japanese and English and he did not understand Japanese, so he stopped her. He said she was jumping between languages, and he could not understand what she was trying to say.

Even Liani did not know what she was saying and asked her mother if she was an alien. This made Kuri slow down, and explain better so that both could understand her. After her slight pause, she said the authorities were so optimistic with this major arrest of the largest known network, the authorities felt they could within the next two years, finally put an end to the criminal networks that had long plagued the Japanese people and in particular Tokyo. They hoped the citizens of their great city would finally speak up to the authorities, to put an end to this plague once and for all. Kuri was quite happy, this was some of the best news she had heard from Japan in her lifetime.

She continue with the descendants of Ronin were not all dishonorable as samurai, and could possibly regain their samurai status with the right people to help. It would mean them voluntarily stopping their criminal network to take true employment, but if they did so voluntarily, Tokyo would not have enough proof to take other actions against their particular network. Some were never honorable people, even as Samurai, following the leadership of their shogun; but they would know that themselves, and be among those the authorities would continue to pursue. What it does mean, is Tokyo is finally in a position to put an end to this type of activity, and maybe the Japanese people could have some time to consider where else they could improve upon; especially in the treatment of their women.

Kuri was so happy that after getting Liani to sleep for the night she felt up to some of her own pleasures, and it was a wonderful night for the both of them.

Tim went to work each day and on the third day he received a call from Detective Marshall who was still in Hong Kong. He started out by saying, "Do not suppose one of your company jets is in Hong Kong, so I do not have to return via commercial flights. Tim said it was highly unlikely, and would probably take longer to get one there than to just take his commercial flight home. The Detective simply said, it could not hurt to ask and told him commercial flying was nowhere near as nice as it was on their private planes. He then went on to explain the real reason to have called him. "Artimus Robbins was found guilty on all charges, including attempted murder. He would be administered the death penalty by law in Hong Kong, since two of his criminal acts occurred in that city. The Hong Kong military had already contacted the US military, to have his penalty administered by the US military. He would be executed by the same means he committed murder, and although rather quick, it would be from the same government he supposedly used to acquire the equipment for his criminal activities. The US military will send a single individual with the equipment to administer the penalty, and return with the equipment. They did not authorize it to be used by any other government or military worldwide.

Tim said "I was hoping for a more painful and methodical approach to account for what he put the communication technician from Hong Kong through, but I will have to accept the means selected." Detective Marshall said, "At least justice has been served, and in this case, it would not have happened without your detailed description in your testimony. Well done I might add, and I truly found it has been a pleasure working with you, I wish all my own people had your skills in memory." Tim said, "It would be nice, but it unfortunately is not something that can be taught or learned, you either have it or you don't, and it starts right from birth."

Detective Marshall: "Just so you hear it from me, you were instrumental in this case finding closure. In all the time I have been here, and all my associates agreed, they never had so much assistance in the finding the suspect most guilty of a crime. If the authorities worldwide were working with the list you had to start with, we most likely would not have more than 200,000 names eliminated that were never suspects to begin with. Do not ever think that all your effort has gone without the appreciation of myself and the entire Seattle police department. Words cannot not justify my own gratitude. Now it is time to head home, I surely hope the wife has not drunk all the Cognac in the four days I have been away, I hate to think about trying to find 500 WC to get a bottle to celebrate the outcome of this going on over three years now."

The vidphone connection was broken, and the vidphone retracted before Tim could reply to the detective's potential need for Cognac. Tim was fairly certain he should have some left, since it had not been a year. The day also included Trask being in for his weekly check on the company, and he was pleased to hear that the problem that had plagued them for over three and a half years was resolved, but then it dawned on him that Tim might want to return to retirement with his family. Trask asked, "With that bit of good news are you going to tell me your going back to retirement?" Tim replied with his own question, "Are you telling me you're also psychic?" Trask said, "No, just trying to figure out how in the hell this company is going to operate without you, you have made us largely single handedly, what we have become. I cannot argue your logic, considering all the trouble this last round has created, largely for you. You took the bull by the horns and ran with it to completion though, I cannot say I would have been able to do it the same way, and with as slow as the authorities were even with your input, it may have gone unresolved with me taking the lead. I would have never considered using our own analysts to investigate, or even taken it upon myself to go to Hong Kong, to insure the suspect was found and in custody.

Additionally, I would have likely denied the use of company planes and a police detective under company care for over a month in Hong Kong, being the same detective that detained me for the better part of a day, keeping me from getting things done that may have sped up the entire process. I do hold grudges much longer than you do. As a matter of fact, I would likely return and haunt the medical doctor who could not keep me alive, just to prove I hold a grudge." Tim laughed a bit with that closing remark, "I think rather than being the slow and time consuming means of become dust and feeding the worms, I prefer incineration and get it over with quickly." Trask with his own chuckle said, "Good point, I might concur with you on that note."

Tim finally got around to saying, "To be honest, Trask with a second child well on the way, I believe it is time to be more of a family man than I have been so far to my growing family. My first child Liani who is a doll, has followed Japanese schooling as her mother decided, and had already begun early school. After two months she has already been advanced to the third grade being too far ahead of the curve from her learning appetite. In addition, she has all her mother's beauty and more and by the time she reaches 16, I am going need a stick big enough to swat dinosaurs, to keep all the boys away intent on spoiling her purity."

That got a good belly laugh from Trask, and it took a few minutes for him to respond. Trask once back under control replied, "You do have a way with words at times, and I will certainly miss that. You telling me at the young age of three, you can already tell your little girl is going to be drop dead gorgeous. I do not envy you one bit there my friend. On the other hand, that is one big stick you are talking about, can you even lift it?" Tim said, "I believe I will have plenty of encouragement from the drooling male population of Seattle, so I will certainly give it my best effort." Trask went to ask, "Who will bring us all the codes to keep our systems up to speed on the Information Gateway." Tim replied, "You only need one MIT graduate in your company to accomplish that." Trask replied, "You know Information Security is a very demanding occupation, and MIT graduates are not exactly beating down our doors here to get on board." Tim: "Am I the only one in the entire company?" Trask said, "You certainly are the only one in Seattle where the information needs to be, I cannot say all of our east coast satellite offices are MIT free, but none of them have come forward to show they have the initiative to even look." Tim said, "I guess it will be up to me to put out feelers, via a vidphone recording to find out if any other MIT graduates are employed." Trask said, "How is you come up with all the ideas while I sit looking like I am sucking my thumb? And it just pops right out of your head like it was the only conceivable way to think on this subject." Tim: "It does just pop into my head, but I am not sure it is the only way to think it over, but that is just how my mind works, covering all the possibilities in an instant and picking the best option. I cannot help it sometimes, it just is what it is." Trask said, "I surely wish my mind worked like that, I need lots of input to weigh out the positives and negatives, to make a decision based on the best foreseeable outcome. All of them usually have negatives, but some have less severe consequences as a result of a decision. Anyway, if you have not been kept up to speed at your last proposal, business is booming while we work out the drawbacks on the big businesses that would really produce the big money, but also the headaches. We are having a problem figuring out with customized clients, how to determine at which point additional systems need to be added into the communications AI network, before efficiency is less than desired. Since it is variable input, it has made it difficult to determine. Got any ideas on that problem?" Tim: With a variable input your capacity will be reached differently depending on the client's needs, as a matter of being prepared, you should have two or three AI systems sitting in wait to be put into the network, when it is necessary. Have the AI systems at least prepped with the standard code needed to operate any communications system we use, and then you can add the variables once put into the network. It may be necessary for an AI to only handle one input TRU address and its information where as it can turn it over to the appropriate AI with that client's variables. Key to the equation will be always having ready and waiting AI computers, at least until business starts to stagnate. With at least one spare always on hand, in the unlikely event of a failure, you will have a backup AI computer waiting to fill in for the one requiring repair or even replacement."

Trask: "I do not understand why we pay these people so much money when I only have to ask you." Tim: "That would be largely because they did not pay attention to technology, and figure out how to best utilize it for this specific application. Your technology people who are all top notch, specialize in technology, not the utilization of it for a specific purpose. On the other hand, I nor you could have integrated a single computer to a robotic humanoid." Trask: "Point taken, but again it is so much simpler to just ask you. Guess it is time to change the subject a little bit, the robotic humanoids as you refer to them, have made it to all the offices around the globe, and the technology team is working on the offices that required more than the original dozen. The largest portion of those are within the US with only a couple of exception. Their task ought to be completed at nearly the same time as you return to retirement, although I am not sure that mini vacation you got was truly retirement. Also the analyst's remodeling project is underway, and the Seattle office will need to use 50% percent of the 34th floor and the other 50 percent will be consumed by communications. That leaves us with no additional expansion room should it be needed. The plan as it is right now, especially with all the current tenants inquiring about the building addition, a fair percentage would prefer not to leave this building, but would like more prestigious office space as their particular businesses have somewhat flourished. They would like to display it through their office space. The general concept here is, with the expansion completed, which will take a fair amount of time, working that high in the air and adding to a building's height is not the simplest project. Relocating those to the new floor wishing to do so will open up some space, to contain it to only 33rd floor we may need to relocate other offices at our cost to free up the entire floor. That will allow us additional expansion should the communication group continue to expand beyond the room we have on the 34th floor. So once again all of your ideas are being put to use."

Tim: "I did not provide all of those ideas, I only proposed one, and three recruits provided the necessary proof over the all-white everything rooms. My original suggestions were denied, I did not provide the substantiating proof the analysts did to convince the board a change needed to be made. I did suggest larger rooms to accommodate humanoid computer systems, but that should have been obvious without the suggestion. Finally, JP asked me if I knew a design consultant, but the expansion to the building was already planned, just needed the plan in design to go forward. All I did was bring my brother into the picture; and he entirely on his own, got the deal based on his design and his firm's stellar reputation."

Tim and Trask had spent the entire morning in conversation. Tim decided to ask Trask if he would like lunch and it was time for Tim to cover the lunch. Trask saw no harm in it and the pair of them headed to the restaurant and arrived in the standard five minutes. Menus were brought, Cognac was ordered, and Tim tried not to rekindle the conversation they had been having. He asked Trask how his wife was since he seldom got to see her and Trask except for all of two occasions.

Trask: "She is doing well, and keeps both of us busy on the days she does not have her get together with her friends. And you are good with many things, but changing the subject is not your specialty, but no worries, I pretty much exhausted my backwards ways to get you to change your mind. To be honest, I can truly understand your reasons and after this last ordeal that largely got done, with your fail to resolve will not happen again attitude, it had to be overbearing at times. I will not promise you that you will never be needed again, but we will not go there until the time comes. Honestly nearly six months advanced noticed will let me try to find someone suitable to take the chair for a while. I believe though this once a week I come in for a day, is far better than getting weekly reports from Loretta, although she was correct about you running a tighter ship than I did. With that, I conclude my meager attempts to persuade you. Aside from the fact you did a marvelous job in your tenure."

They placed their orders and Trask finally said, "You said something about a second child well on the way at the start of this conversation. Did Kuri ask to know whether it was a boy or another girl?" Tim said, "She asked specifically not to know and wanted it to be a bit of a surprise, but she claims it felt different this time and therefore must be a boy. I do not know how a woman can tell, but she is uncannily accurate about her premonitions. Her reasoning for not knowing made a good deal of sense to me. She said, since nothing could really be obtained until the baby was born and certain dimensions were documented, before diapers and clothing could be obtained to fit a little better. I could not argue that, the only thing is if it is a boy, most of the baby clothes obtained for Liani cannot be used for a boy. At least the ones that did not have to be discarded due to stains and stuff that would no longer come out of her clothing, when she was younger. At three she has finally learned to use dinner utensils more efficiently although the fingers still are her first choice." Trask said, "Yes it is amazing how long some children take to using dinner utensils completely without fingers. I think my son was eight before he finally made the full conversion. At one point, I even told him if he continued to use his fingers, I was going buy him a pet bowl to replace his dinnerware." Tim: "I hope you got a better reaction from your wife than I got last night being candid." Trask: "Aside from a sarcastic retort from mine, it was life as usual in the Trask household what about you, what did you say?"

Tim: "I was simply honest about having to be ready with a big stick to beat the boys away from the door so Liani could get into in her own house, seeing she was going to be even more beautiful than her mother." Trask: "I do not see anything so terrible about that, what was your penalty?" Tim: "I got a punch to the arm and told that it was an awful thing to say to my own daughter. The biggest problem, was she hit me so hard for the first time in my life I had a visible bruise." Trask: "You're kidding, is Kuri that strong?" Tim: "Considering she has been doing her mediation routine since she was six years old, she is far stronger than she appears." Trask did not understand meditation routine and Tim told him it was a martial arts exercise for the specific purpose of bringing mind and body into perfect harmony. Tim told him since he did not do his yet today, and he had been, usually because since the investigation concluded, he was often bored out of his mind.

Tim: "When we get back to the office, since it has been so exciting as of late, I will let you hold down the fort while I do my routine. You may watch if you like, but Kuri has a much better routine than I do. When I went to Tokyo for the training seminar, part of Kuri's arranged activities after work, included two martial arts exhibits, which were performed by masters of the martial arts in Japan. It was impressive to say the least. The first night, which I think that would be at least 5 years ago, included her grandfather, who taught Kuri her martial arts, provided a 45 minute routine that was flawless. The most impressive part of the whole evening was all the masters, regardless of age, had the physique of young men in their 20's. Kuri grandfather at the time was 81 years of age and as Kuri said, did not look a day over 45. He has been doing his routine also from the age of six. Kuri said it had been refined and minor alteration made; but the essence of the routine remains the same. She also made a point that none of the master's routines would include the family secrets, they would remain within the family only. I have only met him once since we were married, and it was not a long visit."

The meal arrived and the food was consumed with a second Cognac to finish it off. Tim took care of the charges, and they returned a few minutes later than a normal lunchtime, but it was hardly excessive at five minutes at the most. Once in the office, Trask took the CEO seat which was common on his day in the office each week. Tim went to a more open area in the extremely large room, and went about his one hour and ten minute exercise routine. There were no disturbances, and Trask apparently watched the entire exercise, Tim had quickly reach his point of mental and physical harmony and was fairly oblivious to anything around him. That included Trask's awed expression over the routine he was performing. Tim returned to his seat across from Trask. Trask: That was impressive and you say Kuri's is even better. How long did you have to work on the last part where you hold your leg in the air for like five minutes each?"

Tim: "That is a multiple headed question really, keep in mind, I was performing a lesser routine for several years before Kuri helped me modify it into what it is now, it still is not entirely of Japanese martial arts skills, it is a mix of my original Tai Chi which is Chinese in origins, with some Japanese skill intermixed. When Kuri had me start the last part of the exercise, it took me over a month to hold it for the five minute duration. That was doing the routine every night of every day."

Nora made her presence made aware of by asking, "I have seen you doing this thing for close to two months now, and does it ever change or vary in the slightest?" Tim said, "No, Nora that is kind of the point of a meditation exercise." Nora: Did you say meditation or medication?" This had both Tim and Trask literally howling with laughter. All the while Nora was asking, "What is so funny, might I ask?"

It was even loud enough for a passing system member to pop his head in, before a rapid exit to loudly say, "Must be nice to be able to sit around and shoot the shit!" This really did nothing more than extend the laughter longer, although a bit more subdued?

Tim said to Trask, "I cannot figure out an explanation for Nora who had no concept of either meditation or medication and either explanation sounds similar." Trask said, "I think you might be on to something there, because I think it sounds good until I put them together, and it does sound like two methods to achieve the same results." I really think we should have your three year old explain it to her."

Tim: "That would prove interesting since she has no real idea what the difference is either. Nora, meditation is a state of mental and physical harmony, while medication usually comes in the shape of a pill from a pharmacy. Does that help answer your question?" Nora said, "Not really, since I have no requirement that needs either." Tim said, "Sorry, I have no better explanation than that and it is one of those small things that only makes sense to humans, I guess." Nora, "Yes, it would seem."

At least it made the remaining part of the day disappear quickly as it was now time to depart for home for both Trask and Tim. As they left, Loretta was returning from her nightly visit to the ladies room prior to leaving, and the three, all being parked in close proximity to one another, Tim and Trask escorted Loretta to her vehicle.

The last two days of the week in all retrospect, were simply too quiet for Tim. He found himself searching for things to keep himself occupied, and even paid a visit to the medical staff, largely to see how Rebecca Robbins was doing in her position and if she resumed her education, as well as find a home of her own. Doctor Ward said she was doing quite well and handling her limited sessions with analysts with true compassion. She really did try to find ways to help the few analysts that felt the stress was a little too high. Again, it was largely stress from outside of work; but Rebecca always tried to picture herself in the situation described, to provide a possible means of combating the problem, or at least a method to reduce it to just a bad day and the next one would be better. Rebecca told him she had obtained a modest home, and was using her computer system to get her additional levels of degrees in the medical profession, but this time she had more purpose and direction for her specialty in the medical profession. Since she was by Doctor Ward's opinion a perfect match to psychological therapy, and was trying to get her master's degree and hoped also PhD.

The weekend arrived as Tim went home to insure family time was in his immediate future.

CHAPTER

22

The first thing decided with the family, they would go to Tokyo for a week for some time in the home there. Liani could still follow her schooling program with the computer at that house, and they could try to get in some visits and shopping. They would leave on the week after the next, to give notice at GSC that since Tim had not used any of his paid time off, he would get a couple of trips completed before Kuri was unable. He would also extend his time for that event to a week from five days. The other trip he would schedule for a month later would be to Hong Kong, where only he had been previously. With the advanced notice, he could see if Cho and Yo-li could join them a least one evening for dinner. Since they also knew the sights better than he, they may be available for that as well, or in the very least have some good suggestions.

It was also decided that for dinner Saturday night, which was the next day, they would go to Liani's grandfather's restaurant, where she could pick anything she wanted outside of sake. Liani asked what that was, and Tim explained the best he could, it was rice wine that required her being 21 years of age in order to drink it. She had a ways to go for that milestone in her young life. Also, the next morning or early afternoon they would need to get luggage for Kuri and Liani's clothing to take with them on their two upcoming trips. He was relatively certain that he did not have enough for all of their clothes and personal effects for trips lasting a week. He informed them that they could pick anything they liked, as long as it could be received before next Friday when he hoped they could leave after he got home from work to give them as much time in Tokyo as they could fit in. This was all agreed upon, and the plan was in motion. Kuri said for Friday, she would make a large lunch, so they did not need to eat again until they were on the plane to Tokyo.

Dinner that evening was not terribly complex, but chicken cordon bleu, was always a tasty meal, and would not interfere with the going to the Japanese restaurant the next evening. The evening news was rather mundane, but in many ways that was a good thing. No major catastrophes, or criminal activities reported were a good sign of the world being seemingly at peace. The biggest story of the night was an animal rescue of someone's pet being trapped in a sink hole that emerged in a state that had forever had that problem. It was all the way on the other coast from Seattle. The pet was rescued without any injuries, but the unstable ground gave way with the pet simply walking over the top of it, and dropped 15 feet. The dog was partially stuck in loose ground, but did not have the ground slide in over the top of it. The rescue team took every precaution to insure the safe recovery of the animal, and being a relatively small dog, the single person who went in with support ropes and harnesses, was able to free the dog and hold it to be pulled back up to the more stable ground surface. It was the most exciting bit of new offered for the night. The news broadcast would do a repeat of the story for each of the nightly broadcast, which only told Tim they were hard pressed for other stories that evening.

The following morning, after a good breakfast which everyone requested, they went to the shop that had the best selection of luggage. Kuri decided to get her and Liani matching bags, each capable of holding about 10 days of clothing provided they packed them correctly. She only got one personal effects piece, knowing she had all of her own hygiene products in Tokyo. Tim had some too but always took his to be sure. Liani did not have any, so hers would get brought along, and since they were planning on shopping some, new ones would be obtained for the following trips. Shopping would also include Tim and Kuri having some clothing always in Tokyo, but Liani still growing would need to bring clothes along until the time came she was not changing sizes frequently. It was perfectly normal childhood growth that would have peaks and valleys, but that also would occur later. Tim covered the charges for the luggage, which included a means to transport that many bags in a single trip. It only cost him 800 WC which Tim thought to be modest and all the pieces were at the store, so he took them to the transport and they returned home. Liani was glad to have the day off from schooling, but still had the desire to go over some of the more advance material she was learning from the very start, without any preparation from her parents. Largely because her rapid advancement was not anticipated this early in her development. She only spent an hour on the computer for the entire day. She was getting better at negotiating the stairs, but Kuri or Tim made certain she did not have any unnecessary mishaps like missing a step and falling down the rest of them. Liani, remained relatively cautious when traversing the stairs, so it made it fairly simple for Tim or Kuri to be first down to make sure nothing happened. Tim figured before six months had passed, she would feel comfortable taking steps without any help and likely anyone's knowledge.

The weekend went by quickly, the dinner at Hiro's Authentic Japanese Restaurant was a big hit with Liani, as she tasted her grandfather recipe for the first time. She order something more of a rice mix and sweet and tangy type single dish meal, but also tasted some of her mother's dinner selection and the teriyaki steak entrée of Tim's. When she tried the rice side dish that was included in the steak meal, she told her father it tasted just like his. Tim said that is because he told her grandfather everything he used to make it, after her grandfather told him what he needed to correct. He said to Liani, as far as he knew, this one restaurant was the only one to use all of his ingredients, the ones in Japan had a couple items missing. Hiro did find using real mushrooms would give it nearly the same flavor as the home grown clutee Tim used. It required a specific type of mushroom to accomplish it. Apparently not all mushrooms have entirely the same flavor. Tim never really noticed that before.

On the first day of the work week after greeting Loretta and all his computers, Tim went to JP to inform him of his upcoming time off, which would account for 15 days of his allotted paid time off. Tim then made sure the company private jets would be available, and if they were able to stay the entire week in wait, to make sure it was not the same crew that got to go the last time it occurred in Tokyo. Tim knew there was never any guarantees for holding a plane out of the country, whether it would need to go elsewhere. For this reason, he made sure the plane would be there for departure, which for both trips would be Sunday morning approximately 10 AM local time. This was to allow the whole family the necessary rest time to return to a more daily routine. Tim also knew the two places they were going to visit were hardly the most severe jet lag trips. Still a little extra time to acclimate to the Seattle time zone should be allowed. Tim also made sure the crew assigned were aware of a three year old child being a part of the passenger list. After that he arranged the hotel accommodation in Hong Kong. With it being far enough in advance, they offered him a luxury suite, at his normal room price to help with having a young child. He had no reason to turn down the offer and accepted.

After all those arrangement were completed, he used the IG to see the latest offerings in mobile computers, thinking Liani would best be served in Hong Kong, not to miss an entire week of her schooling. They were far less expensive than his computer desk, but he was unsure of the power type used in Hong Kong. He checked to see which ones had the largest variety of adapters for power to it when it was stationed in one place for a week. He knew if they ever went to St. Petersburg, that alternating current was primary there as well as Sierra. He check into that information also, but it turned out the descriptions were either too vague, or an individual needed to know precisely the adapter they needed. Tim decided to have Nora contact one of the local computer stores to better clarify his unknown needs. Nora made the vidphone connection for him, but Tim did the conversing with the sales person. He made it truly simple. He explained that the DC adapter to power was universally the same everywhere that used it. They offered an adapter kit that the DC adapter plugged into the adapter appropriate to the power source outlet. They only knew of four still used in different countries, and the kit included all four. It did not come with any computer system, but the cost was not excessively high. The outlet adapter that the DC connector plugged into was the voltage control and turned the incoming AC to the DC voltage required by all computers. It was highly unlikely he could damage his computer by inserting the DC connection into the power source, as the two types simply had different designs that were incompatible. Tim decided with the help he received, he would get the computer from there. He asked about the one he thought best for Liani and they kept them on hand, as they were quite popular among people with school children attending classes from home.

Tim told them that was his precise reason for getting it. They then inquired to how old she was and he told them, they wondered where she was attending school at such a young age. He said she was in the Japanese school system as required by her mother. They asked if that was the normal age for children there and Tim confirmed it was, and his little girl was already advanced to the third grade, in the first two months of school. They asked if she was some type of prodigy, and Tim said just enthusiastic about learning. She was too young to be tested for anything more at this point in time.

Tim ordered the computer and two sets of adapters to be safe, and if he ever needed them he would have them. He provided his information necessary to complete the transaction and they told him they would be at the store to pick up at his earliest convenience. Tim figured it would be that evening on his way home. It would only make him about 10 minutes late, as long as he did not have to wait long. He called Kuri to say he might be a little later than normal just to keep her abreast of the day, and did not tell her why, as he wanted her to be surprised as much as Liani. He also found out when checking his funds he received a 3 million WC bonus and although sure of why, he thought he made it clear to share it with the people who were doing the majority of the work. He would have to inquire from Trask on his day in the office, knowing the board members did communicate more than once each month for the meeting.

The rest of the day was rather boring once again, and Tim performed his routine to help with his boredom. He did not know if two a day routines were doing anything more to him, but he found it to be a marvelous way to kill some time. It also put him in a frame of mind to better cope with the lack of things to do, since his biggest issues had reached closure. He wondered if the sentence for Artimus Robbins would coincide with his visit to Hong Kong, but it was a news item that was sufficient to at least get a mention in the nightly news. He thought it especially true since Artimus Robbins was raised in Seattle.

The best thing about his last six or less months, was he had two trips with the family planned, and the arrival of a newborn to look forward to. Also that was not work related, but that was where he needed to be for at least 40 hours each week with so little to do he was creating his own, to occupy his time. The first two days of the week passed without a single incident to divert him from his feeling of wondering why he was even here. When Tim arrived Wednesday, Trask was already in the office and as soon as Tim showed up, Trask said, "Now Nora!" Nora went immediately into her method that pleased Trask to call a meeting.

Tim said, "Is it not a little early for that, I bet all the system people have not even got into their offices yet?" Trask did not think it was that early, and found out it was still 10 minutes before the official start of the workday. Trask said, "Damn, premature out of the gate that is only supposed to happen to young teen boys." Tim only provided the expected chuckle with Trask's comment. Trask did not have a single head show up in the doorway either. Tim asked, "Why are you here so early anyway?" Trask said, "I got up early apparently, but I did not see it that way when I glanced at the time, I thought it was an hour later than it was, rushing to get ready and leave for the office, I never looked at the time again. It did not even dawn on me I was here before you, I simply assumed you were elsewhere in the building, and thought you would show up soon, which of course you did."

Tim jokingly said maybe he should start paying more attention to his bucket list if his mind was going, the rest was sure to follow. Trask said he might be right about that, of course going from 50 hours a week to none back to one day a week was hopefully more in the factor. Tim really did not know how that worked, except for paid time off which never seemed to last long enough to do all he would have like while away. Just a single week was not enough time to develop too many bad habits.

After Tim had been there fifteen minutes, Trask asked Nora to call the meeting again now that everyone should really be here. After giving Trask a little bit of static about his continual requests for the same thing, she complied with Trask's request.

Unlike the first time, all the system people showed up and Trask told Jon Franks he could bypass this meeting not to be offensive, but he simply needed more company time under his belt to be considered in this particular instance.

Trask started out by thanking everyone for coming so quickly, like they had a choice was Tim's thought. Trask: "As much as I regret this coming event, you all should know that Tim will not be renewing his fifth year as CEO contract. In all retrospect to his situation, I cannot find any fault in his decision. He has individually done more to shape and keep this company on the top of the security world, all the while going through some of the highest stress related problems in any known position ever created in any business. Compound that with his diligence to get to the bottom of the first major breach this company monitored, although fortunately we offer no such service at the time. Tim also does not like being beat and learned from it and came up with ways to combat it from happening again. Tim brought about first, the AI simulator to verify if questionable codes were always being used successfully. This led to his proposal to the AI network throughout all the major offices. It concluded with the direct AI to satellite configuration currently in use. None of this would have happened, if left to the rest of us to come up with a plan to put into use to best fit our particular needs, as a security monitoring leader. At the end of his 10 years, although eligible to retire spent his 11th year as Director and it was without a supervisor or Assistant director to aid him in looking into the needs of analysts and clients alike. He also had made the continuing effort to reduce analyst stress, as he himself felt too many analyst were being institutionalized as a result of stress overload syndrome. For those of you unfamiliar with this, literally it means the person who has this is likely going to be incapable of any type of activity that required thought or decision making. The mind at this point is broken, and it remains the one thing the medical people the world over cannot fix. His first proposal for the stress issues was to incorporate an acupuncture specialist in all the office, a solution he discovered on his first global excursion to all the other major offices. This offered a much quicker help to those overly stressed by their analysis work. Seemingly there are no permanent solutions, or one time medications to perform magic in that problem. After that he even encouraged other analysts to see this specialist by going himself to find out what it was all about. He suffered no stress, but the medical department released to the general population that he had been there and it spiraled from there. As account responsibilities continued to grow so did the stress issues, Tim although not the originator of the voice package idea, found the two solutions for an outside vendor to incorporate to make him quite successful. He did not limit his good ideas to simply Global Security Corporation, but his ultimate goal was for analysts to achieve enough time to retire with the abilities to appreciate life. A joke, has turned into the most successful of all the stress relief issues with the use of robotic humanoids to allow analyst to feel like they had another person to talk to within their soundproofed rooms.

Tim has never stopped providing valuable ideas and proposals from his first day, and to this very day, does not think himself so special, as I know he is. His latest proposal is already reaping rewards by using our communications network to help businesses, from home based to large business with restricted access systems. In more ways than I care to count and occasionally admit, Tim has shaped this company into what we are, far ahead and beyond any vision I had with the other nine owners.

The reason for this meeting is really to determine who among you feel they can handle the duties of being the CEO. I select you folks, as all of you have been here more than 10 years, whereas few of the analysts have reached that plateau and only one was not so stressed to continue on another 5 years. Tim managed to make it that far when 95 percent of the analysts he started with failed to do so. The five percent that managed the 10 years in Seattle, did not believe they would last a day longer in this business and were grateful to have a retirement program to live off comfortably for the remaining days they had to finally live a life.

To make this a little shorter, with Tim's attention to the wellbeing of analysts, the use of technology specifically to improve security, and giving the AI systems the largest percentage of the work, the stress levels in this organization have been reduced to the same factor of any other job. What this means for any of you who feel they can improve this company even further, your workload as the CEO has become far less stressful than when either I or Tim held the helm. Also as an owner, I plan to continue to be in this very office once each week, which helps me keep up with the changes that take place. For any of you that know Loretta in the entry office area, she will keep me abreast of problems that arrive and go without being addressed properly. She is extremely attentive and knows just about everything that occurs on a day to day basis. The sad truth is, the only thing she ever told me while Tim was at the helm, is he ran an even tighter ship than I did. Tim will still be here for a little more than 5 months I believe, so you have time to give this some thought. If you yourself do not feel it is for you; but think one of your associates is better suited, please let me know. The position offer is closed to only you in this room, and although none of you are specifically security analysts, you should all understand how to best serve this entire organization not confine it to your particular specialty in the information world. That is vital, as this entire company is founded on a team effort and the principles that come with it. You all may return to your normal purpose for being here and give the matter some thought. I look forward to seeing or hearing from you again soon, although I am only here for sure on Wednesday of each week, Loretta will know how to reach me."

After everyone left without any comment, he said, "Trask, you could have also offered that if they had any questions concerning the CEO position, I would be happy to assist in any way I can." Trask said, "Did not think about that, you would do that?" Tim said, "If it will help get the best person for it I certainly would, although I cannot help them when out of the country on paid time off." Trask: When is that?" Tim: "Friday, after work I go home get the family and luggage and go to the airfield back second Sunday, then repeat 4 weeks later. First to Tokyo, and then to Hong Kong, since we have a house in Tokyo, and I have been the only one in the family to see Hong Kong. Also I increased my time for when the second child is due, to a full week. Since the primary duty I have had since bringing the investigation to closure is combating boredom." Trask: "Yes, It certainly has become much more serene here, in was a madhouse in the first years, not entirely unlike being an analyst for the entire day. Biggest advantage to being here as opposed to the analysts' area, it was much less stress related, but definitely really busy, largely with client calls for both existing and potential. Largely for explanations on what was the responsibility of Global and the actual customer or to be client. Some were unnecessary, as it was a CEO or president too lazy to read through their well explained contracts. Some was preliminary research from potential clients, and this I fully understand and highly approve to be honest. Only spending one day a week here I cannot say anything concerning boredom. I can say from your perspective, after the amount of activity you involved yourself with on a daily basis, this could be far too great of a letdown from wondering how much you cannot get done today, so it is here tomorrow."

Tim: "One other thing I need to address while you are here. When the communication monitoring was put into activity, I thought we agreed on, the bonus should be shared among the communications technicians, as they had far more involved in making this service profitable than any others, including myself. So why did I get a 3 Million WC bonus?" Trask: "The board members decided you were entitled to a one-time bonus, which I believe was equal to the total, split among the communications technicians. They will get subsequent bonuses as the profits continue to rise and with already over 400,000 home businesses, following the single parameter plan to protect them from unauthorized access, they overrode me on this occasion. You will have to really take it up with all of them at the next board meeting, but with you now announcing your departure from the CEO position and company, I would not expect you'll change their minds. Especially since the suggestion started from the financial people of this company, which is a very rare thing indeed." Tim: "Why is it so rare for financial departments to make a suggestion, just out of curiosity?" Trask: "I truly believe it is ingrained in them all from birth the motto of 'it is better to receive than give' as the shortest and most accurate explanation."

Tim: "That is some difficult motto to overcome, I will give you that, so bringing this up is a waste of time at the next board meeting, I take it?" Trask: "Pretty much." Tim decided to do a little IG research into articles and possible technology although he did not expect much from technology at this point, outside of maybe a more advanced brain development in AI and semi-intelligent computer systems. He immediately found one article that was worth mentioning to Trask. Tim: "Trask, this article here say the cloud is officially dead." Trask: "Really, that is sooner than I suspected or anticipated, what else does it say?" Tim: "According to the company that setup the long used information network known as the cloud, they have announced in two weeks the remaining service will be terminated. It is strongly suggested to obtain the TRU for the Information Gateway or do without any service at all. Company officials announced today, that due to the excessive loss of business in the system, due to the more advanced and faster Information Gateway, it is no longer feasible to maintain and keep all the equipment running optimally without a major rate increase to those still using it. The necessary fees for the limited number of people still using the cloud, would exceed the annual income of the median family income. As a result, the company that has long been the only information network provider for nearly 90 years, will terminate all business practices and close their doors forever. It has been a good long run as far as this company is concerned, but simply cannot compete with the light speed transmissions of the Information Gateway, and would like to thank all the people across the world for their long patronage."

Trask: "WOW, that about covers it all. I had not truly expected that to take place for another 10 years, thinking many residences would still be using it for the little bit of time they need to access the Information Gateway. Still, that has to be the fastest transition in the history of moving information from one location to another via computers."

Tim: "It has been nearly 14 years since IG first appeared." Trask: "True, and a medium change as well, but if memory serves, it took nearly 40 years for the cloud to put its predecessor into the position they are in now." Tim: "I guess I better check on the grandparents tonight to make sure they are not still not using the cloud, not sure how much they use their computers, although I know they do. Since the equipment used for either is not highly visible, better make sure they know what is happening in case." Trask: "That would probably be a good idea, but I will bet this type of information will reach just about every conceivable news broadcast in the world, not simply the information highway." Tim: "You are likely correct, I just think it is better to be safe and make sure they are aware of it." Especially since I will be leaving for a week with the family to go remember what the house in Tokyo looks like. It seems like it has been forever since we were there last, although I am sure Kuri will tell me otherwise."

Trask: "Must be nice to have a getaway in some other country, although I have seen your home and you are not as overindulgent as so many others, I have to concede I belong in that category to some degree, but my son surely did. I think it cost me five times as much to build his house than ours. He has an exercise room with all the equipment conceivable, probably larger than the first house I was at when I had to see your samurai sword." Tim: "I guess it must be nice to have your father take care of it all for you." Trask: "Do not get me wrong, I told him up front I would build his home, but he had to be able to cover all the monthly expenses and still have something left to save up for retirement. I do not give him anything weekly, monthly or even annually, outside of a Christmas and birthday present."

That outside of really small talk, concluded the conversation for the remainder of the day. Tim had done his meditation routine to get through the lack of things that required his direct attention. He did check with his grandparents and they had already switched over to the IG, as the cloud cost was rising and it was becoming more costly to use than the IG.

The last two days of the work week were no different, The AI network was running optimally, and keeping business running with precision and efficiency. He used one hour out of the last two days to arrange a conference vidphone connection to all the major office directors. That was largely to confirm that the analyst monitor system had been relocated to the medical staff offices, where the people most qualified to keep a watch for stress issues to arise. Each director had confirmed it was done, but with the robotic computer systems now in place, stress levels were not much different than any other office for any other business. The medical staff was offering their services to address stress related issues outside of the work related problems. For the most part those were the result of two different issues. First was marital problems, which for the biggest part was couples who simply could not learn to live with one another. The medical staff offered a number of scenario solutions, but said the best way to get the final solution was to seek help from a marriage counselor, more specialized in that area of counseling. The other was a result of financial overindulgence, this particular area was a result of people who could not truly handle financial matters. They had either no concept of how to account for funds over a time period, or simply had thought they were wealthier than they really were. Global Security Corporation still remained one of the highest paying jobs analysts could get anywhere in the world. With the high pay, often came over spending from many first job pays, with the unrealistic attitudes, there was always more of that to come. As a result, they bought homes far too large and Tim learned not all designers and construction groups used by them, had the high standards his did. As a result, the maintenance was excessively high and homes were continually requiring major repairs, far before they should have had any repairs. He also told them he would be retiring when his contract was fulfilled.

With the vidphone conference concluded, he finished up his time at the office before the family was to depart for Tokyo. The only thing out of routine even at home was to help pack the luggage Thursday evening, to be prepared for a quick departure when he arrived home after work Friday.

Tim made it home right on schedule, greeted his lovely wife and daughter who were all ready to go. Tim gathered the luggage on the luggage cart, and took it to the transport to load it. Returned to escort the ladies to their selected seats, made sure the entry system was attended to and started out to the airfield, with a plane waiting for them. Once arriving, Tim got Kuri and Liani into the passenger waiting area to take the transport to a parking location, and bring the luggage with him. He was quick with getting it done, found the plane already completed pre-flighted, and waiting for the passengers to board for engine start up. He having used the company jets frequently enough to know all the different crews, noticed it was indeed not the same group who last had the opportunity to visit and see Tokyo, until he got to see the attendant.

This was after they were seated, and the plane was leaving the ground, so Tim asked why she was on this trip with a different crew. She said she enjoyed Tokyo so much she got to switch with the normal attendant with this crew, because the other attendant was not interested in an extended stay out of the country. She was dealing with some problems at home that needed her attention. The attendant did not go into detail on the problems, and Tim thought it best not to inquire further.

It was after the plane reached its cruising altitude, the attendant inquired about drinks, and said they had obtained grape juice for Liani, since Tim told them it was her favorite. They also made sure Kuri and Liani had the banana cream pie for desert, even though Tim made no such request. The meal half way to Tokyo was an Italian chicken recipe on a bed of spaghetti, with sides of applesauce and a mixed vegetable with some form of sauce. It was pretty good food for any plane service, but Tim knew they cooked it in the kitchen on the plane. For Liani, they made her sirloin patties cut in to small bites, with macaroni salad and a side of applesauce. Liani enjoyed every bit of it, and it was something he did not make at home.

Kuri after the meal was finished including the desert, said she arranged with her grandfather a day for them to take Liani to him for a good portion of the day, so they could make the trip to his house, and return for sauna time. Her grandfather was going to give her preview martial arts lessons, so she could see what she would be learning from her mother in a few years, when she was six years of age. Since the trip to her grandfather's house was an hour in each direction, Liani would be there a large part of the day to get to know her great grandfather better, as well as meet her great grandmother. Tim thought this was a good way to do it, since they had nobody else to watch Liani for some time in the sauna house. Tim had simply assumed they would not get to go there this trip, since Liani was considered too young to enter it.

Kuri also said while they were shopping during this trip, she thought it would be a good idea to get Liani some dresses. Kuri said it would be something she would not outgrow as fast as other clothes, and would need something presentable to wear to have restaurant food in Hong Kong. Tim agreed, it would be a good thing to prepare for, although Liani had never worn a dress before. Kuri said it was easier than most of the other clothes she wore, and would learn quickly to dress herself with one lesson. Tim could not argue with that, as Liani was learning everything quickly. Kuri even had her making up some things she missed with her advancement in school grades, and was trying to get her into the same time of starting the next grade, where she would have classmates to see and hear and talk with a little. That was as long as her classmates did not start with Japanese as their first language instead of English. Kuri said it was not uncommon for some Japanese household to reverse the language, because it was used solely within their own household. Tim did not know this, but figured Kuri knew what she was talking about being far more familiar with Tokyo, and the remainder of Japan.

The five and a half hour flight was at its end, and Tim went to get the transport rental to load up the luggage and his wife and child. They departed to the home that awaited them. Once they arrived, Kuri unpacked most of Liani's clothing to get the computer for her to start her school lesson, to get back more time for her in the schooling she was behind on, but in reality was taking her next lesson. Tim went to check on the food stocks and what spoilage may have occurred since the last visit. Aside from some fruits and vegetables, most of the stocks were in good condition. They did need a numbers of items to get through the week for dinners and breakfast. Tim asked Kuri if the grocer nearby was where she obtained English muffins before, and Kuri told him it was not, it was a grocery closer to her parent's restaurant and he could get everything else they needed at the one close by, but the next day when they went shopping with Liani to get dresses they could stop at that grocer for muffins. He agreed and left to the local grocer to get some fish and meats, fruits and vegetables as well as some waffles for Liani's favorite breakfast. He told Kuri he should not be gone too long, but did not know if it was crowded this time of day and week in Tokyo, but knew the best times in Seattle. He left and obtained everything he needed to get through the week of cooking in the Tokyo home. He even found some blueberry syrup for the waffles, which was the syrup to disappear the fastest in Seattle. He returned to the house and put everything away except for the dinner items for tonight's lighter meal, having already had a large lunch on the plane. Also with the time difference it was nearly that time.

The week in Tokyo went by too fast with everything accomplished, including clothes left behind for Tim and Kuri, as well as one dress for Liani. They did not know how quickly they would get back with Kuri well into her pregnancy, and the quick growth of Liani, although the dress should not be outgrown as rapidly as other clothing items. The other dresses were for her trip to Hong Kong now three weeks away. The larger luggage pieces were stuffed so full it took both Tim and Kuri to get them completely closed for the return trip. Fortunately, they both were still feeling the lingering effects of the day at the sauna, but it would end before Tim had to leave for work.

The return trip was also without event, but the attendant told them all about her sight-seeing and checking out the Tokyo hot spots. She was the guide for the other crew members, and thought everyone truly enjoyed the time in the wonderful city of Tokyo.

Once back to work, Tim found only a single incident which was a stress related problem from one analyst. His was told by Doctor Ward that his frustration led to a long session which was marital issues. He had gone to a marriage counselor with his wife as suggested. Even the counselor was frustrated by his wife's refusal to compromise on anything for the sake of the marriage. It was deemed her actions would be considered mental spousal abuse to her husband if she refuse to compromise. She still did not budge on her stand in the marriage, as a result the counselor said before it became a physical abuse, the marriage should be terminated, or end very badly for one of them. The husband was very frustrated about the whole thing, and could not understand why she was unwilling to do anything to keep the marriage moving forward. After filing the papers from the both of them, he got upset with his robotic computer, and was brought into the medical staff, with the help of the director to get his situation a bit more subdued. He was then turned over to the acupuncture specialist for a rather lengthy session for them both. Once that was done, the analyst was far more capable of looking at his situation and accepting it before one of the two went too far in the abuse category.

It was not something Tim ever expected to hear from his medical staff considering all the former work related stress problems. He was glad the analyst was attended to, and happy that the monitoring by the medical staff as opposed to director could result in immediate action.

The following Wednesday for Trask's day in the office, he announced that he had been given only two candidates for the CEO position. One being Tim Topeki as most everyone in the group had been under his supervision for a good while. The other was his son, who did not apply himself, but he announced while at the house, he was taking steps to leave Global Security Corporation, to form his own small business. It seems from his demonstration video on the information gateway that his idea had a far larger demand, than just in GSC offices. Since he was the person to retrofit the computer systems into the robotic humanoids, he had built a prototype in his own home, and provided a demonstration video of it capabilities. It was done in the exercise room to show the strength and maneuverability of the robotic systems. He even kept the part that destroyed one piece of equipment, because it demonstrated how heavy a robotic computer system was. Apparently he tried to have it run on a treadmill to show its speed as well. As soon as the robotic system got onto the treadmill it completely collapsed and was turned into instant recycling material. Jonathan seeing this as something to take advantage of, used it to inform potential clients, that the system could not be used in work environments without solid flooring, such as wood over a lower level below. He then emphasized that the robotic humanoid before retrofit, weighed in excess of 550 pounds, and although the computer was not excessively heavy as a unit, with all the additions to the robotic unit to consider at least a 600 pound weight, if the surface to be used is not capable of supporting that type of weight.

At any rate he indicated his response had been overwhelmingly in his favor, and could easily make 10 times more money independently from

GSC. I cannot fault him in pursuing something worthwhile, it is how I raised him, to not expect everything handed to him by his father, so he could waste his life away."

Tim: "Does that mean I should start grooming Tim Topeki for the position or is the jury still out looking into all possibilities?" Trask: "I will hold off until you have returned from your Hong Kong trip before doing any such thing, and may have someone else interested before that to determine the best choice instead of by default."

Tim just said he would wait until Trask had a specific candidate selected, because there were many areas to consider any of them to be efficient in all of it. Also the pretense of being prepared for any type of event to occur, even if it never occurs to have a plan of attack. It was much better to have a plan for something never to happen, than to be caught in chase mode. Trask said even he never looked that far into advance and that was likely why Loretta also said Tim ran an even better ship than he.

CHAPTER
23

Tim's time in the office until the trip to Hong Kong for a week was by Tim's opinion the longest year in his life. Even though it was less than three weeks after the meeting with Trask it seemed to him, it equaled a full year. Friday morning Tim doubled checked that the private company jet was indeed expecting them, they were ready to go all with the hopes of a stay over in Hong Kong for the entire time. At the end of the workday Friday, and having everything already packed and waiting, he arrived home just a little early to have the ladies ready and waiting.

Tim got the luggage into the transport, followed by Kuri and Liani, insured the entry system was set and departed to the airfield. He got everything into the lobby before parking the transport, and was even quicker this time than the previous trip. The plane was prepped for take-off, and just ready for the passengers to get fully seated. Even Liani was ready to go, and Kuri could not tell her anything of what to expect, because it was her first time ever to Hong Kong. Tim also reconnected with Cho to see what they had in the works as far as plans. Cho said, he and a very pregnant Yo-li would meet them in the hotel lobby for dinner, and since they had Liani with them, it would be one of the good Cantonese restaurants, not too terribly far from the hotel. He let Kuri and Liani know that there was a good chance that Cho and his wife would be waiting in the lobby when they arrived, and instead of doing a typical check in, have the luggage taken to the room so they could go directly to dinner from the lobby. The flight included a better than average luncheon meal, which the crew realized with the time of departure from Seattle it would be a nearly dinnertime in Hong Kong. Everything was available twenty-four hours a day, every day.

The hotel transportation was prompt, and speedy in getting the Frantz family to the hotel, often used by global Security Corporation. He requested his luggage taken to his room or suite was reconfirmed by the desk, and he left a fair gratuity for the valet who performed the deed. Tim had seen and gave a wave to Cho and Yo-li, before going to the front desk with the immediate needs taken care of, he informed the front desk he would be back after dinner with friends waiting, to finish the check-in process. He and Kuri with Liani in hand went to go meet the awaiting friends. Kuri had met Cho in Seattle once and Tim reminded her, just in case, but she remembered him. Tim started by introducing Kuri and Yo-li, and asked them, due to Liani's young age, to introduce themselves by the name they felt comfortable with for a three year old girl. He did not want to assume incorrectly, but both Cho and Yo-li chose to go by first names. Liani asked Yo-li if her name was one or two words. Yo-li said it was hyphenated and asked if Liani knew what that was. Liani said she thought it meant it had a dash in it. Yo-li said for a three year old she was amazingly smart, and asked whether she had started school already. Liani said she had, and was advanced to third grade after two months into the school. Yo-li asked if she was trying to rival her father. Liani said she was not, her father knew everything. Tim laughed, and said he wished he knew half that much, but thanked Liani for thinking that about him. When Cho and Yo-li rose to head to the restaurant they had selected, Tim agreed with Cho about Yo-li and had to ask her when she was due. Yo-li said two weeks, and Kuri said, "Now that is an overgrown melon." Which got all of them but Liani laughing, because she did not understand the joke in the slightest. Liani asked what an overgrown melon was, and Yo-li being a long time professor, went into teaching mode, and said it was a long time Chinese and apparently Japanese reference to a woman in my condition, which is with another life growing inside this large bump. Tim asked if the walk was going to be any problem for her, and Yo-li said outside of being careful how she stepped, since she could not see her own feet, she would be fine. Yo-li in turn asked Kuri when her new bundle of joy was due. Kuri said she still had close to more than three months, but her melon was not as large the first time, and was not sure how much different this one would be, but it was definitely different.

They arrived at the restaurant, and the ladies got to take waiting seats, until a table could be put together for all of them, and asked if the young one needed a high chair or a seat addition to raise her up to table height. Kuri said the seat addition should do fine. While they waited, Kuri and Yo-li talked about pregnancy Yo-li saying it was quite possibly twins, or a prodigy drummer within from all the kicking going on. Kuri believed because of the difference between Liani and this one, she thought it would be a boy. Yo-li said her kicking became noticeable at five months, and her doctor said it was common with twins to have it start early, as they tried to gain space to move a little bit. Yo-li said in all honesty, she was not a five star hotel. Kuri was rather amazed at Yo-li's sense of humor, and asked what she did before having a family. Yo-li said she was a professor at the best technical college in Hong Kong, and Cho was once her student. She asked if Yo-li was who all the code went to when she was in Seattle, trying to help get as much code put together in week with Cho's leadership. Yo-li confirmed she was, and the last update and exclusivity to Global, made it possible for her Cho to finally get the family thing started.

The table was ready, and the five of them were taken to it, Tim got Liani into the extra tall seat; but it did allow her to be more at a proper table height. Tim liked the idea and thought with all the kids for the next Christmas dinner it might come in handy. Cho suggested a particular menu item for Liani, as it was a most unique sauce and it came with both chicken and pork in the meal. Cho said it was a dark cherry colored sauce that was hardly the normal color for Cantonese sweet and sour, but a little sweeter than most and really tasty. Kuri said it sounded good for her also, she had a fancy toward sweets for some reason, and it was particular noticeable to her when she was pregnant. Orders were given and drinks ordered, nothing too high powered, and juice for Liani, but it would not be grape. The server also asked if chop sticks or utensils were needed. Kuri said, it had been quite some time since she used chop sticks and got them, saying she could steal Tim's if she forgot how to use them. Cho and Yo-li also got chop sticks. Tim said he just got Liani able to use a fork better, and was not going to introduce her to chop sticks just yet, he would let

Kuri do that in good time. He had utensils for himself and Liani, neither ever having used chopsticks.

The table conversation got to be more involved with Yo-li and Kuri learning about the others heritage and ancestry. Liani, although not saying much was intently listening as she was learning some subtle differences between being Japanese or Chinese. Tim was also learning and finding as peoples, they had much in common. The biggest difference seemed to stem from the way their countries were shape from those in power long ago. They both referred to different periods in their histories as dynasties, and it seemed that the struggles of the working class of both, were by and large identical. Kuri got to spend time talking about being samurai ancestry, in which Liani piped in with saying her great grandfather said her father was samurai by marriage. This was totally new to Tim, he certainly did nothing to earn such an honor. Kuri said being samurai by marriage is honorable, but not quite the same as by ancestry. Liani learned she was also samurai being brought in this world by her mother and father, and would always be samurai, whereas Tim would be samurai for as long as he and Kuri were together. Even in Japan, some marriages fail, although it is usually not by divorce, but by a violent end. Kuri hoped that Japan would come to realize the importance of women, before her time came to its conclusion.

The meals had arrived, and conversation largely came to a halt, as the aroma of food from the kitchens was winning as far as all their stomachs were concerned. Liani and Kuri were both very happy with their meal, and it was truly a delight. Kuri asked Cho if this restaurant was a family restaurant with some Japanese heritage. Cho did not know and inquired why. Kuri said she thought the unique flavor to this particular meal was a result of blending teriyaki sauce into it. It also accounted for it darker coloring. Cho said he was not too familiar with teriyaki sauce, as there were so few Japanese food establishments in Hong Kong. He also admitted if Yo-li was not such a good cook, he would starve, because he had no idea how to do anything as far as cooking was concerned. Kuri said even though her father was a master chef, it was not until Tim showed her and fully explained the basics, she was also terrible at cooking.

Kuri also said Tim was still much better than she was, but she had learned to do a number of things since he gave her instructions. Liani was quite pleased with her meal and asked her father if he knew how to make it at home also. Tim told her since he had something different it was unlikely, but he did know how to make some Cantonese style meals at home.

With the conclusion of dinner, and Tim covering all the charges, Yo-li and Cho returned to their own place of residence, largely because Yo-li was tiring out for one day. It was decided that they would get together again later in the week for another evening, and Yo-li had someplace in mind that Tim had eaten before, but Kuri and Liani had not. It was the Spanish and Portuguese restaurant, because there were a number of meals not highly spicy. Kuri could eat some spicy foods, but Liani was not overly happy about them. It did take a few more years for children to really find out if they had a like or dislike to them. Also some people never could. It simply did not agree with their internal systems.

Tim, Liani and Kuri took their time returning to the hotel, as Kuri was checking some of the shops on the return trip. Not entering any, but trying to see through shop windows what was offered inside and worth making a visit to later on. Once back to the hotel, they all needed to be scanned to have access to the room they had awaiting them. Tim had to lift Liani for the scan, and wondered if she would even be able to access the room without another lift. She would not be allowed to wander the hotel unattended by at least one of her parents. This was not hotel policy, it was Tim's and Kuri's policy for a three year old.

Once in the hotel room, and everything was unpacked and hung. Tim informed Kuri and Liani that while they were here, and looking around Hong Kong, they would notice a large number of vending carts along the way. All of them would offer samples of the foods they serve, and some of them may even have a wonderful aroma. Do not take any samples or ask to eat at a vending cart. The items sold may be described as a chicken or pork but is likely not. The vending carts use questionable food supplies at least as far as the meats are concerned. Liani asked what he meant. Tim said, "If you noticed while we were walking to and from the restaurant with Cho and Yo-li, there is a serious lack of small animals in this city". Liani just said, "oh Yuk".

It was late, and time for everyone to get some rest, the suite had a second bed for Liani and she with Kuri's assistance completed the evening hygiene ritual before getting put to bed. She was asleep in no time at all. Tim and Kuri did the same and also retired for the evening, although a bit early for Hong Kong, they were up much longer coming from a different time zone, especially Tim who put in a full day at the office.

The nice thing about paid time off, is there is not a set schedule of events, it was a good thing too. All of them slept much later than what is normal for any of them. It was still morning, but rising at 9:30 AM was quite out of character for Tim. His rising was all it took for everyone else to be up and wondering why it was so late in the morning. Liani would normally be well into to her schooling, and everyone would have had breakfast. Once the cleaning ritual was completed by them all and they were dressed, it was time for some breakfast before it was lunchtime. Due to the lateness of the day, Tim figured today would be only breakfast and dinner for them all, and it was likely to occur in the hotel restaurant for today.

They all arrived in the restaurant and were seated. The morning crowds were quite diminished, and except for only a few small groups, the restaurant was relatively empty. Tim let everyone know ahead of time that this was the restaurant where he first tasted the hash browns he tried to learn to make for quite some time, before discovering the secret. Hash browns were definitely on everyone's list, Tim also got the Hong Kong omelet and so did Kuri, but Liani went with scrambled eggs and some bacon. Tim got English muffins and preserves, coffee hoping it was not awful. Liani got flavored milk and Kuri tea.

All the food was cooked fresh, since it was closing in on lunchtime for the locals and business visitors. Tim had the charges added to his hotel bill as was customary for him while traveling, and asked what they wanted to do now that they had eaten. Kuri decided since Liani was already late for starting her school day, they might as well see some of the shops they had passed coming from the restaurant the night before. Liani would start her school day after they returned. They went to half a dozen shops, and although a few things seemed interesting to Kuri, they returned to the hotel empty handed. Nothing impressed her so much that she had to have it. As far as clothing items were concerned, she thought she had found considerably better made items in both Tokyo and Seattle, and said she would not buy any clothing items here, even if she needed them.

Back at the hotel, the one thing apparent with Kuri's second pregnancy, she did not have her normal endurance for any given day. So while Tim and Liani got the school day started, Kuri took a short nap to try to recover some of her missing energy levels. Kuri only slept for an hour, and feeling more energized, performed her meditation routine first before taking over with Liani's schooling assistance, so Tim could do his. He only got to do one the day before; but at least he did not miss a day entirely. Once he was completed, and although Liani still had more lessons for the day to complete, it was time for dinner, and he took them all back to the hotel restaurant, where it was an evening that did not solely offer local cuisine. It was not one that Tim had previously, and wondered if it was something new for the restaurant. It was a mix of eastern European and Russian foods for the menu selections. It was not something Tim had an extensive experience with. He had a few things and when in St. Petersburg knew that cooking with vodka was involved in many of their recipes, but he was uncertain if this restaurant was aware of that specifically.

He inquired when the server appeared with the menus for the evening. The server said that it was used in half of the Russian selections, but none of the others. Tim was only familiar with five of the entrees, and had to read through the descriptions to learn the best thing to get for Liani. Many of them were noodle based meals as opposed to rice or spaghetti. All of them had some type of sauce, and finding something that he thought Liani would like every little bit of, was proving challenging. He determined from the choices the one that Liani would like most of the ingredients was the stuffed cabbages. He did not believe she would enjoy the sauerkraut that came in the mixture, but knew that cooked cabbage tasted far different than as simply part of stir fry or salad.

He chose to have a steak marinated in spices and vodka that was quite good, and Kuri decided to follow his lead, and thought it was good, although much different from teriyaki steak. Liani liked at least the tomato based cabbages, and the meat inside but left as much sauerkraut as she could separate from her item. She did get some as it was impossible to remove completely, but there was enough sauce and other flavor to disguise it. Once the meal was completed, and the charges added to his room, they returned to finish up Liani's schooling for the day. She only had two more hours left to finish that day, and was not going to do any catching up for the day. Tim had placed the nightly news broadcast on with the UK broadcast he knew about.

Kuri watched it while Tim oversaw Liani who did not really need much assistance. The news broadcast said there was another major arrest in Tokyo resulting in another 150 arrests to the underground criminal network. Kuri made sure everyone knew that it had happened, but did not detail it until Liani had completed her schooling for the day.

Kuri said in the last month there had been nearly 500 criminal network members removed from the problem. It was more progress than they had achieved in the last 200 years. She also wondered what brought about the sudden change, knowing it took so long to find the heart of the different leaders. It was highly unlikely that the authorities had significantly increased their numbers, as Japan forever had far too little. Largely a result of the high cost of having an abundance of law enforcement, as well as the danger factor for the pay they received. Tokyo did have undercover people, but so seldom did they accomplish so much in such a short time. She asked Tim if he knew who else was left in Tokyo, since she thought most of the people she knew had gone into retirement. Tim said, as far as he knew Soo Kawasaki was still director in Tokyo as he had not heard otherwise, although he had not checked in some time.

Kuri said she would try to call the next day, during business hours since Tokyo and Hong Kong were not greatly different. It would be too late to expect her to be there now.

After the nightly news, and Liani finishing her schooling for the day. Tim and Kuri had Liani prepare for bedtime, just so the following day would be more in line with what was normal. Tim and Kuri checked up on her and once again once she was in bed it did not take long for her to be asleep. They watched a little more of the entertainment selections, but found little to truly interest them and retired early themselves.

The rest of the week started much earlier, and Liani got all her schooling completed on time, with a small portion of catch up included. Dinner with Cho and Yo-li was quite good, and Liani loved her chimichanga the way Tim had it ordered with guacamole and sour cream and no salsa. Although, she did find the tortilla chips good with the mild salsa. While

Tim had hot salsa, and Cho extra hot, with Yo-li and Kuri using medium. Yo-li admitted since becoming pregnant, she was not able to consume her normal hot spicy level, and learned quickly to reduce it for the time being. She did not know for certain if it was only due to the pregnancy, or if her system was changed permanently from the changes as a result of being pregnant.

Every day in Hong Kong had a short shopping excursion; but the results were largely the same, Kuri not finding anything that truly caught her fancy. She finally leveled with Tim she was looking for something of historic significance to represent that she had been there. Tim said he wished she would have told him much sooner, because Hong Kong itself had none. Virtually every inch of the small island was used, and it was necessary for almost everything historical to be replaced with bigger and more modern to aid in the lack of space to expand anywhere. His first trip to Hong Kong received much the same disappointment, as she was experiencing but he learned, largely after his first search, from Cho. As a matter of economics, old goes away to make room for the new. There are only two historical buildings, which are in combination a museum pertaining to the English, who were the first to populate this small island. They were considered to be traders as far as the Chinese were concerned, and the English royalty thought them more pirates, but because of the uniqueness in the goods they traded, were given some flexibility over absolute law. Aside from that small area, all of Hong Kong has gone to the modern to overcome the past.

Kuri only said she wished he had said something sooner also, and wondered if the historic museum offered anything as keepsakes. Tim said they offered a lot of information about the two different families, but if there was any type of keepsake, it would more resemble England not Hong Kong. Tim said it was important to remember that as independent as Hong Kong may seem, it was still a Chinese territory.

Once they returned home from Hong Kong, and soon back to a normal routine with Tim returning to Global Security, to finish out his time before going into retirement, Tim spent time with Tim Topeki to get him familiar with his expect duties as CEO. In the first couple of months, it was largely a question and answer period to determine if Tim Topeki was truly prepared to be the single person to take responsibility for everything the company did. Largely during that time Tim found he was not as ready as he, Tim Topeki himself thought. Timothy Frantz continually gave him scenarios to determine how prepared he was in the event something came up, requiring his immediate action. It took over a month and half for Tim to think ahead to prepare himself, and understand he needed a plan before something occurred. He had to be prepared, simply because reacting was not enough to keep clients safe, or the company's reputation intact. Timothy was not trying to make Topeki's life difficult, it was really a matter of the better prepared somebody was for any given possibility, the better chance of putting it to a quick halt. He stressed the importance to Tim Topeki that even if the event never occurred in reality, he had to have planned steps to take, to overcome any setback they encountered. Tim Topeki was finally getting the importance behind this process and also had to learn how to pay attention to areas of the Global Security Corporation's overall program, not simply the single area he was most familiar with. When the time came for Tim to take his paid time off for the birth of the second child in his family, Tim Topeki was close to being in full control of any possible scenario.

Tim left the office the day before Kuri was due to be present for the second child's expected arrival. He figured that Kuri and the doctor knew more in the timing of the birth than he ever would. His arrangement was to have a week off, and after reviewing his already taken time off, he had more days left than he thought, and did not want to waste them. He extended this week to two weeks, to insure Kuri had more time to recover, as this pregnancy was much harder on her than the first. She was having difficulty regaining her endurance each and every day prior to the arrival date. When pregnant with Liani, she had no such difficulties, and did not know if it was because she believed this to be a boy, or just she was getting older without any real outward signs of it. She was still incredibly strong, and in good physical condition, it was only her energy level that seem to be slighted. She even altered her mediation routine a month earlier than with Liani, to insure no complications. The only thing it complicated, was her energy level was slightly lower than prior to the alteration.

The following morning, Tim made sure of who could watch over Liani, while he took Kuri to the hospital. He found his mother was going to be in and out all day, but his grandmother, Liani's great grandmother, was more than willing, and so enjoyed having her around; even though she was long past the time of helping Liani with her school work. Liani during the last couple of months had almost caught up to where she should be in school in relation to the rest who would move onto fourth grade. After taking Liani to her great grandmother's house until he could return from the hospital, he took Kuri to her expected location selected by her doctor.

They arrived at the hospital at 11 AM, and it was not under emergency conditions. At approximately 2:30 PM Kuri gave birth with Tim present to Tobias Chankwan-Frantz. The first male, as predicted by Kuri, was brought into the world. Tim honored Kuri's samurai ancestry and remained the only family member without a hyphenated name, but it was imperative to samurai ancestry to forever keep the samurai name. Tim did not mind in the least bit, it presented no real issues to him and he still felt Kuri was the most wonderful woman he could have ever met in his entire life. It was not too terribly long after the birth and first feeding from mother that Kuri was in desperate need of some rest. As the first time, every six hours until Kuri and child could leave the hospital, and return to their home, Toby was brought to Kuri for his feeding. At least the hospital took care of all the other things necessary for a new born infant. After Kuri had completed the feeding, and given some time to rest, he told her, he would be back tomorrow with Liani to see how she was doing, and maybe let Liani meet her new brother.

Tim returned to the lake properties and let his grandparents know the newest member to the Frantz family was Tobias, Toby for the short version, and that Liani now had a brother. Liani did not know what to make of that just yet, and Tim let her know that tomorrow they would go together to the hospital to see Kuri, and hopefully meet her new brother.

Tim took Liani back to their own house, since there was still a little time before he needed to start dinner for only two, he was wondering if he remembered how to cook for less, called his mother to let her know of the latest addition. He would need to get Toby's weight and size tomorrow to have some clothes and diapers for when he came home with his mother. Since Kuri was worn out easier, he thought maybe she could get more on track to her normal vigorous self. It would be something to be concerned about if she could not, and hoped he did not have to travel that path, and it was all due to this pregnancy. After his quick call to his mother, he made sure Liani was in the entertainment room, and he did put the first nightly news broadcast on. Tim never quite understood a three year old's fascination with the nightly news, but it kept her from getting into mischief. Tim went about preparing dinner, and decided too much or not, he would make the chicken bake casserole that Liani always enjoyed, although she did ask why he never made Chimichangas for dinner.

He had to tell Liani first he had no recipe for them, and second it required something special he did not have to make them correctly, and it was easier to go find a place that already made them. Liani then asked if you could get them already made, why she does not remember ever having them before? Tim said this was the last question he would answer for tonight, knowing fully well it could become an endless cycle. She said agreed, and Tim continued to say he did not know if she was ready to try them before, because they often included some rather hot spicy salsa. Hotter than the salsa she had with her tortilla chips. Tim could see she was pondering that next question, and he reminded her no more questions tonight. Which did not deter her from thinking them up for the next night. Tim was beginning to wonder if he put his mother through this during his youngest years, or if his abilities came at a later age.

Tim had checked on her schooling accomplishments for the day, and she being with great grandmother she made it a point to include some catching up school as her mother also had her do. After dinner, and the standard clean up performed by Tim. He and Liani selected an animated Disney movie she had not seen in this version, it was a rather old movie that had gone through the latest restoration to bring it into the present video optimization. It was one Tim had only seen under previous variations, and it was with one of Disney's oldest known characters. The movie starred Mikey Mouse as the sorcerer's apprentice. It was a remarkable story with all things considered to make such a movie at the time this one was done. Liani was pleased with the movie, even though she was already wise enough to know that a mouse was not really that cute, nor could they speak. Just the same, she enjoyed how the story was presented using animated characters, which were not people. At the conclusion, Tim had her prepare for bed, and knowing fully well she preferred her mother for assistance, he told her he would only help her if she yelled for him to come help. She thought that was acceptable, and saw no reason for his help outside of getting her hygiene stuff down low enough for her reach it. After getting her hygiene items down from the cabinet and on the sink counter, he said he would not even be in her room, he would stay outside in the hall unless she needed him.

He was doing his best to let her feel a little more grown up than she could be at the age of three. He also knew after he went back to work to complete the remaining six weeks before retirement, Kuri might need her help. The only other assistance requested by Liani was to put her items back, but Tim said she would need them again when she awoke, and he could do it then after she finished, and he tucked her in with a kiss on the forehead. She had already got into bed and somewhat settled.

The next three days were very much identical except for the meals, they left for the hospital around 9 AM and stayed until 1:30. Liani got to meet her new brother Toby and Kuri asked Liani if she would like to hold him, and Liani politely declined since she did not feel she was big enough to do it just now. Kuri was not disappointed by the answer, and made sure Liani could at least get a good close look at her baby brother. Tim got to hold his new son for only 15 minutes, before he wanted to go back to his mother. Each day was much the same. The doctor had decided to keep Kuri one extra day to recover more of her energy, which was taking longer to get back this time. It was a concern to Tim, and had at least a moment to talk with the doctor alone. The doctor said it was not entirely uncommon, but if it persisted more than a month, she would need to run some tests. Tim asked if the common practice of only two children in Japan was more than population control measures. The doctor did not know, but could do some research that would not be made available on the information gateway. It was not something she ever considered previously, as she did not have any other ladies from Japan in her list of patients.

Kuri arrived home with Tobias (Toby) on the fourth day, Tim had gone the first return day and got the measurements of his son and he and Liani picked out some sleepers and diapers and other items for him to be at home. Once home, things were a bit hectic for a whole week, with an infant who was waking every three hours, and loudly saying he was up. Tim did everything he could to help Kuri regain her energy level, but he could not feed the baby. This was one thing Kuri had to do with the means she intended for his first 4 months, before starting to change it over. Tim only had including the weekend, three days of time off left, before Toby became a little more comfortable with his new surroundings. Liani being awoken rather often was only staying on schedule with her school, and had not been able to get any more catching up done. Kuri had not resumed her full routine; but was doing her modified version to regain her strength, but her stamina and energy were not returning as quickly as she was expecting.

The last three days flew by, and in what seemed like the blink of an eye he was getting ready for work on Monday morning. He was a little bit tired, but nothing too bad. He arrived and greeted Loretta, and once in the office the three computer systems were also made aware of his having returned. He was in the middle of his meditation routine he used to pass the time, when Tim Topeki entered the office. Somewhat oblivious to anything beyond his exercise, Tim Topeki was there 10 minutes before he noticed. Since prior to his time off, Tim Topeki had not ever entered prior to after lunch.

Timothy Frantz stopped his routine to ask Tim Topeki if there was something wrong, since he was not in his office before afternoon. Tim told him there was nothing wrong, he had a talk with Trask over his training for the CEO position. Tim said to Tim Topeki, that he had him prepared over and beyond what Trask himself would have done. He thought the training had Tim Topeki better prepared than he had prepared the current CEO, who was getting ready to retire. Timothy said he could only suggest he create and plan mentally for as many possible scenarios as he could imagine, for any possible area which the company operated. He also reminded Tim Topeki that of the many areas that were in use on this organization, that did not equate to a service provided to clients. Such as the medical staff and virus and information protection inbound to GSC. The more you can imagine to occur, even if it never did, you are mentally prepared to take action, instead of reacting to any given situation. He told Tim Topeki he would be here another six weeks to assist in any other questions or preparations he felt need more work. Other than that he did not see a reason for Tim Topeki to make a daily appearance, unless he thought otherwise.

The last six weeks for Timothy Frantz were exceptionally busy, but not at work. The latest arrival to the Chankwan-Frantz household was far crankier than his older sister was after being brought home. He continued with waking every three hours to inform the household he was either hungry or needed other attention to his discomfort. It resulted in Liani not being able to get any more caught up to her school schedule, and she was performing at a lower level than prior to having a younger brother. As a result of Kuri's last visit to the doctor, and being told Tobias had absolutely no health issues to be concerned with, the doctor told Kuri he was very much normal to most infants. Liani was on the other hand, apparently more willing to adapt to her surroundings from the very start, and was in a very small percentage of all children to do so quickly. Kuri was told she and Tim had to discover the ways that created an environment that Toby was happier in. This led to Tim taking Toby to the lower level for one hour each night to listen to music. It was not excessively loud to help calm the young boy, but it did start to improve his adjustments to being in the world, and particularly the house.

Tim's last week included a final meeting with Trask and Tim Topeki, soon to be CEO. Trask had found no other MIT security graduates in Global Security Corporation although there were some, all were minors in security with the major in something else in the general information profession. Tim agreed, he would contact Trask when he found any new codes to have tested by the Celini brothers. He would check the MIT site once a month, but only call in when he found something new to report. He said it was not entirely out of the question to go six months without a single new code. With that concession made, Trask wished him a happy retirement and hopefully a long lived one since he still had the option to ask Tim back to take the reins once again.

One month beyond retirement, and being home for a much larger portion of the time. Tobias was finally being more comfortable in his newest surroundings and sleeping longer between his attention notices to the household. He still was not really happy with the unidentifiable substances in baby food containers, and the biggest challenge there, was once in his mouth, getting him to keep in his mouth. At least until he swallowed it, instead of seeing how much he could get back onto the highchair table in front of him.

Also during his first month, largely from being in the house during more daylight hours than before, he discovered his windows were rather dingy, and not so crystal clear. He had to find out from his mother, who never told him before that windows needed to be cleaned periodically both inside and out. She told him the proper items to obtain for all of his houses. And should be done at least once each year, and sometime more, depending on what the outdoors and weather brought. With Tobias and Kuri still attending to an infant, Tim did not have any idea when they would get to return to Tokyo for at least a week in that home. The other home had not been visited in quite some time also and it was way past due.

The day he obtained the materials suggested by his mother, he made sure Kuri and Liani would be good for a few hours, while he went to check out the other house and try to do some window cleaning there. They thought they would be fine. He found the job for the windows took a little longer than he thought it would, but with the correct materials suggested, all the windows looked like new, when he completed the task. Almost everything in the kitchen environment cooling system had reached spoilage, so he took care of that with the outdoor incinerating device, and made sure the trap was cleaned before returning to the lake home.

The following day, the window cleaning was done at the lake/pond home, where at least Kuri could get him if needed for anything. Once that was completed, he once again found all the windows looked like new, and the vision was greatly improved. Liani had only two more months of schooling to complete her third grade, and was still a little over two weeks behind the fourth grade start up time for having classmates in the fourth grade. She would shortened it to only one week at the end of the term for most. The Japanese school system only had a six week summer break between school years. Kuri and Liani decided that she would only have five weeks, and finish her one week short, to start with the other fourth grade student. She would be one week short of her fourth birthday. Kuri also said, she would during her five weeks off get some basic Japanese vocabulary as some of her classmates would have that as their primary language. It was not going to be Japanese in five weeks, it would give her enough of the words to know a little about what was being said. The fourth grade was where Japanese would be taught as a part of her lessons. She would not read or write in Japanese for some time, but start the process in the sixth grade, and it took most students until the tenth grade to truly write and read Japanese fully. Liani would learn both languages, and next time she saw her great grandmother, understand better she was not saying hello so much.

Tim was fully into retirement mode by the end of his second month away from work. Kuri had learned from her doctor that Tim had requested her to do some research into a third child in Japan, to see if she was capable of having more children. The doctor informed her that research from over two hundred years ago was initiated by the Japanese government, which led to a time of what seemed to the people as population control. The research conducted over fifty years suggests that although a seemingly population control endeavor by the government, it was not truly the case. Although the government may not have provided the people with a suitable explanation, it was a means to keep more people than loose. It seems for many centuries, a third child resulted in the death of the birth mother, and often the new child before reaching the age of three. Whether it is genetic to the Japanese was not conclusive. It did suggest that since for thousands of years the Japanese people were isolated from many outsiders that it may be unique to the Japanese. The doctor said she knew Kuri wanted to have more than two children. Considering how much it took out of her from the second birth, before she had a third child planned, the doctor wanted to do some rather extensive testing to determine if she first could survive it, and second have a third healthy child. On the bright side, Kuri had one major advantage for a heathy child, that being she was not married to a Japanese man. But no child should have to go through life without a mother from the very start. That led to major issues, not typically physical but in mental development and health. The guilt of a child feeling responsible for his mother's death at birth, is one of the most difficult mental issues to truly resolve. They are aware of it from almost the beginning, but have no way to communicate other than crying their guilt. Often by the time other family members can discuss it with the child, all they do is reinforce the guilt, and some compound it by placing blame on the child. "As I said, no child should have to start out life in this fashion, so the tests will need to be done." The doctor finished up with.

Kuri and Tim had a long discussion over this and was a little unhappy that he asked about it with her doctor, and never let her know. She also said, she would never have considered it was a problem, and not simply a control for the number of people living on a single island. Ultimately Tim and Kuri considered it best after Tobias had reached age three the testing would be done. She would only have another child if the test result were favorable, and she would not consider having a fourth any longer. Besides by the time a fourth child could be considered, Kuri may be too old to have additional children without her being in jeopardy of the horrific results for her and another child.

He was settling into his retirement quite well, and the only thing he really altered in his routines, he and Liani gathered wood from the forest area and he spent far more time using his outdoor wood grill for dinner. Steaks whether beef, tuna or salmon all had a wonderful taste with hickory used in the grilling process. He also found it created better chicken dinners, but he still had to use the kitchen for whatever accompanied the grill selection.

He just wondered if being retired was going to last like it would for most other people when the decision was made. Admittedly, most of them were considerably older than in their later thirties. He did add one other thing to his agenda while in retirement. He enrolled in MIT's PhD program for information security, and resumed his education. He was not in a major hurry to complete it, especially having a family and so many other things to do throughout each day. His first class told him he knew far beyond what they were going to educate on, but continued for the document, that came at his conclusion.

***

WATCH FOR THE FINAL INSTALLMENT TO THE CYBER TRILOGY, CYBER RECALL.

Lightning Source UK Ltd.
Milton Keynes UK
UKHW010633100821
388622UK00001B/22